END OF THE
WORLD BLUES

END OF THE WORLD BLUES

JON COURTENAY GRIMWOOD

The right of Jon Courtenay Grimwood to be identified as the
author of this work has been asserted by him in accordance
with the Copyright, Designs and Patents Act 1988.

First published in Great Britain in 2006
by Gollancz
An imprint of the Orion Publishing Group Ltd,
Orion House, 5 Upper St Martin's Lane,
London, WC2H 9EA
An Hachette Livre UK company

This edition published in Great Britain in 2007 by Gollancz

1 3 5 7 9 10 8 6 4 2

A CIP catalogue record for this book
is available from the British Library.

ISBN 978 0 57507 9 533

Typeset by Deltatype Ltd, Birkenhead, Merseyside

Printed and bound at
Mackays of Chatham plc, Chatham, Kent

The Orion Publishing Group's policy is to use papers that
are natural, renewable and recyclable products and made
from wood grown in sustainable forests. The logging and
manufacturing processes are expected to conform to the
environmental regulations of the country of origin.

'End of the world or not, peonies, azaleas and camellias
will still produce beautiful flowers ...'
Hagakure Kikigaki (Way of the Samurai)

PROLOGUE
Friday 22 December

'That looks heavy.'

Glancing round, the girl saw a porter in the grey-green uniform of the Tokyo Metro, complete with smart white gloves. He was smiling.

'No,' she said. 'It's fine.'

'If you're sure?'

'I'm certain,' said Nijie, more firmly than was polite. *Kids today,* she could see him think. *No manners.*

Having wrestled her case into a left-luggage locker at Shinjuku Sanchome, Nijie Kitagawa slammed its steel door and fed 2000 yen into a slot. She followed this with two 500 yen coins and checked the door was tight.

The longest she could leave her case was three days. After that, she'd need to change lockers. As Nijie was fifteen and official statistics suggested she should live to the age of eighty-three, this meant she'd need to swap lockers 8273 times before she died.

Mind you, official statistics could be wrong.

Alternatively she could spend its contents. On that basis, the girl could afford to take $100 a day for the rest of her life, minus the $500 she'd already used. $15,000,000 was a lot of money to steal, particularly for someone her age.

It was Friday, 22nd of December, the last day of school term and Nijie's friends would be wondering where she was, Nijie could imagine their conversation.

She'd left a cup of saké, her videophone and her high-school identity card at a roadside shrine for luck, before entering the station. As an afterthought, Nijie had swapped her card for five $100 bills, anchoring them with her door keys. So now her card lay in a gutter where it belonged. A girl with brown eyes, her hair in bunches, still smiling as people trod down.

1

The first train was for Ginza, from where it would run the loop to Ikeburuku, giving her twenty-four stations before she needed to change. Getting a corner seat was lucky, because the metro was crowded with Christmas shoppers carrying white-painted twigs and plastic snowmen. So Nijie sat quietly, working out what to do next. After a while she remembered to keep her knees together.

Opposite her, a woman with that day's *Asahi Shimbun* was tutting to her husband about the Kitagawa killings, while a photograph of a man with swept-back hair stared from its front page. Tony Kitagawa looked better in black and white, certainly a lot better than when Nijie last saw him.

'*I am a cat*,' she announced.

Across the aisle a boy in the blue tunic of a local high school glanced up, only to smile as he recognised her words. '*As yet I have no name*,' he said, finishing the quote for her.

Nijie burst into tears.

When she next looked he was gone. Maybe he was late for school, maybe the start times had changed or perhaps she'd been on the train longer than she realised. Looking around, Nijie decided it was a different train.

Station names changed and smartly-dressed men got on or off, and when every seat but the one next to her was taken, even that one filled up. Having finished her crying, Nijie sniffed, being far too carefully brought up to blow her nose in public.

Her old life had gone. She needed a new name and somewhere to hide. Most of all she needed to stop crying and pull herself together. Reciting lines from *I Am A Cat* was perhaps not the best way to achieve this, but the story came from her grandmother, who'd read it aloud one winter night many years before.

At the end of the line, the girl climbed out of her seat, crossed the platform and waited for the train to take her back. The station was suburban neat, its trees pruned into elegant shapes and a clock above the tracks counted off the seconds until her train would arrive.

When the clock hit zero, Nijie felt it happen, like paper ripping inside her. Several things previously muddled became clear. *Neko* meant cat, while *niku* meant meat; she was both of those.

Neku?

Yes, she thought, that was it. She was Lady Neku. And suddenly, the girl who became Lady Neku understood she'd never really been anyone else.

*

When the salaryman opposite began staring, Neku moved her magazine to obstruct his view of her knees. It was early afternoon, the metro was full of Christmas shoppers and Neku was several hours into her new life.

At this, the man shifted to get a better look and Neku decided subtlety wasn't going to work. 'Pervert,' she announced loudly. When no one paid any attention, Neku stood up and repeated herself, only this time she pointed.

The man got off at the next stop.

Although what actually happened was that he got off, the woman sitting next to Neku changed seats and two grandmothers opposite spent the next three stops muttering to each other.

Well, said their glance, *What did you expect? Looking like that.*

Shrugging, Neku raised a pencil and began to give herself eyebrows. Her cheeks stung from skin bleach but she ignored it. The tube said apply over the course of two weeks, use not more than an inch and start with a sensitivity test. To be helpful, the makers even printed a line with the daily measurement.

Neku had applied half the tube, before deciding this was a bad idea and washing most of it off. Far from lightening her complexion, the cream had made her skin blotchy, so now Neku wore foundation to hide a rash, which rather defeated the object ...

Pulling out a black lipstick, she slashed a line across her face and a goth girl began to appear in the reflection opposite. White face, strong eyebrows and a pastiche geisha pout. Neku sat too far from her own reflection to see the silver bolt recently fixed through her tongue, but she could still taste its metal and blood.

She wore a fat amber ring on her right hand, a black plastic watch and a bracelet made from glass beads threaded onto silver mesh. Five gold hoops ran the rim of one aching ear and beneath her ripped blouse she could feel flesh try to shrivel beneath the bolts now skewering it. The first boy to touch her, and he'd barely glanced at Nijie's breasts as he swabbed on surgical spirit, reached for a metal clamp and thrust a spike through each nipple.

Pain meant nothing.

Remember that, Neku told herself.

She was not like the other kids arriving at Harajuku Bridge with their fantasy identities hidden in Liz Lisa bags. Little suburban show-offs who unpacked their alter egos each weekend, flashing white knickers as they made up their faces or struggled into thigh boots, lace tops or ripped silver jeans. She was Lady Neku, the original; the others were just copies.

Swirling her cloak and raising her chin, Neku left the station by its first exit, ignored a poster featuring a winged, haloed and very happy Santa Claus, and dodged two foreigners busy unpacking fake Rolex from a box on the corner. Harajuku Bridge was famous for its costume play gangs who gathered each day to parade their outlandish clothes; but the sky was getting dark, it was beginning to drizzle and most of the spectators had already gone home.

No matter.

A group of three *cos-play* glanced up and scowled when they realised the stranger in the scarlet cloak was no one they knew. Neku kept walking, sleet on her face.

They'd know her soon enough.

Korea issues complaint at Tokyo Olympic bid. Faceless corpse found on London motorway. So said the paper she tossed onto a bench, earning a glare from an old man and more tuts from a group of women. It was the front page that irritated Neku.

Public Outrage Mounts.

She didn't need their outrage, approval or anything else to tell her what she already knew. *In a bizarre suicide pact, the family of Tony Kitagawa was found dead on a beach near Koyurugi Point.*

Neku sighed.

Beyond the bridge a path split, one direction heading to the Meiji-jingu shrine. It was here a family had gathered, fifteen years earlier for the marriage of a son to an Italian girl he'd met in New York. A union strange enough to bring the Kitagawa clan together for the first time in five years.

It had been brief, this marriage; and there'd been only one child, a daughter, nobody important. It had not even been his first marriage, so the girl was sent to live with her half brothers, part of the family but never quite equal. She had her gender, her foreign looks and her mixed blood to thank for this.

Neku was glad that girl was dead.

Around her, winter-bare maples dripped with drizzle and swayed slowly in the chill wind as gravel shifted wetly under foot. A stream beneath a tiny bridge had swollen, where rotted leaves created a natural dam, and a black man with an old-fashioned twig broom was busy trying to brush the leaves away.

4

At the turning to a café, Neku made herself turn back. The black man had been staring at her anyway, as if to say someone dressed like her did not belong on the gravel paths leading to the Meiji Shrine, and he was right. She belonged on the bridge with the other girls, that gaggle of giggles and spite.

A couple of *cos-play* glanced up and Neku looked right through them, rolling her shoulders and letting her arms hang loose. These were *ijime-ko*, suburban kids with unconvincing sneers, the kind of people who regarded pulling each other's hair as a fight bad enough to talk about for days.

Neku had seen real fights.

'Careful where you walk.'

When Neku stepped too close to a line of carefully-arranged cosmetics their owner didn't even bother to be polite. Just barked his order and went back to choosing a lipstick from a line of seven laid out in a row. Shu Uemura, Chanel, Dior, Shiseido and Bourjois ...

Neku wondered if he'd even checked the colours or just bought by label.

'You hear me?'

'Oh yes,' she said. 'I hear you.'

Kicking over his lipsticks, Neku stamped on the boy's wrist before he had time to scramble away. Bones broke and Neku tried not to smile as a gaggle of girls parted to let her through. That was all it ever took, according to the Kitagawa brothers. One punch, one bullet, one kick ... Precedent was everything, only the Kitagawa were dead and no amount of precedent was going to change that.

In front of Meiji-jingumae Station two uniformed officers were questioning the foreign couple who'd obviously only just finished unpacking their consignment of fake Rolex. When Neku paused to watch, the eldest of the two police officers waved her away.

Go, his look said.

It didn't say, *We've been looking for you.* And it didn't say, *Stop right there, while I call base to see if you're a runaway.* It just said, *Who cares if you're upset? Go away. We're too busy to bother with stupidly-dressed children.*

Neku did as the look said.

5

PART ONE

CHAPTER I
August 2003

Later, Kit Nouveau was to realise that his world unravelled in Tokyo, six months after a *cos-play* stuffed large amounts of money into a locker that could be opened with a cheap screwdriver, had anyone known what it contained. Until then, he'd thought it ended fifteen years earlier, at 10.38 p.m., on Friday 15 August 2003, behind an old barn on the chalk hills above Middle Morton, a small town in Hampshire.

Who knew? Certainly not the nineteen-year-old squaddie leaning against the barn's wooden wall. He'd come to the party with his latest girlfriend, a high-breasted Welsh girl called Amy who had a filthy laugh and, he hoped, filthy habits. Only she was inside sulking and the girl whose bandana top he'd just undone was going out with someone else.

'Hey,' said Kit. 'It's okay.'

Pushing him away, the girl retied a ribbon. 'No,' she said. 'It's not.' Mary O'Mally wore lipstick, black eyeliner and bare legs under a frayed white miniskirt. Both make-up and attitude having been put on in a bus shelter, roughly halfway between her parents' house and the barn. She'd cut her hair since Kit last saw her and had red highlights put in.

Under his own waxed jacket Kit wore a Switchblade Lies T-shirt, with jeans and biker boots. His fair hair had been cropped and the faintest trace of a blond, very non-regulation goatee ghosted his chin.

Inside the hut someone took off *Original Pirate Material* and slung on *Tight Smile,* jacking up the volume.

'Wait,' said Kit, when Mary tried to say something. And they both listened to the bass line, as Vita Brevis thumbed a Vintage 5-string; then came Art Nouveau, splintering Vita's bass line with a three-chord crash, and Kit found himself fingering fret shapes onto empty air.

Mary grinned.

'I'll walk you home,' he said.

'Kit ...'

Undoing her top had been stupid but old habits died hard. Josh was a nice guy, in a rich-boy kind of way, but Mary was Kit's ex-girlfriend and he still occasionally dreamed about her. Reassuring dreams, at least reassuring to someone who'd puked his way through an Iraqi firefight, put his sniper training into practice and was on compassionate leave, while his Colonel worked out what to do about an incident no one really wanted to make the papers.

'I'd better go back.'

'Okay,' said Kit.

'You coming with me?'

Shaking his head, Kit said 'Better not. Can you get Josh to give Amy a lift home? And, you know ...' Kit stopped, wondering how to put his thoughts into words.

'What?' said Mary.

'You know. If you and Josh ever ...'

'If we?'

'If you split up,' said Kit, 'then maybe we could try again?' His voice trailed off as he realised Mary wanted to slap him, which wouldn't be the first time. 'I know,' he said, holding up his hands.

'No you don't,' she said, dirty blonde hair brushing bare shoulders as she shook her head, each shake fiercer than the one before. *'You have no fucking idea.'*

Mary and Kit went out for five months, right up to the start of last year's exams. She'd just about convinced her mother that Kit and band practice weren't about to ruin her GCSEs when Kit broke up Switchblade Lies, dumped Mary and talked himself onto a thirteen-week Army Preparation Course, all in the same afternoon.

Josh was the one who picked up the pieces and walked Mary to her exams and convinced her life could still be good. Josh was the one Mary's mother liked, though she'd probably have liked him more if his mother hadn't been Korean.

'It was just a thought,' said Kit.

'Yeah,' said Mary. 'A shit one.' And there it might have rested, except the moon chose that moment to slip between clouds, and Mary caught the tears in eyes of the boy opposite.

'You broke it off,' she said crossly.

'It's not that.'

'What then?'

'I don't know,' said Kit. 'Life, I guess ... You'd better go back inside. Josh will be wondering where you've gone.'

'He doesn't own me.'

'Hey,' said Kit. 'No one owns you, I know that. No one owns me. No one owns anyone. We just get to borrow each other for a while.'

She glared at him. 'Did you make that up?'

'Yeah, I think so.' Kit thought about it. 'At least, I don't think it's stolen from anybody else.'

Kit and Mary ended up pushing his Kawasaki between them, while the moon stretched an elongated couple and bike onto Blackboy Lane and night winds whispered through fields on the far side of the hedge.

The barn, which was lapboard, stained black and had been built before any of them had been born, the pub to which the hut belonged and the three farm cottages that made up Wintersprint were half a mile behind. Two of the cottages had been knocked together to make a house. It was his mother's idea.

'What are you thinking?'

'About Mum.'

Anyone else would have left it there. 'Do you regret giving evidence?'

Kit's mother had been American, an artist from New York. His father was small-town Hampshire, a sergeant on the local police force. It would have been hard to find two people more unsuited. Their marriage had been coming apart for most of Kit's childhood; certainly for as long as he could remember, and Kit had a good memory.

One night, three years before, his parents had argued, which was nothing new. And Kit's mother had demanded a divorce, which was also nothing new. Only this time she meant it, which was ... A jogger found her at the foot of Ashley chalk pit, her skull broken and her ribs badly fractured. She'd been dead for roughly two hours, according to the coroner.

Suicide, said his father.

Kit was interviewed and told the inspector what he'd heard. Which was far more than he'd ever wanted to hear. When asked, *It was the first such argument, wasn't it?* He said no. And kept saying no, all the way through to appearing as a witness for the prosecution in court.

Kit's evidence was tainted, that was the position of the defence. He'd had his own argument with his father, a day earlier. A fierce and vicious argument, that saw Sergeant Newton forced to physically restrain his son. This was the boy's revenge. A twisted attempt to use the death of his mother to hurt his father, a man who was already heartbroken by the loss. The jury believed the defence, and Kit and his father had not spoken since, not a single word. Although, until Kit enlisted, they'd shared the same house.

'You don't think that maybe ...'

'No,' said Kit, *'I don't.'*

She glanced away, moonlight on her face. Kit saw it happen. She glanced aside and bit her lip. *Say it,* he wanted to tell her. Only Mary wouldn't and if he was honest Kit wasn't sure he wanted it said. Being wrong about his father was as bad as being right.

'A pity,' said Mary, some time later.

'What? about my mother?'

'No,' she said, sighing. 'About the band.'

Art Nouveau, Vita Brevis and Joshua Treece ... Kit managed a smile. 'Not really,' he said. 'We were shit. None of us could even play.'

'That's harsh,' said the girl who'd briefly been *Vita Brevis – bass/vocals/keyboards/lyrics.*

'We were worse than shit.'

One single, a week's air play on local radio and a final fumble with Mary in the back of a transit, while Josh pretended to sleep and Colonel Treece kept his eyes on the road. Kit had bought the Kawasaki with money he got selling his guitar and the only thing he'd kept was his new name, although the *Art* bit of that had gone the way of his hair.

'You want a cigarette?'

'No,' said Kit, 'I've given up.' Kicking his bike onto its stand, he took the packet from her fingers and tapped one free, lighting it with a high-chrome Zippo that read, *Iraq 2003, the Democracy in Action Tour.* He'd borrowed it from an American sergeant, who was still waiting for him to give it back.

'Here,' he said.

'You know,' said Mary. 'We should get out of the road.'

So Kit rolled his bike through a gap in the hedge and parked it up again. In the old days people would have read meaning into the jagged clouds and back-lit sky, the wind that dragged shivers from both their bodies and a moon as cold and clear as a world trapped in the cross hairs of a gun sight.

'Time to go,' said Kit, watching Mary grind her cigarette underfoot.

Mary raised her eyebrows.

'Curfew, remember?' As if either of them could forget. One of the

reasons Mary's mother disliked Kit was that he treated her rules as something negotiable, rather than laws set in stone.

'They're away.'

Kit looked at her.

'Yeah,' she said. 'You wouldn't believe the lecture I got.'

'I would. No friends back to the house and no staying out all night. Your dad knows exactly how many beers there are in the fridge and the level of every bottle in the drinks cupboard. I've had it,' he added, when she looked surprised. 'That time my parents went to London.'

Back in the days when my mother was alive.

'The weekend you had the party?'

Yeah, that weekend.

Clouds continued to scuttle across the sky and eleven o'clock came and went, measured in bells carried on the wind from the village below. At Mary's insistence, they counted off the bells, but called the first bell *two* and ended at *twelve* to muddle the devil.

'Don't ask,' she said. 'Blame my grandmother.'

A battered red Mini came by, followed by a taxi. It looked at if those unable to squeeze into Josh's car had banded together to get a cab. Amy was among them.

When the next round of bells began, Mary and Kit counted them from *two* to *thirteen* and then stood up. It was meant to be a simple thank-you for watching the clouds, letting him count bells and not holding their last argument against him. A farewell to what had been, little more.

Leaning forward, Kit took Mary's face in his hands. He expected a kiss, a shrug and to walk her home. A snog for old time's sake. Something by way of goodbye. Only, something happened.

As Mary's hand came up to touch his face, his fingers brushed the bare skin of her waist and a circuit closed between them, the shiver of excitement catching them both by surprise. Her lips tasted of cheap cigarettes and expensive brandy that she'd stolen from home. She said nothing when his hand found the knot on her bandeau top for a second time and even less when he reached for the buttons on her skirt. He was her first, something unexpected.

'I thought you and Josh ...'

Mary said nothing, just raised herself on one elbow and stared until Kit looked away. 'No,' she said, into his silence.

Slivers of daylight had begun to warm the chalk hills around them. A maroon Volvo trundled out of the village, headed for Southampton or

London. Its headlights sweeping blindly over the spot where Mary and Kit lay.

'Sorry,' said Kit. 'Wrong question.'

Reaching over, Mary patted his face. 'You don't say.'

CHAPTER 2
Friday 8 June

The bar occupied the second floor of a narrow building in Roppongi, behind a tourist drag of burger bars, clothes shops and strip joints running south from Almond crossing. The building stood low on a slope, in an area full of crooked, dirty alleyways, one of few such areas remaining in Roppongi or anywhere else.

A small patch of cinder-block parking occupied what was once a garden, but because the original garden sloped away from the road, a wall had been built and ground infilled to make space for three cars. This had been done back in the 1950s, when most of Tokyo was still a bomb site, and Allied soldiers were abandoning Roppongi to the bar owners and pimps who'd kept them so well entertained.

Nowadays the cinder patch was empty by day and home to a row of motorcycles at night. And this area, directly opposite the cemetery, smelt slightly of sewage, because the whole of Roppongi smelt of sewage in summer. Mixed with the odour of noodles, it was one of Tokyo's signature smells.

The man who stared from Pirate Mary's basement window inhaled a deeper sourness, one that danced in wisps of smoke from the heated foil in his fingers. Kit Nouveau kept his habit on a tight leash, limiting himself to one fix a day, but the dragon was restless and beginning to strain against its chains. One of them was winning and Kit guessed it wasn't him.

Crumpling blackened foil, Kit tossed it into a bin and went to fetch his wife. 'Come inside,' he told Yoshi, shrugging himself into a bike jacket. 'I need to go.'

'Okay,' she said. 'I'm leaving at nine.'

'I'll be back,' Kit promised.

Yoshi Tanaka nodded, not really seeing her husband. She was wearing

15

a blue yukata, tied clumsily around her narrow waist with the belt from something else. Her feet were bare and clay splattered, and she'd twisted her sweat-darkened hair into a knot and fastened it with a yellow rubber band. In her hand was an unfired bowl, unlike any work of hers he'd ever seen.

'What are you doing?' Kit's voice must have been abrupt, because his question made Yoshi flip her gaze towards him. Her eyes were as glazed as the pots she usually made.

'Getting rid of it,' she said.

There were so many things wrong with this Kit barely knew where to begin, so he started with the first thing that came to mind. 'You never waste clay,' he said. 'I thought you told me it brought bad luck.'

Yoshi scowled.

'Anyway,' said Kit. 'What's wrong with it?'

He watched her think. And just when he was sure her thoughts had turned to something else altogether, Yoshi glanced at the bowl and began to shake her head.

'It's not me,' she said.

This, for Yoshi, was a statement of such overwhelming egotism that Kit was shocked. 'It's beautiful,' he said. 'Look at the thing ...'

She peered at it doubtfully.

'Bring it inside,' said Kit. 'If you still hate it tomorrow we'll bin it.' He led his wife through the basement door and into the utility room. It was no cooler inside than out, but at least Yoshi was away from direct sun and no longer standing semi-naked in full view of the street.

Sweat slicked Yoshi's face and gathered in the valley between her breasts, she'd been awake for thirty-two hours and treddling her potter's wheel for almost fifteen of those. A stranger could have told how exhausted she was from the way her eyes kept sliding out of focus.

'Get some sleep,' Kit suggested. 'Before we open again.'

Pirate Mary's was one of five Irish bars in Roppongi. An area that still traded on its reputation for seediness and sex but which was rapidly becoming smarter than expats like Kit really liked. Exclusive designers opened as fast as brothels shut. The tiny cemetery behind Kit's bar had started appearing on postcards, and the prostitutes walking Gaien-Higashi-dori now wore faux rather than real fur in winter, so as not to upset their clients' sensibilities.

One day, the real Roppongi, with its hostess bars and filthy courtyards would vanish forever, like Montmartre or London's Soho before it, leaving an ersatz theme park of perversion lite. In the meantime, the

Irish bars pulled in regular crowds, with Pirate Mary's gathering one of the largest.

'Come on,' he said. 'Let's get you settled.'

Footsteps followed Kit up three flights of stairs and when he led Yoshi into their bedroom he was relieved to discover that she'd left the bowl behind. 'I'll set the alarm clock for you.'

Her nod was slight.

Lifting the yukata from her shoulders, Kit steered his wife towards a naked lavatory in the corner and watched her piss. She didn't bother to clean her teeth in the basin or remove the smear of lip gloss that served as make-up. When she finally moved it was to examine herself in a long mirror.

'You can stop,' he said.

Yoshi shook her head. 'No,' she said. 'I can't.'

Rope burns circled her wrists, thighs and breasts. The knots had been too loose the first time and she'd made him tie them all again. It was a regular ritual, one he still failed to understand.

Outside on the balcony her treadle was sticky with slops and the bucket of raw clay had been left uncovered. So Kit found a cloth, ran it under water and protected the clay. Having done that, he cut the slops from her table and cleaned its wheel with the edge of a wooden blade, flicking the scrapings on the floor to dry. He could sweep them up later.

Yoshi was asleep by the time he finished.

The new bowl was where Yoshi left it, next to one of the bins on the cinder patch beside the bar. She'd been carrying it clumsily and her thumb had smudged a dark print beneath the rim, the bowl already dry enough to produce a white bloom around the edge.

Kit's first instinct was to run the bowl under a tap, but its rim was so thin that it looked as if it might bend at the slightest pressure. So he put the bowl on a tray, found some gauze and soaked this in water and draped it over the bowl, protecting both with a large upturned cake tin. As an afterthought he put the cake tin in a cupboard by the back door, checked the front door was also locked and went to get his motorbike.

'Noovoo-san ...'

The old man who tended the graveyard was waiting for Kit by the railings. In his arms, Ito-san carried a long bundle of prayer sticks, stained with age.

'Mr Ito.'

'Police were here.'

'What?' said Kit. He should have said, *I'm sorry, who ...? And thank you for letting me know.* But all he wanted to do was arrive in time for his language lesson.

'Police,' Mr Ito said. 'From the ward office. One kept trying the door. I said you were probably out.'

Mr Ito seemed embarrassed.

'It's okay,' said Kit. 'Thank you for telling me.'

Ito-san gave a brief bow.

CHAPTER 3
Friday 8 June

'Oniji-chan,' said Kit, 'I probably shouldn't ask this but where's your husband?'

Elegant, middle-aged and happily naked, the Japanese woman lifted herself onto one elbow, revealing a heavy breast. 'He's busy.'

Kit considered that.

'What kind of busy?' he asked finally. There were many things about Mrs Oniji's life that puzzled him. Including why her husband spent so little time with his wife.

'Torturing someone.'

'God ...' Kit sat up in bed. 'Why?'

Mrs Oniji shrugged. 'I don't know,' she said. 'I never ask.' She smiled. 'Does my answer make you feel afraid?'

When Kit shook his head, Mrs Oniji sighed.

'It should,' she said, 'but then I'm not sure you feel much anything.' She paused. 'Is that correct?'

'Just about,' said Kit. '*Much about anything* or *anything much* would be better ...'

'Ahh,' said Mrs Oniji. 'I see.'

Later, when they'd made love again, rinsed themselves under a power shower and returned to the bed, because Mrs Oniji's little room had only a futon for furniture, Kit put his hand on Mrs Oniji's stomach and felt it rumble.

'We should eat.'

Mrs Oniji rolled over to stare into the pale blue of his eyes. She seemed puzzled. 'Is that an order?'

'No,' said Kit. 'More of a suggestion. An order would be, W*e must eat now*, or *You will eat*.'

Mrs Oniji smiled. 'I'll remember that,' she said. Having understood its meaning and how the phrase should be used Mrs Oniji would undoubtedly return to it, probably the next time they met. 'You know,' she said a minute later. 'There is no food in this house. However, I have booked a restaurant.'

Kit's heart sank.

The bed on which he and Mrs Oniji lay was a hundred and fifty years old and as uncomfortable as the day it was made. It sat in the upstairs room of a wooden house in the lanes behind Aoyama-dori. The building originally belonged to her grandfather, and if Mrs Oniji's husband ever knew his wife owned it he'd forgotten.

Everything Kit knew about Mr Oniji he'd learnt from Mrs Oniji, relayed to him in increasingly complex and confident sentences. Oniji Kisho had interests in construction and shipping, both of which kept him very busy. Also, *fuzoku*, the ejaculation industry. He owned a hostess bar in Roppongi, five soapland brothels, a large love hotel in Kabukicho, and Bottomless Kup, a franchise where ostentatiously subservient waitresses waxed their pubic hair and served coffee, without knickers.

He also liked gold watches and ceramics, but hated golf. Which was a problem because he owned a golf course in sight of Mount Fuji. The members, who paid handsomely for their membership, would have liked their chairman to play.

When Kit first arrived in Tokyo it was to work for an exclusive and very expensive language school that catered for the wives of high-ranking executives expecting to be sent overseas.

The job was well paid and secure in the way that only Japanese jobs back then could be. It was also fantastically boring. Although what finally drove Kit out were the classroom posters, one of which read, *talent requires reformatting what you know*. Having identified the Japanese as the world's first post-modern race, Per Sorenson had created post-modern language tuition, ideally suited to a country where people inevitably told you something by telling you something else.

Kit's second job paid substantially less but catered for a wider variety of students, one of whom was Mrs Oniji. It was only later that Kit discovered A1 Language Learning was owned by her husband.

When Kit resigned from A1 it was on the understanding he would continue to give Mrs Oniji her monthly lesson; and that was ten years ago. She'd been thirty-one and he'd been twenty-three. The arrangement had continued happily until six months earlier, when somehow they'd ended up in bed.

'Are you happy?'

It was unusual for Mrs Oniji to ask such questions. And the fact she felt able to ask a question quite that personal came as a shock.

'Why?' asked Kit.

'Just wondered,' she said.

Pushing her down, Kit pulled aside the sheet and stilled the hand that came up to cover her breasts. 'I'm not unhappy,' he said, positioning himself over her.

Mrs Oniji sighed. 'That makes two of us, *I guess...*'

Most people when they mention Tokyo mean the twenty-three wards. Although, metropolitan Tokyo is actually formed of twenty-three wards, twenty-six cities, three towns, one village and two islands. For Mrs Oniji the city was smaller still, contained within only three wards: Chiyoda-ku, Chuo-ku and Minato-ku.

Within these could be found the restaurants of Akasaka, the shopping district of Ginza, and Maranouchi itself, the centre of all things commercial and political. It was in Maranouchi that Oniji Kisho had offices.

Inevitably enough, the restaurant to which she took Kit was in Akasaka, set back behind Hitosuki-dori and separated from the bustle of the street by wooden fencing and a quiet garden. In its courtyard a senior and junior salaryman were finishing one of those clipped conversations that looked – to outsiders – like the verbal equivalent of a punishment beating. Whatever was said, the younger of the two bowed deeply and turned for the exit, standing aside to let Mrs Oniji pass.

Kit doubted she even noticed.

Walking into the restaurant was like walking into a bamboo grove, because dried lengths had been used to divide the low room into waiting area, bar area and restaurant proper. Not by making walls, because that would be far too obvious, it had been used to suggest where walls might be, as if each upwards stroke of bamboo existed to provide structural supports for a wall that had never been built.

Maybe the lengths were real, or perhaps they were cast from resin. Whatever, the light within each was bright enough to illuminate its skin like neon bars to a cage. There were three dozen such strands, rising from a slate floor and disappearing into the ceiling. The tables were also slate, the chairs wooden. A length of counter was lined with rattan stools, each claimed by someone smart enough to pass muster. The tables might need reservations, but despite complaints Café Ryokan resolutely refused to take reservations for places at the bar.

It was a million miles from Pirate Mary's in Roppongi, where *bozozoku* bikers mixed with Western expatriates, Tokyo's art crowd and a smattering of Japanese students who believed, sometimes rightly, that they were living dangerously.

'Another saké?'

Kit shrugged, caught himself and smiled. 'Sounds neat ...'

The Japanese woman opposite repeated the words to herself and Kit could see her think them through, consider all possible meanings to be found in the phrase and fail to come up with one that made sense of being offered a drink.

'Slang?'

Nodding, Kit watched her file away the words for later use.

We should eat,' she said.

Fragments of sea urchin slid across Kit's bowl, and even black pepper did little to improve their taste, which was over-rich and slimy to the tongue.

This was, he knew, the entire point of eating *ezobarfun*. Its texture being as important as its taste, maybe more important. He could tell himself *ezobarfun* tasted like Mrs Oniji at the mid-point of her cycle, but still his throat tightened with every fresh piece. No amount of saké was enough to wash it down, and he was drinking a lot of saké.

'Slowly,' said Mrs Oniji. 'It is best to eat *ezobarfun* slowly.'

Kit looked up from his bowl.

'Savour it,' she suggested.

He nodded doubtfully.

'You like this place?'

Ordinarily yes, he wanted to say. Only today he was late home and Mrs Oniji and he had at least another three courses to go. The mistake had been in not booking a restaurant himself. Nonetheless, Kit understood the compliment she was paying in bringing him here.

'It's very elegant,' he said. 'Very sophisticated.'

'Elegant,' said Mrs Oniji, turning the word over in her mouth. 'Sophisticated.' She got the stress slightly wrong both times and swallowed the middle of her second word, but her English was still infinitely more impressive than Kit's Japanese, which consisted of five hundred or so words or phrases and could be reduced to the three that mattered.

Domo Arigato, Dozo, Shumimasen.

Thank you/Excuse me/I'm sorry.

'There is a difference?'

'Between ...?'

He'd been too abrupt. 'Let me see,' he said, pushing his bowl aside, while he explained why the arrangement of bamboo in the rock garden outside was elegant while the American woman at the bar was sophisticated. The weather, clothes, food, Impressionist art and books, these were the things Mrs Oniji and Kit discussed during their weekly meetings.

'I thought, perhaps,' said Mrs Oniji. 'We could go late-night shopping …' She waited for Kit to nod, his acceptance that this was a good idea. 'I need a dress for New York.'

He could hear the simple pride in that sentence. She was flying to America for a week's holiday, with her sister, her sister-in-law and her mother. Her husband was too busy to make the trip, Oniji Kisho was always too busy, but his would be the money that paid for first-class flights, the hotel near Central Park and, quite probably, the presents that all three women would buy him at the Takashimaya department store on New York's Fifth Avenue.

Standing up, Kit pulled back Mrs Oniji's chair. He had been her English tutor for ten years, her friend for three and her lover only recently. He was not proud of cheating on his wife, but life with Yoshi was infinitely more complicated than most people realised.

Neither Mrs Oniji nor Kit noticed the man who watched them collect their coats and it would have made little difference if they had. Hiroshi Sato had been selected for the absolute averageness of his looks, height, hair and complexion.

He was near invisible.

Waiting a few seconds, Oniji Kisho's personal assistant pushed back his stool, dropped a 10,000 yen note onto the counter and followed the couple outside.

CHAPTER 4
Friday 8 June

Below a cast-iron street light that rusted in the shadow of an overpass built for Tokyo's 1964 Olympics (and scheduled for demolition should Japan win the next Olympic bid), on a corner by Best Soul Burger and a bit beyond where the Shuto Expressway 3 forks west to Shibuya or south towards the ersatz Parisian splendour of the Tokyo Tower, a *cos-play-zoku* in a faded red cloak made knives appear and disappear.

The knives came into being between the girl's first finger and thumb and disappeared at a flick of her wrist. She wore white gloves with the fingers cut away and was watched only by a cat.

At least that was tonight's audience until Mr Oniji's personal assistant arrived.

'Clever,' he said.

The girl bowed, bent quickly to scoop up half the coins the man dropped into her plastic coffee cup, and tossed one of her knives high into the air, before catching it behind her back.

He noticed, almost too late, that the girl in the cloak and white-lace wedding dress kept her eyes shut. 'Isn't that dangerous?'

'Not really.'

Hiroshi Sato kept watching anyway. Although what he really watched was the alley beyond the girl, where the foreigner headed for home. Mr Oniji's instructions had been very clear, Sato was to observe without being seen.

The job had begun five hours earlier. When Mr Nouveau ambled out of Pirate Mary's, conversed briefly with an old man and climbed onto a Kawasaki W650, which he rode north. Having paid a Brazilian mechanic in advance, Mr Nouveau left his W650 at a machine shop on Akasaka-dori, walking the rest of the way, to arrive at a tiny wooden house near Temechi-dori at 4.30 exactly, the time given for Mrs Oniji's lesson.

Two and a half hours later, Mrs Oniji and her tutor had left the house. A short while later they reached a well-known restaurant, where they sat at a corner table. Mrs Oniji did the bulk of the talking and Hiroshi Sato regarded this as appropriate, since she was the one practising her conversation. After this, they went shopping.

The boss had not asked for a full report. He had merely told Hiroshi Sato where the foreigner lived and when the lesson would begin and ordered him to follow the man. He had not told Hiroshi Sato to write a report or make notes. Although Mr Sato was making them anyway, just in case. So far as he could tell, nothing unseemly was taking place. Whether walking, talking or eating, the boss's wife and the foreigner treated each other with polite respect.

Leaving the *cos-play* to her knives, Mr Sato abandoned the corner near Best Soul Burger for air conditioning inside. He nodded absent-mindedly at the sing-song *'irasahimase'* greeting from a Korean girl behind the counter and ordered a teriyaki burger. When it came, by itself on a white plate, with a thick soy and plum sauce, he carried it to a table away from a window and began to expand his notes.

Even if windows had let Hiroshi Sato watch the alley outside, it's unlikely he'd have noticed the tramp who staggered from a Club Kitty doorway. This was the man who'd watched Mr Sato break off his careful if over-obvious shadowing of the drunken foreigner. It was even less likely Mr Sato would have noticed the cat, which ambled over to look at the homeless man at a nod from the *cos-play*.

'Trouble?' Neku asked.

'Think so,' said the cat. At least, that's what she thought he said.

The cat might not be able to name days of the week, but he knew good days from bad, and until Neku appeared the cat had been suffering bad traffic, weird weather and a row of metal bins where plastic ones used to be.

This was a problem, because the cat had been able to lift plastic lids. In fact, since he first stopped to watch the juggling girl two months earlier, those bins had been where he ate every night. The cat wasn't to know his eating habits had led to a call from the Citizens Recycling Society, suggesting Best Soul adopt metal bins as good practice suggested.

'You're odd,' the cat said.

'And you're not?' said Neku, twisting her hair into a knot and fixing it in place with two long ivory pins. The blades she slipped into her pocket.

'Where are we going?' asked the cat. Although, what he actually said was, *Now . . . ?*

'Work.'

The cat scowled.

'I've got this,' Neku said, reaching into her pocket for smoked eel. '*Unagi* set,' she added, 'you eat it.' They walked in silence, with Neku taking cold boiled rice for herself and tossing the cat slivers of meat from her bento box, applauding every time the cat caught a fragment before it hit the ground.

'All gone,' she told him.

Having checked to make sure she told the truth, the cat twisted between Neku's ankles, almost tripping her.

'Sorry,' said Neku, 'I need to be alone now.'

So the cat asked, *Why?* Which he did with a simple twitch of his whiskers and a quarter turn of one ear.

'Hunting,' said the girl.

At this the cat looked interested. 'More food?'

Neku shook her head. 'Enemies . . .'

'Ahh,' said the cat. Food, hunting, sex and fighting, such things he understood. Conversation waited for none of those.

'Good to meet you,' said Neku

The cat nodded and watched her walk away. He liked her cloak, which was long and lined with shiny stuff. And he'd liked the eel, very much. After a few seconds' thought, the cat trotted after her.

Violent crime is still rare in Japan. That's the official version. The truth is somewhat more complex, though nothing like as grim as the hipper guide books suggest, with their dark rumours about heavily-massaged figures and officially-sanctioned under reporting. Violence happens. It's still relatively common within families, between senior and junior classes in school and remains the currency of choice inside gangs, but it occurs within rigidly defined hierarchies. Everybody understands that.

It felt out of place on darkened steps leading to a Roppongi graveyard.

Maybe this was why Kit was so slow to realise he was being followed. Alternatively, his slowness might have been down to the saké sweating itself out of his body and making him stumble on the steps, already aware he was too late to do anything but hope Yoshi had left No Neck in charge, and gone to visit her sister as originally planned.

He was inside his own thoughts, oblivious to the cloying humidity around him. His life was not right, it was not even wrong, it just was ... And had been that way for so long Kit found it impossible to imagine life being any different. So he didn't try, he just put one foot in front of another and wished himself home.

Neku sighed. If she'd been hunting she would have struck by now, so much time wasted on tracking was merely silly; unless the tramp with the Colt was having doubts? This seemed possible, because the gap between hunter and prey remained the same ten paces as it had been a minute earlier, only now the hunter was glancing back, as if aware he too might be followed.

And he was, for reasons that probably made sense only if you were Neku, the original ... The foreigner gave her coffee. He'd never actually asked if she liked coffee, but every morning, when he returned from his walk, he presented her with a cup, giving Neku a slight bow. Once she changed doorways just to see what would happen and he arrived at her new doorway, carrying her cup, as if that was where she always slept.

And before this, he'd given her 5000 yen. At a kiosk on the way to the Meiji shrine. One day when he was feeling sad and Neku was feeling scared. In the early days when she was still getting used to being herself. It was unacceptable that someone should hunt him.

The Rolex was a fake but it was a good fake, triple-wrapped white gold, with a pearl face and appliqué numbers, Korean made. Kit stared drunkenly at the man's Colt automatic, then at his own watch. 'Okay,' said Kit, deciding to do what he was told. 'It's yours.'

This was not the response his mugger had been expecting.

'Drop it.'

When Kit bent, the man shook his head. 'Drop it,' he said.

The fake Rolex hit the dirt with a thud, then bounced against the railings of the graveyard to become lost in darkness.

'Now your wallet.'

Extracting a small leather billfold, Kit flipped it open, peered inside and shrugged. 50,000 yen. About the price of a good meal in Akasaka, a week's heroin or a proper service for his bike. Hardly worth getting killed over.

'No,' said the man, when Kit got ready to drop it. 'Hand the thing to me.'

Kit did as he was told.

His mugger man was openly sneering now.

27

'And the rest.'

Kit began to search his own pockets. Nothing but keys to the bar and a handful of coins, mostly 500 yen coins or lower. It was only when he dipped his hand into the inside pocket of his wax jacket that Kit hesitated, although he imagined the expression on his face was surprise.

'Come on.'

'It's just a postcard.'

'I don't care,' said the man.

I always thought this is where we'd end up. How wrong can one girl be? Signed with heart, which was really just an M with the first and last down stroke squeezed together. If Mary's card had sentimental value, how come he hadn't answered the thing?

'*Dear Kit, it probably seems a long time ago now . . .*'

She'd got that right.

'Come on,' said the man.

'I'm late,' Kit said.

The man stared at him.

'You've already got my wallet. And my watch. What difference can a postcard make?' Quite why it mattered to Kit was hard to say. Although, from the mugger's scowl it obviously mattered that Kit was refusing to do as he was told.

'Afraid?' the man demanded.

Which was when Kit realised he was shivering. 'Drugs,' said Kit, so matter of factly the mugger actually flushed.

'Fuck that,' he said, raising his gun. 'This should cure you.'

And just as Kit decided that perhaps it wasn't worth dying for a postcard of Amsterdam, his world exploded into a hurricane of white lace and scarlet silk, the mugger's gunshot going wide as the *cos-play* spun between Kit and the weapon, knocking it aside. Silver hair shook free and an ivory hair pin punched home, freezing a facial nerve as it ruptured the mugger's eardrum and entered his brain.

As Kit watched, the homeless man sank to his knees and tipped forward, coming to rest with his head against the railings. The last thing he did was stare at the *cos-play* who'd dropped to a crouch beside him.

'Too slow,' she told him. 'Way too slow.'

'What have you done?' asked Kit.

'Spiked him,' she said. 'Simple, neat and looks to the untrained eye like an aneurysm.'

'What about that?' said Kit, nodding to the juggling knife now sticking from the man's ribs.

'Oh shit,' she said. 'Instinctive overkill ... I'm Lady Neku,' she added, before executing a small bow and offering her hand. When Kit shook, he couldn't help noticing that her fingers were sticky.

'You all right?' asked Neku.

'Drugs,' he said it without thinking. 'I've got a ...' Kit looked at the dead body, and then from the *cos-play* to the black cat who'd just appeared behind her. 'Is this for real?' he said. 'I mean, is any of this happening?'

Neku shrugged. 'It's as real as anything else on this planet.'

CHAPTER 5
Friday 8 June

When Kit looked again the girl was gone and so was her cat. The body, however, was very definitely still there.

'Oh fuck,' said Kit, a fairly useless thing to say.

Picking up his watch, Kit threaded his wrist through its metal strap and managed to click the catch on his third attempt. It was ten minutes after midnight, which meant it was actually fifteen, because the watch could be guaranteed to lose five minutes in a day. Apart from a splatter pattern, his wallet looked fine, so Kit pocketed that too, having first wiped it on the dead man's jacket.

If this was shock ...

A hot night wind, a dead body and the shakes.

I should call the police, thought Kit, only what would he say? *I was about to be shot when a cos-play saved me. No, I don't know why.* Actually, he didn't know why he was being mugged either. His clothes were cheap, his fake Rolex out of sight and there had to be better targets out there.

He'd seen bodies before, of course. Watched the living die through the cross hairs of a sniper rifle, each hit walled off in an area of his mind Kit no longer visited. Before that there was Josh, looking neater than he'd ever looked when alive, hair combed and shoes shined, wearing a tweed jacket he'd have hated.

Getting mugged, that was also shocking. And yet, it was the ease with which the *cos-play* turned the homeless man to meat ... A spike through the ear and a blade to his side, before victim or Kit even knew it had happened.

That was the real shock.

He should leave before someone saw him standing next to a body and called the police anyway. In the time it took Kit to think this, he put a dozen paces between himself and the dead man, only to turn back. Had the girl been wearing gloves? Most *cos-play-zoku* did. Long black gloves that went up to their elbows, white lace mittens or some atrocity of chain mail and steel. What if her gloves had been fingerless? Some of the kids wore those. She'd have left fingerprints.

The drunken conversation Kit had with himself halted him on the edge of flight. In the end he went back, because if he decided to leave he'd only waste more time frozen to the spot, worrying it was the wrong choice.

Kit knew himself well.

Trying to look as if he'd only just stumbled over the body, Kit touched a hand to the man's throat and then reached for the knife, but it refused to move. Eventually he remembered to twist its handle and the blade slid free with a sucking sound.

'*Nouveau-san . . .*'

Kit turned at his name and found himself staring into the worried eyes of Mr Ito, who still carried his rickety home-made brush. The man bowed and, after a second, Kit remembered his own manners and bowed back.

Sweeping the cemetery might actually be Mr Ito's job. Although it seemed more likely that the old man did it from respect or out of love for his dead wife. Whichever, he was there most hours of the day, dressed in a traditional jacket and wearing wooden clogs that were down at the heel.

'A thief,' said Kit.

The old man looked at the corpse.

'I didn't kill him,' Kit added, wanting to make this clear. The old man glanced from the dead mugger to the thin blade in Kit's hand.

'It was someone else,' said Kit.

'Ahh,' the man nodded, something clicking into place behind his eyes. 'It was someone else. I understand.'

'It *was* someone else.'

'*Hai.*' A little bow. 'Yes, I understand. Someone else.' Glancing anxiously at the blade in Kit's hand, he asked. 'Did I see this someone?'

Kit sighed. 'I'm going now,' he said. 'You might want to call the police.'

The man thought about that. 'Might I?' he asked finally. 'Only they were here again.' He paused. 'Apparently, I didn't see them either.'

CHAPTER 6
Friday 8 June

An *uyoku* van blocked the steps to Pirate Mary's parking lot. *Revere the throne, Expel the barbarian,* announced lettering down both sides. Unlike most such vans, which were black with a gold chrysanthemum, this one was gold with the imperial chrysanthemum picked out in black. It still had a revolving foghorn though, bolted to the cabin roof, ready to harangue people on all sides.

The van was empty, all its doors locked.

Kit shrugged. He was drunk, tired and stank of someone else's wife; which was probably just as well, at least being drunk was, because had Kit been sober he'd be terrified. Not about the fascist van, but about the dead man behind him and the *cos-play's* blade hanging heavy in his pocket.

Three Suzuki cruisers, all chopped beyond recognition, blocked the truck's access to the alley. So its driver would need to climb two flights of stairs to Pirate Mary's, track down three drunk *bozozoku* bikers and persuade them to let him out. The faithful-sword-to-the-throne was going to require all the luck he could get.

Kit knew he should go in. And yet . . .

From habit, he reached into his back pocket for a multitool, flipped out the flat-blade screwdriver and began to refix Pirate Mary's history to the alley walls, someone was forever trying to steal it. Towards the end of the 1500s a single figure controlled the seas around Ireland, her name was Gráinne Ni Mhaille, known to Elizabeth Tudor, the Queen of England, as Grace O'Malley and to Elizabeth's government as *a wicked director of thieves and murderers.*

She held hostage Elizabeth's ships, raided villages on the English mainland, stole cattle and forced Elizabeth to the negotiating table. Máirín Ni Mhaille was Grace O'Malley's eldest daughter, better known as Pirate Mary. Some reports said she ended on the gallows in Dublin, others that she took James Stuart's offer of a small castle on the Connemara coast. A revisionist version, recorded by the bishop of Santiago, had her repenting of her sins and living out her final years as a nun in Spain.

About half of that was true. The rest Kit had invented after he bought the narrow wooden building in Roppongi and begun fitting out its second floor as an Irish pub. Such is the nature of history that Máirín ending her days at a Spanish convent now featured as fact in a TV documentary examining the links between Ireland and Spain.

Buying the house had been Yoshi's idea. Cold and brilliant Yoshi, who blew into Kit's life and left him standing, because unlike her other lovers he let her blow right through him. He'd asked Yoshi once, near the beginning, if something terrible had happened in her childhood and she'd given a smile both slight and mocking.

'So simplistic,' she said.

A day later she asked him if that was his excuse. Kit intended to tell her about his mother, but talked about being a sniper instead.

'A *rurouni*,' said Yoshi, at the end of it. 'A *rurouni* and a *hitokiri*. A killer and a traveller with no destination.'

Within three days she'd made the *Kawakami Gensai* sequence, a series of twelve pots in shades of desert yellow, slashed across the sides with quick flicks of a knife. And the sequence sold within hours of going on display in Mitsukoshi, the majority going to private collectors, although one ended up in New York's Metropolitan Museum.

It had taken two years to repair the wreck of a building, but they'd done it eventually. Another six months were lost in creating a bar, installing the loos and white-washing wooden walls. The sign came last, painted by a small Vietnamese woman who owned a tattoo parlour behind the Almond coffee shop. She did it from a tatty snapshot of Mary O'Mally and a postcard showing the Disney version of Captain Hook.

Pirate Mary's – Tokyo's Best Irish Bar. No one but Kit knew where Máirín Ni Mhaille got her face.

CHAPTER 7
Friday 8 June

'*Dozo* ...'

The *bozozoku* glanced round, ready to take offence, recognised his host and decided to move aside, albeit reluctantly and without bothering to take his hand from the knickers of a girl in a tartan skirt.

Oh well, thought Kit, *it gives the place colour.* Dope thickened the stairs around him and a snatch of jig, ripped from an old *Riverdance* DVD, ran on a wall screen outside the bar.

Without thinking about it, Kit tucked the *cos-play's* knife above the lintel, where he usually left a spare key. Then he took a deep breath and pushed open the pub door. The room stank of warm beer and too much skunk. Someone had ripped a chrome grille off the jukebox in the hope of making it louder, and two *bozozoku* in leathers and replica WW2 helmets had crashed a table of art students and were coming on to the girls. No Neck was meant to be having a word with his friends about that.

'Kit, mate. Over here ...'

People began calling before Kit even shut the door. Yoshi was still here, working the Guinness pumps, a job she hated. No Neck was definitely missing and the food cabinet was entirely empty.

'Listen ...' It was Gaz, a Scouser who ran a studio by day, with a sideline in *portfolios* by night. Every would-be hostess who staggered off a plane at Narita already knew she was selling her breast size, hair colour and smile. When Gaz suggested life could be better as a model most were happy to believe it.

He charged them camera use, studio time, the use of cheap clothes and the services of a bad make-up artist. Model cards came extra. *Cards* being the best shot printed up with the model's name, age and vital statistics.

These lied as often as Gaz did.

Kit didn't really dislike him. He was just one of those people … One of a thousand expats who'd dragged their unhappiness to the other side of the world, expecting everything to be different and never quite got over the fact it felt the same. At least Kit had arrived with no such expectations.

'Sweet fuck,' said Gaz, cancelling what he was about to say. 'You look wrecked.'

'Yeah,' Kit said. 'Tough night, catch you later.'

Until Micki appeared Kit really thought he might make it across the smoky room without being stopped. She looked about twelve but then she also looked like a boy. Her twenty-first birthday had been at Pirate Mary's, courtesy of her friends in the *bozozoku*.

'I'm so sorry,' said Micki, bowing. 'My fault.'

'What is?'

'Everything,' she said, and promptly burst into tears.

Kit took a deep breath. 'What happened?'

'Yoshi-san fired No Neck.'

'She what …?'

'When he wouldn't leave, she called the police.' Tears were streaming down the Japanese girl's face. 'They hit No Neck with sticks,' she said, 'very hard.'

'The police?'

Micki nodded, her mouth a tight butterfly of misery. Tommy No Neck had been chapter leader with the Rebels, Australia's most notorious gang of bikers. And he was the only foreigner Kit knew who rode with the *bozozoku*, Japan's very own speed tribe.

'Yoshi …'

Looking up from her pump, Yoshi glanced back long enough to check a glass was full and slapped the lever, delivering a pint of Caffreys to the counter with a slight bang. For Yoshi, this counted as full-on rage.

'Kit,' she said, just his name.

'About No Neck …'

'Leave it,' said Yoshi. 'I'm not having this discussion.'

'He's my best friend.'

'That's why he sells drugs, drinks beer without paying for it and steals money from the till.'

'Small change,' Kit said.

'Also packets of cigarettes, whole boxes of condoms, whisky from the cabinet. He treats this pub like he owns it.'

'Okay,' said Kit, 'we'll discuss this later.'

Shaking her head, Yoshi said, 'No, we won't. There's nothing to discuss.' She glanced at her watch. Almost an hour after midnight. Officially the bar shut at 11 p.m.. In practice, because his clientele were mostly foreign and the *bozozoku* fought only among themselves, the police overlooked the fact he stayed open late. Whether that arrangement would last beyond their arrest of No Neck was another matter.

'You want me to ring the bell?'

Yoshi shrugged.

'Last orders,' Kit shouted at noisy crowd. Ten minutes after this, he rang the bell for *drinking up* and ten minutes after that he called *time*, simultaneously turning up all the house lights. Calling time was tradition, and tradition was what Tokyo's Irish pubs sold.

It was as he hooked back the doors and began to herd his customers towards the stairwell that Kit finally heard the furious howl of a police siren, coming closer by the second. Mr Ito, it seemed, had left the body for someone else to find.

Yoshi and he cleaned the bar together, Kit taking four trays on which newly-pulled pints were placed and tipping their slops into a bucket. He collected up the glasses and emptied the ashtrays into a plastic bag, tying it tightly. Yoshi wanted to say something. It was the way she stood, with one foot forward and her arms awkward at her sides.

'You were late,' she said.

'Yes,' said Kit, 'I know. Something happened ...'

'I was meant to see Yuko tonight.'

Yuko and Yoshi, the Tanaka twins. Yuko was younger, conventionally pretty and had married Tek Tamagusuku, a well-known property developer. Yoshi was famous, so famous that complete strangers turned up begging Yoshi to sell her pots to them. It had taken Kit years to work out what she wanted from him and why they were still together. He kept her family away, apart from Yuko.

'You were meant to ...?'

'*I told you*,' Yoshi said. 'Tamagusuku-san's in London. So Yuko invited me to supper. I was meant to stay the night. I even bought the baby presents.' This wasn't as big a commitment as it sounded. Yoshi spent her life buying presents for Yuko's children.

'*You promised*,' said Yoshi.

That was the problem. Yoshi kept her promises. If she said she was going to do something she did it. Kit was into territory he understood, without actually feeling the intricate web of Japanese emotions that accompanied it.

36

'About No Neck ...'

'I fired him.' Yoshi said crossly. 'He kept saying you'd be back. I asked him where you were. He wouldn't tell me.'

'I was giving an English lesson.'

Yoshi shook her head. 'No,' she said, 'that was over hours ago. Why wouldn't No Neck tell me?'

'He didn't know,' said Kit. 'Mrs Oniji booked a table at Red Bamboo. You know how long those things take.'

'You're lying.' Yoshi's eyes were large with tears.

'No. I'm not ... Look,' Kit said, 'why don't we get you a taxi. Yuko will understand.'

'It's too late,' said Yoshi.

He hoped she was talking about the taxi.

CHAPTER 8
Friday 8 June

Neku's cloak was actually a coat. That is, it was cut with sleeves rather than mere slits through which to put one's arms. Although its sleeves were very short, almost vestigial. The garment appeared to be modelled on one worn by *Vampire Hunter D* in an old film, with an upturned collar and a silk lining that glistened wetly as Neku climbed the stairs towards Pirate Mary's.

In an ideal world the cloak would keep her warm at night, wrap itself around her against the rain and harden to a shell should anyone try to kick her while she slept. But in an ideal world Neku wouldn't be sleeping in doorways in the first place and she was in this world, so her cloak just flapped, although it still managed to look better than she did.

Wrapping the cloak around her, Neku knocked politely at the half-open door of the bar. '*Sumimasen* ...?'

'We're shut.'

The voice was flat to the point of being hostile. So Neku knocked again, because she wasn't sure what else to do, then put her head round the edge. The bar was empty, chairs upended on tables and the tiles wet from having been recently mopped.

'I told you, we're ...' The woman looked up and whoever she was expecting to see saw someone else.

'*Yoshi.*'

Seeing the woman blink, Neku realised that perhaps she should have called the woman something more formal. Yet Yoshi was famous. People wrote about her in *Tokyo Today*. How could Neku not know her name?

'Who are you?'

'Lady Neku,' said Neku, bowing slightly. 'In exile on this world.'

Yoshi scowled. 'I don't have time for games,' she said. 'If someone's told you about the bar job I'll need to know your proper name. And you will call me *madame*.'

'Bar job?'

'You didn't come about No Neck's job?'

Neku shook her head. 'Your man,' she said, looking around. 'Is he here?'

'Why?' demanded Yoshi.

'Because we have business.'

'You have …?'

Watching the other woman's eyes open, Neku wondered what this famous potter saw. A curve of cheek? A single line encompassing Neku's nose, mouth and chin? When Neku caught herself in a shop window she saw a ragged *cos-play*, with flattish face and hunched shoulders. The lithe and deadly assassin Neku remembered had been missing for a while.

'What business?' Yoshi demanded.

'He has something of mine.'

'Of yours?' Yoshi must have known how lame that sounded, Neku decided, because the woman blushed and then shook her head in irritation. 'What?' Yoshi demanded. 'What could Kit-san possibly have of yours?'

My knife.

This seemed an inappropriate thing to say, so Neku just shrugged. 'He borrowed something,' she said. 'I want it back.' She looked round for somewhere to sit.

'He's out,' said Yoshi. 'Banking tonight's cash. You can't wait here.' She seemed torn between insisting Neku leave and a need to ask more questions. And it was obvious, at least to the younger of the two, that the fewer questions anyone asked the better.

'I'll be downstairs,' said Neku.

'Wait …' Yoshi held up one hand. 'This *thing*, when did he borrow it?'

Well, Neku almost said, *it wasn't exactly borrow*. She'd gone back for her knife the second she realised it was missing and found the body, still warm and slumped against the railings, only her knife was gone and the police were due to arrive. So she'd come here because this was where the cat said the foreigner lived, and because her knife was important.

'About an hour ago,' said Neku, then wondered what she'd said.

When Kit got back he found the outside light still on. That was his first warning all was not right. His second was that the *cos-play* sat on Pirate

Mary's bottom step, wrapped in her cloak. Kit's third and final clue came when Yoshi threw an ashtray from the top of the stairwell. She threw it badly, possibly because tears ruined her aim. It was also possible she intended to miss.

'How could you ...'

'What?' Kit asked.

'Look at her,' said Yoshi.

Neku clambered to her feet. 'I'm sorry,' she said, 'I didn't meant to cause problems.'

'She's just a kid,' said Yoshi.

Neku's chin came up at that. 'No, I'm not.'

Kit looked between Yoshi and the *cos-play,* who were now glaring at each other. 'God,' he said. 'Yoshi. How could you even ...'

The girl stamped, it was a very childish gesture. 'Look,' she said, holding out her hand. 'Just give it back.' Her fingernails beneath her lace gloves were bitten and broken, the gloves themselves were torn.

Pulling 15,000 yen from his wallet, Kit held the notes out to her. 'Find somewhere to sleep,' he said. 'Have a shower. Get something to eat.'

'I want my ...'

'I don't have anything of yours,' said Kit. Turning to Yoshi, he shrugged. 'She's a street kid,' he said. 'I've given her a couple of coffees, bought her a bowl of noodles, that's all.'

'Kit ...'

He hadn't expected Neku to know his name.

'Leave,' he told her. 'Before we call the police.'

'You wouldn't dare.'

'Try me,' said Kit. What else could he say? Yoshi was within listening distance.

CHAPTER 9
Saturday 9 June

When Kit got back after locking the door to the alley where the bins were kept, and the door at the stairs, which let customers into Pirate Mary's, he found the dishwasher rumbling and Yoshi nowhere in sight. So he checked the window locks, wiped down the counter one final time and began to type out a note advertising No Neck's job, since this looked like being the price Yoshi intended to extract for making peace.

'You okay?' he asked, having tracked Yoshi down to the bathroom. A question too stupid to merit an answer.

'Tomorrow,' she said, 'we'll talk tomorrow.'

Kit shut the bathroom door on his way out. He shut it softly, climbed the stairs to the next level and walked out onto the balcony, to watch Tokyo's lights twinkle like a mat of stars around him. He no longer felt drunk, he no longer felt afraid. Kit was coming to accept that he no longer felt anything very much at all.

The bath was large enough for two adults to sit upright, and so deep when filled that the level would reach their necks. Made from cast iron, it had been dragged to the third floor years earlier and sunk so far through the floor that it protruded into the area below, which was the bar these days. Above the bath was a shower that took water from a rain tank on the roof. The spray was warm in summer and cold in winter, which was the way Yoshi liked it.

The house had belonged to a grandfather on her mother's side, and when Kit put up the money it had been to buy a wreck of a building from Yoshi's cousin, the old man's heir. The price still being low enough to make the rest of Yoshi's family mutter.

It was her grandfather who originally dragged the metal bath to the third floor, before the walls had even been put in place. The bath was destined for the top floor, but her grandfather settled on the floor below, having decided that getting it so far was a miracle.

Such a bath would never now get planning permission. Partly this was because its weight made the cast-iron bath unsuitable for a wooden-framed house and partly because mains cabling ran close to one side. But mostly it was because the bath was heated by a gas burner bolted directly to its rim.

Naked flame played on metal and this heated the water. The only time Yoshi slipped as a child she burnt herself so badly the scar on her hip was still there, although growing had shrunk it to the size of a flower.

As always, Yoshi showered before taking a bath. Her other grandfather had squatted naked at an outside tap and rinsed himself with a cloth, but most of the old man's children and grandchildren had grown up with showers. Kit was the first person Yoshi met who actually washed in the bath and he stopped the moment he understood how much this upset her.

She was no fool. Yoshi knew Kit didn't love her. At least, not any longer. He was fond of her and put up with her moods and bound her tightly when she demanded it, but that wasn't love. He admired her work, the way she had of throwing pots so fine they looked too fragile to exist. And he admired her body, which was lean and spare and his whenever he wanted. But he didn't love her. Which was fine, because she'd always been honest about not loving him.

Discarding her dressing gown once the water was hot, Yoshi sank beneath its surface, letting the heat make her sleepy. And as she sat, with the water up to her neck, barely half awake and trying not to get the pages of her paperback wet, the frivolous flickering of a billion stars fought the city's sodium glare for the right to the night sky beyond her window. Silent backdrop to the street noise of Roppongi.

Drunken tourists leaving a club. A motorbike at the lights, something large. The dying howl of a cop car and an amplified order to *behave properly*. A woman in a house opposite having sex, more noisily than was strictly necessary. Yoshi knew her city and its sounds. Kit might insist he belonged here. So he'd told her, right at the beginning, the summer he arrived at Narita with one suit, three battered Murakami paperbacks and a Berlitz phrase book. She'd been right not to believe him.

She heard a cat first, then a bin going over.

'Kit . . .?'

Yoshi listened in vain for his answer.

'You want to check that?'

The cat was expected, round here there was always a cat; but the bin was heavy, too large she'd have thought to be knocked over by an animal that small. Sighing, Yoshi climbed out of the bath and reached for her dressing gown, without bothering to dry herself first. She shuffled on some slippers and climbed the single flight of stairs to their bedroom to fetch her husband.

The sheet was thrown back and his yukata was missing from its hook on the door. Since it was hardly worth going back in her bath, Yoshi collected her book of poems, relit the gas to heat the water for Kit and returned to the bedroom, climbing wearily into bed.

Outside a car started up and a cat yowled, wooden walls creaked, as they often did, and a metallic clang at ground level told Yoshi that Kit had opened the grille which covered Pirate Mary's rear door. She fell asleep to thoughts of Yuko, her sister's new baby and how she'd telephone in the morning to apologise.

CHAPTER 10
Saturday 9 June

Kit wore the wax jacket over his sarong, though he'd forgotten to put on shoes. The baseball bat in his hand came from a stall in Asakusa and was so old it had a facsimile of Babe Ruth's signature, the words *1948 memorial edition* and *produced in occupied Japan* stamped into the handle.

Flicking on the overhead lights, Kit said, 'I know you're in here.'

Halogen strips stuttered into life overhead, revealing three microwaves, a Zanuzi deep fat fryer, an industrial-size dishwasher and a butcher's block that had been there when he and Yoshi bought the building.

Other than this his kitchen was empty.

Bat in hand, Kit returned to the bar, realising too late that he'd just provided a perfect target for anybody now hidden behind the door.

'I'm armed,' he added.

Kit recognised the snort before he saw the girl. She was over by a window, wrapped in the folds of her cloak. It would have made more sense to Kit to discard the thing before she broke in, but then he wasn't fifteen or a *cos-play-zoku* and who knew what rules they worked to?

'Found it,' she said, holding up her knife. 'That's all I wanted.' Neku did something clever with her fingers and the blade disappeared, only to pop back into being when she reversed the movement.

'See,' she said. 'Not hard.'

Another twist of the wrist and it was gone again.

'I'm leaving now.'

Kit nodded.

'I won't be back.'

'That works for me,' he said.

'Okay, I'm off.' Neku hesitated on the edge of leaving. 'Can I ask you something?'

'You can ask …'

'How did you know I was down here?'

'That bin lid,' Kit said. 'You shouldn't have knocked it over.'

Neku looked puzzled. 'I haven't been near the bins,' she said, before shifting to her next question. 'And why did you buy me coffee?'

'You looked cold,' said Kit.

She sighed. 'You know,' said Neku. 'I'm not sure I'm ever going to understand this world.'

'I'll see you out,' he said.

Stepping onto cinderblock, Neku flicked open her cloak and twisted one hand, summoning the knife she'd taken from the bar. A flick of her other wrist and she had the second knife. With a twirl, she cut one blade through the air and then cut again with the other, folding them out of sight with a simple twist of her fingers.

And then – and this is where it became impossible – Neku forced her fingers into the cut in the air and began to prise it apart, the tips of her fingers vanishing from sight.

'Wait,' Kit demanded.

Neku shook her head.

'Please,' said Kit.

'You're drunk,' she told him. 'And the drugs are eating what little you have left inside. Go to bed, get some sleep … I'm going home.' Neku didn't sound very happy about this.

'No,' he said, 'not yet …'

Kit shouldn't have touched her. That was his first mistake. He reached out and tried to grab her arm, his fingers closing on her wrist, and then Neku was behind him, beside him and in front, a blur of movement that ended with Kit sitting in the dirt holding Neku's broken bracelet, a wicked knife gash disfiguring the palm of his left hand.

…Incredible heat.

Bone splintering as a boy flipped backwards, his ancient Lee Enfield tracing a parabola before it hit desert behind him, Kit's cross hairs already hunting their next target …

…Silver night and no stars. A wedding dress in the dirt, the body within it also discarded. A web of ropes holding the sky in place.

A girl on her bed, knees pulled up to her chin and her arms wrapped tight around her legs, in tears and naked …

'Shit,' said Neku, shaking her head. 'I so didn't need to know that.'

As the air around her began to shimmer, Neku rammed her hands into the haze and began to drag it apart, one arm disappearing as she began to squeeze through the gap.

'Come back,' Kit demanded. 'I need ...'

And then what he needed stopped mattering. Because glass exploded from the upper windows behind them and the front of Pirate Mary's peeled away, fragments of broken boards splintering across the street. The broken ceiling of the bar, now open to view, curled billows of smoke into a downward roll.

Made almost entirely of wood, the old building did what wooden buildings do best, it began to burn. Dark and oily, from seven decades of paint, the smoke billowed above the fire. Kit didn't remember climbing to his feet or charging towards the stairs. And he barely registered the flames that forced his retreat, into the grip of Mr Ito.

'Who has the keys?'

Kit looked blank.

'That van,' said Mr Ito. 'It will block the fire engine. We must move it.' He shook Kit's shoulder. 'Come on, who has the keys?'

'I don't know.' Pulling free, Kit screamed, *'Yoshi.'*

A wall of flames roared back.

'My wife,' said Kit.

Hands dragged him away and when Kit looked again there was no doorway from which to be dragged. The fury had swallowed every detail within its flames.

A fire officer was demanding answers. Try as he might, Kit couldn't remember having been asked a question. After a second, he understood.

'Hai,' he said. The two Iwatani burners in the kitchen used butane. Yes, there were spare bottles stacked near the grille. Four, maybe five. But what he really needed to do was find ...

'Yoshi,' he yelled.

The next time he tried to break free, a girl in a white coat appeared at a nod from the officer and snapped open her leather bag. The jab took less than five seconds to disconnect Kit from the chaos around him.

CHAPTER 11
nawa-no-ukiyo
(floating rope world)

Stumbling through the door, Lady Neku, otherwise known as Baroness Nawa-no-ukiyo, Countess High Strange and chatelaine of Schloss Omga, fell to her knees and threw up all over mother-of-pearl floor tiles. What she'd seen inside his head clung to her like static, and he'd taken memories from her. Lady Neku could still feel the holes.

'Fuck.'

Polyglot, polygoyle . . .

Polyandrous?

Double fuck. She wasn't allowed to forget what shape those tiles were meant to be, remembering stuff like that was her job.

Lady Neku was also Duchesse de Temps Perdu. Sometime around the start of the last millennia there had been a bout of title inflation. Hyper-inflation, her grandfather said sniffily, guards became captains, captains became generals and the fugees got rights. Although, to be honest, they were no more free than before.

When Lady Neku looked again the tiles were triangular.

'Stop it,' she told Schloss Omga, her family's castle.

Maybe the castle was listening, or maybe it just got bored and decided to stop the architectural equivalent of twiddling its hair. Whatever, next time Lady Neku looked, the tiles in her bedroom had changed back to polygons and that was the last change of the day.

Dragging herself to her feet, Lady Neku stared around her. The vomit was already gone, swallowed by the floor and fed back to the castle. Schloss Omga was good at telling the difference between living organics and waste. It hardly ever got this wrong.

'Shit.'

She felt sick. Hell, she'd been sick. The damage to her shadow must be worse than she thought. Lady Neku turned the cloak over in her hands until she found a small tear. He shouldn't have grabbed her like that, she'd almost let the rip close around her. And then where would she have been?

Dead, obviously.

So cross was Lady Neku at having damaged the red cloak that it took her five minutes to notice her memory bracelet was missing, and another five to realise her real body wasn't in the room waiting for her. No back-up beads and no original from which to burn more. This was serious. Actually, it was beyond serious.

She'd left her body on a chair beside the door. At first she imagined her bedroom had just tidied it away, but all her wardrobes were empty. So she checked the room she'd used as a child, just in case household gods were being more forgetful than usual, only her body wasn't there either.

'Castle,' Neku demanded.

All she got by way of answer was an echoing emptiness in her head.

'Come on,' she said.

Again silence.

This was not unusual. The Katchatka family castle could sulk for decades if really pushed, and everyone but Neku regarded Schloss Omga as irretrievably senile and did their best to ignore it. *Work arounds*, her Lady Mother called them.

Work arounds involved cutting new doors rather than waiting for them to grow and quarrying storage space out of the bloody flesh beneath the council chamber, rather than asking the living core of the castle to withdraw.

Just to be certain she hadn't overlooked her body, Lady Neku checked the first bedroom again, walking along each wall in turn and opening every wardrobe. The castle knew she was looking because wardrobes started to appear that she'd never even seen before. Needless to say, all were empty.

The castle could imitate marble and manage a very good approximation of granite, which seemed to be constructed from the glue it used to stick itself to the slopes of their mountain, but what Schloss Omga really liked was mother-of-pearl. Neku imagined this was because it had originally been a snail. Although, obviously enough, it had only been a snail in the sense that her ancestors had been human.

They were talking a very long time back. Certainly pre-Cenoarchean, if not actually pre-Cenoproterozoic.

All of the wardrobes that appeared out of her walls were made from mother-of-pearl, many extruded into intricate rococo shapes that Lady Neku recognised from the library. Either the castle had remembered how to do this stuff, or she was being shown work that no one had seen for generations.

Art had been the topic of the only real conversation she and the castle ever had, though that talk had been rather one-sided. Mostly because few of the castle's thoughts seemed to make sense. Half a million years glitched between humanity's first flint blade and its first image, on a cave wall. Before pictures had been beads and before beads, pigments to make colour. This indicated a conceptual lag between technology and art, which reflected a slowness in the species to understand the importance of symbolic thought. Which was, apparently, the basis for all sentient behavioural organisation.

At this point the castle had paused. Which was Lady Neku's cue to think of something intelligent to say. So she'd wondered, *what's flint?* And the conversation had been over. Personally, she thought it impressive she'd known what a human was ... Humans were fugees, unless it was the other way round.

'These are wild,' said Lady Neku, running her fingers across a pair of flying babies holding a heart pierced by an arrow. Not to mention, *kitsch* and *hyper-clichéd*. Although Lady Neku refrained from saying this. The castle could be sensitive about such comments.

Having examined all the alcoves, cupboards and wardrobes, Lady Neku climbed inside the largest, so the castle could impress her with its false back and spiral stairs up to an entire floor that waited empty and anxious. Lady Neku knew this, having been shown the wardrobe before. Its style and the winding stairs had an organic smoothness that spoke of her family's very earliest years at the end of the world.

It wasn't really the end of the world, of course ... That would be when the planet turned to cinder and the last wisps of atmosphere burnt off, as the seas would do first, given time. Meanwhile, six overworlds kept the sun at bay and protected the planet as best they could.

Six families owned the off-world habitats, the biggest of which was High Strange, belonging to her family, the Katchatka. And a mesh of sky ropes held a mantle of silver gauze in place exactly a hundred kilometres above the world's surface.

Her brother Petro, who was oldest, said the ropes were alien and no one knew what the mantle around the planet was meant to do. Antonio disagreed, because Antonio always disagreed with Petro. It was Nico, the youngest of her brothers, who took Lady Neku's question seriously. He

49

said the gossamer ate charged particles and the ropes created a magnetic field, which was why it was bad that their bit of sky had ripped.

Lady Neku had a theory about this. Mind you, she had a theory about everything and she was aware her body was still missing. She was merely avoiding panic and trying to approach the matter in a grown-up fashion. Lady Neku's theory said the earliest styles of furniture were fluid and organic because this reflected confidence in the future.

Her family were explorers, new to the end of the world and owners of what remained of human time, which could still be counted in tens of millennia. Not much, maybe, for a planet that had already existed for countless billions of years but it was enough.

When the sky tore, doubts set in. As the fugees stopped coming, the need for reassurance became stronger, hence the regression into fussier styles, an explosion in pointless titles and an endless recycling of cultures long gone. Of course, *fugee* was a misnomer. They were temporal exiles, removed from their own cultures. Although it had taken Lady Neku's family more centuries than was sensible to realise that they themselves were also exiles, as much imprisoned as the fugees they ruled.

If the cupboard was warm and the stairs warmer, the suite of rooms into which Lady Neku made herself venture was claustrophobic beyond description.

'Hot,' she said.

Inside her head Lady Neku felt the castle agree and instantly felt guilty. She wasn't the one endlessly crawling up a slope, trying to get away from the shrinking lakes, methane pockets and somatolite mats of the dead lands. No one lived in the castle these days, all her family preferred High Strange.

'Need to go home,' said Lady Neku, and felt the castle signal its understanding. She had more of Schloss Omga's attention than she remembered having been given before. 'My body,' she added, trying to keep the hope out of her thoughts. 'Don't suppose you remember where you put it?'

'Didn't,' said the castle.

'Didn't what?' asked Lady Neku.

The castle thought about that. It thought about it while Lady Neku retraced her steps to the twist of stairs. It thought about it while she scrabbled her way down the stairs and out of the cupboard, rank with sweat that stuck her dress to her spine and made hair feel disgusting. And it thought about it while she stripped off her dress, gloves and knickers and watched them dissolve into a puddle on the floor.

There had been a time when Schloss Omga was not alive. Lady Neku knew this because her brother Nico had told her. Walls had been spun from simple shell, the rooms had been soulless, many of them barely sentient. It seemed unlikely but Neku had come to understand something about Nico. However much he might tease her, Nico never lied.

'So,' said Neku, when she felt the castle's attention begin to drift. 'About my body ...?'

'Not me,' said the castle.

'You're sure?'

'Quite.' It seemed certain about that.

With a sigh, Lady Neku broke the connection and let the castle return its attention to whatever had been occupying it when she first interrupted; crawling up its slope most probably. All that now remained of Lady Neku's clothes was the cloak. This would never dissolve or need cleaning and that was its virtue. The garment was indestructible and guaranteed to protect its wearer from family explosions, black ice and electric rain ...

She'd listened to the label once, hidden in a doorway in Shinjuku, one afternoon when she was very bored. It had kept talking until she had to tell it to stop. And yet, guarantee or not, her cloak was now damaged. Which, Lady Neku guessed was what one should expect if one caught it on a rip in time.

Because Lady Neku was stubborn, and being stubborn often did unnecessary things because she'd already decided to do them, she rechecked the wardrobes in her room. There were a hundred and thirteen, which was at least seventy more than normal.

Among these was her new favourite, the mother-of-pearl wardrobe with the winged cherubs. Neku checked this last, just in case the castle was trying to tell her something, but it was as empty as the others. Her body was definitely gone.

Unless ...?

Now that was a thought.

Her mother was perfectly capable of having taken Lady Neku's current *real* as a way of telling her daughter it was time to grow up. There was only one problem with this. It would mean, firstly, that Lady Katchatka knew her daughter had been breaking bounds. Secondly, it would require Lady Katchatka to visit the Schloss in person, something that had not occurred in Lady Neku's lifetime.

The corridor down to her mother's castle quarters twisted more than was strictly necessary to accommodate the spiral nature of Schloss

Omga. Sometimes it seemed that the castle wasted too much effort trying to match form, not so much to function as original inspiration.

'My Lady?'

Silence greeted her.

So Lady Neku waited enough time to be polite and then called again. The Katchatka were a very formal family. Dust covered the table and something sticky smeared the oiled paper screen dividing her mother's study in two. Forbidden from touching or changing anything in Lady Katchatka's room, the castle had chosen to assume this rule applied to cleaning it as well.

When it became clear that not even servants had visited her mother's quarters for weeks, if not longer, Lady Neku turned to go, turned back and went with her original choice, making herself walk away without another glance.

'Castle,' said Lady Neku. 'Prepare me a lift to High Strange.'

'Madame. The overworld is empty.'

Lady Neku wondered if she'd heard that correctly. 'Patch me through,' she demanded. 'Do it now.'

'Link made,' said the castle.

Having tried to contact her mother, Lady Neku tried each of her brothers in turn, starting with Nico, her favourite. 'Where are they?' she asked. When Schloss Omga failed to reply, she asked again.

'I haven't seen them,' the castle admitted. 'Not since ...'

'Since what?'

'Your wedding,' said the castle. And Lady Neku found herself kneeling on the tiles, vomiting again. Polyglot, polygoyle ...

Polyandrous?

There was so much Lady Neku needed to remember. So much she needed to forget.

A naked girl sifted hot rubble with her bare hands. She was watched by a cat. A sign on a fence behind them read, *Danger – Keep Out*. The girl clawed at the dirt so frantically that anyone observing would imagine she fought to save a life. But when she finally sat back on her haunches, darkness between her knees and in her eyes ...

'Fever,' someone said, when Kit whispered Neku's name. 'Drug induced, we're investigating.'

'Also,' another voice announced. 'Cuts, bruises and minor burns.' If they were so minor, Kit wondered, why was he lying naked on a foam sheet being sprayed with electrolysed water, whatever that was.

After the voices came a darkness both cool and forgiving. When Kit woke he had a plaster cast on one arm, bandages around his ribs and was wired to a monitor. A fat blood bag hung from a hook above his head, its tube feeding into his left wrist. Another tube, with a twist valve, seemed to be draining old blood.

Kit looked around for someone to plunge him back into the darkness but the room was empty.

Outside the window a blue sky hung above a small garden filled with plum and cherry trees. The fruit on the plum trees was green, and that was how Kit knew he'd been lost in darkness for days rather than weeks. The ion-rich skies of his dreams, the heat and the matrix of silver threads that hung static overhead were nowhere to be seen. An ugly gash across the palm of his right hand had been stitched shut.

Kit Nouveau, read a tag on his arm. It was written in kanji.

He was in hospital, Kit realised, then wondered if he already knew this. He was in hospital because ...

The Korean orderly who came running wore a green uniform that hid her hair under a square cap. She was on her knees and wiping up Kit's vomit before the nurse behind her even made it through the door. The nurse had one of those upside-down watches, which she flipped up to note the time, then wrote something on a board hooked to the end of his bed.

'*Yoshi*,' said Kit.

'Tell them he's awake.'

Hesitating on the edge of wiping up the last of Kit's mess, the orderly jumped to her feet at a barked order from the nurse. When she returned it was with a suited man and the floor cloth was still in her hand.

'They're coming,' he said.

The first policeman had the glossy-peaked cap of a regular officer. As did the man behind, although he also had a shiny stripe down the outside of his trousers. The third officer wore a soft cap that proclaimed him a detective. But it was the last man, the one in the suit Kit really noticed.

His hair was grey and worn cropped. Heavy glasses hid eyes that were flat and watchful, the eyes of an Ainu hunter from the northern islands. A man whose ancestors would have grown used to watching their boats sunk and houses ripped apart by storms, who knew what it was like to rebuild life from the ground up. It seemed strange that such a man could rise so high in the Tokyo police.

Now was when the newcomer should announce that he was with the Organised Crime Squad. He would tell Kit that Yoshi was dead and his bar destroyed – and ask about recent enemies, unpaid bills or protection payments overdue. Although, perhaps, he would ask first about a dead tramp found against cemetery railings near the bar.

Kit tried to think of a suitable answer, but his head was empty and what could he say anyway? That a *cos-play-zoku* with a neat line in juggling knives had broken into his bar looking for the murder weapon, then cut open thin air to crawl inside ...

As for Yoshi.

'Here,' said the man.

Reaching for the tissue, Kit snagged his wrist on a drip tube and three people started forward at once, only to hesitate. It was the nurse who replaced the drip, renewed the sticking plaster holding the needle in place and wiped Kit's eyes for him. At a nod from the man she opened a buff folder and extracted a MRI scan, clipping it to a light box on the wall.

'Show me,' he said.

Stepping aside, she pointed to a smudge of shadow. 'Brodmann's area

10, in the rostral prefrontal cortex.' She seemed to be reciting words from memory.

'Dangerous?'

The nurse shook her head. 'Just unusual.'

'What is?' Kit demanded.

'Unexpected development within your prefrontal white matter,' said the man, then offered his hand. From the shock on the faces of the uniformed officers, this courtesy was a surprise. 'I'm Mr Oniji,' he added. 'I believe you know my wife.'

Darkness felt welcome.

When Kit woke someone was sliding a needle from his arm. 'His body's coping with drug withdrawal,' said the someone. 'He'll probably go under again, so you might want to ask your questions now.'

'Right,' said Mr Oniji. 'About these lessons.'

'English lessons,' said Kit, working hard to pull himself together. 'She's good.' It seemed best not to mention the time Mrs Oniji rendered the saying, *Out of sight, out of mind*, as, *invisible/insane*. 'Hard working,' said Kit. 'Extremely conscientious.'

'I'm sure she is,' said Mr Oniji. 'She's good at many things.' He paused. 'Did you know she was a marine biologist?'

'No,' said Kit, he could confidently say this had passed him by.

'Eleven kilometres down, the gap between biology, chemistry and physics becomes immaterial.' Mr Oniji smiled. 'Or so she told me on our first date. She was working on *foraminifera*, which are billions of years old. Unless that's just microbes in general.'

He hesitated, as if he'd forgotten what he intended to say. After a moment, he glanced at the officers, a fact that left them looking unhappy. All the same they went. The orderly, the nurse and the suited administrator followed without having to be asked.

'May I sit?'

'Of course,' said Kit, 'I'm sorry.' He nodded to a chair in the corner. It was steel, with raw leather and bead highlights. Dragging it across the floor, Mr Oniji positioned himself close to Kit's bed. When he sat it was formally, his back straight and his legs together, his elbows on the arms of the chair, his hands flat and angled slightly inwards where they rested on each knee.

'How good is your Japanese?'

'Good enough,' said Kit.

Mr Oniji nodded. 'There are things I need to say,' he said. 'We can speak in English if that is better for you?'

Kit shook his head.

'Okay,' said Mr Oniji. 'The most important thing I have to say is this ... You need to leave Tokyo.'

'Tokyo?'

'Japan,' Mr Oniji said, amending his words. 'I suggest you go soon. Visit Australia or Thailand. Take a holiday ...'

'For how long?'

'A month, two months, maybe longer.' The Japanese man ran one hand through his salt and pepper hair, wiping his fingers on a tissue. He looked tired, but determined. 'It is not safe for you to remain here.'

Was that a threat? Kit wondered.

Straightening the jacket of his suit, Mr Oniji brushed invisible dust from one knee of his trousers and shot the cuffs of his shirt, revealing simple gold cufflinks. The oyabun was nervous, Kit realised. An idea that seemed absurd.

'My wife will have told you I am High Yakusa. Maybe she's said I am rarely at home and have little to do with her family or my own. If she has not already told you then you have probably deduced we have no children ...'

When Kit nodded, Mr Oniji smiled.

'Only the last of those is true,' said Mr Oniji. 'We have no children.' He paused, choosing his words with care. 'Have you ever done anything you really regret? No,' he said. 'No need to reply. I can see the answer in your eyes.'

Mr Oniji took a sip of water from a fresh glass on Kit's bedside locker.

'My regret,' he said, 'is marrying my wife ...' He must have decided he'd either said too much or too little, because after a slight hesitation, he added. 'I knew from the beginning we were not suited.'

'So why marry?'

'You know how it is,' said Mr Oniji. 'She was young and pretty and I needed a wife.'

'But you didn't love her?'

Whether Mr Oniji looked sad for himself, his wife or the world in general was hard to say. 'This is difficult,' he said. 'Women have never been of much interest to me. Unfortunately, a wife was necessary. I should have told her,' he added, 'Explained things. That is my regret.'

'Why tell me?'

'The police will want to ask you questions' said Mr Oniji. 'They will ask you, because they always ask, if you have any enemies ...'

56

'I don't,' said Kit.

Mr Oniji's smile was tight. 'Everyone has enemies,' he said. 'I would like to make clear that I am not one of them. Also, there is the possibility of arson. If that is true, I had nothing to do with it.'

Early next morning a Korean orderly carried a small book and a business card into Kit's room and presented the card first, his fingertips barely touching its edges as he offered the object to Kit.

Hiroshi Sato, second assistant to Mr Oniji, presented his compliments. Should Mr Nouveau wish to send a message to Mr Oniji, he could do so through the good offices of Mr Sato. An e-mail and telephone number were both given on the card. Quite why Kit might need this went unsaid.

The book had been wrapped by a professional. A sheet of hand-laid paper, folded so every edge formed a perfect line was wrapped into the covers and tied in place with a length of dried grass. The grass bisected the book twice, the angle between each length chosen with care.

On the front of the book was a wood-block illustration of a samurai in a wolf-skin coat. *In the Shadow of Leaves* announced the title. The date was 1934, the language English. It had been printed by the Board of Tourist Industry, on behalf of Japanese Governmental Railways.

'The essence of speaking is in not speaking at all. If you think you can accomplish a task without words then do so ... When compelled to choose between death now or death later, choose now. It just is ...'

There were eighty-six pages of such aphorisms, with five more wood-block prints and a fold-out map of feudal Japan. Mr Oniji's note was tucked between the cover and the title page. *Read this,* he said.

Some hours later, just as Kit was finishing *In the Shadow of Leaves* for the second time a nurse arrived to change the staples in his face. Her name was Lucy, at least that was the name on her badge, and until she began tossing ant-like pincers of plastic into an enamel dish Kit hadn't even known his face had staples.

When this was done, she fixed two metal splints to his right ankle, braced the splints with steel crossbars and fed strips of foam over the braces and under the crossbars, hardening the padding with a UV light wand.

'Monday,' she said, when Kit asked what day it was. She shaved him very carefully, helped him to the lavatory and waited, telling him to lean on her when he walked back to his room. 'Now I'm going to give you a blanket bath,' Lucy announced when Kit was back in his bed.

'I can manage a shower.'

'No.' Lucy shook her head. 'You're much too weak. In fact, you can barely answer questions.'

'Questions?'

Unbuttoning his pyjama top, Lucy extracted a sterile flannel from its foil wrapper and dunked the flannel into a basin that had appeared on the locker beside Kit's bed. She wiped his face and neck, washed under his arms and across the top of his chest, taking care not to wet the bandages over his ribs.

'A cut,' she said, in answer to his question. 'Metal shrapnel from the explosion. You were lucky.' Lucy must have caught the shock on Kit's face, because she smiled. 'It barely grazed your side,' she said. 'And it was hot enough to sear the edges of the wound.'

After she'd washed his chest, she washed his back and undid his pyjama bottoms. 'You stink,' she said, when he tried to protest. She said this firmly, but with a smile. 'A major from the National Police is going to question you. His arrival is unexpected and he intends to catch you unaware. We will, as a hospital, make the strongest protest possible.'

'If it's unexpected …'

'Then how do we know?'

Kit nodded.

'I believe the manager had a call from police HQ.'

When Kit looked puzzled, Lucy sighed. 'Mr Oniji owns this hospital,' she said. 'He owns many things in Tokyo and his contacts are good.' Having washed Kit's legs, genitals and backside with casual competence, the nurse dried him with a different cloth and helped him into a fresh pair of pyjama bottoms.

A few minutes later Kit was sat up in bed, new drips inserted into one wrist and the window open to let in the warm breeze. His leg, with the new ankle cast, had been attached to a system of pulleys.

'You are Christopher Alan Nouveau, known as Kit …?'

'Yes,' said Kit, with a wince. Maybe trying to pull himself up in bed was a mistake, what with the traction weights tugging on his ankle.

'Hurt?'

Kit nodded.

The officer wore fawn slacks and a tweed sports coat. His hair was dark and swept back, worn slightly longer than Kit expected, and he carried a small leather bag, halfway between a wallet and a brief case.

'I'm Major Yamota,' announced the young man, carefully handing Kit his card.

Major Tom Yamota
Organised Crime Section/Tokyo Branch

Inside the leather carry case was a voice recorder, obviously far too hi-tech to bother with anything like buttons, since Major Yamota merely put the machine on the locker beside Kit's bed and began talking.

'So,' he said. 'I gather you were badly injured in the explosion. Also, that you've only recently regained consciousness?'

At least two things were wrong with this suggestion. The most obvious being that Kit had been conscious almost from the time he was brought in for treatment. Well, more or less.

'The hospital told us you were unfit for questioning. The local police agreed. We have been waiting for almost a week.' Major Yamota did not seem happy about this.

'Unfit ...?'

'You can speak Japanese? You understand what I'm saying?'

Kit nodded.

'Good,' the major glanced down at a notebook. Since he was having trouble deciphering the characters, the notes had to be compiled by someone else. 'You've lived in Japan for twelve years. Your wife owned Pirate Mary's. You were happily married. This is what I've been told by the local force. Is that correct?'

'I owned the bar.'

The major looked up. 'Ms Tanaka's sister says Ms Yoshi owned it. Also,' Major Yamota scowled at the notes. 'My department can find no official record of your marriage.'

'We got hitched in San Francisco,' said Kit. 'Yoshi was going to register the marriage with the *shimin ka* on our return.'

'Still,' he said. 'No record exists. Why do you think that is?'

'I don't know. Maybe Yoshi never got round to it.'

Major Yamota chewed his lip. 'And you're certain,' he said. 'About having no enemies?'

Kit thought of Mr Oniji and his promise that Yoshi's death had nothing to do with him. And he thought of the strange *cos-play* returning to collect her knife, neither seemed like an enemy to him.

'None,' Kit said.

After a final question, about any enemies Yoshi might have, Major Yamota stood up, bowed very slightly and left without bothering to say goodbye.

CHAPTER 13
Friday 15 June

'Put the following statements in order of descending incongruity ...' On screen the final round of a trivia quiz kicked off and a man in black suit and dark glasses began to read from his list.

Since Kit was the only other person in the room, he got up and changed channels. A teen drama, in which three school friends tried to talk a new girl out of throwing herself off the roof. A comedy cop show about an ex-Yakusa turned detective and a documentary about spawning eels. He'd lived too long in Tokyo to find anything about that selection unusual.

In Kit's hand was a photograph, found tucked into the back of his wallet. One of those thumbnail pictures that everyone was printing out back when camera phones were still news. It showed a girl with dirty blonde hair, a smile to kill and wide eyes, wrapped up in a face that was all cheekbones.

She looked more fragile than he remembered.

As fifteen minutes crawled towards thirty and finally became forty-five, Kit stood up from his bench in Roppongi's police station, and decided to see what happened if he tried to leave. At which point a young officer stuck his head round the door and glanced from Kit to the suitcase he'd just picked up. Kit was pretty sure it was an officer he'd seen at the hospital.

'Are you all right?'

Rather sheepishly, Kit nodded.

'Major Yamota won't be much longer.'

'What's he doing?' asked Kit, quickly adding. 'Of course, I realise he's very busy.'

For a second it looked as if the young man was about to say that Major Yamota was doing something both important and secret. Instead, he shrugged. 'Who knows,' the man said. 'He's from Organised.'

It seemed the junior officer was there to inspect the level in the water cooler and check the coffee machine was functioning. As the water cooler was virtually empty, the officer removed its old bottle, upended a fresh one and left Kit to his thoughts and memories. In an ideal world, of course, he'd have left the rubbish and taken the memories.

The day before Yoshi died, Kit and Yoshi made love, if that was the right word. Kit bound nine metres of cord around his wife's body, in a complicated pattern that went between her legs and around her neck, squeezed both breasts and constricted her hips, before coming to a knot over her belly button.

Edo cord bondage.

On the days she really needed to lose herself, Yoshi had Kit hoist her from the floor, in the *gyaku-ebi-tsuri* position. For this they used a single rope, a hook attached to the storeroom ceiling and a pulley bought from a chandler in Chiba, where her brother-in-law got fittings for his precious yacht.

That morning was simpler. Kit just bound Yoshi tight, lay her flat on a tatami mat and left her alone for an hour. Then he untied her and helped her shower, telling her to get some rest. The next time they saw each other, she was standing by the bins behind Pirate Mary's, about to destroy a pot so perfect it was almost not there ...

On screen a Korean girl raced towards a finish line, with her mouth open and one hand stretched desperately for a Japanese child waiting to start the next lap. The Korean was too self-conscious to run happily, her bust thick beneath a black tracksuit. Although ten girls ran at any one time, five in black and five in white, the camera stayed with the girl at the back, its focus tight to her upper body. In the final seconds, it flipped to the face of the girl she needed to reach.

Although this one ran herself into the ground, rolling onto her side to gasp for air, the race was already lost. When she raised her face for the camera, her eyes had flooded with tears. Child by child, the camera cut from one losing face to another, twenty-five schoolgirls in black, every single one crying.

What was interesting was that the Korean – who was large by Japanese standards, but would pass unnoticed on the streets of any capital in the Western world – had known her team was losing before she even began to run, as had the girl who took her place. Yet both had run themselves into gasping despair at not being able to close the gap. Maybe that was how Yoshi felt.

A police car had collected Kit from hospital and delivered him to this room on the ground floor of the new Azabu Police Station. A courtesy, that was how his transport arrangements had been presented. Equally, there had been no suggestion Kit might refuse the ride.

He would have signed himself out of hospital days before, but this suggestion had produced the administrator. A small man in a dark suit and tortoise-shell glasses who appeared in the doorway and announced, politely but firmly, that the doctors insisted Kit stay in bed for at least a week. He still needed to recover.

'From this?' said Kit, indicating the cast on his left arm.

The small man had smiled.

'Is it really broken?' Kit's fingers worked perfectly, and apart from a dull ache in the elbow, his arm felt fine. The worst thing that could be said was that his skin itched like fuck beneath the plaster.

'We have X-rays showing a minor fracture. Nothing too serious.' The man spoke with a Hokkaido accent, the extra stress on each Z added a harshness to words someone from Tokyo would have left soft.

'What about my ankle?' Kit said.

The administrator appeared to think about this. 'All right,' he said. 'The cast on that can come off.' He hesitated. 'You were killing yourself with drugs,' he said finally. 'I don't expect you to believe that because addicts never do, until they become ex-addicts. Only you know which side of that line you now stand.'

The arrival of a police driver at lunchtime the following day was enough to make the administrator reappear, flanked by two technical assistants who looked as if they'd been chosen mostly for the width of their shoulders. Standing once again in Kit's doorway, the administrator looked as if he personally intended to stop his patient and the police officer from leaving.

'I am troubled by this,' said the small man. He looked at the driver, who nodded to indicate that the administrator's reservations had been noted. 'Obviously, we are happy to do everything we can to help the authorities, but ...'

'I have my orders,' said the driver.

The administrator sighed, his sigh obviously intended to indicate both his unease and the fact the matter was now out of his hands. 'I'll have his cases sent to the station,' he said. It was all Kit could do not to ask, What cases?

Half an hour after Kit arrived at the police station, still in pyjamas and a dressing gown, a pair of matching leather suitcases turned up, full of clothes in his size. A brown envelope tucked into the top of his case contained a broken watch, a broken bead bracelet and Kit's wallet, minus its last twist of heroin. Mind you, the wallet bulged with money, far more than when Kit had been bundled into an ambulance outside Pirate Mary's.

His old war jacket was missing.

So now Kit wore dark cotton trousers, a pale blue shirt with short sleeves and a tan leather belt. Not his style at all, but they seemed to play well with everyone who came through the waiting-room door.

'If you're ready?'

'If I'm ...?' Kit shut his mouth and followed a young policewoman along a corridor and up a flight of stairs. It was obvious that the carpet in the public areas was more expensive than the carpet in areas seen only by the police and those they brought in for interview.

'Ah,' said Major Yamota. 'There you are ... This won't take long.' Nodding to his assistant, he waited while the junior officer spread papers and photographs across a desk. The photographs mostly showed the ruins of Kit's bar. The papers were more varied, with one whole pile relating only to Yoshi, everything from a certified copy of her family register to school certificates and a newspaper article about her status as one of Japan's rising stars.

The paper Major Yamota actually wanted was an official-looking document from the Tokyo Institute of Police Science, Investigation Division/Explosions. 'It was an accident,' said Major Yamota, holding up the report. 'A gas explosion. All the evidence is in here.'

'Evidence?'

'Of fire patterns,' said the Major. 'Smoke signatures and burning rates. Deeply regrettable, but still an accident.'

Kit held out his hand. 'May I see the report?'

Major Yamota's mouth twisted.

He had, Kit realised, just insulted the man. An insult so deep that it that would have been regarded as utterly unforgivable had Kit not been *gaijin*. As such, his crassness was excused on the simple grounds that it would be unreasonable to expect better from a foreigner.

'I'll have a copy made.'

'Thank you,' said Kit. 'And the rest?' he asked, indicating the papers and files spread across the desk.

'Let's see,' Major Yamota said. He gathered up a couple of forms and hesitated for a second over a third, before selecting it and a handful of other pieces of paper. 'All of these you can read. Unfortunately, to see reports relating directly to Miss Tanaka you will need her family's permission.'

A stab of a button produced Major Yamota's assistant, who rushed away the bundle of forms. Seconds later the sound of a photocopier could be heard through the walls.

'Why do I need their permission?' Kit demanded.

'Because of the complication,' said Major Yamota, and before Kit could ask which complication, the Major told him. 'It seems the two of you were not married.'

'But we ...'

'Under Japanese law,' said the Major. 'Citizens who wed abroad must register their marriage with the relevant ward office within a year. This did not happen. As you were not actually married to Miss Tanaka your rights to information are limited by statutory regulation. Her family also have the right to claim her remains. I should probably tell you,' he added, 'that the funeral was yesterday.'

'In Tokyo?'

'No,' said Major Yamota. 'They took her home.'

Kit knew where Yoshi's sister lived and that Yoshi had an aunt in Kobe. Yoshi and Kit had shared a bed, lived in the same house and together run a bar but he still didn't know where she'd been born. Some shitty little village in the hills ... That was what Yoshi said, when he asked her in the early days.

He had no idea which village or which hills.

CHAPTER 14
Friday 15 June

Major Yamota cut Kit loose from Azabu station with two suitcases full of clothes he hadn't chosen and a replacement resident's permit. He had some money in his wallet and about 2,000,000 yen in his savings, roughly £10,000. Without it ever being put into words, Mr Oniji had made it clear that Kit's job teaching English to Mrs Oniji was now over. At the door to his office, Major Yamota asked Kit where he intended to go.

'Back to the bar,' Kit said.

The Major opened his mouth to say something, then changed his mind. *This is no longer my business*, said the expression on his face. That Kit could read Major Yamota's expression was a surprise. Maybe Kit had learnt more from his time in Tokyo than he thought.

The wind outside was warm and stank of the river, which was a slightly sour smell, like that of an unwashed dog. It was years since Kit had smoked anything but the dragon, but a slot machine stood outside the steps to the metro and he found himself feeding coins into the slot before he even realised what he was doing.

Crumpling cellophane, Kit pushed the wrapper deep into his pocket and realised he still needed a light.

'Here,' said a boy. He looked about thirteen, bleach-blond hair and brutally ripped jeans. Too old to be out this early from school, but still young enough to offer his lighter to a foreigner standing on a street corner with an unlit cigarette.

'*Domo arigato*,' said Kit.

The truant brushed away his thanks. 'Tourist?'

'Probably more than I realised.'

'I'm sorry?'

'Nothing,' said Kit. He smiled at the boy. 'Your English is very good ...'

The boy nodded. In the end, because Kit was unable to face the ruins of Pirate Mary's, the boy found him a taxi. None of this was put into words. Instead, the boy looked at Kit's suitcase, looked at the crowds streaming around them and smiled sympathetically. Putting up an arm, he pulled an empty taxi out of the afternoon traffic as if performing magic and stepped back so the automatic doors could open.

'Green for occupied, red for empty,' said the boy. 'Don't tip.'

Nodding to show he understood, Kit watched the boy wave brightly as the taxi pulled away. It felt really shitty to check he still had his wallet, but Kit checked anyway.

The taxi dropped him outside the Shinjuku branch of Mitsukoshi, next to a bank of ATM machines and a street down from Ryuchi's Burger Bar. There was a two-star hotel above the bar, run by Ryuchi's mother and catering mainly for sex tourists too nervous to base themselves in the heart of Kabuki-cho. Mrs Keita knew all the local girls and kept an eye on their comings and goings, having once been one herself. On occasion, she would even call their pimps if punters got ugly or things looked like getting out of hand.

'*Konban wa,*' Kit said, reaching the top of the stairs.

Mrs Keita glanced up from her paper and Kit caught the moment she recognised him. Very carefully, Mrs Keita folded her copy of the *Asahi Evening News*, although she'd quite obviously finished it, right down to doodling little squares across the sports section at the back.

'Can I help you?'

It wasn't the reply Kit had been expecting.

'It's Kit Nouveau,' he said. 'Ryuchi's friend.'

The woman nodded.

'I need a room,' said Kit, 'for a week, maybe more. Until ...' He expected her to say something about Pirate Mary's. At the very least to mention Yoshi, but the woman remained silent.

'A room,' repeated Kit.

'Very difficult,' she said, consulting her ledger. 'Unfortunately we're fully booked.' She made a pretence of studying the ledger to make sure, shifting her bulk onto her elbows as she poured over its pages. 'Sadly,' she said, 'they're all taken. You could try ...'

She recommended a love hotel at the edge of the Golden Gai shopping mall, once site of Kabuki-cho's most notorious maze of *nomiya* bars, jazz clubs and pigeons permanently drunk on salaryman vomit. The Moonlight Venus got by on location alone, being within spitting distance of two soaplands, a strip club and a branch of Bottomless Kup. It was sleazy even by Piss Alley standards.

Opening his wallet, Kit extracted 50,000 yen. 'Surely you must have one room?'

Mrs Keita regarded the money wistfully, something very close to regret crossing her wide face. 'Unfortunately not,' she said. It seemed unlikely, given Mrs Keita's hotel had never been booked out in its long and insalubrious life. This was the place that charged a group of Germans floor space in the boiler room, when a cyclone ripped away the hotel's roof and made their original room unusable.

'Okay,' Kit said. 'No problem.'

Hair bleached and a new stud through his lip, Ryuchi leant against a wall by the counter, a position undoubtedly chosen so he could watch a young Filipina flash fry a tuna burger. Having drenched the nugget of yellow fin with mango relish, she sprinkled chopped coriander over the top.

'One to go,' she said.

So low slung were the girl's jeans that it looked only a matter of time before gravity eventually won. Mind you, Kit still reckoned Ryuchi could have done more than glance across at him and then look back.

'Hi,' said Kit. 'How's it going?'

Ryuchi had spent two summers in London in the late nineties, which had frozen his personal style and command of English into something resembling a manga interpretation of post-Rock lite.

'Fine,' Ryuchi replied.

'You got a moment? said Kit, wanting to ask what he'd done to offend Ryuchi's mother, a woman who made a living out of being almost entirely unshockable. 'I could buy you a beer.'

'I'm kinda busy ...' Ryuchi shrugged. 'You know, work to do.'

There was one customer in the café, a foreigner in a dark suit scrawling something into a black notebook with a silver pen. He'd finished his tuna burger in a couple of bites and was now trying to wipe mango relish from his book's cover.

'Supplies,' said Ryuchi, noting Kit's glance. 'I've got to fetch the supplies.'

'Sure,' Kit said. 'Maybe see you later.'

'Yeah.' Ryuchi's wave of the hand was casual, the tightness around his eyes anything but. 'Good luck.'

The transvestite behind the counter at Moonlight Venus named a price for a room that was outrageous, halving it when Kit turned away, and halving it again when he reached the door.

'We don't get much call for all nighters,' s/he said, adjusting a flowered kimono.

Kit kept his comments to himself and went to check a cluster of back-lit photographs on the wall. There were twenty-five photographs, each showing a different room. The lit ones were free. He could have a room draped in black satin, red velvet, silver rubber or ivory-coloured faux fur. Two of the rooms were old school/high concept, one mirrored on all four walls, its ceiling and floor, the other done out like a stage set from *Casablanca*, complete with miniature grand piano.

The final room on offer was the one Kit chose. It was pink, had a school desk and came with a free pair of fluffy handcuffs. Other than that, it looked relatively normal.

Barely large enough to qualify as a real room, the box-like space Kit rented for the night offered a double bed, a video screen and – a nice touch – a kettle, a black lacquered tray and two incredibly delicate tea cups. Three condoms and a pack of what claimed to be obstetrical wipes were hidden inside a Hello Kitty box next to the kettle.

The handcuffs hung from a hook above the bed. They were sealed into a plastic bag and came with a little note asking that the cuffs be used in a manner that was both thoughtful and safe. Consent is mandatory, said the note.

On the back of the door were two other notes. The first announced that Moonlight Venus had been licensed, under the Entertainment & Amusement Trades Control Law (Revised), the second reminded patrons that criminal gangs were forbidden to block-book hotels.

Having unpacked and then repacked both leather cases, to see exactly what was in each, Kit tried to sleep, wrapping himself in a sheet and dimming the lights; but sleep was difficult to find, largely because the couple in the room next door were obviously new to each other and still excited.

Cardboard thin walls left little to the imagination, from rising moans that became shouts to the slap of flesh against flesh and the laughter of release. So Kit listened for a while and let his thoughts wander, none of them being important enough to be dragged back for questioning. Technically speaking, he was fucked, how much thought did it take to work that out?

His wife was dead, not that she was his wife. His bar was burnt. His friends had turned into strangers. He would like someone to blame, but was afraid that if he examined that thought too hard he'd discover the someone was himself.

Couples came and went, with a peak at just after midnight and another at around four, when some of the hostess bars closed. Pretty soon the noise of people making love, having sex and sometimes just talking to each other blurred into the background, became familiar and finally slipped out of Kit's mind altogether.

Bizarrely enough, he fell to sleep smiling.

CHAPTER 15
nawa-no-ukiyo

Lady Neku walked very slowly round herself as she'd been two years earlier. It was a salutary lesson. Her eyes were instantly forgettable, and if she had shape beneath those cheeks, it was only because bones were a biological necessity, required to keep her smug little face from collapsing.

Average height, slightly above average weight, her shoulders accentuated the broadness of her back; even her breasts managed to be too large for her age, while being too small for the ribs over which they lay.

As for her pubic hair.

This grew like lichen, if lichen was black and wiry and glinted in the castle's light. She'd hated that body and still did, but today's hatred was as nothing to what she felt when it was first presented to her. It was only after Lady Neku killed herself for the third time that her mother agreed she could change.

'Shit,' she said, kicking the thing.

The glass tube in which it floated rang like a bell.

At the age of three, Lady Neku had blonde hair and eyes the colour of a cold summer sky. At five, her hair was silver, like the spires of High Strange seen on a cloudless night and her eyes the amber of a Baltic morning.

Her mother loved her best between those two ages, and looking at herself Lady Neku could understand why. She'd been beautiful, a faithful shadow, willing to trot from meeting to meeting or sit in silence while Lady Katchatka worked at her desk.

At nine, Lady Neku had black hair, white skin and brown eyes. It was a very ordinary look. A transition point between the fading prettiness of her seven-year-old self and the cruel plainness of her body aged eleven. Lady Neku knew exactly why this had happened, her mother could forgive anything except competition for attention from Antonio, Nico and Petro.

Lady Neku's whole history was in the figures who stood blank-eyed and empty before her. The tiny, blonde-haired infant, the silver-haired girl … She could take any of them back, revert to the child she'd once been. Five orphaned bodies, neither living nor dead, just existing at the point where she abandoned them.

She'd taken this body she wore. At least, Lady Neku was pretty sure she had. Walked out of the night and into a squalid little house. A dozen faces had watched as she looked round the tiny room and chose a girl of roughly her own age.

'You're bleeding,' they said, rising from the table. And then one of them realised who Lady Neku was and concern turned to fear.

'Don't,' they said.

'Take me instead,' said one. A woman who looked old enough to be Lady Neku's mother, though she was probably no older than her visitor. Time was counted differently among fugees.

'Please,' said the woman. 'Choose me.'

'I'm sorry,' Lady Neku said. 'You're not the one I want.' And she walked round to the far side of the table, where three children sat frozen on a bench. The youngest, a boy of about ten, stood to defend his sister and Lady Neku felt a tightness in her throat and tears come into her own eyes.

So brave, so stupid.

When she put her fingers to the boy's temples, it was gently, and she lowered him to the dirt so he didn't bang his head on the way down.

His mind was simple, barely more than a single emotion and the most banal level of self knowledge … fugees and family shared their origins, but at times like this even Lady Neku had trouble believing them the same.

'I'll bring her back,' Lady Neku told the mother.

'As what …?' It seemed the girl's father had finally found his voice. 'What will she be?' He glared at his wife. 'We don't want her back, you understand … We won't take her.'

Touching the girl on her shoulder, Lady Neku led her from the house, leaving the family arguing behind her. They were dirt poor, they had to be. Anyone richer would have been somewhere else. Only the poor still lived near the surface, where even the thickest ceilings struggled to keep back the heat outside and where fugees went unprotected from people like her.

It hurt Lady Neku to think of herself as a predator. *'Guardians,'* she said to the girl. *'Custodians.'*

These words were unknown to the child.

'Keepers,' said Lady Neku.

She understood that one.

'What's your name?'

'Mai ...'

'Well Mai, I'm not going to hurt you,' Lady Neku promised. 'And I'll bring you back ...'

Mai chewed her lip while she considered what the keeper said. The girl was sweet and simple, the blood flushing her filthy cheeks a saline echo of the sea that originally spawned all life. For a fugee she was almost beautiful. Compared to Lady Neku, she was the drabbest moth to a butterfly.

'Really?' said Mai.

'Promise,' Lady Neku said, reaching out to touch the girl's cheek. Without even meaning to, she lied.

CHAPTER 16
Saturday 16 June

The laws governing the playing of pinball in Tokyo's arcades are as complex as the game is simple. The player buys a handful of *pachinko* balls and launches them into a table, using each ball's speed to negotiate its way through a forest of pins and into a winning hole, if all goes well. There are no flippers. Selecting the speed is the only skill in what is otherwise a game of chance.

Because *pachinko* relies on chance it is illegal to play for money. At least, that's the pretence. The winnings pay out in additional steel balls, which can be exchanged at a counter for prizes, such as playing cards, stuffed toys and decorative dolls. At an entirely different counter, usually outside the pachinko parlour, the toys can be 'sold' for money.

According to No Neck, the arcades were a perfect way to pass time while waiting for other more interesting things to happen. And since the biggest pachinko parlour in Roppongi was Pachinko Paradise, that was where Kit tried first, once a taxi had decanted him into the Saturday morning crowd near Almond crossing.

He was almost within sight of Azabu Police Station, but Kit wasn't worried. If Major Yamota wanted Kit the police would just pick him up again. How hard would it be to find a shell-shocked thirty-five-year-old Englishman in Tokyo? He didn't look Japanese, he didn't look Korean and he certainly didn't look like a tourist ...

The suit helped with that. He'd found it the night before, in the second of the leather cases, and it had been the only thing he'd kept, apart from a black T-shirt and the shoes obviously. The rest he'd sold – including the cases – to the transvestite behind the counter at Moonlight Venus, getting what Kit thought was a good price; until he saw the suit for sale in a Mitsukoshi window and realised he'd probably just been robbed blind.

Having tried Pachinko Paradise, Kit stuck his head through the entrance of a couple of noodle bars on Gaien-Higashi-dori, before walking south towards the Family Mart on the corner, where Micki worked. His plan to leave a note for No Neck was unnecessary, because the man was already there, his bulbous body stuffed into a white T-shirt and jeans. Even his tattoos looked stretched.

No Neck was busy examining a brightly-coloured bubble pack that included dayglo dark glasses, a water bottle and a bush hat, with a clip-on sun flap at the back.

Have a Happy Summer, announced a banner. *Buy Our Holiday Beach Side Set.* From the way the man was examining the packet No Neck seemed about to take the banner at its word. He was wearing dark glasses of his own ... Large ones, presumably to hide the purple bruising around his eyes.

'No Neck,' said Kit.

The other man said nothing, what could he realistically say? No Neck might be sorry at Yoshi's death but she had still fired him and had him beaten up by the Tokyo police. So Kit picked up a beach set of his own and turned it over, wondering what he was missing. 'You really interested in this?'

'I've got a granddaughter,' said No Neck. 'It's her birthday soon.'

'When?'

'Don't know. They won't tell me.' He looked at Kit, then glanced at the bubble pack in his own hand. 'I send the presents to her grandma.'

'And she sends them on?'

'Maybe ... Never had a letter back.' No Neck kept his gaze on the Beach Set, until Kit finally realised this was because the biker was close to tears and doing his best to hide that fact.

'Need a razor,' said Kit, 'back in a second.'

Shit happened and then everyone pretended it hadn't. Life was easier that way. Yoshi's death. No Neck's family. Kit's mother. All that shit in Iraq. A month or so before the incident with the truck, Kit took shrapnel below one knee. The cut was nothing, six inches of bone showing where metal split flesh.

When a medic arrived Kit stood to salute and went down sideways. It was instinct that made him stand, nothing more. The reptilian bit of his brain still firing after everything more intelligent went into shock.

The medic told her major, who told the colonel. Since this was better than the reports he usually got, about squaddies drunk on cheap beer and boredom, flogging bits of uniform on eBay to sad fucks back home, the old man came to see Kit for himself, dragging some obedient hack behind him like a shadow.

Having told Kit not to stand this time, he shook Kit's hand and stamped out again. The picture made the front of the *Sun*, page two in the *Mail*, page five of the *Daily Telegraph* and page seven of the *Mirror*.

That was when he got the first postcard. *Saw the photograph. Sorry you were injured. Look after yourself. All the best. Mary.* So many hollow spaces between so few words.

He wrote back but got no reply.

Picking out the cheapest razor, Kit carried it to the checkout and was collecting his change when No Neck joined the queue, still clutching a Beach Side Fun Set.

'I didn't do it,' said No Neck, the moment they got outside. 'Okay? And I'm genuinely sorry about ...' He stopped before he could tell Kit what, though they both knew.

'You didn't do what?'

'Bomb Pirate Mary's. You know me. I wouldn't do something like that. We're friends.' The huge man close to tears again.

'No one bombed the bar,' said Kit. 'It was a gas explosion. I've read the ...'

No Neck shook his head. 'You seen what's left of your bar?'

'Not yet.'

'A right fucking mess,' said No Neck. 'You did time in Iraq, right? It's okay,' he added quickly. 'Been there, done that, got my own tattoo ...' Pulling up his sleeve, he flashed a faded dagger inside a wreath. 'Shit, you know how it goes.'

Yeah, Kit did.

'Someone wanted a job done,' said No Neck. 'Take a look at the wreckage if you don't believe me. Phosphorus and plastique. A really nasty mixture.'

Only most of the wreckage was gone and a truck was hauling away the last of the rubble, leaving charred timbers and a skip full of earth by the time Kit and No Neck reached the site where Pirate Mary's had been. The last bit of actual building still standing was a far corner, at the bottom of the slope. Most of this was fire-blackened concrete but a single jagged post stuck defiantly into the air.

A sign on the alley wall announced *Pirate Mary's Irish Tavern* and pointed to a building that wasn't there.

Kit vomited.

It wasn't the sight of the blackened ruins nor the fact Yoshi had died here. A fact made infinitely more real by being there. It was the smell. The stink of charcoal and death. Yoshi's body was gone, but other things had died here, rats or birds, mice and other rodents. He could smell the corruption, that unmistakable, utterly cloying signature of dead flesh.

'Fuck.' Kit wiped his mouth with the back of his hand.

'You okay?' said No Neck, before shaking his head. 'Shit, sorry ... Of course you're not okay.'

'It's the smell,' said Kit, spitting.

No Neck looked at him. 'What smell?' he asked.

A thickset man in a hard hat tried to wave Kit away as he approached two Brazilians busy heaving chunks of concrete into a fresh skip. 'Please stay back,' he said. 'We're working.'

'Yeah?' said No Neck. 'Well we're ...'

Kit stepped between them. 'This was my bar,' he said. 'My wife died here.'

Whatever the foreman saw in Kit's eyes was enough for him to order the Brazilians to stop working. 'We're going to take a break,' he said. 'We'll be back in ten minutes.' Left unspoken was the fact this was all the time Kit would get.

'I thought you owned this place,' said No Neck, as he watched the crew head uphill towards Roppongi's main drag.

'Yeah,' said Kit.

'So you've just sold it, right?'

Kit shook his head. 'I know nothing about this,' he said. He looked around at the scattered rubble, the half-filled skip and a silent pneumatic drill. 'No one's mentioned this at all.'

CHAPTER 17
Monday 18 June

At 5.30 a.m a man in the next capsule coughed himself awake, flicked down the video screen in his roof and began to drum his nails as he waited for the news.

Japan's biggest fraud trial collapses, CEO Osamu Nakamura too ill to give evidence. File closes on Katagawa family suicide. Washington, London and Moscow ramp up their war on narco-terrorism.

And then Kit heard Yoshi's name.

At Christies in New York an example of work by Ms Yoshi Tanaka sells for an unprecedented sum ...

Ten minutes later the same man began to shave with a loud and erratic razor. About half an hour after this, a woman on the female-only floor farted loudly and spent the next five minutes chuckling to herself.

By 7.30 a.m, the sole guest at Executive Start Capsule Hotel was Kit, and he'd been awake all night, trying to work out why Yuko wouldn't take his calls. So he rolled up the blind covering his glass door and scrambled out, manoeuvring himself over the lip, because the capsules were stacked two deep along a corridor and he'd chosen an upper one.

Of course, Kit could have taken a room at the Tokyo Hilton, on the far side of Shinjuku station, about half a mile west of where he was. He still had Mr Oniji's money, mostly untouched. But in his own way Kit was saying goodbye to a city that had been saying goodbye to itself for as long as he could remember. A trial separation from Tokyo felt as lonely as leaving a lover.

It was only as he sweated out last night's beer in a communal sauna that Kit realised he'd obviously taken Mr Oniji's advice to heart. Until then, he'd have said he had no intention of going anywhere. Kit was still wondering about that as he showered. And then, when he'd put it off for as long as possible, he shaved carefully, dressed and checked himself in the mirror.

Hollow eyes stared back. Other than that, he'd do.

The sub-manager at Kyoto Credit Bank was apologetic. Ms Tanaka's sister and brother-in-law had closed her account a week earlier and emptied the strong box Ms Tanaka had been renting. The joint account Mr Nouveau held with Ms Tanaka still existed. Unfortunately, under Japanese law, it was now frozen until a certificate of probate was filed at the ward office. He believed from what Ms Tanaka's brother-in-law said that this would be very soon.

On his way to the door, not just of his office but the bank itself, the sub-manager added his profound regret at the incalculable loss of an Important Intangible Cultural Property and so much of her work. When Kit told him that most of Yoshi's recent pieces were on tour in New York, the man looked almost relieved.

'A tragic loss nevertheless.'

Nodding, Kit shook hands, bowed briefly and cut across the road, headed for No Neck's waiting Speedmaster. It was either that or kick shit out of KCB's sub-manager.

'Okay,' said No Neck, after Kit told him what had happened. 'Next stop, her lawyers.'

The woman behind the desk at Yamanoto & Co was so embarrassed at Kit's arrival that she sat frozen at her counter, repeating Yoshi's name to herself, while she fretted about what to do next. She was still glitching when a young woman in a dark suit stopped to listen, overheard Yoshi's name and introduced herself.

'Suzuki,' she said, offering his hand. 'Ako Suzuki. Mr Togo's senior assistant.'

'Suzuki-san ...'

'Perhaps,' said the young woman, 'it might be best if we used Mr Togo's office?' She gestured to a cherrywood door behind her.

'I'll see you outside,' said No Neck.

Having turned down the offer of both tea and coffee, Kit accepted a glass of water, because turning this down would only have produced the offer of fruit juice or something else. When his water finally arrived, brought by the receptionist, it came in a glass, with ice and a slice of lemon and Kit and Ms Suzuki had just agreed it was a pity Mr Togo was not here himself, that the spring blossom around Inokashira Pond had been spectacular and the weather was surprisingly humid, even for June.

Only when Kit had sipped from his glass did Mr Togo's assistant put both her hands on the table and bow, very slightly. 'We are sorry,' she said, 'for your loss.' The language Ms Suzuki used was so formal Kit barely understood what she said. He waited for her to add something about Yoshi's work or the fact Ms Tanaka was the best potter of her generation. Instead she just reached across the desk for a desk diary.

'Mr Togo had the meeting on Tuesday with Mr Tamagusuku,' she said, flicking back a couple of pages. 'Ms Tanaka's brother-in-law said he would update you on what was said. I imagine he's been in touch?'

Kit shook his head.

'Ahh ...' Ms Suzuki considered the diary in front of her very carefully. As if it might explain why. 'That is unfortunate.'

She shuffled a few pages and then shuffled back again, got up and went to a filing cabinet, only to turn round and come back again. Although young, Ms Suzuki did not look like the kind of woman who got flustered.

'There was a will,' she said. 'We gave it to Mr Tamagusuku.' Of course there was. Of course they did.

Artists in the west were meant to be untidy and driven by inner demons. Yoshi had demons, all right. Only she'd probably kept their details filed in the order in which they first appeared.

'You had more than one copy,' Kit stated.

Ms Suzuki stared at him.

'I know Yoshi,' said Kit. 'She'd have asked Mr Togo to notarise two copies, then she'd have filed another with her bank, kept a spare at home, and for all I know, given a final copy to Yuko ...'

He caught Ms Suzuki's glance and thought about what he'd said.

'Okay, maybe not that last one,' admitted Kit, because then Yuko's husband wouldn't have been in such a hurry to collect the original.

'Forgive me for asking,' she said. 'How long were ...' Ms Suzuki caught herself. 'How long did you and Yoshi live together?'

'Ten years.'

Ms Suzuki made notes on a piece of paper. 'No children?'

Kit shook his head.

'Probably for the best.'

When Kit looked surprised, he got a short lecture on single mothers and Japanese inheritance law, followed by a longer lecture on probate for childless couples, both married and unmarried. As Yoshi's parents were dead, Kit would have inherited three-quarters, with Yuko sharing the rest. Unfortunately, the situation with unmarried couples was not nearly so favourable …

Which raised a whole new set of questions. Such as, if Yoshi was really so organised, how come she filed multiple copies of her will, while failing to register their marriage at the ward office as she'd promised she would?

CHAPTER 18
Wednesday 20 June

'Guinness or Caffreys?' No Neck asked.

Kit nodded, without thinking, and reached the last free table in Paddy's Tavern a second or so before three Australian backpackers, who took one look at No Neck's tattoos and the bleakness in Kit's face and decided they'd rather stand at the bar.

No Neck sighed. 'I'll get Guinness,' he said.

Slitting open a buff envelope, Kit shook its contents onto the rickety table in front of him. It was just before 1 p.m., two days after Kit met Ms Suzuki and the promised copy of Yoshi's will had finally been cleared with Mr Togo himself for collecting.

Getting the beers in while Kit read the will was No Neck's idea of tact. A gesture No Neck promptly ruined by banging two pints of Guinness onto the table and demanding to know exactly what the will said.

'Nothing good,' said Kit, killing half of his pint in one go. Having skim-read the document, he read it again more carefully. Ms Suzuki had kindly included a notarised English translation, but Kit felt he should read the original. It was handwritten and the writing was Yoshi's own. There was something harsh about knowing this was probably the last piece of her writing he'd see.

Yoshi's will was a very simple document, little more than a single page. She left everything to her sister. There was no reference to a loan from Kit and the bar was barely mentioned. The will had been drafted three months earlier and Kit didn't recognise the name of either witness.

'You okay?' asked No Neck.

'Sure,' said Kit. 'Everything's great.'

No Neck left to get another two beers without being asked. And when he came back it was with the beers, a bowl of udon noodles and a pair of disposable chopsticks. 'Eat,' he said, dumping his tray on the table in front of Kit.

'What about you?'

'Micki made noodles for breakfast,' said No Neck. 'You look as if you haven't eaten in weeks.'

'Micki?'

The huge man actually blushed. 'She's looking after me,' he said. 'Just a temporary thing.'

The trucks were gone and the jackhammer stood silent when Kit and No Neck reached the site where Pirate Mary's had been. Someone had swept grit from the road and piled it into a heap. A handful of cigarette ends and a broken polystyrene cup were caught in the sweepings and now mixed with dirt like artefacts from some strange archaeological dig. The concrete foundations Kit saw on his last visit had been reduced to rubble and carried away.

Coming soon, announced a sign. *Executive manshon. 9 apartments. South facing.* A picture on the board showed an elegant block filling the area where Pirate Mary's and its parking space had been.

Where jagged foundation once stood a jackhammer had exposed a well. The slab that originally closed off the well shaft was cracked down the middle and someone had used a crowbar to shift the smaller of two pieces. Kit knew this because the bar still stood beside a broken section of slab and both leant against the low wall around the well.

'You can't go in,' No Neck protested, when Kit tried the new metal gate.

'I own this place.'

'Maybe,' said No Neck. 'But it's still padlocked. Talk to Mr Suzuki in the morning ...'

'I own this place,' repeated Kit, rattling the fence. He felt hands grip his shoulders from behind and the *bozozoku* lifted him aside.

'Leave it,' said No Neck. 'Learn when to walk away.'

'I can't,' said Kit.

Dark eyes looked at Kit from a face that would scare hardened criminals, the light from a street lamp falling across the *bozozoku*'s cheek like a scar. 'This matters that much?' he said.

'Yes,' said Kit, 'it does.'

'You want to tell me why?' The *bozozoku* stood between Kit and the gate, his head bent slightly to show that he was ready to listen. Kit knew almost nothing about No Neck and the man knew even less about him, it was one of the things that let them remain friends.

'I mean,' said No Neck. 'It's not as if you and Yoshi even liked each other.'

'It's not just Yoshi,' admitted Kit. 'It's the way it's all getting white-washed. No bomb, tragic accident. No bar, new apartments. I feel like a ghost in my own life. I want the bar back.'

No Neck considered that.

'Okay,' he said.

The metal fence was designed so that sections locked together. It should have been possible to separate one section from another merely by lifting. Unfortunately practice turned out to be very different to theory.

An old woman in a yukata had appeared from one of the few remaining wooden houses, a building even more ramshackle than the bar had been. And Mr Ito now stood at the edge of the darkened graveyard, leaning on his broom. Both were watching intently and neither looked like being much help.

'We need more people,' Kit said, looking round.

'Tomorrow,' promised No Neck. 'We'll have lots of people. Let me make some calls first.'

'Want to talk about Yoshi?' asked No Neck, a few hours later. After one of the many calls he'd promised to make delivered them to another bar. With No Neck it was always a bar, unless that was just Tokyo.

'No,' Kit said. 'I don't think I do.'

'Okay,' said No Neck. 'You ever wondered what it was you and Yoshi had in common?'

'I just said ...'

'You're not talking about it,' said No Neck. 'I am. You ever wonder?'

Kit shook his head.

'Nothing,' said No Neck. 'That was what you had in common ... All those empty rooms. No television, no radio, no computers. Four floors of your own building in central Tokyo and the only room you bothered to decorate was the bar. Everything else was just storage space, without the storage.'

'Yeah,' said Kit. 'Probably.'

'Does that sound like a marriage to you?'

Kit looked at him.

'She didn't register it,' No Neck said. 'Because that way she got to walk away ...'

'If things went wrong.'

No Neck nodded.

'Look,' said Kit. 'You want to tell me what happened that night?'

Kit and No Neck were sat in Seventh Gear, a biker shack on the north west edge of Kabuki-cho, built under a raised section of the Seibu Shinjuku line. And Kit had earned his share of stares and comments just by pushing his way through its bead curtain. No Neck had to do some quick talking, his share of stares, shoulder slapping and arm gripping before Kit's presence became accepted.

'Sure,' said No Neck, taking off his shades to reveal bruises purple enough to make a Goth rainbow. 'Why not? She shopped me to the cops. The cops decided to beat the crap out of me, repeatedly.'

'Shit,' said Kit. 'You know why?'

No Neck snorted. 'Why do you think?' he said. 'By then, they wanted me to sign a confession saying my friends bombed your bar.'

'They gave you a translation?'

'I can read Japanese.'

Kit stared at him. 'You're worse than me,' he said. 'Everyone knows that.'

No Neck looked embarrassed. 'I can read it,' he said. 'And talk Japanese, if I must.'

'So why the *me no speaks* stuff?'

'Think about it,' said No Neck, 'why does Micki keep coming round to my apartment?'

'To teach you ...' Kit stopped.

'Yeah.' The huge man smiled. 'I've been here for twenty-five years,' he said, 'remember Madori? Namiko? Mai? They all wanted to teach me Japanese. You'd be surprised how many of those lessons ended up in bed.'

Actually, Kit wouldn't.

'The police knew it wasn't me,' said No Neck, with a shrug. 'But it would have been tidier. One *gaijin* bombs another, famous Japanese artist caught in the conflict ... They came very close,' No Neck added.

'Close to what?'

'Getting their confession.' Upending his bottle, No Neck killed what was left of his Kirin. 'Not sure what changed,' he said. 'One moment some psycho has me in a cell, the next there's a knock at the door and I'm alone on the floor with footprints on my face.' The Australian checked he really had finished his beer and got up to fetch another.

When No Neck returned it was with four Kirin and a saucer of chilli nuts. 'The bastard didn't even bother to come back,' he said, sounding more fucked off by that than anything else. 'Just left me on the floor in my own piss. A uniform kicked me free. Gave me back my wallet, permit and resident's card and told me to behave myself in future. He looked about twelve ...'

'It could have been worse,' said Kit. 'They could have shipped you back to Sydney.' For reasons unspecified, the *bozozoku* had let it be known that returning home could be fatal.

'Ex-wife,' said No Neck, as if hearing Kit's thought. 'Turkish, big family, half a dozen brothers.' Reaching for the chilli nuts, he emptied the saucer with a single scoop and swallowed the lot, pulling a face. 'Her father hated how it began and loathed how it ended.'

'How did it start?'

'In a school gym.'

Kit looked at No Neck. 'I was teaching,' said No Neck. 'She wasn't ...'

It was a long story, not pretty and the only thing No Neck would say in his defence was that he'd loved the girl. She'd been six months under legal and he'd married her as soon as he was allowed. Things had gone downhill from there.

'You know how many bodies I buried in the first Iraq war?'

Kit shook his head.

'Nor do I,' said No Neck, 'there were that many, kids and conscripts ... We just bulldozed sand over the top. I always thought that was my worst and then Maryam announced she was leaving and taking the kids.'

He caught Kit's look, the unspoken question. 'I was drinking,' he admitted. 'Spending too much time with the Rebels. Things were rough.'

'So you ended up here?'

'There are worse places,' said No Neck, glancing round. He nodded to a couple of *bozozoku* in the far corner. One was wearing a white headband with shades, the other just had the shades. 'These guys are family,' No Neck said, thumping his ribs over the heart. 'Know what I mean?'

The Australian was missing when Kit got back from taking a piss. Although Kit found him easily enough, over in the far corner with the guy wearing a headband. 'Meet Micki's brother Tetsuo. He's going to help us shift that fence.'

Kit shook, trying not to wince at the other man's grip.

'According to Tetsuo,' said No Neck, 'someone out there is looking for you.'

'Police?'

Micki's brother and No Neck exchanged glances. 'No,' said Tetsuo. 'A *gaijin*, someone like you ... A woman.' He thought about it some more. 'An old woman.'

'Has this woman said why?'

Tetsuo shook his head. 'No,' he said. 'She just said whoever finds you gets half-a-million yen. So, if you want help tomorrow shifting that fence ...'

The *bozozoku* escort was presented as a compliment, an honour guard to escort Kit and No Neck through the neon squalor of North Shinjuku. 'Tell her, I'll come by the Hilton for my money,' said Tetsuo, and No Neck nodded.

Like most bars in the city Pom Pom Palace had a lurid sign. Only this one was bleached almost white by time and advertised girls who probably hadn't danced in years. A Korean in a shiny tuxedo opened a door at the bottom of some steps and began bowing them inside.

'You're expected,' he said.

A girl was on stage under a single light. She wore a silver g-string and white gloves and was dancing, fairly badly, to *Jenny Was A Friend Of Mine*. Half a dozen Italian tourists sat round a formica table in front of the stage. The table looked as if it had been salvaged from a sandwich shop. And the Italians looked like they'd been expecting rather more for their money.

There was something intrinsically sad about Shinjuku. A vacuum-packed hollowness that no quantity of neon could hide. Roppongi was the same, only there the sadness was older and more Western. All that movement to so little purpose. A million strangers searching for a cure to the darkness behind their eyes in the void between someone else's legs.

It could be on film, behind glass in a peek booth, printed out and pasted on walls; or it could be on stage under a single light, looking down at strangers, beyond caring why the strangers stared back.

Rock and Roll Lies.

Another band, another nearly forgotten track, another girl about to dance. Wrapping one arm around Kit's shoulders, No Neck said. 'Come on. Let's get this over with.'

'You knew about this?'

'Not until just now,' said No Neck. 'Well, maybe a little. I'd heard someone was asking for you.' He shook his head sadly. 'I mean, that's not exactly news. But I figured ...'

'You figured what?'

The huge Australian seemed embarrassed. 'You know, someone wanted to finish what they started. Except Tetsuo says it's not like that at all. This woman wants to hire you. And, God knows, you need something to stop you coming apart.'

'I'm fine,' Kit said.

No Neck sighed. 'Take a look at yourself,' he suggested.

'So they found you ...' The woman who stood up from the corner table looked her guest up and down, as one might look at a cut of meat in the butchers, before arguing about price. Which was entirely fitting because Kate O'Mally began life in a butcher's shop, before her lack of squeamishness and facility with a blade let her move into more profitable areas, allegedly.

She looked older than Kit remembered and was wearing a tweed sports coat, utterly out of keeping with her surroundings. But then, Mary's mother never had known how to dress.

The last time they'd talked, the woman had threatened to have Kit's legs broken and his testicles crushed with pliers if he went near Mary again. Kate O'Mally had found her daughter bent over a lavatory, vomiting. Mary thought she might be pregnant.

As one half-naked girl replaced another on stage and silence stretched thin between No Neck, Kit and Mrs O'Mally, Kit finally remembered the woman's promise of when they'd next meet.

'I guess,' he said. 'This means hell's finally frozen over.'

CHAPTER 19
Wednesday 20 June

Slung under a concrete overhang, in a building designed by Hiroshi-Oe and built by one of his followers, the top-floor bar of Kate O'Mally's hotel looked out on a handful of lanes running south from Akasaka Mitsuke. At first sight these looked to be a typically working-class jumble of thin alleys, short cross lanes, red paper lanterns and a mix of ramen shops, chemists and *pachinko* parlours. The kind of area that could once be found almost anywhere.

Appearances were wrong. Akasaka was a favourite haunt for senior staff from Japan's civil service, which explained the prices in some of the *kaiseki ryori* restaurants.

'Pretty, isn't it?' said Kate O'Mally.

And Kit knew hell really had frozen over. The Kate O'Mally he remembered would never have bothered with small talk.

'Very,' said Kit. 'I knew the wife of the man who owns most of it, once.'

Kate went back to her whisky. The bar in which they both sat was panelled in dark oak, had low leather sofas and coffee tables made from fat slabs of industrial glass.

As with most Tokyo hotels, the waiting staff were female and dressed with such discretion they were almost transparent with good taste. A heavy pall of cigar smoke hung cloud-like around them, from three cigars that had been whisked away the moment their stubs hit the ashtray in front of Kate.

'Sherry and vanilla,' said Kate, sniffing her glass.

It smelt like whisky to Kit.

So now they sat, not quite opposite each other. Their bowl of rice crackers was empty and the suits in the corner had abandoned their conversation for a club in one of the alleys beyond the main road. Kit had watched them go.

Every so often, Kate would lean forward and then change her mind about whatever she'd been about to say. Having slipped another Cuban cigar from a leather holder, Kate sliced it with a silver cutter and lit it using a gold Ronson. She stubbed the cigar out within three puffs and it vanished a second later.

'Just say it,' he said. 'This place closes in half an hour. After that, I'm going home.'

'And where would that be?' said Kate. 'I've seen the ruins, and your bloody pub sign. You used my daughter's face.' She shook her head angrily. 'You think she'd like that?'

Kit's smile was cold. 'You think I'd care?'

Kate turned away.

Outside the picture window a Kawasaki cruiser had stopped at the lights far below, its modified pipes echoing off the concrete canyon around it, loud enough to shake windows twenty-eight floors above. A steady stream of Kawasakis, Harleys and chopped Hondas had been rolling past the hotel. No Neck's idea of keeping his eye on a friend.

'I'm not a fool,' said Kate. 'I always knew it was you.'

'Yeah ...' Kit nodded. 'So you said.' Pushing back his chair, he watched the Kawasaki jump the lights as a police cruiser pulled up behind. What had been a noise violation became something more serious.

'I'm off,' he said. 'You can settle the bill.'

Kate tossed down a Y50,000 note without bothering to check the denomination. 'I'm coming too,' she said. They took the lift in silence. Kit in his new clothes, Kate with her drunk's face, hair curled so tight it fitted like a helmet. She wore too many gold rings and a Rolex better suited to a deep-sea diver. For all her wealth she seemed as ill at ease in her clothes as Kit felt in his skin.

'Finished staring?'

'Yeah,' said Kit. 'I guess age nails us all in the end.' He looked Kate in the face, rather than watching her in the mirrored wall of the lift. 'I used to be afraid of you,' he said. 'Everyone was.'

'Not Mary.'

'Oh yes,' said Kit. 'Especially Mary. Ask her.'

'I can't fucking ask.' Whatever time had failed to do, his words completed. The jaw always held so rigid began to tremble and Kate's eyes, usually flint-like, spilled with tears. As the lift reached the lobby Kate retreated to the safety of an inside corner.

Leaning past the lift girl, Kit punched the *floor 28* button for himself. 'Forgotten something,' he told a waitress, when he walked back into the bar. Kate was still staring fiercely ahead when Kit returned, while the lift attendant did her best to act as if everything was normal.

One can learn a lot about someone in the time it takes a lift to descend two dozen floors, a lot about how their life came apart. It didn't even take that many words.

'You've quarrelled?'

'Mary's dead.

'Oh shit,' said Kit, half a dozen floors passing as he reached for his next question. 'She got sick?'

'No,' said Kate. 'Although, that would be bad enough.'

'A car accident?'

'Killed herself,' Kate said. 'Wrote a note, changed her clothes, bought a ticket and stepped off the side of the Ostend ferry. She left this ...' The woman dug into her jacket to retrieve an envelope just as the lift reached the ground.

'Police,' said Kate, nodding to a slit in the envelope's flap. 'Not me. I wasn't going to come,' she added. 'Even if I did I wasn't going to find you. Only Pat insisted.'

Patrick Robbe-Duras, Kit could remember him. A small man with a Dublin accent that had survived twenty-five years of life in London and the home counties. Mary had adored her father.

'Mr Duras made you?'

'Said it was what she wanted. Only I don't think Mary had any fucking idea what she ...'

'We should move,' Kit said, stepping forward to stop the lift doors from closing again. 'Come on.' He led Kate out of the Otis and nodded his thanks to the lift girl, who bowed, smiled and hit a button to shut their problems out of her life. Drunks got special dispensation in Tokyo, which was just as well, there were usually enough of them.

'Ramen,' said Kit. 'A bit like spaghetti. Eat the shrimp and noodles, then drink the soup. It'll help soak up the alcohol.'

'I know what ramen are,' Kate said. 'Mary took me to Wagamama.'

They sat in a tiny café under an arch in Asakusa, delivered there by a reluctant taxi. If the driver noticed the ancient Speedmaster trailing him, he probably put it down to some *bozozoku* having fun at his expense. The café was the only place Kit knew for sure would be open at 3 a.m on a weekday. Well, there were strip joints in Kabuki-cho, the *kaiseki ryori* of Akasaka and enough hostess bars in Shinjuku to keep an army of suits happy, only Kit was looking for something more discreet.

'Is this all anyone does in Tokyo?'

Kit looked puzzled.

'Eat and drink,' said Kate. 'Stay out all night partying?'

He considered mentioning the lack of living space, the fact love hotels existed because so many couples still lived with their parents, the way worlds overlapped, the conflict between public and private pleasures and the part communal drinking played in establishing hierarchies, then decided not to bother. Kate was just being difficult for the sake of it.

'Drink the pink stuff,' he said.

Surprisingly, Kate did as she was told, tipping back a glass of sugar water mixed with amino acids. It was reputed to cure drunkenness, improve mental function and extend life. Kate looked like she needed all three.

'Okay,' said Kit, 'now give me Mary's letter.'

Kate hesitated, as he knew she would.

Bringing a bowl to his lips, Kit slurped down his broth. 'I understand,' he said. 'You hate me. You don't want to be here. You're only here because of Pat. Now show me the letter.'

Kate dug into her pocket.

Somehow, given Kate's reappearance in his life, Kit had expected to see his own name. Instead Mary had addressed her letter to everyone and no one at the same time. *To whom it may concern.* Taking the envelope, Kit extracted a key and a single sheet of cheap paper. *I'm sorry, I know it's selfish, but life has become impossible.* Misery laid out on the page in words written a thousand times before.

Kate's reason for being in Tokyo came in the final paragraph. And, having read it, Kit could understand why Kate had been reluctant to make the trip. Given how she felt about him it must have hurt just getting on the plane.

Mary had owned a flat in central London, an art gallery in Canterville Mews, five goldfish and cat called Miu. The cat was being looked after by Pat, the goldfish had gone to a friend. The art gallery was run by a half-Czech woman called Sylvia and could look after itself. All of these, however, now belonged to Kit.

'Is this legal?'

'That's all you can ask?' Kate's voice was raw. *'Is it legal'* The bang as she slammed down her bowl was enough to make a market porter at the next table stare across. A nod from Kit and the man in overalls and yellow boots went back to his paper, foreigners forgotten.

'What do you want me to say?' asked Kit. 'You think I want her flat and all this other shit?' Reaching deep into his wallet, Kit slid out a thumbnail print he'd forgotten until recently was even there. He pushed it over to Kate, who glanced down, grabbed the square of cardboard and held it close to her face.

It was a cruel thing to do, Kit knew that. It was meant to be cruel.

'That's how I remember Mary,' he said. *'That's* the Mary I knew.' Without asking, Kit reached over and took back his photograph.

Thursday 16th May 2002, a single day of blazing sunshine, trapped between a day of drizzle and an almighty thunder storm. The Doves were top of the album charts. Slipknot, White Stripes and Mercury Rev were scheduled to play Reading. He'd just bought new strings for his guitar. Mary was still going out with him. All the bad stuff was yet to come. The one perfect day of his life.

'Who took the picture?' demanded Kate.

'Who do you think?' said Kit. 'Josh, obviously ...'

Josh with his new Nokia, photographing his best mate and his best mate's girl, sat almost facing each other. So bohemian, beneath an early summer sky. As if Mary's naked top and Kit's faux casual insolence in the face of a camera phone meant all other restraints had been lost.

They looked like the kids they'd been. Only one had to be old to think like that and Kit wasn't, not really; just tired and drunk and doing his best to hold Kate's news at bay. 'Why are you really here?'

'Because I told Pat I'd find you.'

'You could have lied,' Kit said, 'holed up in a hotel, told him I'd left for somewhere else.'

'I did,' said Kate. 'Twice. The last time was a month ago.'

She drank off the rest of her broth, without seeming to notice it was cold and picked up a disposable chopstick, which was crude enough to have split down one edge when separated from its pair.

Years back, yanking her fingers apart, Yoshi had described how, until he met her sister, Yuko's new husband had *hashi* his way through office ladies. It turned out she meant split open, used one time only and tossed away. Every time Kit used disposable chopsticks he thought of Mr Tamagusuku.

'Cheap,' Kate said, putting down one chopstick and snapping the other in two. She regarded the jagged end with interest and Kit felt himself tense.

'Maybe back then,' she said. 'Not now.'

'So why come looking a third time?' asked Kit, returning to what really worried him.

'I've told you,' said Kate. 'Pat.'

'What about him?' Kit prompted.

Kate O'Mally took a deep breath. Kit thought it was a sigh until he saw her shoulders lock and she blew the air out again. It was frustration that drove the breath from her body with the force of a punch.

'We've separated,' she said. 'Happened about five years ago. Still stay it touch. Well, we did, mostly about Mary. He thinks she's still alive.'

Putting down his green tea, Kit waited.

'I know for a fact,' said Kate. 'My daughter stepped off a ferry into the sea. The police, the coroner, all Mary's friends … We know that's the truth. Only Pat refuses to believe it.'

'Why?'

'Why do you think? Because he can't stand the thought of Mary drowning herself.' From the scowl on Kate O'Mally's face she wasn't handling the truth much better herself. This was a woman who'd used pliers as a negotiating tool, Kit reminded himself. Now was probably not the time to start feeling pity.

'What?' demanded Kate.

'Just remembering,' Kit told her.

'Pat says Mary wouldn't kill herself.' Kate sighed. 'He says suicide wasn't in Mary's character.'

'So what does he think happened?'

'He told the police he believes she was kidnapped and murdered.'

'Then there should be a body or a ransom note.'

'That's what they said.' Kate shrugged. 'An inspector came down from London. I think Pat had been giving them trouble. You know, calling them with new ideas and suggestions. You remember Mary's cousin Mike?'

Kit shook his head, not that it made any difference.

'Surprise me,' said Kate sourly. 'He took over the business a few years back.' She grimaced. 'Good at it too, much smoother than me. Anyway, he called. It turned out he'd been in contact with Mary all those years she wouldn't even talk to me.'

Mary wouldn't …

'Why did he call?'

'To say I should do what Pat wanted.' From the flatness in Kate's voice, it sounded as if her nephew had said a lot of other things as well.

An early wash of dawn was weakening neon beyond the café's curtain, turning the lights from a mating display to a jumble of glass tubes and tatty flex. Across the street a group of Chinese cleaners were tumbling out of a white van, in a clatter of mops and pails, their conversation fractured by the rattle of early-morning trains overhead.

No Neck's motorbike was parked up and Kit knew the *bozozoku* would be watching from somewhere nearby, the man and his machine were rarely parted for long.

'Come on,' said Kit, 'let's get you back to your hotel.'

Pushing back her chair, Kate reached for her coat, forcing her arm through its sleeve on her third attempt. 'I've got a better idea,' she said. 'You can show me the sights.'

CHAPTER 20
nawa-no-ukiyo

Stumbling through the door, Lady Neku, otherwise known as Baroness Nawa-no-ukiyo, Countess High Strange and chatelaine of Schloss Omga, fell to her knees and vomited all over slate tiles. What she'd seen clung to her like smoke, her thoughts were rubble through which the last wisps of necessity demanded she search.

'Fuck.'

Hoplite, heliocentric ...

Hemispherical?

Double fuck. There was something important she needed to tell her brother Nico. Only she'd forgotten it already.

Lady Neku was naked, her fingers bled from broken nails. A scratch on her ankles had obviously oozed liquid and then sealed itself. From what she could tell the glue her body had produced was ... was ... *Tied to extra-cellular matrix receptors, linked to the initiation of granulation tissue formation.*

She jumped, shocked that the castle had been the one to speak first. 'You're back,' it said. 'Did you get what you were after?'

'What was I after?' asked Lady Neku.

The castle sighed. 'Obviously not,' it said.

Squatting naked like some fugee, Lady Neku let the tiles melt around her and felt herself sink into the floor, until the level came up to her neck. It was wet and warm but not unpleasant, like damp flesh on damp flesh, which is what it was, Lady Neku realised.

'Can you mend me?' she asked.

'Define mend.'

'Repair the cuts and heal the bruises.' She felt the castle's amusement. 'I can still do the small stuff,' it said. 'It's the bigger stuff ...'

'What bigger stuff?'

96

'Neku,' it said, and Lady Neku realised this was the first time Schloss Omga had ever called her by name. 'You're sweet, but not very bright.'

'I'm more intelligent than my brothers,' Lady Neku said crossly.

'Yes,' said the castle, 'there is always that.'

Later, when the aches had gone, Lady Neku dipped her head beneath the tiles and let Schloss Omga heal the scratches on her face. 'Thank you,' she said, clambering out of a fleshy softness that returned itself to tile once she'd climbed free. 'I need to find Nico now.'

'Neku ...'

'Yes?' said Lady Neku, realising she hadn't yet asked the castle for her clothes back. 'What?'

'You know,' Schloss Omga said. 'You need to think really hard about why you're still wearing that body.'

'You know why,' said Lady Neku. 'Someone stole my real one.'

'Were you wearing this body when you left just now?'

Lady Neku nodded.

'What about the time before?' prompted the castle. 'What were you wearing then?'

She thought about it, she really did. And in thinking about this Neku realised something else. She'd gone back to get her memory bracelet, because how could she function without it? Only, her wrist was still bare. Which meant ...

'You should go back,' said the castle.

'To find my memories?'

'That too,' said Schloss Omga. 'Though there are better reasons. Meanwhile, I want you to think really hard about why looking for Nico is a bad idea.'

'But I've lost ...'

'Doesn't matter,' said the castle. 'All memories get filed twice, once in the bracelet and once in your head. Use the wetware,' it said. 'And start now, while your mind is still imprinted on that body. Begin with something simple, something recent. What's the very last thing you can remember?'

'Waking,' said Lady Neku.

'Where was this?'

'In my bedroom. Someone asked me a question.'

'Begin there,' said the castle. 'Try to recall what happened next.'

She was asleep in her room at High Strange, a circular room at the top of a spire. In the old days the spires were called spindles and there was

97

a lot of history attached to them, but Lady Neku did her best to ignore it.

Lady Neku chose her room because it looked towards the stars, what few remained within her light cone, rather than towards the Earth which a room at the other end of the spire would have done.

Her mother had an earth room as tradition demanded, so the head of the family could view the lands she protected. Although the Katchatka did little to protect anyone these days, now that the sails of *nawa-no-ukiyo* were ripped and the sun was free to lay waste to their segment.

How strange, everyone said, when Lady Neku chose that room. Which was odd, because it seemed to make perfect sense for her to live as far from her family as possible.

Words woke her on the night she remembered. Unexpected, because she'd added a filter to her thoughts to keep her brothers away.

'Neku ... Hey, you there?'

She recognised his voice instantly. Young, well spoken and slightly arch. *I mean,* she thought, how many boys/excluding brothers were there in High Strange?

None.

And how many boys in the overworlds?

Thirty-eight, working to a tolerance of two years either way. Eleven of these were blood related within the last three generations. Of the remaining twenty-seven, just over half were habitually female. Not that Lady Neku had anything against flipping genders, obviously. That left thirteen spread across six segments. Two of those segments were hostile and Lady Neku knew of their five possibilities from records only. Which left eight boys, ranging in age from thirteen to seventeen. Who were, almost without exception, contemptible in their hunger to make friends with her. The exception was Perfect.

This wasn't his real name. That was something so absurd he refused to use it when introducing himself. If segment titles had suffered from inflation, then names in the Menham Segment had suffered worse still. Lady Neku had her own suspicions about why this had happened.

'Neku?'

'Yes,' she said. 'I'm here.'

'Oh, right.' Per sounded puzzled. 'You sound different.'

The fact they were even talking would be regarded as an outrage by Lady Neku's mother. That Lady Neku and Per one day planned to meet, albeit at ground level ...

'Take a guess why?'

'Don't know,' Per said, sounding cross. 'I'm rubbish at guessing games. Your throat's sore?'

'Close,' said Lady Neku. 'I cut it with Nico's knife.'

'You ...?'

'I want a new body. My dear Lady Mother won't give me one.'

Perfect Lord Menham was eighteen months older than Lady Neku and given to pretending he'd spent years doing things she'd only dreamed up yesterday. Except that whoever told Per that girls liked *dissolute, damned* and *dangerous* (and Lady Neku's bet was on his sister), should also have told him there was no point asking questions if he was going to be shocked by the answers.

'It's healing,' she said. 'Worst luck. Why did you call me?'

'The d'Alamberts,' said Per.

Information flowed from the web of beads around Lady Neku's wrist, maps of d'Alambert influence and schematics showing their sections of the rope world, flicking across her mind until she told the information to stop.

'What about them?' demanded Lady Neku, more crossly than was polite.

'It's just,' said Per, 'I've heard ...'

Whatever Perfect had heard was obviously so stupid he decided not to say it; because Lady Neku suddenly got a head full of static and then silence. When she was certain Per was gone, she tried to call Nico, Petro and Antonio in turn, but apparently her brothers didn't want to talk to her either.

CHAPTER 21
Thursday 21 June

Kit intended to leave Kate where she slept, he really did. The bench was large, Shinjuku Chuo Park was safe, not even the homeless would disturb a middle-aged woman snoring drunkenly in front of an artificial waterfall, under the gaze of a lost Mandarin duck.

The last thing he needed was Kate O'Mally bringing her hangover to his meeting with Tetsuo, who really was going to help Kit with his problems in Roppongi ... Well, according to No Neck.

All Kit had to do was walk away. He could fold Mary's letter back into its envelope and place the envelope inside Kate's coat, and leave the woman to her sadness and a hangover that would do little to ruin a day already ruined from the moment she woke.

It was so tempting.

He owed her nothing. After all, Kate O'Mally was the person he'd once promised to destroy, in a fit of teenage bravado. Only life had already done that for him. Her daughter was dead, Kate's relationship with Patrick Robbe-Duras was ended and the house above Middle Morton echoed with so much loneliness she could barely stand to live there.

Who knew Kate could be so poetic? So honest about the horror she was facing. It was that honesty which put its hook into Kit's flesh. So that every time he stood up to walk away, sharp tugs of guilt sat him down again. It was her honesty, and one final admission.

'You know,' said Kate, when they first reached the bench. 'There's another possibility.'

'There is?'

'Pat originally thought Mary was running away.'

'From what?' asked Kit.

The face Kate turned to Kit was ravaged by alcohol, guilt and a level of self-awareness more cruel than anything a teenage Kit could have wished on her. 'From me,' she said. 'And you know what Pat said? *Better late than never ...*'

It took the duck an hour to realise the couple on the bench were useless as a source of food and get cross. By then, the sun had got stuck behind the government buildings to Kit's right and the roads around the little park become crowded with traffic. Carbon monoxide mixed with the sour smell of campfires from a collection of blue plastic tents nearby. It was no longer early and the homeless were hanging out their blankets to air or washing shirts in the splash pool of the waterfall.

Mrs Oniji had once explained to Kit that ducks divide into *ahiru* and *kamo*, those that are white and those that are not, but then Mrs Oniji used different words for water, depending on whether it was hot, cold or merely warm. Maybe she'd miss the lessons? Kit hoped so, at least he thought he did.

'Shoo,' Kit told the duck. One tiny eye peered at him from a slash of white like plate armour along the side of its head. After a moment, the duck decided to leave anyway.

When it came, the ring-tone was loud enough to make Kit jump. Tokyo was a city of videophones that doubled as DVDs, diaries and e-mail organisers. The big problem for tourists was that only Japanese-registered phones seemed to work. One needed to rent a phone on arrival and top it up with credit.

It seemed that Kate O'Mally had.

The longer Kit ignored the phone, the louder the ring-tone became, and the less likely it seemed that Kate would wake. In the end, Kit simply reached into her pocket and found the phone, flicking it to voice only.

'Hello ...?' All Kit got was an echo of his own voice and the sense of distance which satellite lag imparts, technology making the world tiny and then guaranteeing it felt very large again.

'Hello,' repeated Kit.

Satellite distance, and a taste of something else.

'Katie?'

'No,' said Kit, 'She's sleeping.'

For a moment it sounded as if the man at the other end had broken the connection and then Kit heard his own name, the authorised version. 'Christopher Newton?'

'Nouveau,' said Kit, without even thinking. 'And it's Kit.' Only then did he realise who was on the other end of the line.

'Oh fuck,' said Patrick Robbe-Duras. 'Katie found you.'

'Yes,' said Kit. 'That she did.'

'She's been looking for months. You know, I told her you'd probably moved. For all we knew you were in Australia or back in England.'

'Mr Duras ...'

'Patrick,' said the man. 'Call me Patrick.' He hesitated. 'Katie's already told you what this is about?'

'Of course,' Kit said. 'You believe Mary's still alive and you want me to find her.'

There was a silence. 'That's what she said?'

'Yes,' said Kit. 'Did I get it wrong?'

'You could say that ...' Patrick Robbe-Duras said. His voice ghostly, made distant by more than the 5000 nautical miles and fifteen bitter years between them. 'My daughter killed herself. She booked a ferry, left her shoes by the railings and stepped into the sea. Katie is the one who believes Mary is alive. She's the one who's spent the last six months of her life trying to find you. And you know why?'

Only, Kit had stopped listening.

Water tumbled from the long lip of the artificial fall onto carefully-placed rocks below, watched only by a duck, Kit and a homeless couple, both of whom had stripped to the waist before washing themselves in its pool. At Kit's side, Kate O'Mally slept off a hangover that would have felled a man half her age, while Kit gripped her phone in trembling fingers, already thumbing its off button.

Six months. Late December.

'Oh fuck,' Kit said, vomiting udon noodles, green tea and alcohol onto the paving at his feet, as Pat's words finally managed what Yoshi's death had been unable to achieve, make Kit face what had really happened.

I'm not sure if this is going to reach you. I hope so. There are some things I really should have told you at the time ... When she'd written that, the inhabitants of Middle Morton had already burnt their famous bonfire. In Tokyo, the *koyou* season was over, each day's news no longer ending with an update on the autumn foliage. And Mary O'Mally, the only person he'd ever really loved, was preparing to kill herself.

Kit tried to remember the date of its postmark, thought about it some more and realised he could. He could also remember the day her card arrived. It was the day he fucked Namiko and the day he went to pray at the Meiji-jingu shrine. Although it began as the day he woke to discover Yoshi had gone for a walk.

CHAPTER 22
flashback to Winter

The dampness in Pirate Mary's storeroom was made worse by a broken window, which let rain dribble down the inside of one wall. Yoshi said she liked the cold, because everyone from Hokkaido liked the cold.

Kit often wondered if that was true.

The sunken bath had been given a little room of its own near the stairs, but everything else on the third floor was stripped back to bare walls and rafters, so that any footsteps across the floor could be heard clearly in the bar below.

A long bench, an expensive black leather and steel punishment rack and something that looked like medieval stocks comprised its only furniture. All three had arrived with Yoshi and never been used, at least not during the years that Kit had known her.

A hook in the ceiling, a coil of rope, carefully boiled to silk-like softness and a twelve-foot length of bamboo, made up the three items that Yoshi still used. The bamboo pole was the most versatile, being utilised in more ways than Kit would have thought possible.

It was five weeks since Yoshi had even looked at a potter's wheel. She'd served behind the bar at Pirate Mary's, talked ceramics to first year students at the Tokyo Design School and cooked impossibly complicated dishes involving three kinds of eel and two types of noodle. She took to walking in the Meiji gardens to watch crimson leaves fall from the winter trees. When that failed, she tracked Kit down to the bar, where he was mending a beer pump and told him she wanted tying.

That was the deal. She always asked, Kit wasn't expected to volunteer. Like most such deals it was unspoken and possibly entirely unconscious.

'You know,' said Yoshi, as she stripped off her yukata. 'All I want is an empty mind ...' She looked for a second as if she was about to ask, *Is that so unreasonable?*

She began to relax the moment the ropes began to constrict her body. Her eyes glazed and turned inwards and the tightness around her eyes smoothed away.

'Thank you,' she said, when the final knot was tied.

'Shhh ...' Kit touched his finger to her lips.

Yoshi smiled.

Her needs had little to do with masochism and even less to do with sex, at least in any way Kit understood those terms. *Edo Rope Bondage* was Yoshi's way of reaching clarity and if Yoshi lacked clarity, well, for Yoshi, work was what made life worth living.

She was still smiling as he went back to mending his pump. A hour and a half later, about ten minutes after Kit unbound her, the sound of Yoshi's wheel could be heard as it spun steadily. A hour after that Kit decided he might as well take himself for a walk.

'Nouveau-san.' The post boy held out one white gloved hand and bowed slightly. The dark blue uniform he wore already looked familiar, though the firm he represented was new. A dozen stories had already run about the fall in standards now that Japan's post office was privately run. To Kit the service seemed immaculate.

Barely noticing the boy's bow, Kit took the card and flipped it over, his thoughts already on which of a dozen tasks he needed to do first. And then Kit saw the writing, read Mary's message before realising he'd even done so, and everything else ceased to matter.

'About the baby,' wrote Mary. *'I lied.'*

Usually it was No Neck who wanted Kit's help getting drunk. This time round, Mary's postcard still clutched in one hand, Kit went in search of the other man. Although, in Kit's defence, he really did think he just needed to talk.

No Neck was doing what he usually did on Tuesday afternoons: handing out highly-inaccurate flyers to any tourist stupid enough to think Roppongi was a place worth visiting in daylight.

'Doing okay?' No Neck asked three Swedish backpackers.

Glancing round, they saw a shaven-headed man with a tattooed ring of barbed wire around one naked bicep. In the hot days of summer No Neck wore a singlet to show off his abs. In winter, he added a waistcoat to the mix. If one got close enough, which was not necessarily a good idea, it was possible to see frayed stitches across the back, where a three-part patch had once announced his nomad status within Australia's Rebel MC.

'Here,' said No Neck, thrusting out one hand.

All new girls, said his latest flyer. *Highly trained & highly professional.* Which was code for, *have danced before/not sex workers*. Both these statements were open to argument, but were included to convince the local police that Bernie's Bar was clean, tourist-friendly and not going to give them trouble.

'Filthy,' said No Neck to the backpackers. 'Absolutely filthy. You guys been to Bangkok?'

All three nodded.

'Infinitely dirtier,' No Neck said. 'Show this at the door for a twenty percent reduction.'

They took a flyer each.

'Not quite fun for all the family,' he told an American couple, 'but not far off. A bit like burlesque, only the Japanese version.'

Taking a flyer, the man gave it to his wife. A hundred paces down the road, the woman handed the flyer back to her husband, who dumped it into a bin.

'Can't win them all,' said Kit.

The deal was that No Neck got 500 yen for each tourist who arrived at Bernie's Bar clutching a flyer. If he got arrested then someone he met on the street sub-contracted the work, the club had never seen him and certainly hadn't employed him. It was a convenient fiction.

'Want a drink?

No Neck glanced from the flyers in his hand towards the entrance to Kaballero Kantina, which happened to be just across the street. Beer money or free beer? If Kit had been feeling less upset it would probably have been funny.

'Come on,' he said. It was enough.

Stuffing the rest of the flyers into his sleeveless jacket No Neck wrapped one heavy arm around Kit's shoulders and waded into the traffic.

'Let me see if I've got this right,' said No Neck. 'You get your best friend's girlfriend pregnant, freak out when she tells you and blame your friend when her psycho Ma comes calling?'

Kit nodded.

'What I don't understand,' No Neck said, taking a pull at his bottle, 'is why your ex-friend had nothing to say about this.'

'Because he was dead.'

That got everyone's attention. Kit had intended this to be a quiet drink, but the crowd around their table was growing, and No Neck wouldn't let the matter lie.

'Crashed his bike,' added Kit, before No Neck had time to ask.

'Fuck,' No Neck said, 'that's harsh. Did he know about you and …?'

That was No Neck for you. The *bozozoku* could always be relied on to go straight to the heart of the matter, and having got there, rip it out and dump it on the table in a bloody puddle so everyone else could get a good look.

'Yeah,' said Kit, admitting the unthinkable. 'I think he did.'

No Neck picked up his empty bottle and peered at it. The signal Kit should buy everyone another round. At present, *everyone* included Kit, No Neck, Micki and Namiko, a girl No Neck used to fuck, before he started going out with Micki.

'Get some nachos,' suggested Namiko.

Having eaten half the nachos and emptied his next bottle, No Neck wiped his mouth on the back of his hand and sat back, considering. 'Okay,' he said. 'She told you she was pregnant, then she told you she wasn't and now she says she was.'

Kit nodded.

'Fucking hell,' said No Neck. 'What happened about the baby?'

'*I took care of things myself*,' Kit quoted, then returned the card to its resting place in his pocket. 'Pretty obvious, isn't it?'

'It was a test,' said Micki.

'Yeah,' Kit said. 'I worked that out myself.'

'And you fucked up,' said No Neck.

Sat next to him, Micki looked as if she was about to burst into tears. So Kit went to the bar and bought a final round without being asked, paid for the nachos and went back to the table to tell the others that he needed to take a walk.

'Want company?' No Neck asked.

'No.' Kit shook his head. 'Stay here. I'll catch you all later.'

'I need a walk,' said Namiko, pushing back her chair. 'And it's good you're upset.'

Kit looked at her.

'If you weren't,' said Namiko. 'That would say bad things about you.' Slipping her arm through his, she steered him towards the door.

'Where are we going?' Kit asked.

'For that walk,' said Namiko.

They went to her room, which was in a small tenement block above an American diner that specialised in post-Rock and late forties GI Kitsch.

That was where he'd seen her originally, Kit realised. She used to wait tables.

The room was tiny, which was the way with such rooms, and most of its space was filled with computer screens, old laptops and a jumble of wires. 'I farm,' Namiko said, catching Kit's glance.

'Make much?'

'Enough,' said Namiko, handing him a scrap of paper in English. It contained a list of powers, weapons and gold required by a fourteen-year-old in California, who wanted to skip straight to the end of new computer game. The deal was done through eBay and the fee had already been paid.

'Not bad,' Kit said.

Namiko smiled. 'You want a drink?'

'Not really,' he said. 'I've had plenty.'

So Namiko put the Kirin back in her fridge and ran a tap long enough to get the water cold. Having washed out her mouth, she gave the glass to Kit, who drank a couple of sour mouthfuls before doing the same. He couldn't remember saying he needed sex. He certainly couldn't remember propositioning her. Though Namiko seemed pretty certain that was why he'd come to her room.

'The sheets are none too clean,' she said.

Kit shrugged. The whole room was filthy. It seemed unlikely her sheets would be anything else.

'You like me?' asked Namiko.

He nodded, because this seemed the right response.

'Good,' said Namiko. 'I've always liked you. You're not like the others.'

Of course I am, Kit thought. *Why else would I be here?*

Namiko stripped easily, with none of the embarrassment he associated with Japanese girls. And her body was riper than he expected, heavy breasts tipped with dark nipples set into stretched circles. Her belly protruded over a tuft of thick pubic hair.

When Kit was done, Namiko shifted him off her and sucked him hard and clean, then rolled him onto his back and straddled him.

'My turn,' she said.

It was only later that she produced a twist of paper and shook out the dirty brown powder inside. 'You ever tried this?' asked Namiko, 'like real heroin, but cheaper. Doesn't dissolve in water,' she added, when Kit looked puzzled. 'You smoke this stuff instead ...'

CHAPTER 23
Thursday 21 June

'Find yourself a seat,' suggested Kate, dumping her flight bag next to a recliner in the BA lounge at Narita. So Kit left his own case on a chair overlooking the darkened runway and nodded towards a bank of computer screens in the corner. 'I'll be back in a moment.'

'Sure,' said Kate, settling herself down.

Kit was able to use the lounge because Kate O'Mally had paid for business class flights for the both of them. Having found herself a copy of yesterday's *Mail*, Kate was preparing to tut over some celebrity outrage and sip from a glass of mineral water on the table next to her. A Nurofen packet rested beside her glass and an unopened cheese sandwich rested next to that.

The morning's tears in Shinjuku Chuo Park were gone and not to be mentioned, Kate had made that clear. She was, it was fair to say, back to being the demanding, hard-eyed bitch that everyone who knew her expected. Which explained why Kit felt the need to kill time at a screen while Kate skimmed her paper on the other side of the room.

The first e-mail Kit opened was from Micki. It showed a kitten drinking milk from a saucer, which was roughly what he'd expect from No Neck's girlfriend. The second was from No Neck himself, and said simply, *Watch this space!*

It was the third e-mail that was unexpected. Micki's brother Tetsuo had registered Kit with the *Asahi Shimbun* news site and given his interests as *motorcycles*, *urban development* and *political dissent*. A link in the e-mail fed to a story *Asahi Shimbun* apparently thought he might like.

Kit read it in mounting disbelief. Late that afternoon a hard core of *bozozoku* had ripped down the fences protecting a building site in

108

Roppongi and occupied the area, surrounding it with totally unnecessary burning braziers and a ring of motorbikes. Anyone who touched one bike touched them all.

No Neck could be seen in the accompanying photograph, but only just. The most obvious character was Tetsuo, stood in the middle wearing a studded jacket and a white headband. He was carrying a bodukan, while the boy directly behind held a flag. After a second, Kit realised it wasn't a boy at all. It was Micki, wearing sunglasses and a biker jacket several sizes too big.

'Fuck,' said Kit, earning himself a stare from a woman on the next terminal. So this was what No Neck meant when he said Tetsuo had an idea. In response to Kit's query as to what, No Neck had replied, 'the 47 Ronin.'

Quite how that translated into this ...? Kit was still wondering, when a frenzy of bowing at the door caught his attention. Both receptionists came out from behind the desk and ushered a young Japanese man into the executive lounge. In his arms he held a cardboard box tied with string. Nothing else, no briefcase, suit-carrier nor overnight bag. None of the badges of status carried by every other passenger in the room. Just a battered box from Circle K.

Sapporo Ichiban (Chicken) Noodles. 24 x 100gm, read the stencilling on its side.

Looking round, Hiroshi Sato saw Kit at the terminal and said something to one of the women. She disappeared behind her desk and when she returned it was to whisper something in the man's ear.

The man nodded.

'Nouveau-san?'

Kit bowed.

'Mr Oniji asked me to give you this.' Mr Sato held out the box, waiting for Kit to take it. He should take the thing, Kit knew that. People were watching ...

'Do you know what it is?'

The young man shook his head, but he was lying. Hiroshi Sato knew all right.

What now? wondered Kit.

The box was packed with straw made from a flat-bladed grass. The choice of material was probably significant, almost everything in Tokyo was. Thrusting his hands into the straw, Kit closed his fingers around something and began to pull.

'Nouveau-san!'

So real was the young man's horror that Kit let go of whatever he held and began to unpack the straw instead.

'What's in there?' demanded Kate, curiosity having finally forced her to abandon her place near the window.

'How would I know?' Kit asked.

Handful after handful of dried grass piled up on a glass table until Kit could finally see what Mr Oniji had sent after him. A small bowl, twisted very slightly along one edge where gravity had touched the rim. Flame blackened its inside, but the underneath was fired to the colour of ash. A smudge had been fixed by heat into its base, Yoshi's fingerprint fossilised like an ancient shell into rock.

'Fuck,' he said.

Looking round, Kit realised the entire lounge had come to a standstill. Middle-aged men, well-dressed women, complete strangers, even Kate O'Mally; all of them reduced to awed silence.

'It's beautiful,' said Kit, speaking entirely to himself.

The young man nodded. 'Her best work,' he said. 'Unlike anything before it. It has ...' He hesitated, searching for the right words. 'A quality we believe only great artists achieve. Mr Oniji is at a loss to know how it survived the fire.'

'In a cake tin,' Kit said flatly.

Hiroshi Sato stared at him.

'I put it in a ceramic cake tin.'

The young man considered this. 'Still,' he said, 'its survival is unusual. When the museum at Kobe was destroyed by an inferno many thousands of priceless ceramics cracked in the flames.'

A woman behind him began nodding.

'The bowl was unfired,' said Kit, deciding this would make a difference. 'And covered with a damp cloth ...' Now Kit came to look, he could see the blackness inside the bowl carried a weave where cotton had smouldered and fallen to ash.

'Who found it?' Kit demanded.

Mr Sato looked embarrassed. 'No one seems to know,' he said, shuffling immaculately shined shoes. 'It was left with a note on the doorstep of a small town house in Akasaka.'

'This house, did it belong to someone known to Mr Oniji?'

Hiroshi Sato's nod was so slight as to be almost invisible.

So beautiful. Cold and beautiful and fragile and able to survive the ruining of his life, the bowl had Kit's attention and held his gaze. Everything he'd loved and respected about Yoshi was represented in that bowl.

As was everything he'd feared and failed to understand.

'You take it,' he told Hiroshi Sato.

The man opened his mouth.

'Return it with my heartfelt thanks. Ask Mr Oniji to keep the bowl safe.'

Very carefully, as if suddenly aware he might drop it, Hiroshi Sato took the bowl from Kit and put it back in the noodle box. Then he began to pack the box with thin-bladed straw, while all the passengers and both of the women from behind the desk continued to watch in silence.

CHAPTER 24
Friday 22 June

The battle began at dawn. In a blaze of outrage, long-focus lenses and electronic flash. A couple of police vans pulled up, blocking the road south from Roppongi's main drag. Having arrived, they proceeded to do nothing. Which was fine with the *bozozoku*, because it let them concentrate on one enemy at a time.

A row of bikes had been positioned to face away from the road, as if the owners planned to ride straight into Pirate Mary's cinderblock parking area. At five minutes before noon, as baseball-bat wielding *chimpira* entered the narrow road that ran along the lower edge of the graveyard, a girl carrying a cat slipped between two bikes and headed away from the coming confrontation. A second later, another girl followed. Although she went unwillingly, still complaining and almost in tears.

'We should ...' Micki said.

But the ranks had already closed. Namiko left first because of the cat and because no one really knew why she was there in the first place. Micki went, under extreme protest, because her brother Tetsuo felt girls shouldn't fight.

Micki had her own opinions on that. Which she was fucked if she was going to keep to herself.

'Go,' said Tetsuo. 'This is going to get ugly.'

She went, low-level Yakusa thugs with clubs parting under the eye of the cameras to let her though.

'Wait up,' Micki said.

Namiko kept going.

'Wait,' demanded Micki, then added. 'Out of my way ...' But she was talking to a photographer who'd decided to get close and much too personal. Small, male and not her favourite person, the man fired his flash right in Micki's face.

112

'Fuck *off*,' said Micki, using up most of her English.

Gaz Maguire, erstwhile provider of *portfolios* to would-be models, grinned, stepped sideways to block Micki's path again and snapped another shot at the exact moment Micki stuck one finger up and scowled at the camera. 'Perfect,' he said. 'Thank you.'

Gaz was about to say something else when Namiko shoved him aside, grabbed Micki by the shoulder and dragged her away from the photographers that had begun to gather around her.

'That's enough,' said Namiko crossly, passing the cat to Micki. 'Come on, we need to get out of here.'

'What's going to happen?'

Namiko snorted. 'They'll fight,' she said, stepping around a vast stone torii near the entrance to the graveyard. Gravel crunched underfoot as they walked towards an old man leaning on a broom.

'*Konichiwa*,' said the old man.

'*Konichiwa*,' Micki and Namiko said together. Everyone bowed. After names had been exchanged, Mr Ito made space for them by moving a pile of prayer sticks he'd leant against a moss-covered tomb. 'Big fight,' he said. 'But over soon.'

'How do you know?' asked Micki.

'*Bozozoku*,' said Mr Ito, appearing to weigh the word in one hand. 'Little monkeys ...' He juggled his hands slightly, before finding the first heavier. 'As long as the police stay quiet this will be quick.'

Mr Ito was right. As a first wave of yelling *chimpira* charged towards the bikes, the *bozozoku* fired up their engines, blipped the throttles and hit switches crudely wired to the handlebars.

Micki grinned. 'Afterburners,' she said. As flame lanced from each of the bikes, a *chimpira* dropped his bat and began clutching his ankle.

'Clever,' Mr Ito said. 'Also inventive.'

What was most interesting was that the police continued to do nothing

True, they'd left their vans. But that was the only movement they made, apart from securing both ends of the street and moving the press back slightly. And yet, in their black-vizored riot helmets, body armour and studded gauntlets they looked easily the most frightening of the three groups gathered at the site of Kit's old bar.

'When it's over,' said Mr Ito. 'That's when they'll move.'

Micki looked at him.

'I lived through the Sixties,' he said, with a smile. 'You watch. They'll arrest the losers.'

113

Ito-san's prophecy probably explained why the police eventually climbed back into their riot vehicles, having done little more than watch, keep casual spectators off the street and stop the photographers from getting themselves hurt. Because when the battle ended, everything was pretty much as it had been.

Paramedics treated five *chimpira* with burns, but since all the burns were below the knee, the journalists were refusing to take the injuries seriously. A couple of *bozozoku* had broken heads and one *chimpira* had been carried away unconscious, his colleagues angrily refusing offers of medical help.

'Interesting,' said Mr Ito.

'What is?' asked Micki.

'Most things,' he said. 'Particularly this.'

CHAPTER 25
Friday 22 June

Five miles above Siberia, with the clouds below the plane set out like a slab of ice, the youngest of the Japanese cabin crew brought Neku a copy of *TunaBelly* to sign.

Approaching diffidently, the girl dropped to a crouch beside Neku's seat, before producing the battered paperback.

'I wondered, perhaps ...?'

Without a word, Neku produced a pen and opened the book at its title page. *TunaBelly* was a million-selling novel about teenage lust, love and murder set in the half-lit world of Tokyo's Tsukiji market. It featured drugs, graphic sex and a working-class boy who loved a twenty-eight-year-old Yakusa hit woman against his better judgement. The neatly made-up girl knelt holding the book looked exactly like Neku's idea of the target reader.

Cherry, read the nametag on her jacket. So Neku inscribed the book to Cherry, added her best wishes and signed the title page with a scrawl.

It was as well the real Mika Aiko was a recluse. This was the third copy of *TunaBelly* to be thrust at Neku since she presented herself at the check-in counter with a regular ticket and a fake passport. If anyone had known what Aiko really looked like then Neku would have been in trouble. As it was, the fake passport was a good one, its biological data was spot on, and fame, even borrowed fame, was becoming addictive. Not least for its ability to clear problems out of the way.

If the woman at the check-in counter had got her way Neku would now be travelling business class, maybe even first.

'No,' Neku had insisted.

'We must, please,' the woman had said. 'It would be terrible for us to make Mika Aiko ...'

Neku's first excuse having faltered against the woman's certainty that

115

anonymity could be guaranteed wherever Miss Aiko sat, Neku admitted that her real reason for wanting to travel economy, was because this was how her next heroine would fly on a similar trip to London.

After that everything was easy. Neku was given a choice of the remaining seats and chose one right at the back – near the toilets – where no one could sit behind her. So far Neku had refused offers of wine, gin and beer and turned away a meal one of the crew tried to serve her an hour after take-off. This seemed to be entirely what the cabin crew expected of a media brat travelling as incognito as five piercings, red hair and a ripped skirt allowed.

'Miss Aiko?'

Having checked her celebrity passenger really was awake, the stewardess who'd wanted her book signed wondered if Miss Aiko would like to see the cockpit. Since refusing seemed rude, Neku agreed – and found herself being escorted though a darkened cabin towards the front.

A handful of people watched their screens in Premium Economy and a solitary man in Business was stubbornly working at his laptop, surrounded by darkness. Most of the beds in First were empty, with the only bed actually occupied carrying two people, though they slept chastely, curled around each other and half covered by a blue blanket.

Neku smiled, though mostly her amusement was reserved for Kit Nouveau and his companion. They were on this plane, as she'd been told to expect, on the far side of Business, their seats ratcheted back and their feet on flip-up stools. The woman slept with a whisky glass clutched in one hand. Nouveau-san had a copy of *Hagakure Kikigaki* open on his lap.

Those two were the reason she'd refused an upgrade. Neku didn't want to be seen yet, and just agreeing to come forward like this had taken more nerve than she expected.

It had been Kit's friend who told Neku where Kit was going and why. She'd found him in a *gaijin* bar, along with two girls, half a dozen *bozozoku*, an English photographer called Gaz, a black cat and a map of Roppongi, which was spread out across a table. It was the third Irish bar she'd tried.

'Ah,' said the huge man. 'It's the Goth kid.'

A couple of *bozozoku* looked up.

'Which kid?' demanded one.

'That one,' he said, nodding towards the door. 'She's friends with Kit.'

A girl snorted.

Making herself approach the table, Neku bowed slightly. 'Can I talk to you?'

The man pointed to a stool at the next table and made dragging motions, indicating that Neku should join them.

'Not here,' said Neku.

The man sighed.

His name was No Neck and his first kiss tasted of beer. There wasn't a second, because Neku had turned her face away by then. 'It wasn't like that,' Neku said, when he asked how long Neku and Kit had been friends.

'Wasn't it?' No Neck looked doubtful. 'You sure? I mean, everyone knows he had a Japanese lover.'

'Yoshi,' said Neku.

No Neck shook his head. 'Yoshi wasn't his mistress. Not sure what she was,' he added, half sobered by Neku's mention of the dead woman. 'It was complicated, that relationship.' No Neck stared at Neku, suddenly seeing her. 'Until I saw you,' he said. 'I wasn't sure Kit did normal ...'

'I'm seventeen,' said Neku, adding another two years to her age.

'Yeah,' said No Neck. 'That's what I mean.'

'Are you all right?' Cherry was looking anxiously at her celebrity passenger, who'd stalled a handful of steps from the cabin door.

'Just thinking,' said Neku, about what was not for sharing. Life was complicated and death made it more so. Kit Nouveau owed her a life, which meant he was bound to her. Although Neku wasn't sure Kit understood that. But in saving him, she'd assumed responsibility for his happiness. She wasn't sure he understood that either.

He also had her memory beads, or what was left of them. At least, Neku hoped he had.

'Through here,' said Cherry, knocking twice on a door.

Neku heard the sound of a lock being flicked on the far side. It made sense to secure the doors, she supposed. Neku might have been anyone.

'Is this Miss Aiko?'

The stewardess nodded.

Somehow, Neku had expected the pilot to be a man. Maybe middle-aged, with swept back hair going grey at the temples. Instead the woman wearing the Captain's uniform looked young and businesslike.

'Konichiwa,' said the Captain.

Neku bowed slightly. 'Konichiwa,' she offered in turn. Since it was dark in the main part of the plane but daylight outside, *konichiwa* was just as good as *konbanwa* or *ohayo gozaimasu*. It being neither morning, afternoon or evening, but something out of time in between.

'God,' said the Captain. 'Will you look at those studs.' Her words were for the co-pilot beside her. 'That's what Annabel wants. You wouldn't believe the fights we've been having.'

'How old is your daughter?' asked Neku.

It was meant as a simple question. Although, from the shock on the Captain's face, Neku assumed her question had been taken as criticism. And then Neku understood the truth was simpler still. The Captain simply hadn't expected Neku to be able to cope with colloquial English.

'I spent …' Neku paused. She had no idea if Mika Aiko had spent time in America or England. And while the captain was unlikely to know, it was possible Cherry might. 'I learn languages fast,' Neku said, then smiled.

Like all the best lies it was impossible to refute. Not least, because it happened to be true.

CHAPTER 26
nawa-no-ukiyo

Chaos began with six words, Lady Neku could remember that much. It was a simple enough statement ... Little to suggest her life was about to change irrevocably. *Your mother is looking for you.*

The voice came from an alcove, where a marble statue glared at the floor of a corridor few even knew existed. The corridor was wider than it was tall, windowless and lit with flickering globes set into a low ceiling.

Lady Neku sneezed, dust had that effect on her.

A simple maintenance duct under a hydroponic farm, before title inflation hit High Strange and the farm became the Stroll Garden and the duct acquired statues, the metal tube ran the entire length of a bigger spur, from one side of the ring right the way through to the other. Doors sealed the duct where it left the spire, clumsy welds holding them in place, though these looked newer than the seamless joins found on most doors leading off the maintenance tunnels.

She'd been five when she first found the corridor, maybe six, when her hair was still faded silver and her eyes strange enough to make her brothers look away. She gained entrance by kicking the back off a cupboard and stepping into a circular room. The room had three other doors, two of them leading to other cupboards and the third to this corridor.

It was, she felt, an impressive find – although it would have been more impressive if she hadn't kicked the backs off a dozen other cupboards first. And it wasn't just cupboards, there was that panelling in her mother's study and a huge portrait of the first Duke of High Strange. Lady Neku had been certain the painting hid a secret door.

Lady Neku had spent much of her sixth year trying to discover if the lights in her corridor were always on or if they lit as she entered. She also wondered why the dust remained, when spiderbots automatically ingested dust everywhere else.

It was months before she realised High Strange put the dust there especially for her. The access tunnel was sealed at both ends. She was the only person, so far as she knew, to know it existed. No way could that much dust settle in the days between her visits.

'Your mother is looking for you,' said a second statue. 'As are your brothers.'

The figure was naked, wore winged sandals and had his hair twisted into a marble topknot. He was the latest addition to the corridor's collection and looked exactly like Nico.

'My brothers?' That did surprise Lady Neku. Most weeks she could be forgiven for believing her brothers had forgotten she even existed.

'Your brothers,' insisted the statue. 'And your mother.'

Lady Neku sighed.

Miss a couple of meals, skip a week's worth of lessons, cut your throat and everyone wanted a bit of your hide. Lady Neku ran through the things she might have done wrong. On balance, she'd have to say she'd been pretty good. Maybe it was her most recent trip to the Schloss? *Only ... I mean*, she thought, *they couldn't possibly know about that.*

Of course not.

Scuffing dust, Lady Neku slid her way to the middle of the corridor and finished with a quick twirl that left her dizzy and slightly breathless in front of a double helix of steps. The spiral came out behind a tapestry in the audience chamber above. Up close one could see that the tapestry of a girl with unicorn was stitched, but from a distance the picture looked like a painting.

It was very old.

Millions of years had been mentioned. Right back to the far side of the Great White, when there was only one inhabited planet and this was it. Of course, millions was relative. Like most things to do with time, it all depended on how fast you were going, who was doing the counting and where they stood.

On that basis, her great-great-great-great grandfather had been nine hundred and ninety-nine thousand, three hundred and twenty when he died, which was ridiculous, because everyone knew he'd died young.

History only made sense if one discounted the jump. Always assuming one could define *jump* in a way that actually made sense. It seemed to Lady Neku that the originators had undertaken the temporal equivalent of fly tipping. Small wonder her world now came with its own exclusion zone.

In a galaxy rich with life no one came calling and the last people to be shifted forward were the families themselves; falling into a world where the future had arrived before them.

It was a cheap trick, that was what her mother said.

'Where are my brothers?' Lady Neku demanded.

A simple answer would have been enough. Instead she got a visual of her mother's study, with its amber-panelled walls, old carpets and stained glass windows. Lady Katchatka sat in a gilded chair beneath a huge mirror, her greying hair brushed back from a ravaged face. There were wooden stools set out for the boys, but they still sat at her feet. Lady Katchatka was stroking Petro's hair as she might stroke a cat, absent-mindedly and only half aware.

'Who was the last to see her?'

That was Nico, the youngest. A good three years older than his sister, he looked younger, his face still round with childhood and his dark hair worn so it flopped elegantly into one eye. 'Well?' he demanded, brushing imaginary dust from a black velvet sleeve.

Petro and Antonio shrugged as one.

'You know what she's like,' said Petro. 'I'm not even sure this is a good idea.'

The fingers stroking his hair stopped their caress.

'I can see its good points,' he said quickly. 'I'm just worried about what will happen if the plan goes wrong.'

'It won't,' said Lady Katchatka. 'All she has to do is shut up and smile. How hard can that be?'

'For Neku ...?' said Antonio, only to drop into silence the moment he realised her question was rhetorical.

'What interests me,' Nico said, 'is what you're going to tell her. I mean, this is Neku. When did she last do anything expected of her? As far as she's concerned, we might as well not exist.'

I wish, thought Lady Neku. 'Do they know I'm watching?' she asked, not bothering to vocalise her question. 'No ... What I mean is ... Oh fuck, you know what I mean.'

'They don't know you're watching,' said High Strange. 'Besides,' it said, 'you're not, I am.'

'There's a difference?'

'Once upon a time,' said High Strange. 'Humans believed the earth was flat.' Before Lady Neku could protest that she already knew this, High Strange dipped the lights around Lady Neku, then relit them. She was meant to listen, Lady Neku realised.

'They believed the earth was flat because it looked flat.'

121

'Well, obviously,' began Lady Neku, then stopped, 'Sorry,' she said, realising she'd interrupted anyway.

'No,' said the voice. 'Go on. What shape is the earth?'

'Round,' said Lady Neku.

'How do you know?'

'Because I can see it from most of the windows.' She stopped, wondering why the voice laughed.

'People see only what they expect to see,' it said. 'To you, the planet is round, because that's how it looks. You need to ask yourself how it looks to people who live under its surface.'

Lady Neku thought about that. 'Flat,' she said finally. She wasn't convinced by this answer, but it seemed to be the answer expected. 'Although they know it's round.'

'How?'

'Because we tell them.'

'You tell them lots of things. Since the bulk of what you say is lies, why should they know which fragments are true? You say they are here for their own good. You say you exist to protect them. How simple do you think these people are?'

'Very,' said Lady Neku.

High Strange sighed. 'You should go,' it said. 'You know how your Lady Mother hates to be kept waiting.'

'Okay,' said Lady Neku, then hesitated. 'What does believing the earth is flat have to do with my mother?

'Think about it,' said the voice. 'And tidy yourself up before you go in.'

Obviously enough, since Lady Neku was officially unaware that her mother wanted to see her, and since her mother's study was not somewhere the girl would usually go she needed to find a reason to visit.

'Fish,' she told her cat.

This was enough to get the animal's attention.

'Real?'

'Of course,' promised Lady Neku, wondering where she'd get fresh fish this time. Her mistake had been to feed the animal Nico's goldfish, no matter how much her cat begged.

'Now?'

'Later,' she said firmly.

All the cat had to do was get comprehensively lost. Since High Strange had 119 levels in the spire alone, twelve spars, ninety knot rooms in the ring to handle karman lines and more maintenance tunnels than anyone had ever bothered to count, that should be relatively easy.

Once the cat had sloped off, adding extra demands and sub-clauses tied to any late delivery of its food, Lady Neku took a shower. The water was warm and undoubtedly tasteless, but she still kept her mouth firmly shut. Lady Neku used water because Nico once told her about a great aunt who was cooked so thoroughly in a malfunctioning cleanser that flesh fell from her bones.

A week later, he stopped her in a corridor and wondered, idly, if she realised the liquid in which she now bathed was distilled from his piss? An hour passed before Lady Neku started to worry about how Nico knew she'd begun taking showers.

Having dried herself, Neku dressed in a simple white frock and combed her hair until it fell around her shoulders. She debated using a silk scarf to hide the scar on her throat and decided against.

The stairs down to her mother's study were empty. Lady Neku stopped, rephrasing that thought. There were no members of her immediate family on the stairs. There were, however, numerous servitors, a guard and a kitchen girl. All looking slightly breathless, as fugees did when placed in high orbit. The girl had been crying.

'It's okay,' said Lady Neku. 'You can tell me if something's wrong.'

The girl kept her mouth shut and her eyes on her feet.

'Or not.' Having opened the study door, Lady Neku barged her way into the room and froze just inside.

'I'm ...' She caught herself. 'Lady Mother.' The curtsey Neku sketched was almost elegant. 'Lord Brothers.'

Lady Katchatka's smile spoke of deep thoughts and dark plans. Her smile and her eyes were two of Lady Katchatka's strongest assets. Her daughter took care not to smile back.

'You're late,' said Nico.

'For what?' Lady Neku did a good job of looking puzzled. Since all four of them regarded her as an idiot, this took remarkably little effort. She just pulled a face and her brothers and mother imposed their own meanings onto the expression.

'My message,' Lady Katchatka said.

'What ...?' Lady Neku bowed her head. She had no wish to get slapped. 'I'm sorry,' she said. 'I must have missed the call.' Neku saw her mother blink and knew she was checking with the major domo.

'I sent it an hour ago.'

'Ah …' Neku took time to consider this. 'I've been looking for my cat.' What correlation there could be between the cat being missing and the call went unspecified, but no one asked her to explain. One of the great advantages of being the family idiot was that she had very little to live up to.

'Did you try asking the *kami*?' said Nico, with a smirk.

'*Nico,*' their mother's voice was sharp.

'Just wondering,' he said.

'Well stop.' Lady Katchatka glared round at the boys, softening her gaze as it reached her daughter, which worried Lady Neku greatly. 'We'll have no such talk … You can go,' she told Nico. 'You can all go.' She meant the boys. 'Your sister and I have a wedding to discuss.'

CHAPTER 27
Saturday 23 June

'Next ...'

The immigration officer at Heathrow flicked through the Japanese girl's passport to check the stamp marks, uncovering New York, Paris and Milan. After this, he matched her face to the smiling photograph and took fingerprints, checking these confirmed a 12-point match with the example held on her passport's digital strip.

The fingerprints tallied. And the passport definitely showed the young girl shuffling her feet in front of him, though her hair looked shorter, having been pinned back before the picture was taken. Neku was pleased with that touch. She already knew the digital strip said all the right things, down to height, weight, original hair colour and iris pattern. So far no one had checked these, but it was good to know the details were correct if they did.

Besides, what else was she going to do with all that stolen cash, if not give a fistful of it to Tetsuo for top of the range fakes? Invest it, buy herself an apartment in Maranouchi, give the stuff back? She could just imagine trying. *Hi, I'm no longer the person who took your money. These days I'm someone else... No, honestly.*

'Why are you here?'

'Holiday,' said Neku.

'And you're staying at ...' The officer examined the form Neku had filled out on the plane. 'Flat 7, 5 Hogarth Mews, Fitzrovia?'

'North of Soho,' said Neku brightly. 'A friend of the family. I'm using his flat.' She'd got the address from No Neck, who'd been given it by Kit.

'Do you plan to find work in England?'

It was one of those trick questions. Neku knew it was a trick question because the man left slight a gap between each word and watched her eyes.

'I intend to write.'

While he was still thinking this one through, Neku unzipped her shoulder bag and dumped a paperback of *TunaBelly* in front of him. When he still looked blank, she took back her passport and opened it, pointing out the match between names.

'It contains a clear and troubling truth,' Neku announced, translating the cover quote.

The man looked blank.

'You know *fan boys*,' said Neku.

He looked blanker still.

'They love manga, video games, fighting beauty ...' He was muddled, Neku could tell by his strange green eyes. 'Fan boys,' she said. 'People think they want to fuck fighting beauty, anime gun-wielding girls. No, *otaku* want to *be* fighting beauty. *Bishojo*, cute teenage girls, they want to be fighting beauty too. So everyone liked this book, even old people ...'

'You wrote this?'

Neku nodded, watching him check her date of birth and work out her age.

'Right,' he said, 'I see.'

Quite what he saw went unsaid, but it probably didn't matter. He stamped her passport with an inky square and handed it back to her. No one stopped her in customs, which was probably just as well because Neku had lined the bottom of her shoulder bag with $10,000 in hundred dollar notes, three bundles at a time wrapped in dust covers stolen from hardback books.

Having debated what to do with the rest of her haul, given that she could only leave her bag in a locker for three days at a time, Neku had come up with a solution that was either extremely clever or unbelievably stupid, only time would tell. She took the bag to Mrs Oniji, along with the bowl dug from the ruins of Pirate Mary's.

 She told the woman how she found the bowl, then suggested by implication that the bag belonged to Kit Nouveau. The bowl was to be a present for Mr Oniji, a man famous for collecting ceramics. Neku would let her know what to do with the bag.

After Mrs Oniji got over her initial surprise, which divided into three parts

1) that Neku knew where she lived

2) that Neku knew about her friendship with the Englishman

3) that Neku thought it might be a good idea to give Mr Oniji the bowl

She invited Neku inside and offered the girl tea.

A metro ran from Heathrow airport to one of the most famous underground stations in London. She knew this because it was in a magazine stuck into the back of the seat in front of her on the plane. The magazine said using the London metro system was very easy, which turned out to be a lie. By the time the third train was ready to leave, Neku had planned her route, bought a ticket, found a seat and settled herself in for the journey.

If the train was dirty the stations through which it passed were worse. As for Piccadilly Circus ... This was one of the world's greatest tourist areas, London's equivalent of Ginza, or so it said in the magazine. Neku wasn't sure what she expected, but English people came somewhere near the top of her list.

A dozen people jostled Neku as she left the station. One man even moved her aside on the escalator, as if shifting some inanimate object out of his way. The steps streamed with all races and colours and no one seemed to notice the mix of languages or the wild and wide variety of clothes. Identifying groups was impossible, because everyone seemed to be a group of their own. And yet how could all these people know who they were without a framework to define them?

'You might want to move.'

'I might ...?'

'Come on,' said the boy in a black suit. 'Let me get you out of here.' He led Neku away from the steps and around a fat metal rail that existed to stop people stepping into the road. It didn't work, because men kept jumping over it.

'Japanese?' asked the boy.

Neku nodded, which seemed easier than trying to explain why he was both right and wrong.

'Thought so,' he said. 'You look Japanese.'

When Neku touched her face, he smiled. 'No,' he said. 'Your clothes.'

'My ...?' Neku glanced at herself in a shop window. Catching glimpses of herself in the occasional gap between other people's reflections. He was right, she did look very foreign. Too *mote*, much too soft and cutesy for this city.

'I'm Neku,' she said, making a decision.

'Charlie ...' He shook her hand, and grinned as Neku gave a bow. 'Let me buy you a latte,' he said, then stopped, seeing her smile. 'What?' Charlie demanded.

'Just wondering,' Neku said, as she linked her arm though his. 'What it is about strange men and coffee.'

'I'll just be late,' said Charlie, putting a tray down on the table. 'God knows, they owe me.'

Neku looked puzzled.

'I work at the Virgin Megastore,' he said. 'Weekends only.'

On the café table next to the tray was a *Time Out*, a *Cosmopolitan* and a *GQ* ... Those had been the magazines Neku recognised. Also on the table was a *Mirror*, *Mail* and *Times*, plus a free paper and a magazine she'd bought from a homeless man with a dog on her way to the café in Oxford Street.

'This city smells,' she told Charlie.

He looked offended.

'All cities smell,' Neku said hastily.

'Of what?' he asked, sliding a chip into the mobile they'd picked up three doors before Caffè Nero, after Neku suddenly stopped dead in front of Vids4U and nearly caused a pile up of pedestrians.

'It varies,' she said, adding, 'I'm serious,' when Charlie glanced up. 'London smells of coffee and cars and women's perfume. Also sweat.'

'And Tokyo?'

'Noodles,' she said, 'and sewage.'

Charlie looked mollified. 'Your battery needs a charge,' he said. 'But you've got enough to last until then. Plug the phone in overnight, okay?'

'And I can just buy more credit?'

'Sure,' said Charlie, 'that's not a problem.' He glanced round the busy café and then looked at his watch. 'I should move,' he said, sounding reluctant. 'Maybe we could get coffee again sometime ...'

When Charlie left it was with Neku's new phone number and a promise they'd meet soon. 'All those magazines,' he said, as he hovered on the edge of going. 'Are you trying to catch up on our culture?'

'On your world,' said Neku, glad that he smiled.

She started with *The Times*, because that looked the most serious and she believed in getting the difficult jobs over first, then she read the *Mail* and the *Mirror* and all the magazines.

Black was back, Cartagena was the new Bogotá, Rome still believed it might win the Olympic bid and bikers had rioted in Tokyo. The M25 corpse was currently unidentified and fifteen men had been arrested in Leeds. The police were refusing to say on what charge ...

At the end of it all, having read every single sentence of every single paragraph, Neku wasn't sure she was all that much wiser, but at least the film posters she'd seen on London bus shelters and the pictures on other people's T-shirts had finally begun to make sense.

The laptop Neku bought from a second-hand shop in Tottenham Court Road came with web access, obviously enough. The small Indian woman behind the counter even threw in six months free connection when she realised Neku intended to pay cash, albeit dollars rather than local currency. After that, Neku went clothes shopping, had her hair cut and dropped her piercings in a bin. Well, the facial ones anyway.

A man in a taxi looked put out when Neku asked to be taken to Hogarth Mews. At first, Neku thought this was because of how she dressed, although there were many girls out shopping dressed far more strangely, and in some cases barely dressed at all. And then Neku decided it was because she was Japanese, but couldn't see why that would worry him, since he looked African.

It was only when he turned down one street, turned up another and stopped outside an arch that Neku realised she'd been less than two minutes walk from where she needed to be.

'Thank you,' she said, giving the man twenty dollars. When it looked as if he was about to complain, she handed him another twenty.

He drove off without saying goodbye.

CHAPTER 28
Saturday 23 June

Hogarth Mews ended at a red door in a white wall, shortly after the little courtyard turned abruptly right. Four other houses made up the mews, three to the left of the entrance, and one almost directly on the right. The last house, the one with the red door, was around the corner and invisible from the street.

This house had six windows. One of them was at ground level and this had iron bars covering a rotting window frame. On the plus side, all the other windows to number 5 Hogarth Mews had flower boxes and the front door had been painted recently enough to still be sticky.

Putting down her shopping Neku examined the buzzers. Not a name or a number between the lot of them. Choosing one at random, she pushed hard and when no one answered, she pushed it again. On her third try someone shouted from inside. At Neku's fifth attempt, footsteps were heard and a woman with paint in her hair yanked open the door. Whatever she expected to see it obviously wasn't a smartly-dressed young Japanese girl in black jeans, white sneakers and black Banana Yoshimoto T-shirt, all from RetroMetro in Covent Garden.

Bowing deeply, Neku smiled. 'I'm sorry,' she said. 'Could you repeat that?'

'The buzzers,' said the woman, then stopped. 'It doesn't matter ...'

'What about them?'

'Fucking broken,' said the woman. 'Doesn't matter which one you choose, they all ring.' She flicked ash from her cigarette, dragged a last gasp from its stub and dropped the filter onto cobbles, crushing it under her bare heel. 'Someone's going to have to mend it, probably me.'

Neku decided not to explain that she had, in fact, been ringing all of them.

'Which flat were you after?'

'The top one,' said Neku, 'I'm looking for Kit Nouveau.'

The English woman was blonde, with long curling hair and jeans far tighter than those Neku wore. She had on a man's shirt, with the tails untucked and enough buttons undone at the neck for Neku to see her breasts, which were very small. Vermilion paint smudged her cheek. Her teeth when she smiled were slightly yellow.

'Are you sure you've got the right flat?'

Pulling No Neck's note from her pocket, Neku checked the address. Flat 7, 5 Hogarth Mews, Fitzrovia, London, WC1 ... As an afterthought, she handed over the note.

'Right,' said the woman, 'I guess this means Mary sold the place.'

'No,' said Neku. 'Mary committed suicide.'

Over a gin in a courtyard that had been glassed over to make a small studio, Neku told Mary's story as No Neck had told it to her, complete with the holes and contradictions he'd appeared not to see. But first Sophie Van Allen, artist and bell mender, introduced herself, having finally remembered that she didn't know Neku's name.

'Really ... *Lady Neku*,' said Sophie, sounding impressed. 'I didn't know the Japanese went in for that stuff.'

The gin, when Sophie fetched it, came in tooth mugs and the crisps were still in their packet rather than a bowl, but she listened attentively as Neku relayed all the things No Neck had told her, about Mary stepping off the side of a ferry and about how Mary hadn't seen Kit for fifteen years but had still left him everything she owned.

'That's love, I guess,' said Neku.

Sophie's face twisted.

'You don't agree?'

'Can't have pleased the cokehead.'

Neku waited politely for Sophie to realise she had absolutely no idea who that might be ... 'Mary's boyfriend,' explained Sophie. 'Too pretty for his own good. You know how it is. Looks get to be a problem in the end, because you end up relying on them just around the time they begin to fade.'

It sounded to Neku as if the woman might be talking about herself.

'I thought,' said Sophie, 'you know, that Mary and Ben had just moved in together. Happens all the time in London. Couples share, but keep their own flats just in case the shit starts flying. Common sense really.'

'Didn't you notice the police?' Neku said, then wondered if that was too rude. 'I mean, when they searched the flat?'

'They might have come by,' Sophie admitted. 'You know, collect a sample of Mary's writing, that kind of stuff. When did you say this happened?' Sophie counted back on her fingers to reach an answer. 'I was in Italy,' she said, nodding to herself. 'Christmas in Florence.'

'Really,' said Neku. 'When did you get back?'

'About five weeks ago.'

Taking a sip of almost-neat gin, Neku grimaced. Nothing would surprise her and the English woman's natural habitat seemed to be squalor. At least it was, to judge from the empty cups and the unwashed plates that stacked a dozen deep, with forks still protruding between each plate. Pizza boxes covered the floor like tiles. How anyone could eat that much take-out while remaining thin was beyond Neku.

A row of five canvasses stood drying against one wall, all showing a variation of the same picture. The subject was topless, had wild blonde hair and nipples so dark they were almost black. So far as Neku could tell, that woman was currently drinking gin opposite her.

'Self portraits,' said Sophie, catching Neku's gaze. 'For an exhibition in Amsterdam. *33/33 @ Thirty Three* ... That's my age,' she added. 'Thirty-three oils showing me aged thirty-three, to be exhibited at Gallery 3+30.'

'Where are the others? asked Neku.

'I haven't painted them yet.'

Putting her cup down among the others, Neku stood. 'I'm sorry,' she said. 'I should let you get on with you work.'

'Guess so,' said Sophie. '*Who* did you say you were meeting?'

'Kit Nouveau.'

'And he owns the flat now?'

Neku nodded.

'Okay,' said Sophie, 'I don't meant to be nosy – but you're a friend of his, right?' It was hard to tell from the way Sophie said *friend* if the word was meant to carry more than its obvious meaning.

'He used to buy me coffee.'

Sophie smiled. 'I'll get you a spare key.'

None of the lights in the flat worked because the electricity was off, as was the gas. Water still ran from the taps in its tiny kitchen and even smaller bathroom. Obviously enough, it ran cold. So Neku took a cold shower and then used the lavatory, which was incredibly primitive but still flushed and refilled on demand.

It was the lavatory that told Neku the police had been, because they'd removed its lid and left the thing propped against a shower cubicle. Also, the bed was on its side, the under-sink cupboard was open and someone had turned out most of Mary's drawers, without bothering to repack any of the clothes.

That was the flat – a bedroom, a kitchen and a shower room. Neku had expected something bigger. A frosted-glass door across the landing had bolts above and below its glass, with an old key sticking from a battered lock. Since the note asking people to keep this door shut was signed Mary, and that meant its secrets had to belong to flat 7, Neku yanked back the bolts, twisted the key and found herself on a small roof garden.

Ex-roof garden, really. Dead lavender spiked from a terracotta pot. An old ceramic sink had been filled with peat and planted with ... 'Mint,' Neku decided, dropping crumbled leaves to the floor.

It was pretty, the garden; walled and elegant and not really overlooked, unless you included an office block three streets away and the Post Office Tower. What was more, it had a tiny wooden shed built against the far wall. She could sleep there, Neku decided. In the meantime she might as well clear up.

CHAPTER 29
Saturday 23 June

'Look,' said Patrick Robbe-Duras. 'Have you any idea how badly you hurt Mary?' Liver spots covered the back of his hands, which were so thin that his fingers looked like twigs wrapped in wet paper. Nevertheless, Pat shook off Kit's attempt to take the tray with an abrupt shake of his head.

'Well?'

There were those who said Pat was the brains behind the move to unite half a dozen areas of London into one rigidly-controlled fiefdom. They were usually people who'd never actually met his ex-partner.

'Yes,' said Kit. 'I have. It was unforgivable.'

He waited while Pat put a tray on the table, and waited some more for Pat to remove two cups and place them on slate coasters. Kit was having trouble reconciling this cardigan-wearing old man with the dapper, tweed-coated figure he remembered from his childhood.

'I'm glad you know that,' said Pat. 'If you'd denied it, I was planning to get very cross.' They were sat at a pine table in a long kitchen, with low ceilings and leaded windows that stared out across sloping lawns, towards the stump of an old cherry tree and a silver twist of river beyond.

For all that he'd been born in Dublin and shared most of his adult life with Kate O'Mally, the man quietly sipping tea had obviously become a Londoner at heart, with a Londoner's dreams of retiring to a little cottage in the country.

'You don't approve?'

'A little too pretty for me.'

'You and Mary both,' said Pat. 'She hated this place. Too chi-chi, too neat, too everything really.'

'Still, you like it. That's what matters.'

'Actually,' said the man, 'It leaves me cold. That was what made Mary so cross.'

'So why buy it?'

Pat sighed. 'You visited Seven Chimneys,' he said. 'Damn it, that was probably where ... No,' he said, 'let's not even go there. You visited the house. So you must know why I bought this.'

'Because it couldn't be more different?'

'Story of my life,' said Pat. 'You should have seen my first wife.'

'Quiet, discreet, understated?'

Pat Robbe-Duras nodded. 'It was a disaster. She took my surname so Katie wouldn't ... My family hated that. Not that Katie could have children, as it turned out.'

Kit looked at him.

'Mary was adopted,' said Pat. 'Surely she told you?'

'No,' Kit said. 'Never. You don't regret not ...'

'I adored Mary,' said Pat. 'And Katie is the love of my life.' He looked at Kit, and shook her head, almost gently. 'We separated only because I insisted,' said Pat. 'I'm dying. I'd have thought that was obvious to anyone. Come on, let me show you the garden.'

The lawns were cut by a boy who came in on Wednesdays. A woman came in from the village to clean the house on Mondays and Fridays. Dr Porteus tried to drop by on Tuesdays and, if possible, on Thursdays as well. Mary used to come down some weekends. The police drove by a couple of times a week to check everything was okay, and the farmer who owned the fields next door kept half a dozen Charolais cattle in Pat's paddock, and was around every other day.

'So you can see,' Pat said, as he stopped by the stump of the cherry, 'you're lucky to find me alone.' He nodded at a battered oak bench, indicating that Kit should sit. 'There are a couple of questions I'd like to ask you.'

'You can ask,' said Kit.

'The first,' said Pat. 'Is why you hung up on me in Tokyo.'

'I was busy being sick,' said Kit, which was close enough to the truth to do. He'd have hung up anyway, probably.

'But you'd already been told that Mary was dead.'

'Yes,' Kit said. 'But not when it happened.'

Pale blue eyes hooked into his. Watery and old, framed by lower lids that drooped and brows so low they must limit what Pat Robbe-Duras could actually see. It wasn't a cold or even angry gaze, more curious, as if the man had moved beyond extremes, despite his earlier threats of anger.

'The date matters?'

'Mary wrote,' said Kit. 'She sent me a postcard.'

'When?' Such a simple word.

Kit took a deep breath. 'The week before she killed herself.'

'Are you going to tell me what it said?'

'No,' said Kit, shaking his head. 'But I promise you one thing. It didn't mention suicide or give a reason for doing what she did.'

'Assuming she did.'

'I thought you were the one who …?'

Pat leant back on his bench and stared at a twist of silver river. A willow draped its branches into the water and a flotilla of baby coots were chirping their way around rushes on the far bank. It looked idyllic, if you liked that sort of thing. When Pat finally spoke his voice was flat, stripped of all emotion.

'Mary's dead,' he said. 'I'm just not sure it was suicide. That's what I wanted to see you about. Let me be honest … I never expected Kate to find you. But telling her to keep looking beat having her disturb the police with mad theories about what was really going on in Mary's life.'

'Which was …?'

'What you'll find out for me,' said Pat, reaching for Kit's wrist.

Kit unpeeled the old man's fingers. 'People can do things without reason,' he said.

Standing up, Pat said, 'You're wrong. Everything has its own logic. If Mary killed herself I want to know why. Which brings us to my final question. Why would someone like Katie, who considers you ruined her daughter's life, ask Kit Newton for help?'

'Because,' said Kit. 'She's desperate.'

'Thank God,' the old man said. 'At least you understand that much.'

They ate cold chicken in a small dining room with oak boards and a granite over-mantel carved in a flat, almost stark style. A huge gilded mirror had been fixed to the wall with its base resting on two wooden blocks that, in turn, rested on the mantel below.

'Too heavy to hang properly,' said Pat. 'But the room needs the light.'

A couple of early Victorian oil landscapes adorned one wall, above a silver jug which was tarnished with lack of cleaning. The table had wooden pegs in place of screws and a Persian rug covering the floor had a hole in one corner. Kit found it impossible to know if he was looking at discreet poverty or a priceless collection of antiques he was too ignorant to recognise.

'You know,' said Pat. 'I'm grateful you came. I wasn't even sure Katie would pass on my message.'

'It was a close-run thing,' admitted Kit. 'She almost forgot.'

Pat snorted. 'Katie has a memory like an elephant,' he said, reaching for his white wine. 'She never forgets and rarely forgives. If you only understand one thing about Katie O'Mally, understand that. She believes Mary is alive, I don't. I do, however, want to know why my daughter died.'

'Suppose I find out,' said Kit. 'Are you really sure you want the answer?'

'Let's face that when we get to it.'

By the time a taxi arrived to take Kit to the railway station he knew everything Pat knew about his daughter's recent life; which was either surprisingly little or Patrick Robbe-Duras was being less than honest.

Kit knew she'd had a handful of lovers, none of them serious. The longest had been the last, a magazine publisher called Benjamin Flyte. Apparently, Katie had hated him. 'Mind you,' admitted Pat. 'Katie hated all of Mary's boyfriends.'

'And you?' asked Kit. 'How did you feel?'

Pat's smile was sour. 'I'm a pragmatist,' he said. 'After you, anything was an improvement.'

Kit tried to remember how Major Yamota had framed his questions. The way the Japanese detective had approached each fact from a dozen different angles, like a swordsman looking for the perfect strike. It was hard to know if such skill was an art or science. Whichever, Kit lacked the experience to interview deftly and he stumbled instead through what might have been wrong with Mary's life.

By the end of the afternoon Kit knew that Mary's gallery was breaking even, which was more than could be said for most galleries in central London. She seemed happy on the occasions Pat saw her, which was less than he would have liked.

Her flat had been a belated 18th birthday present. Mary having returned home shortly after her actual birthday. She'd been in Amsterdam and Dublin, then gone to Madrid, travelling. At least that was how Mary explained her two year absence.

Mary owned the flat in Hogarth Mews outright, without mortgage. She had an allowance from Kate. Most of what Pat owned was already held in trust for her. She worked the hours she worked because she wanted to.

Nothing Kit discovered came close to suggesting a reason for suicide. Which either meant Pat was keeping silent about something or knew less about Mary than he wanted to believe. Maybe that was true of every family.

As the cab from a local firm pulled into Pat's little drive, crunching gravel in front of his ivy-covered front door, Kit turned back to ask the only question that mattered.

'What aren't you telling me?'

Pat's answer was unexpected. It was also grubby and friable from having been read too many times and had muddy fingerprints across the flap. Kit's name was scrawled across the front of an envelope in ink that had faded with age.

'Take it,' said Pat. 'Better late than never.'

Kit, hi . . .

Reading in the back of the cab made Kit feel sick. So he slipped Mary's letter into its tatty envelope and saved it for the twenty-five minutes he had to wait for a train on a windy platform in the middle of nowhere.

The letter had been given to him without apology.

'You found this after she died?'

'No,' said Pat. 'I've always had it. Mary posted it through your letter box.'

'So how did you get it?'

'Your father. He recognised Mary's writing and kept it. For safety, he said.'

The words inside were simple. Grief, anger and guilt had stripped away any pretence of literary style. Her other notes to him, few as they were, had been clever or witty, carefully worded and designed to impress. All of that was missing. Mary wanted to know what he'd said to Josh the morning before Josh died. She wanted explanations.

'When did he give it to you?'

'After he heard Mary was missing. We'd reported it to the police.'

Yeah, Kit knew all about that. Somehow he'd ended up at the top of their suspect list. It said so in the newspapers.

'Katie was convinced you'd killed her.' It seemed Kit had been saved by a single line on a card posted in Dublin. Even Kate O'Malley had accepted Mary was unlikely to be writing from beyond the grave.

'Did my father say why he kept it?'

'He thought you were a bad influence on Mary.'

'And you,' asked Kit, feeling emptiness in his stomach. 'What did you think?'

Pat smiled sadly. 'Me,' he said. 'I always thought it was the other way round.'

CHAPTER 30
Saturday 23 June

Three hours and two changes of train took Kit to London. And by the time he reached the head of a taxi queue at Waterloo station, he'd added another twenty minutes to this. The sky above the Houses of Parliament was already turning pink as a black cab carried him over the flat greyness of Waterloo bridge. The flood lights on the Savoy Hotel were lit and the river level was low.

It was colder than Tokyo, less humid, but it was still hotter than Kit remembered. What little energy he had after the flight and his meeting with Mary's father had been leached away by reading her letter. He was nine hours behind where his body believed it was and fifteen years removed from the boy to whom that letter had been addressed.

Reading it still hurt.

At first the city was as he remembered; grand buildings gone slightly to seed, a jumble of Victorian hotels and theatres cheek by jowl with office blocks, too much traffic and too little road planning. It was only when he looked back at the National Theatre with its neon lifts rising to the roof gardens that Kit began to accept London had changed. The police checkpoint near Holborn confirmed his view.

Kit took a taxi because he was too tired to find the flat on his own. In his pocket he had a Japanese videophone, as useless in London as its English equivalent was in Tokyo. Also in his pocket was a passport, a leather wallet containing £500 in small notes and the keys Kate O'Mally gave him to Mary's old flat.

Whatever Mary had said in her note about the flat being his, Hogarth Mews was only on loan until Mary wanted the place back, Kate was very clear about that. It had seemed best to nod.

'Okay,' said the taxi driver. 'I'd better drop you here. No room to turn,' he added, while Kit fumbled with the door. This was true. Even if the driver moved the bins waiting at the entrance for next day's rubbish collection, turning inside the mews was still impossible. A silver Porsche took up too much of the available space under the arch. Vivaldi played from a half-open window on the left and someone had watered their flower boxes, so that water dripped like rain onto the car. *Money*, said the Porsche. *Arsehole*, said its parking.

'She's upstairs.'

Turning, Kit found himself facing a blonde woman with tied-back hair, a Gauloise hung from her mouth and a white shirt splattered with paint. Just in case Kit had missed the fact she was artistic, she was holding a fat brush and a multi-hued palate.

Maybe he was being unfair.

'I gave her Mary's spare key.' The woman hovered on the edge of saying something else. 'I'm Sophie,' she added, though this was obviously a prelude to what she really wanted to say.

Shaking hands, Kit found his own fingers sticky with paint. 'Who's upstairs ...?' He began to ask, but Sophie had already moved on.

'I'm sorry,' she said. 'You know ... About Mary. Must have been a real shock. I was away and ...' Sophie stopped. 'I'm just sorry, all right? Really sorry.' She sounded almost cross to find herself explaining things.

'Who's upstairs?' Kit asked.

'The kid. Apparently the electricity to Mary's flat is off, so I've lent her my lighter and a couple of Diptyque candles.'

Which kid?

The obvious question answered itself in a crash of feet on winding stairs and a head suddenly appearing round the corner. Neku had been waiting and listening. She looked defiant rather than nervous.

'Fuck,' said Kit. 'What are you doing here?' Then he took another look at the Japanese girl and blinked. 'And what the hell happened to your hair?'

Sophie snorted. 'I'll leave you to it,' she said.

After Neku's third attempt to explain why she was in London, Kit decided it could wait. He decided this because every attempt to explain reduced Neku to tears that seemed to be of anger. She felt the answer should be obvious. 'Who else knows you're here?' he demanded, settling his back against the railings of the flat's little roof garden.

'No Neck,' said Neku.

Kit was shocked.

'And Mrs Oniji ... I gave her Yoshi's bowl,' Neku added, seeing Kit's look. 'Someone has to look after it. You were in hospital and I was

141

frightened it might, you know ...' She looked sick at the mere thought. 'That would be a disaster.'

'What would?' Kit wanted to know.

'If the bowl broke.'

He took a deep breath. 'Why should it break?'

'It has a crack,' said Neku, 'down one side. Hairline, almost impossible to spot without X-rays.'

Kit stared at her.

'It begins below the rim,' said Neku. 'And runs from there to the base. I've been wondering if the crack is intentional. An artist's acknowledgement of the flaws inherent in all perfection.' Looking at Kit, she said. 'You don't have the faintest idea why this matters, do you?'

'No,' said Kit, going to fetch another jug of water.

Refilling her glass, Neku returned to her cushion. They were watching the sun settle behind slate roofs, as seagulls circled the London sky above and the western edge of the city finally turned from dark pink to purple. Searchlights already swept the sky, clustered above the obvious places – Parliament, Buckingham Palace, Downing Street and the financial centres of the City.

'Are you going to tell me?' Kit asked.

Neku considered the star-specked sky and shivered in the first stirrings of a night wind. This planet was weird, its cities chaotic and its social structures fragmented to the point of being incomprehensible. Every breath she took was probably poisoning her.

'No,' she said finally. 'I don't think I am. You wouldn't understand anyway.' She shrugged, shuffled on her cushion and got up, only to sit down again a few seconds later.

'What's wrong?'

'This body,' she said. 'I just can't get used to it.'

'You will,' said Kit. 'That's just an age thing.'

'Yeah,' said Neku. It was the first time he'd seen her grin.

CHAPTER 31
nawa-no-ukiyo

'Marriage?' So shocked was Lady Neku that she forgot to keep the horror out of her voice, but for once her mother seemed not to notice. The girl could remember that much.

'Happens to us all,' said Lady Katchatka.

'Whom will I marry?'

'Luc d'Alambert. You'll like him.'

Lady Neku froze.

'I've got some pictures,' said her mother, touching the wall. 'Here ...'
I'll like him?

A boy of Lady Neku's age stared out at her. Ash blond hair, pale eyes and skin so thin it was almost marble. Someone must have said something funny out of sight because Luc d'Alambert suddenly grinned. Although a glitch froze his top lip and shut one eye.

'What's wrong with the picture?'

'There's nothing wrong with it,' said Lady Katchatka, waving away the connection. 'Luc has a tiny problem with one side of his face. Nerve damage. We'll have it fixed when he arrives.'

'Why doesn't he have it fixed himself?'

Lady Neku's mother shrugged. 'The d'Alamberts can be odd,' she said. 'His father has firm views on augmentation. As I said, we can have it fixed when Luc arrives.'

Inbreds, throwbacks ... Odd wasn't a word her mother usually applied to the d'Alamberts. Although Neku had heard her use plenty of others. And little about this proposed marriage made sense.

'I thought we hated the d'Alamberts?'

'Neku ...' The reprimand was swallowed. Instead, the elderly woman stood up and walked to a mirror, flicking her fingers so the glass revealed the dusty landscape laid out below. An ocean filled the window's upper corner. It looked sullen and lifeless, matted with purple weed. The waters had been teeming with life once, or so the *kami* insisted. Unfortunately, nowadays the shade cast by High Strange covered less than a quarter of the Katchatka segment, and it was out there, in the naked sunlight, that Schloss Omga could just be seen clinging to the side of a mountain.

'It used to be beautiful,' said Lady Katchatka.

'The desert?'

'Grasslands back then. Grasslands and forest and savannah. The desert came later.'

'Can you remember when the world was different?'

Lady Katchatka glanced at her daughter to see if Neku was serious. 'How old do you think I am?' she asked.

'How old would you need to be?'

Her mother smiled sourly. 'Older than this.'

Lady Neku nodded. 'Mother ...' She was taking a risk using the word without an honorific to formalise it, but from the slight nod she got in reply, it had been a risk worth taking. 'Where will I live?'

'With your husband.'

'Luc d'Alambert?'

It was Lady Katchatka's turn to nod.

'And the wedding?'

'Will be here,' said Lady Katchatka with a smile. 'We will invite the d'Alamberts and the major retainers. I have already ordered our major domo to open up the unused circles of High Strange. It will be magnificent.'

Lady Neku considered this. The idea still troubled her. 'I don't understand,' she said. 'I really thought the d'Alamberts were our ...'

'You don't have to understand.'

She watched her mother rein in her anger and take a very deep breath, the kind most people followed by counting to ten.

'Something must change,' her mother said. 'If it doesn't then the families are going to tear each other apart. No one knows how much longer we can support life, at least at its present level. Five thousand years, ten thousand, maybe more. But first we need peace.' Lady Katchatka shrugged. 'I'm sorry it comes at a price.'

That was when Lady Neku realised the price was her.

Personally Lady Neku doubted if the moon really had been split into six and divided between families like an orange. All reliable records suggested the moon had a mass of 7.35 x 10 22 kg, roughly an eightieth of the original mass of the earth. The total mass of High Strange and the other five knots in *nawa-no-ukiyo*, plus all the karman lines and the sails came to less than half this. So if the habitats had really been grown from segments of moon, then where had the rest of it gone?

Lady Neku raised this with Nico, but he wasn't interested. As for her other two brothers they barely understood the question.

'Moon,' said Lady Neku, leaning against the wall of the duelling room. 'You know, used to go round us like a baby planet back when the days were shorter?'

'Who's us?' Petro asked.

'The earth,' said Lady Neku, nodding towards a window.

'We're not earth,' said Petro. 'We're family.'

'Anyway,' said Antonio. 'Who said days were shorter?' He glanced at Petro, who grinned. 'Oh, I get it,' Antonio said. 'The *kami* told you.'

Both brothers burst into laughter.

Lady Neku left them to their laughter and the fight. Since High Strange could protect itself and fugees were forbidden weapons, training with blades was utterly pointless. Apparently, the sheer pointlessness *was* the point. At least it was according to Nico, who could beat both his brothers without even breaking sweat. *Not caring,* was what he told Lady Neku, when his sister first asked how he managed it. She'd been working hard to copy him ever since.

The d'Alamberts arrived in eleven ships. They arrived on the morning of the third day after her mother told Lady Neku about her marriage and the whole of High Strange gathered to meet them.

'Empty,' said Petro, looking at the ships. 'No one has this many servitors.'

'No,' Nico said. 'I've checked. The major domo says the vessels are full.'

Petro laughed.

'Multiple life signs,' insisted Nico. 'On all of the ships.'

'Animals then. To make them look occupied.'

'Maybe not,' said Antonio. 'It could be ground dwellers.'

'Same thing.'

'But they'd die,' said Lady Neku. Everyone knew ground dwellers grew sick if moved out of their sphere. 'The d'Alamberts wouldn't do that.'

'Who the fuck knows what they'd do?' said Petro, then shut his mouth at a very pointed stare from his mother.

'Look straight ahead,' Lady Katchatka told her daughter. 'And for heaven's sake start smiling.' Lady Neku did as she was ordered.

The first ship was the biggest. It was red and yellow, although the yellow had faded. The ship behind looked newer, being bright red with no contrasting colour, and the ships beyond that were shades of violet, pink and blue. Despite herself, Lady Neku was impressed. She'd never seen a ship that wasn't black.

'Family colours,' said Nico, wrapping his arm about his sister.

She edged away.

'Provincials,' said Petro. 'What can one expect?'

Lady Katchatka shook her head. 'You're wrong,' she said. 'They just like to appear that way. Always remember, looking weak can sometimes be a strength.'

An army poured from the first ship. A hundred men streamed down the ramp. They wore gold and red, carried hand weapons and gazed intently at the family and servitors gathered to meet them. It was only when Lady Neku looked closely that she realised the group included old men and those who were little more than children.

'And this is meant to impress us?' asked Nico.

The hundred men gathered into two lines and turned to face the door of the second ship. 'Lord d'Alambert,' muttered Nico before the door had even begun to open.

'No,' said his mother. 'Luc ...'

'How did you know?' asked Lady Neku, when a thin figure hesitated in the doorway, only to flinch at a command from someone out of sight. Raising his chin, Luc d'Alambert put one foot on the ramp and forced himself to take another step. His subsequent steps came more easily.

'If we let the boy live then the old man will follow.'

Lady Neku looked at her mother in case she was joking. From the look on Lady Katchatka's face, her daughter guessed not. 'Is that how you'd do it?'

'Probably,' said her mother. 'But then I have three sons. Lord d'Alambert has only one.'

The boy in the red jacket walked slowly towards the foot of the ramp, only too aware that all eyes in the hangar were on him. He hesitated slightly at the bottom, before stepping onto the deck.

'What does he think?' said Antonio. 'That we've electrified that exact patch of ground?'

Nico looked interested. 'Is that possible?'

Antonio ruffled his brother's hair. 'Anything's possible,' he said, 'given sufficient will.'

146

Glancing up, Luc d'Alambert caught the entire Katchatka family watching him and looked away. He was shaking, Lady Neku realised. For a second she considered walking out to meet him. Her mother might be furious. On the other hand, her mother might be impressed. The problem with Lady Katchatka was that it was never possible to work out which it would be in advance, and besides there were her brothers' opinions to consider.

Lady Neku decided to stay where she was.

'God,' said Petro, watching the boy walk slowly towards them. 'I'm surprised they didn't drown the little shit at birth.'

Luc d'Alambert was short of stature. Scrawny, with a narrow face and deep set eyes. And his skin … It was pale enough to be almost transparent. A paper cut-out of a real person.

'Lady Katchatka, my lords, Lady Neku …'

Neku liked that she and her mother got name checks while her brothers were lumped in together, although she could tell from the stiffening of Nico's shoulders that he'd already taken offence.

'My Lord Luc …' Somehow, while Lady Neku had been watching Nico, Petro and Antonio and wondering which was going to sneer first, her mother had moved forward to meet the boy.

Shit, thought Lady Neku.

'Go on,' hissed Nico.

She shook her head. Waiting until she was summoned now seemed the safest option. *What did he see?* Lady Neku wondered. What did the boy see when he looked at her mother. A small woman in a black dress who walked with a stick or a monster rumoured to have strangled her husband the moment she tired of him? Harsh times produced harsh people and few came harsher than Isabeau Katchatka, who joined the family as the fourteen-year-old bride to a man thirty years her senior and still ruled endless decades later.

There was another rumour. One that said Nico, Petro and Antonio shared no DNA with the father who died before they were born. If this was true, then the heirs to High Strange had no link to the original family other than name. It also threw an interesting light on an even darker rumour. That Lady Katchatka shared her bed with all three of her sons.

If they came from her body alone, then Lady Katchatka was, if rumour be believed, effectively sleeping with herself. Personally Lady Neku doubted it. According to Nico, the only times he'd shared a bed with his mother, the woman had done nothing but fall asleep and snore.

CHAPTER 32
Sunday 24 June

A house phone started ringing halfway through breakfast. Until then neither Kit nor Neku had realised the flat in Hogarth Mews possessed one. It was Neku who found the thing in an alcove behind a Warhol print near the front door.

A joke, Kit decided, given the endless repetition of silk-screened ears on the print itself.

The phone was ivory white, had a curling cord and was so old it teetered on the edge of being fashionably retro. Although what Kit noticed was a row of keys hanging from hooks on the wall above. It looked like the police hadn't needed to break the locks on Mary's cupboard after all.

'Kit Nouveau,' he said, picking up the receiver.

The laugh at the other end was mocking. 'How much longer are you going to keep calling yourself that?' demanded Kate, sounding herself now she was back on home ground.

'Until I can be bothered to change it back.'

'Which will be when?'

'Probably never,' said Kit. 'Maybe sooner. What do you want?' He hadn't intended to be so blunt, but with Kate it was probably the best way to be.

'You saw Pat?'

'Yes, of course. I told you I would.'

'And how was he?'

'Dying,' said Kit.

When Kate spoke again, even Neku, who hovered at Kit's shoulder, could tell the woman was fighting to hold her temper. 'He gave you Mary's original letter?'

'Yes,' admitted Kit. 'He did.'

'I knew he would,' she said. 'Pat always wanted to send that letter on. Unfortunately, by the time he argued me into it you'd vanished. Anyway, I was more worried about tracking down my daughter.'

'Who came back,' said Kit.

'Eventually. So what have you found out so far?'

'*Kate!*'

'Just asking.'

Kit considered what he knew. Wondering what the underlying tidiness of the flat said about Mary's state of mind in the hours before she'd locked the door for the last time, leaving a bag of rubbish forgotten inside. The chaos was superficial, upturned drawers and emptied cases. The carpets had been clean and the floor tiles in the shower room wiped down. Even the wastepaper bin in the bedroom had been emptied.

'She cancelled her milk, gas and electricity,' said Kit. 'But not her telephone. The washing up was done, her washing basket was empty, ditto the fridge, and her cooker's been cleaned.'

Mary had also put unwanted vegetables into a Sainsbury's bag to throw away, then left them by the door. A single flaw to suggest she had bigger things on her mind. Neku had dumped the bag before Kit arrived, only to watch in bemusement as he hauled it back and upended it into the shower cubicle, sorting through a slush of long-rotted lemons, peppers and carrots.

'I thought it would be messier,' said Kit, 'what with a police search and everything.'

'They didn't do one,' Kate said. 'Apparently, once Pat confirmed Mary's writing there was no need.' Her voice made clear exactly what Kate thought about that. 'The police were too busy to come out.'

'Doing what?'

'Whatever they do these days instead of solving crimes. Rounding up people in Bradford probably.'

It took all Kit's will not to snort. Kate O'Mally, ex-crime boss and icon of old London – well, in certain circles – complaining about police inefficiency and their lack of commitment. He wanted to give the woman more ... Some hope, for whichever one of them really believed Mary was still alive, only nothing in the flat suggested she was. All the neatness, the card to Tokyo, cancelling the milk, it looked to Kit like a woman tying up the loose ends of her life.

'Tell me again,' said Kit. 'Why do you ...' He paused, rewording his question. 'What makes Pat think she's alive?'

'Her Visa card,' Kate said. 'Someone used it in Gwent the day after she ...' Kate's voice trailed into silence.

'Took the ferry,' said Kit, finishing the sentence for her. 'What did the police say?'

'Did Mary know her pin numbers by heart? Or might she have written them down. Because her wallet and purse were both missing when her handbag was found.'

'And what was the answer?'

Kit heard a deep sigh. 'Mary couldn't do numbers to save her life.'

'Which means ...'

'I'm aware of what it means,' said Kate, breaking the connection.

Kit had woken that morning to the clatter of dishes and the smell of burning toast. An acrid catch at the back of his throat that had him out of bed before he remembered where he was. Stumbling from Mary's bedroom, still glitching with jet lag, he found himself suddenly face to face with Neku, who seemed to be wearing nothing but a long black jersey. She was scraping carbon into a empty supermarket bag, which she'd suspended from a door handle.

'Built a fire,' she said.

'You've—'

'On the roof. It's okay,' she added. 'I've put it out again.'

'And the bread?'

'Bought it when I couldn't find noodles. There's a shop round the corner that sells knickers, bread, batteries and milk. Also these.' She nodded to an MP3 player and then was when Kit realised he could hear music.

'You didn't.'

Neku saw him gaze at her bare legs. 'As if,' she said, putting the scraped toast onto a plate and putting the plate on the tiny breakfast bar in front of him. 'I'll buy butter tomorrow,' she promised. Huge eyes watched him from across the table. Eyes that were dark and speckled in colours he couldn't remember having seen before.

'What?' Neku asked.

Kit shook his head. 'Come on,' he said. 'You still have to tell me why you followed me.' The shrug she gave was neither sullen nor pointed, simply matter of fact.

'What choice did I have?' she said.

Maybe he was missing something. Actually, thought Kit, it was a fair bet he was missing a lot more than one thing. Where Neku was concerned, he got the feeling everyone missed more than they caught. Her change of image for one thing. She'd gone from the ripped lace of a *cos-play* to black jersey and minimal make-up in a single week.

'You're going to have to tell me sometime,' he said.

'So are you,' said Neku.

'Tell you what?'

'What all this is really about.' And then, luckily for both of them, Kate O'Mally telephoned. About three minutes later Neku's new videophone started buzzing, she took one look at the number, began blushing and retired to the roof garden outside.

Charlie Olifard read maths at Imperial, wrote his own code until he was thirteen, when he got bored and was now trying to work out if the Fibonacci sequence contained an infinite number of primes. In his spare time he mixed music, releasing his work into common ownership so it could be mixed further. He was quite keen on joining GCHQ, but felt most spooks were probably boring by nature. So he was worried what joining GCHQ might say about him.

Neku, by contrast, studied English at a language school behind Oxford Street. At least she did in the version of her life she gave Charlie. But then, according to her new friend life was a mathematical construct, with solutions that made sense only if one first understood the question. So what did lying matter?

'Your English is really good,' Charlie said. 'You must have been studying for years.'

'About six months,' said Neku, blushing when the boy turned to her.

'God,' Charlie said. 'And people claim I'm intelligent ... Now, what was it you wanted to do?' He ran one hand through shaggy blond hair. It was a nervous tic, the hair thing. Neku hoped he'd get over it.

In response to Charlie's original proposal that he show her the London Eye, Neku had suggested meeting outside the Fitzroy Tavern in Charlotte Street. Look rich, artistic and messy, she'd told him.

Neku had to admit he did it rather well.

A battered suede jacket, black jeans, tight T-shirt and a watch that looked old and incredibly expensive. It was the gold Rolex that made Neku wonder if he was all of those things anyway.

'You'll find out,' she said.

Canterville Gallery in Conde Street looked like any other boutique. Positioned between a lingerie shop selling hand-made silk bras and a place offering Moroccan ceramics, it had a green canvas canopy shading its front, bay trees on either side of a glass door and a huge burglar alarm halfway up the wall, which flashed at lazy intervals as Charlie and Neku approached.

Open, announced the sign.

A plastic mannequin in the window helped add to the idea that Canterville Gallery was a simple shop like any other. Although the fact that the mannequin was naked apart from a triangle of pubic hair made from copper nails rather undermined the effect.

'Well,' said Charlie, as Neku reached for the door. 'I take it we're here.'

'Good afternoon.'

A woman in a black dress looked up at Neku's greeting. Having stared for slightly longer than was polite, she remembered to smile. 'Can I help?'

'I hope so,' said Neku. 'I'm a friend of the new owner.' As intended, her words knocked the smile from the other woman's lips.

Charlie shut the door behind him and nodded at the mannequin. 'Is that a Tessa Markham?' he asked.

The woman nodded.

'Thought so,' said Charlie. Of course it was, the mannequin's base had a label at ground level. He'd simply read the thing before entering the shop.

'I'm Charlie Olifard,' he said. 'And this is ...'

'Lady Neku,' said Neku, wondering why Charlie blinked.

'I'm Sylvia,' said the woman. 'I run this place. Can I ask what your particular interest is?'

Neku nodded. 'Of course,' she said. 'I'm thinking of buying it.'

'The Tessa Markham?'

'No,' said Neku. 'The gallery.'

Take a look at the gallery. Be discreet. Kit had said, when finally pestered into giving Neku something to do that didn't involve her making plans to fly home. Something that was impossible, because to do that she needed a home in the first place. *And take a look at Major Yamota's police forms for me.* Neku chose the gallery first because it sounded more fun. Besides, Neku had company. Translating the police forms into English would be a waste of Charlie time.

As for the boast about buying the place, maybe she would; but that wasn't what this was about. Her brothers always said take control from the start. How better to make this woman nervous?

Half a dozen oils hung from one wall. A glass dildo sat in a glass

152

cabinet next to a Benin fetish mask. The dildo featured a spiral of cobalt blue along the shaft, like vapour trails within glass. The African mask had gold studs hammered flat around the edges and looked as old as the glass looked new.

'Murano,' said Sylvia.

'Of course,' said Neku, wondering if Sylvia meant the mask or the paperweight. Stepping back, Neku looked around more openly. It was hard to imagine how anyone could make money from the objects on display. At least, that was what Neku thought until she asked Sylvia the price of the mask. Buying it would take a substantial slice of the money Neku had left with Mrs Oniji. One wouldn't have to sell too many objects like it to pay the bills.

'Can you tell me what happened to Mary?'

'She killed herself.' Sylvia hesitated on the edge of saying something else. 'I don't know why.' Whatever she'd been planning to say, Neku guessed it wasn't that.

'Boyfriend trouble?'

Sylvia shook her head.

'Money?'

The other woman sighed. 'Look,' she said. 'Do you two want a coffee? We close at three on Sunday anyway and there's a place on Goodge Street ...'

CHAPTER 33
Sunday 24 June

Neku let Charlie take her hand on the way back from the café. He did this almost casually, his fingers having brushed hers a few seconds earlier, by accident she'd thought at the time.

'Okay?' he asked.

'Sure,' said Neku, 'I'm fine.' There were obviously a dozen things Charlie wanted to ask her about their visit to the Canterville Gallery, but he kept his peace and said nothing. Neku was impressed. Discretion was a valuable commodity in any man.

'So,' Charlie said. 'Are we going home now?'

Home. Her fingers pulled free as Neku tripped on his word and Charlie stepped out of her reach.

'What's wrong?' he demanded.

'Nothing,' said Neku. She could almost feel his sideways glance, which slid away when she turned to him. So she took Charlie's hand again, smiled and bent her head, listening as he began to talk about some incredibly good band due to play in a basement in Camden. As Charlie's words trailed to a halt Neku realised he'd been inviting her out.

'Sounds good,' she said.

He smiled the rest of the way back to Mary's flat. 'Wow,' said Charlie, as they turned under the arch and he saw the flower boxes, black front doors and tiny white-painted houses that made up Hogarth Mews. 'Cool place.'

'Not bad,' Neku admitted. Pulling the key from her back pocket, Neku opened the front door to find Sophie doing something complicated to a racing bicycle in the hall.

'This is Charlie,' said Neku.

'Hi,' said Sophie, offering her hand; which meant the first thing Neku had to do on reaching the flat was find kitchen paper so Charlie could clean bike chain oil from his fingers.

'She's an artist,' said Neku.

Charlie nodded sourly, as if he'd suspected as much.

There was cola and milk in the fridge, fresh bread in a wooden box next to the sink and a bowl full of pears and bananas on the tiny work surface. Rice and spaghetti had been stacked by the box. Kit had even found instant noodles that came with sachets of miso soup. The only flaw was the fridge being warm, because the electricity still needed to be turned back on, and gas resolutely refusing to hiss from any of the cooker rings.

'You've been cut off?'

'No,' said Neku. 'We're waiting for it to be turned back on.'

Neku should have been able to read his expression. She'd have been able to read him if he was one of her brothers. All the same, it was only when Charlie mouthed *we* that his scowl made sense.

'I share with a friend,' she said. 'It's his flat.'

'Right,' said Charlie. 'I see.'

No, you don't. Instead of saying this Neku took a Coke from the fridge and a couple of wine glasses from the cupboard and led Charlie out onto the roof, where her mattress aired in the sun, her pillow rested against the side of the little wooden hut and her sheet swung gently from a washing line in the breeze. Having dumped her shoulder bag in the hut, Neku returned with a notebook, her ink block and a brush.

So young, she thought, watching Charlie's eyes flick from mattress to hut to pillow. 'You thought Kit and I ...'

'No, I didn't.'

'You did,' Neku said.

Charlie wasn't good at sulking. In fact he lasted less time than it took a wine-glass full of diet cola to lose its bubbles, which was barely any time at all. 'Okay,' he said. 'Maybe I did.'

Neku smiled.

'Can I ask you something?'

She nodded, wondering which of the dozen questions it would be.

'Are you really planning to buy that gallery?'

'No,' Neku said, dripping flat Coke onto a saucer and grinding her ink block into the liquid until it was thick enough to use. She drew a circle, because she always began everything with a circle, then began to note down everything she could remember from her conversation with Sylvia No-Last-Name. 'I was lying ...'

Charlie looked sweetly shocked.

'Unsettle people,' said Neku. 'It's one of the first rules of control. Unsettle them and they'll answer your questions or do what you want because they're too busy being unsettled to close down or object. My brothers taught me that.'

'You have brothers?' Charlie asked. 'How old are they?'

Which was the point Neku burst into tears. And that was how Kit found them. Neku on her knees, an abandoned brush on the tiles in front of her and a boy, all curly blond hair and bat-wing cheekbones frozen with embarrassment as he tried and failed to comfort her.

'Meet Charlie,' said Neku through bitter sobs.

Charlie tried to shake hands.

'What did you do?'

Charlie let his hand drop. 'I asked Neku about her brothers.'

'Brothers?' Kit said.

CHAPTER 34
Monday 25 June

Kit was the one to see Charlie out, offering his hand at the last minute – if only to tell the boy that he didn't hold what happened against him.

'See you some time,' said Kit.

Charlie nodded doubtfully.

When Kit got upstairs the shower was running and there Neku stayed, washing away whatever it was she needed to wash away with an hour's worth of cold water. She came out of the room shivering and wrapped in a towel, trailing wet footprints onto the roof garden, where she spent the rest of the afternoon, plugged into her MP3 player, with a pile of Japanese police files, a notebook and cup of coffee Kit had got from a local café cooling on the tiles in front of her.

The first two times Kit went to see her, she looked up politely and waited, going back to her papers when she realised he was just fussing.

'You knew this woman ... Mrs Kate?' she asked, when he came out a third time, still fussing, with a bowl of instant noodles and a fork, because he'd been unable to find wooden chopsticks. She took the noodles without comment, placing them next to the coffee.

'Kate's mentioned in there?'

Neku nodded. 'Who gave you these files?'

'Major Yamota,' said Kit. 'They're to do with the fire at Pirate Mary's. I wasn't allowed the ones to do with Yoshi.'

'I wondered about that,' Neku said, crossing something off her list. 'Most of these are statements from the fire officer, the first policeman on the scene, the paramedic who gave you a sedative. There's a forensic report from the Police Scientific Bureau, but there are other papers not to do with the fire.'

'They must have got in by mistake,' said Kit.

Neku's mouth twisted. 'Japanese police,' she said, 'don't make that kind of mistake. Not unless they intend to.'

'What are the papers?'

She hesitated. 'A report on a murder. A list of collectors known to buy stolen ceramics. A credit check on Pirate Mary's. One of the reports links you to a career criminal known to be making trips to Tokyo. Kathryn Robbe-Duras, née O'Mally.'

'She never took Pat's name,' said Kit. 'And she's retired.'

'This is the woman No Neck mentioned? The one who called you this morning?'

'Yes,' said Kit.

'She's an old friend?'

Kit shook his head. 'An enemy,' he said. 'An old enemy.'

Neku nodded. It seemed she could understand that.

The buzzer sounded at midnight. Since the row of buttons beside the front door was illuminated and Sophie had already warned Kit that drunks used the courtyard to piss or worse, he ignored it. At which point the noise got louder as whoever it was began to kick the door instead.

Scrambling for his jeans, Kit reached the landing in time to hear Sophie open the door herself. 'Prove it,' he heard her say, and a second later the front door shut and Sophie began stamping her way upstairs. She was swearing.

'It's the police,' she said. 'Well, one of them. A big fucker. Apparently he wants to talk to you.'

'Where is he?'

'Outside. I told him to get a warrant if he wants to come in. Unless, of course, he thinks we're terrorists, in which case I suggested he organise backup and a few guns ...'

'And what did he say?' Kit could imagine what a Japanese policeman would have said. Actually, Kit couldn't, because he doubted anyone in Japan would leave a police officer on the doorstep, far less be that rude to them.

'Some bollocks about Section 44. So I told him I used to be a lawyer.'

'Were you?'

Sophie shrugged. 'A paralegal ... It's close enough. Do you want a witness, because I can stay around if you need?'

'It'll be fine,' promised Kit.

There were a dozen reasons why this was unlikely to be true. Desertion from the British Army had no statute of limitations. So the original arrest warrant was technically valid. And you didn't go AWOL, only to return to the place that issued the arrest warrant unless you were stupid, or had people like Major Yamota suggesting you go back to your own country for a while.

And that was before Kit even factored in Kate O'Mally, his own guilt at Yoshi's death or his memories of Mary.

'You certain?' Sophie asked.

'Sure,' said Kit, nodding his thanks.

'Whatever,' she said. 'Call me if you need me.'

'Mr Noover?'

'Nouveau,' said Kit, looking out into the half darkness. An officer in uniform was backlit by lights from beyond the arch. Flicking on the hall lights, Kit saw the huge man blink.

'Come in,' said Kit.

'You don't want to see my search warrant, sir?'

'Have you got one?'

A sour smile.

'Whatever,' said Kit. 'Come in anyway.'

Without waiting to see if the officer would follow, Kit made his way towards the stairs and heard the front door click behind him. As the two of them passed the door to Sophie's flat, her door opened slightly and then shut again.

'She didn't like me.'

'It's late,' said Kit. 'You worried her.'

'Really, sir? Well, people who don't like the police worry me.'

By the time they reached the top landing the officer was stopping for the occasional rest and gasping for breath, Kit found that oddly reassuring. 'In here,' he said, undoing the door. 'Let me get some candles ... I'm waiting for the electrics to come back on.'

Only a candle was already burning and Neku stood in the kitchen doorway.

'I heard noises,' she said.

A flame lit her fingers, until Kit looked again and the match went out, leaving Neku outlined in flame and a thin sodium haze that filtered between the slats of a wooden blind. It didn't help that Neku was dressed in her black jersey and very little else.

'Go back to bed,' said Kit.

The girl gave him a look, but disappeared as ordered.

'How old is she?' asked the officer.

Kit shrugged. 'I don't know,' he said. 'I've never asked.'

Silence followed this answer. And when Kit finished finding a saucer for the candle, it was to find the huge man staring at him.

'What?' said Kit.

'You send her to your bed and you don't know how old she is? People like you need to be more careful ...' All pretence of politeness was gone, along with the *sirs* the officer had been dropping into his sentences like redundant punctuation.

'She's not going to my bed,' said Kit.

He watched the officer leave the kitchen and count off the exits leading from the tiny hall; front door, half-open bedroom door and one other, from behind which came the flush of a lavatory. As the officer watched, that door opened and Neku stalked out, stared straight through both of them and left the flat. A second later, an unseen door crashed shut, rather louder than was necessary.

'Roof garden,' said Kit. 'She's got a mattress.'

The huge officer ran his fingers through thinning hair and wiped his hands on his trousers. The sheer smallness of Mary's flat seemed to be giving him problems. 'Mattress?' he said, before deciding not to take it further.

Digging into his pocket, the man produced a leather wallet and flipped it open. A badge inside introduced him as Sergeant Samson. That was all Kit had time to see before the sergeant flipped it shut and stuffed the wallet back into his jacket.

'I've got some questions,' he said. 'I'd be grateful if you'd answer them honestly ...'

'If I can,' Kit said.

'You were a friend of Mary O'Mally?' The sergeant obviously had no doubts that Kate's daughter was dead.

Kit nodded, embarrassed to feel almost sick with relief. It seemed the questions were about Mary, rather than him.

'When did you last see her?'

'About three days after the funeral of a friend.'

'And how long ago was this?'

PART TWO

CHAPTER 35
flashback

The love affair of Kit's life began to unravel two weeks after Kit and Mary first made love and three weeks before Josh crashed his bike. It began unravelling in Mary's bedroom at Seven Chimneys with an argument about cars.

'Gently,' she said. Mary wasn't happy to be squatting naked on top of Kit and kept glancing at her stomach. The first two fucks of that day had been great, but this was one too many and it was Kit's fault for being greedy.

'Here,' he said, folding a sheet around her shoulders. 'Better?'

Mary nodded.

It was complicated, because Mary was going out with Josh. Well, technically. Only Josh was in Paris for a fortnight with his parents. So he and Mary would need to talk when Josh got back.

'You love me?'

They'd been through this. The first time a fortnight earlier, beside the potato field, as sun edged its way between two hills and stained the spire of St Peter's with the first rays of dawn. Kit had been impressed Mary waited until after he took off her clothes. 'Of course I do,' said Kit, which had been his answer then.

'Say it,' Mary demanded.

So Kit did.

'Mean it,' she said.

'I'll love you forever,' said Kit, and inside that second it was true.

When he was done, Mary wiped between her legs and folded the soiled tissue inside a clean one, then stuffed three foil wrappers into the crumpled cardboard of a condom packet and folded a tissue around this. She left Kit to collect up the used rubbers and add these to her fist-sized ball of rubbish.

'Take it with you,' said Mary.

Kit looked at her.

'We have a cesspit,' she explained. 'Dad makes enough fuss about the pipes getting clogged with loo paper. He'd freak if he discovered we'd blocked them with these.'

'Okay,' said Kit. It felt odd to be in Mary's bedroom, but not as odd as actually being at her house. Patrick Robbe-Duras and Kate O'Mally kept themselves to themselves. Jumped up, said half the village; the other half wondered which of the two had most to hide.

A high wall ringed the garden and electric gates guarded the entrance with its white pillars and two stone eagles. A turning circle in front of the huge yellow-bricked house was scuffed with tire marks from half a dozen cars and Kit's own motorbike. *Legoland,* Josh's father called it, but obviously not to Mary's face.

A black BMW 5 Series, a red XK Jaguar, a metallic blue Mini Cooper S convertible and a new Land Rover among the vehicles parked outside. They were all still there, visible from Mary's bedroom window.

'How many cars have you got?'

'One,' said Mary, pulling a sheet over her breasts. 'The Mini. The others belong to Mum or Dad. Why?'

'Just wondered.'

'Mum started out dirt poor,' Mary said. 'You need to remember that.'

He'd made her cross, Kit realised. Mary's relationship with her mother was as complicated as his own with his father was simple. Kit hated the man, Kit's father hated him, both of them knew exactly where they stood. 'It doesn't matter,' said Kit. 'I was only wondering.'

'Yeah, right ...'

At the gate Kit had to lean over to punch numbers into a keypad that hid itself beneath a stucco-coloured plastic cover. He entered Mary's birthday from memory, and had just kicked his Kawasaki into gear when Kate O'Mally pulled up on the far side of the gate in a dark Mercedes. Armani sunglasses examined Kit, flicked to his bike and returned to his face.

The thick-set woman was busy lowering her window when Kit blipped his throttle, let slip the clutch and roared out onto Morton Road, only just missing her wing mirror as he went past.

Josh died in an accident on the B342. The evening was warm, the light was still good and the road was dry. His Suzuki went out of control on a bend in the road and crashed into a two-hundred-year-old oak tree near the edge of Woodham Common. He died instantly, at least that was what the police told his parents.

A piece in the *Advertiser* talked about the danger young men on bikes posed to themselves. A kinder piece, under a smiling photograph, highlighted Josh's achievement, the grades he got at A level and the fact he'd been offered at place at Trinity, his father's old college at Oxford.

A picture showed a Josh who was younger by three or four years, in the days before he grew his hair, discovered amphetamines and took to wearing shades. Josh was dressed in a blue blazer, with a white shirt open at the neck. Maybe that was how his family remembered him.

The funeral was delayed by an autopsy, to the outrage of Josh's father. All the autopsy proved was that Josh had not been drinking. At first it seemed the funeral would be private, then someone must have talked to Colonel Treece, because it was agreed the service would be immediate family, but Josh's friends could attend the burial and come back to the house afterwards. Mary O'Mally was the only exception. She got to go to the whole thing.

Mary looked terrible, that was the first thing everyone noticed. As she followed Josh's coffin and its bearers up the lane towards the new graveyard, she looked like someone else. She'd lost weight and dark circles had sunk her eyes into her skull. She was crying, not discreetly, but openly and with sobs that shook her entire body.

Josh's mother, a tiny Korean woman in a dark coat and gloves despite the heat, had one arm around Mary, trying to console her. Kate O'Mally trailed a couple of paces behind her sobbing daughter, looking out of place in a blue skirt and jacket. When she caught Kit watching her daughter, Kate's eyes filled with something very dark indeed.

Mrs Treece, however, simply nodded to Kit, and handed Mary to her mother, as if entrusting the woman with something infinitely fragile, while the pall bearers fiddled with canvas straps and the priest shuffled through an open prayer book, finding his place.

'You're Christopher Newton,' she said.

Kit nodded.

'I remember. You were in Josh's band with Mary ...' Which was one way of putting it. 'So you know Mary well?'

Another nod.

'She's going to need her friends,' said Mrs Treece. 'It's strange,' she added. 'All the things that matter until something like this happens. Josh wanted to stay here with Mary, you know. His father insisted he go with us to Paris. Now all David can remember is the argument.'

David had to be the Colonel.

'Such a waste,' Mrs Treece said, before returning to the graveside. As Kit watched, the Colonel tried to wrap an arm around his wife's shoulder. She shook him off without even noticing what she'd done.

It had taken Josh a week after his return from Paris to track Kit down and thirty seconds and a handful of words to make him go away, there being nothing like the truth for fucking best friends over.

Mary turned up the day after the funeral. Hammering on the door of the cottage in Wintersprint until Kit's father let her in. When Kit got down to the kitchen he found Mary stood with her back to the sink, clutching a barely-touched cup of Brooke Bond and kicking her heel against the cupboard.

Kit's father walked out as Kit came in.

'We need to talk ...'

'Sure,' said Kit, nodding towards the stairs.

'No,' said Mary. 'Not here.'

'Where then?' he asked.

'The church,' she said. 'But I want to put flowers on Josh's grave first.' There was no vase for the wild flowers Mary had picked along the way, so she just put them at the top of the mound, below the mock-marble headstone. Then she turned and looked round the silent graveyard, nodding slowly to herself.

'What?' asked Kit.

'Just remembering.'

He followed her down to the church in silence.

'It looks so empty,' she said, her voice echoing from bare walls and a hammer-beam ceiling. Someone had tidied away yesterday's kneelers and removed the wreaths and fresh flowers, although the table at the back where the book of condolences rested was still there.

Mary's offering had been simple.

A single word.

Sorry.

'You want some time to yourself?'

Mary shook her head, almost crossly. 'I told you,' she said. 'We need to talk. Somewhere private.'

The door to the tower was open and a spiral of stone steps led to the belfry, with a simple wooden ladder leading to a flat roof above. Kit went first, both up the spiral of steps and the ladder. Either the medieval tower was higher than he'd imagined or the hills were lower, because Middle Morton looked smaller than expected.

Slumping down, he put his back to a stone parapet and watched Mary try to work out where to sit. *Okay*, he thought. *If she sits next to me, that means ... If she stays standing ...* She sat exactly opposite, and Kit tried to tell himself that meant nothing at all.

'You want to talk about Josh?'

'No,' said Mary. 'I want to talk about us.' She shifted restlessly and for a moment Kit thought she was about to stand up again, but all she did was twist her head and run one hand across her face. 'We may have a problem.'

'Josh's death?'

Mary sighed. 'Just listen,' she said. 'I'm late ...'

Late for what? Kit almost asked. And then he realised.

'Shit ...'

'Yeah,' she said. 'Shit and fuck and anything else you want to say. But it's still true.'

'But we used condoms,' said Kit, sounding like someone else. 'You can't be pregnant.'

'Not that first time,' said Mary. 'When my parents were away. You remember?' She said this as if daring him to contradict her.

'But I ...' He could recall the stickiness on his fingers and her stomach, where he'd withdrawn before it was too late. 'I pulled out, remember?'

'Listen,' said Mary, 'I'm late. End of story.'

'How late?'

'Late enough.'

'Oh fuck,' said Kit. 'Are you sure it's me?'

Mary stared at him. She raised her head, opened her eyes against the sunlight reflecting from the lead roof on which they both sat and glared at Kit, harder than he'd have thought it possible for anyone to glare.

'I'm just asking,' he said.

'Yeah,' she said. 'It's you.'

'You and Josh ...?'

'Me and Josh nothing,' said Mary, crossly. 'Forget Josh. We need to talk about what we're going to do.'

'Who have you told?'

'Christ,' said Mary. 'I've told no one. Who do you think I've told?'

Kit took a deep breath. 'I've got four hundred and fifty pounds in my savings.' He thought about it. 'That should be enough.'

'For what?'

'You know,' said Kit.

'No,' Mary said. 'I don't know. Tell me. Enough for what?'

167

'To sort things out.'

Mary repeated his words back to herself. She knew exactly what he meant, Kit was sure of that. All the same, she kept repeating his words, until they sounded like an echo of an echo, soiling the air around them.

'I've got to go,' Mary said, climbing to her feet.

'No, wait …' Kit caught her arm, harder than he intended. All the same, the speed with which she turned to wrench herself free shocked both of them.

'Stay here,' she said, from the top of the ladder. 'Give me five minutes. I mean, we wouldn't want to start rumours.'

Her text message arrived next morning. She thanked him for coming to put flowers on Josh's grave, apologised if she'd been bad company and told him not to worry about the other thing. It had been a false alarm. He should have known from her politeness that she lied.

'Look,' said Kit. He wanted to say he was sorry, wanted to say half a dozen things but the words stuck in his throat, so he shuffled his heels on the path and bowed his head to the dead flowers at his feet.

A yew tree had been planted near the gate, a sop to tradition for those still angry that the original site next to St Peter's was no longer used for burials. In fifty years the tree would look as if it belonged. For now it looked what it was, a stripling planted ten years earlier to counter complaints from everyone in the village who thought such things mattered.

None of the graves on the hillside dated much before the mid-1980s. Even then, Josh's parents had to fight to get a plot near the gate and have a plaque commemorating his brief life added to the wall of the Treece family chapel inside the church.

It was late, the wind warm and smelling of summer. Kit had the graveyard to himself, an arbitrary patch of hillside consecrated above St Peter's. Wreaths from three days earlier hid recently-turned earth and a temporary headstone, rag-rolled with grey paint on cheap wood, had been over-painted with Joshua's full name and brief dates. A tiny bunch of wild flowers rotted just below the headstone.

Having tried and failed to apologise, Kit headed home. He took the footpath that skirted the edge of Wicker Copse and came out on Blackboy Lane, turning back to see the whole of the village laid out below him. A breeze blew warm and gentle along Morton valley, barely troubling the leaves, the river curved gently in a twisted ribbon of greenish blue. It was an evening destined for memory, almost too still and too perfect in itself.

Kit knew why he'd stopped. He wanted to cry for Josh, for Mary, for himself and the whole shitty mess they'd made of their friendship; but his eyes remained dry and the simple apology he wanted to make choked his throat. So Kit took off his jacket, and set out for Wintersprint and the cluster of knocked-through cottages he occasionally still called home.

'Kit Newton?'

Nouveau, he almost said.

And then Kit took a look at the man asking and those stood behind him. They'd been waiting at a blind corner screened by brambles on one side and a roofless barn on the other. A spread of elder could be seen through the barn door. Someone had hacked it back to the roots but it stubbornly insisted on resprouting.

The man at the front had gelled hair, a grin and a photograph, which he compared one final time to the boy standing in the middle of the road in front of him.

'Yeah,' said someone behind. 'That's the little fuck.'

There were five of them, perhaps three or four years older than Kit. Hired muscle mostly, track-suit bottoms, branded T-shirts and gold chains. They'd have hated Kit anyway, even if they weren't being paid for the pleasure.

Pulling a spring-loaded cosh from his pocket, gelled hair flicked it to its full length and tapped the end against his own palm. 'One arm and one leg,' he said. 'And I'm to tell you, that's getting off lightly. Feel free to argue, because we can make this as hard or easy as you like.'

'Who sent you?' asked Kit.

The man grinned, and grinned even more when Kit bent to retrieve a broken stick from the roadside. 'Oh well,' he said. 'It's your choice.'

The others stood back, raised their eyebrows at each other or stared around as if the rolling fields behind the barn were some alien landscape. One of them even pulled a phone from his pocket, fingers stabbing at its keys as he kept half his attention on Kit and the rest on some text he was answering.

No one was taking this seriously, Kit realised. Hurting him was just a tick on a list, like filling a car with fuel or remembering to buy beer on the way home. A job they'd been given ....

Somehow that made things worse. 'Who?' Kit demanded.

'Why would I tell you?' Gelled hair tapped the weighted cosh against his hand, anxious to get things moving. 'We're just doing a favour.'

'A favour?'

'How do you think these things work?

'I don't know,' Kit said.

'Well, guess what?' said the man. 'You're about to find out.'

The first swing of the cosh smashed Kit's stick, splintering the wood an inch or two above his fingers. Reversing direction, the man began to sweep the cosh towards Kit's elbow, harnessing all the energy in its coiled handle.

Two histories hung on the flick of that wrist. In the first, Kit's *ulna* smashed under the weight of the blow, a single sliver of bone skewering muscle in what was almost a clean break. This was the most likely outcome, until Kit stepped into the blow and used his arm to block the handle, twisting his body sideways as the weighted end of the cosh snapped round.

Flesh tore, staining the cotton of Kit's shirt, but it was surface damage only, little more than split skin and blood. If the blow had landed, his elbow would be broken, the fight over and his leg next in line. Instead Kit had control of the fight, moving so far into the moment that his sergeant would be proud of him, if the man hadn't already been dead.

Flicking upwards, Kit's own hand was moving before he'd even had time to decide he wanted to fight, the splintered stub of stick he held rising towards the attacker's jaw, ready to be punched through to his brain. But in the last second gelled hair threw back his head, and Kit's stick scored its way across his cheek and splintered against bone overhanging the man's left eye.

Instinct made gelled hair clasp a hand to his face. So it was instinct that drove a splinter of wood the final few millimetres into the man's eye, blinding him. By then the cosh was already in Kit's hands and he'd cracked the knee of the man closest, stepping over him to reach the person behind. Kit smashed his phone, fingers and wrist first, in a single blow, before moving on to a leg.

One arm and one leg, Kit took the price from each of them, swiftly and brutally, sparing only their leader, who was on his knees in the road, his hands covering his face.

'Who sent you?' Kit demanded.

When gelled hair refused to answer, Kit knelt in front of him and gripped the man's little finger, prising his hand away from his face. There was little blood and no sticky liquor running down his cheeks like egg yolk. Just a sliver of wood about the length of a needle protruding from the corner of one eye.

'Tell me,' said Kit, reaching for the splinter.

On his way back to the cottages Kit passed their car. A black Jeep with smoked windows and chrome bars on the front. The glass in the windows was good quality, though it cracked eventually under blows from the cosh, having crazed into tiny diamonds first.

A top-of-the-range, hands-free phone system came with the Jeep, at least it looked ready-built into the dash, so Kit called an ambulance. Leaving the Jeep, he used a bridle path to reach the old main road to London. There was nothing he wanted from his father's cottage at Wintersprint, and he didn't recognise the Kit Nouveau who'd broken all those bones or smashed up the Jeep, though Kit guessed his father had always been there inside him, waiting.

Sometimes, decided Kit, the only safe choice was to walk away from yourself. So he did.

CHAPTER 36

Monday 25 June

'So what did he want?' asked Neku.

'Who?' said Kit, looking up from his bowl. Somehow Neku had found fresh soba noodles in Soho, and breakfast had been waiting when he finally staggered out of the shower.

'That policeman.'

'Not sure,' said Kit.

'But it was about Mary O'Mally's suicide?' Neku's Japanese accent made the first and last parts of Mary's name sound identical.

'I thought it was,' admitted Kit. 'At least to start with. Now I'm not certain.' Aggression and interest had faded from the moment Sergeant Samson realised Kit hadn't seen Mary in years. It blipped again at Kit's mention of a letter and disappeared altogether when Kit admitted this had been six months before and the contents entirely personal.

'She didn't mention boyfriends?' said Sergeant Samson.

A shake of the head was all it took to make the uniformed officer reach for his cap, push back his chrome stool and remember, at the last minute, to thank Kit for the barely touched can of Coke.

'A friend of the family?' asked Sergeant Samson, on his way out. He was nodding towards the roof garden door, which stood slightly open.

'Something like that.'

'How long's she been in the country?'

'Less than a week,' said Kit. 'She'll be going home soon.'

'Just as well. Still, she's pretty. I'll give you that.' The big man paused on the stairs. 'I mean, for a Chink, obviously ...'

Now watching Neku ladle the last of the warm noodles into his bowl, Kit wondered how much of that particular conversation she'd overheard and which part of it was making her alternate between frowns and an anxious smile.

'Mary left a suicide note,' said Neku. 'So why don't her parents believe it?'

'How do you know about the note?'

'You told me,' she said. 'The night I arrived.' Picking up her bowl, Neku carried it over to the sink and ran it under the cold tap, washing away a solitary strand of udon and the last of the miso. When she looked at Kit again something in her eyes was troubled. 'We're not getting very far, are we?'

We? 'I'm not getting anywhere,' he said.

'Why not?'

'Because,' said Kit. 'I'm not sure there's anywhere to get.'

He told Kate O'Mally the same thing when she called half an hour later. It was probably the wrong thing to say, but Kit wanted to be honest. He was also trying to work out if either of Mary's parents really believed she was alive and had started to wonder if they both knew she was dead, just didn't know how to admit it to each other.

'Sergeant Samson,' said Kit, into the static that followed his original admission. 'He came by last night.'

'Never heard of him.'

'Wanted to talk about Mary's recent boyfriends.'

'Why would you know about that?'

'Good question,' said Kit, 'I thought you might have an answer.'

A click was his reply.

Personally Lady Neku doubted if the moon really had been split into six and divided between families like an orange . . .

'I'm going out,' said Kit, opening the door to Neku's wooden hut. The sun was hidden and the clouds thick enough to be cut in slabs. A chill wind ruffled the few plants to survive Mary's absence, but neither the wind, nor the sky, nor the darkness in the little hut seemed to worry Neku. She was inking a diagram and annotations into a notebook, her lips moving in time to the brush.

'My diary,' she said, blowing carefully onto the paper. 'Where are you going?'

'Canterville Gallery.'

'Already been,' said Neku. 'I went with Charlie.'

'You what?' demanded Kit.

'Yesterday afternoon. You asked me. Charlie and I had coffee with the manager, remember?'

Kit shook his head.

173

Neku sighed. 'Are you sure?'

By the time Kit left, they'd established three things. Kit seriously needed to get more sleep, Neku would remain at the flat while he visited the gallery, and if she wanted to help while he was away, she could keep translating the police files or start making a list of Mary's possessions. Actually, they established four things, because they also established that Charlie could come round.

'How do you know he's free?'

'It's the twenty-fifth,' said Neku. 'His term ended on Friday ... He texted me,' she added, when Kit looked blank.

'Where's Charlie now?' asked Kit.

Neku rolled her eyes. 'Outside,' she said, as if that was obvious.

'I've got a question,' said Neku, putting a can of Coke in front of Charlie and placing a bowl of seaweed crackers beside the can. When he put his hands together, in quick thanks for the food, Neku smiled.

'A question?'

'Well, more of a logic puzzle really.'

'Oh, right.' Neku could practically see Charlie relax. 'What is it?'

They sat on Mary's bed, surrounded by clothes pulled from one of the built-in cupboards. At least a third of these were male. A blue suit with a thick chalk stripe, a blazer with five gold buttons on each sleeve, something that might be a rugger shirt if not made from raw silk. Now Neku came to think of it, she'd thought the suit Kit had been wearing looked a little flashy for his taste.

'Suppose the police found a gun,' said Neku.

'This has to do with that woman's suicide?'

'No,' said Neku. 'This has to do with something else. Suppose they found a gun and it had been loaded with ...' She looked at him. 'You might want to write this down,' she said, offering him a notepad. 'Five blanks, two live rounds and one blank ...'

Charlie looked up from his pen. 'Which order,' he asked. 'Five blanks first, or one blank first?'

'Five,' said Neku. 'Definitely five.'

'Okay,' he said. 'What's your question?'

'Why?' said Neku.

After watching Neku for a couple of minutes, while she sorted through the clothes and carefully rehung them by colour, beginning at one end of the visible spectrum and ending at the other, Charlie took his can of Coke, bowl of crackers and logic question out to the roof garden, leaving

Neku to draw up her list of Mary's possessions in peace. By then, of course, Neku had moved onto Mary's bedside locker.

Top drawer.

Seven pairs of knickers, size ten, all M&S, three nylon slips, five bras (34 D, but Europeans were large), an old diary, written in something that wasn't English, Japanese or any other script Neku recognised, a key-ring vibrator and a pink plastic egg.

'Easy reach,' thought Neku, looking from the open drawer to the bed.

Middle drawer.

A dozen black T-shirts from Topshop. Armani jeans, black, size ten and well worn. A black jersey, frayed at the cuffs. And, beneath this a torn copy of Sandra Horley's *The Charm Syndrome*. Someone had taped it back together.

Bottom drawer.

A collection of art magazines. A catalogue from Christies New York, dated 2007. Three copies of *Time Out*, all the same issue and containing a glowing review for a Tessa Markham exhibition at the Canterville Gallery. Removing the bottom drawer only revealed smooth wood beneath, so Neku tipped the whole unit forward to see if the base was hollow. It was, but it was also empty.

Although a Victorian metal fireplace had been removed and the damage plastered over, the gap between the built-in wardrobe's middle door and underlying chimney breast was only deep enough to take shallow shelves.

On the shelves were three black, two pink and one green T-shirt that looked as if it had never been used, more knickers, a bundle of socks and rolled jeans. Nothing else, and certainly nothing interesting. The jeans were size eight. So either Mary used these and kept the Armani jeans in her bedside locker because she couldn't bear to throw them away, or it was the other way round.

A collection of black jackets hung from wooden hangers in the next wardrobe along. All of the jackets were short and most were nipped at the waist. Some had pockets with flaps, others didn't. One of them had a tiny pocket in the lining, low down on the left hand side. It was here Neku found the key.

It was the thirty-eighth pocket she'd searched since Charlie took his logic problem outside and the fifth key she'd found. Although the others had been found in drawers or hanging from nails on the wall. Neku tried to open the obvious items first. A battered flight case under the bed, which was already unlocked … A metal box file, contents missing. Both pointless, since the key was self-evidently meant for a different kind of lock.

So Neku took the key downstairs and knocked at Sophie's door. She wasn't quite sure how she felt about Sophie and suspected the woman felt the same about her, but Neku needed to talk to someone who understood English things.

'What things?' Sophie asked.

Neku held up the key.

Taking it, Sophie stepped back and waved Neku into her studio, which was in chaos. 'Sorry about the mess,' she said.

'I've seen worse,' said Neku, then wondered if she should have been more impressed.

'Right,' said Sophie, 'grab a stool while I make coffee.' And with that the woman disappeared inside, leaving her guest alone in the glassed-over yard that, quite obviously, made up Sophie's life. Would it be rude to say she'd already had enough coffee to last one lifetime? Come to that. would it be rude to open a louvre window? Neku wondered. Or would this ruin the portraits now drying in a row along one wall …

'How do you stand the smell?'

Sophie looked surprised.

'I'm sorry,' said Neku. 'I didn't meant to be rude, it's just …'

Once an overhead window had been opened and Sophie had checked twice that Neku really did like her coffee black and unsweetened, Sophie turned her attention to the little brass key.

'School trunk,' said Sophie finally. 'Maybe a tuck box.'

After she'd explained that one was for uniform and the other for personal possessions, and both were required by children going to boarding school, Sophie remembered to ask where Neku found the key.

'Upstairs.'

And after a few questions, mostly about how she liked London, Neku realised she was meant to go now. So she thanked Sophie for the coffee, trying not to mind the woman's obvious relief when she showed Neku to the door. By the time Neku had climbed the stairs and was letting herself into the flat, she'd reached a conclusion. The first completely firm conclusion she'd reached since leaving home. Pretty much everybody on this planet was weird.

CHAPTER 37
nawa-no-ukiyo

'Lady Neku...'

So many people, almost all of them strangers. Yellow cloaks, red tunics, faded blue hats and belts in a dozen other colours her mother would undoubtedly regard as vulgar. The d'Alambert retainers might look like clowns but they kept their gaze steady and held their ground.

She was being called.

Petro pushed her forward and Lady Neku stumbled to a halt in front of Luc d'Alambert, who bowed. 'My father would like to meet you.'

Lady Neku glanced at her mother.

'Apparently Lord d'Alambert wishes you to board his *yacht*.' The contempt with which Lady Katchatka said that final word revealed what she really thought of the gaudily-painted vessel.

Luc blushed. 'It's protocol,' he insisted.

Well, Lady Neku thought, *that's an end to that.* From introduction to intractable argument inside a single minute. That was quick, even for the Katchatka family.

'Please,' said Luc, the first time Lady Neku could remember anyone saying this. Well, certainly in her lifetime.

'He insists?' she asked.

Luc d'Alambert nodded.

'Well,' said Lady Neku. 'We'd better go.' She watched Luc try to work out if she was mocking him and wondered if she was; maybe a little, Neku mocked everyone while pretending to do the opposite. It made for a shell most people found hard to crack.

'After you,' he said.

If he could descend that ramp to meet the Katchatka family then she could climb it to meet Lord d'Alambert. *I mean*, Lady Neku asked herself. *How hard could it be?* As she neared the top, Lady Neku reminded herself not to ask idiot questions. The answer was *very difficult indeed*. And not just because the d'Alamberts used a slightly tighter logarithm for gravity.

'You all right?'

'Of course I'm ...' Glaring at the boy beside her, Lady Neku got ready to insist she was fine and then shrugged, making do with a small nod.

'He's made it hard,' said Luc. 'On purpose. Even we don't use gravity this dense.'

'Why are you telling me that?'

The boy looked puzzled. 'So you know things will get easier.' Putting his hand under Neku's elbow, Luc d'Alambert helped her climb the last few steps. They could have been any couple, thought Lady Neku, apart from the fact their families hated each other. She was half a head taller and Luc was so pale he might as well have been a ghost. He was right, though. Lady Neku felt her steps get less sticky and her body lighter as she neared the top of the ramp.

'Brace yourself,' said Luc.

A wave of nausea washed over Lady Neku. A churning sickness that abandoned her almost as soon as it began. When she came to, Luc was still supporting her elbow, only now he held it tight.

'Shit,' Lady Neku said.

Luc nodded, although he also glanced towards his father to see whether the thin man standing just inside the doorway had heard. Lord d'Alambert gave little sign of hearing, if he had, he was too busy examining a wall.

It showed a naked ...

Me, Lady Neku realised. As she looked, the scan sank beneath the surface of her breasts, nose, knees and abdomen, sectioning her into wafer-thin silhouettes that flickered and vanished. She saw her beating heart, brain, lungs and spine appear and disappear just as quickly. Until the leading edge of the scan passed through her body, leaving only a faint echo of dissolving buttock, seen from the inside out.

'Come in,' said a voice, and Lady Neku realised she still had a few paces to take. Closing the gap between herself and the old man, Lady Neku made a point of glancing at the darkening wall and then bowed.

Should she have curtsied? Seeing the amusement in the old man's eyes, Lady Neku decided perhaps not. Amusement was good. Certainly better than anger.

'My Lord.'

Luc's father was rumoured to be as old as Neku's mother, though the years had treated him less kindly. His eyes were watery and scales disfigured one side of his face and showed in armour-like rows from beneath his cuffs. She could smell the reptile stink of corruption from where she stood.

'Pretty,' he said, 'Isn't it?'

Harsh eyes warned Luc not to answer. Lord d'Alambert was waiting to see how Neku would reply.

'You're starting to look like a lizard,' she said.

'Very true.' Lord d'Alambert's smile was sour. 'Pretty soon I'll be as cold-blooded as your mother.'

'If it doesn't kill you first.' said Lady Neku, and Lord d'Alambert actually laughed. Although, from the scowls on the faces of his retainers it looked as if most of them had trouble seeing the joke.

'How much longer before you turn?'

'A century,' he said. 'God willing.'

Never show surprise, never show fear, never even pretend to take anything seriously, these rules had been instilled in Lady Neku by her brothers, with slaps and threats and the occasional treat. All the same, she still found it hard to keep the shock from her face. She asked how old Lord d'Alambert was without thinking.

Lady Neku had no idea whether or not he was lying when he told her his age. No way was her mother that old, unless the Katchatkas and d'Alamberts counted their years differently.

'You know why we're here?'

'A marriage,' said Lady Neku.

'Your marriage,' Lord d'Alambert said. He stared at the girl. 'How do you feel about that?'

Lady Neku's shrug was not the most elegant of responses.

Stepping forward, Lord d'Alambert wrapped one arm around the girl's shoulders and steered her away from Luc and the yellow-clad retainers who hovered at the edges of their conversation. Maybe this was planned, thought Lady Neku, maybe all those men in their strange suits and yellow cloaks knew to stand back. These were the d'Alamberts, the oldest of all families. According to her mother, they worked at levels of subtlety so deep even she had trouble extracting the real meaning from their words.

'Tell me honestly,' said Lord d'Alambert. 'How do you feel about this marriage?'

She would have shrugged again, but something in those eyes told

Lady Neku he would return to the question and keep returning to it until she answered.

'Does it matter?' asked Lady Neku.

'Yes,' said the old man. 'Your genes will be mixed with those of my son. Has that been explained to you?'

'Yes,' said Lady Neku.

'We're old-fashioned,' he added, almost sadly. 'Hog-tied by tradition. You will be required to live with us. We will also expect you to birth your own children.'

'I'm not sure I can,' said Lady Neku. 'Our record in that area is not very good.' She hesitated, wondering whether she dare say what was in her mind. 'You've heard the rumours?'

Three generations made by splitting cells.

The old man smiled. His breath was sour and he leant on her arm more heavily than Lady Neku liked. All the same she was shocked to realise she was starting to respect Lord d'Alambert, something so unlikely it made her wonder if he worked at levels more subtle than even her mother realised.

'I've heard the rumours,' said the man. 'And you'll be fine. I had you scanned as you came aboard. There's nothing amiss that can't be cured by inducing the menarche.' He smiled at Lady Neku's expression. 'You carry an ancient Bayer Rochelle mod for elective sterility. No breeding,' he added, when she looked puzzled. 'Until we splice in a key.'

CHAPTER 38

Thursday 28 June

There were three likely answers according to Charlie, another seven possible and thirty-eight more that ranged from technically possible to unlikely, each with its own factor of probability. And though every one could be examined in isolation, it was unrealistic to consider why a handgun clip might hold a mix of live and blank ammunition without tightening the parameters. 'Could the difference between bullet types be seen?'

'Unlikely,' said Neku. 'Clips are mostly closed on all sides.'

'Would the man unload the clip?'

'Doubt it,' she said.

'And the blanks?'

'Crimped,' said Neku, adding. 'No wax plug or fake bullet, just powder, minimal wadding and crimped metal around the top.'

She grinned at the memory, clung tighter to Kit's bike jacket and leant into a bend. Charlie had taken her problem away last Sunday, called her Monday with his request for more information and disappeared for another two days, finally texting yesterday to ask how many answers she'd like.

'Okay,' said Charlie, when she called. 'I can give you probabilities or divide my solutions into unlikely, possible and ...'

'Give me the most obvious answer,' said Neku, ruining his carefully considered presentation. She knew she'd ruined it, because Charlie's voice stumbled to a halt, leaving her alone on the roof with a silent phone and a distant police siren for company.

'Is this real?' he asked finally. 'I mean, does it have something to do with the dead woman?'

'Mary,' said Neku.

'Yes,' Charlie said, 'Mary.'

'No,' said Neku, flicking her Nokia to visual. She caught Charlie's blink as the streaming video came on line, and then the widening of his eyes.

'Neku, you're …'

I'm what? she wondered, before realising he meant shirtless. 'It's hot,' she told him. 'Tokyo has more wind.' He was about to say something else, but just nodded.

'So, it's not about Mary?'

'No,' said Neku. 'Definitely not.'

'But it is for real?' Charlie said, carefully not facing his screen. 'I mean,' he added. 'You don't strike me as interested in the hypothetical.'

Neku smiled, then realised it might have been an insult. 'It's real,' she said. 'I've been trying to work out what it means ever since.' This wasn't strictly true, she'd simply found the fact in a report amid the mess of papers from Major Yamota's office and passed the problem straight to Charlie.

'Okay,' he said, 'first thought, it's obviously intentional.' Charlie must have been glancing at his screen because he responded to Neku's frown. 'If the clip had five blanks and three live shells … Well, that could have been someone not bothering to empty the clip properly, but five blanks, two live, one blank.'

'Suggests what?'

Charlie took a deep breath … 'Taking the five/two combination first,' he said. 'Someone wants to frighten someone, while reserving the means to kill them. Second option, someone wants to frighten someone, then kill them. Third option, someone wants to frighten someone, then kill someone else.'

'Go on,' said Neku.

'There are other possibilities,' said Charlie. 'But I'd need more background. The clip is logical until you consider that last blank. Why load a final blank having loaded two live shells above it?'

'I imagine,' said Neku, 'it all depends on who loaded the clip.'

'On …?'

'How about, scare someone, kill someone else, get killed yourself?'

'Yeah,' said Charlie. 'That works for me.'

He'd wanted to see her again, obviously enough, which was a fair price. At least Neku thought it was, but she had to tell Charlie she was busy next day and that led into telling him about Kate O'Mally and Pat and all the other slivers of information she'd prised out of Kit as reward for translating his wretched forms.

'Call me when you get back?' asked Charlie.

Neku promised she would.

The sky above the downs was a ridiculous shade of blue and the afternoon stank of warm earth, summer and grass. It was all Kit could do not to put out one gloved hand to brush the hedge as he roared past.

The mill at Little Westover looked unchanged. The White Bear, on the corner where Blackboy Lane crossed with the ghost of a Roman road, was festooned with flowers, and its car park as full as ever.

But the old hut had gone.

Kit expected to find overgrown foundations or rotten walls and a broken roof, but it was gone completely. Someone had cleared the site, concreted it over and installed mesh fencing and a steel gate. A Ukrainian tractor and trailer now stood where the hut had been.

For the first half of the ride, Neku had gripped his jacket and held tight. After they stopped at a café and Kit told her how to ride pillion Neku loosened her grip and now leant back, holding plastic handles that protruded from the Kawasaki's cheap seat. They were using Sony earbeads, a modification that had cost almost as much as the old bike. Well, it did, when you threw in the cost of earbead-compatible helmets.

'Okay,' said Neku. 'Who am I?'

Kit twitched his head, then glanced back at the lane in time to see twin walls of cow parsley twist to one side. 'Lean,' he ordered, and felt Neku ride the bend. Of course, being Neku, explaining what she should do to ride pillion had also required him to explain why, so Kit ended up sketching a cross section of wheel onto a paper napkin.

'Precision and deflection,' she said, 'combined with centrifugal force. Simple enough.'

'If you say so.'

Now Neku threw herself into bends, which actually translated as leaning with the bike rather than against it. Kit had ridden these roads a thousand times before, in an earlier life and swept the curves from memory as he headed for Middle Morton and the old humpback bridge, but first he had Wintersprint.

The cottage was still there, although builders had removed the slate roof and added dormer windows. The thatch replacing the slates had been in place long enough to grow moss and turn black along its lower edges. The outside walls had been plastered and painted white. Half tubs, cut from beer barrels, overflowed with flowers on both sides of a glossy black door.

183

'Well?' demanded Neku, her voice loud in his earbead.

'Well, what?'

'How are you going to explain me to Mrs O'Mally?'

'Hell,' said Kit. 'How do I explain you to anyone?'

'You don't.'

Flicking on his indicators, Kit kicked down a couple of gears and coasted to a halt beside a gap in the hedge. The potato field still existed. The earth bank around its edge might look a little flatter and the copse of trees at its far end a little closer than he remembered, but its dark earth was still cut into furrows and a trailer rusted in one corner beneath rotting sacks. A sign by the gate advertised, *pick your own*.

'Why have we stopped?'

'Because I need to stretch my legs,' said Kit.

Having watched him unbolt a five-bar gate. Neku said, 'I'll come with you.'

'No,' said Kit, 'you won't. I need you to stay with the bike.'

Fifteen years had gone and still he stood humbled at the site of a mindless fuck between teenagers, one of them half drunk, the other ramped on speed. A thousand other people would have been having sex that night, ten thousand, a hundred thousand. Yoshi had been wrong. No one could tie you tighter than you could tie yourself and it was the ropes you couldn't see that bound you tightest.

'You're crying,' said Neku, when he returned.

Kit put his helmet back on.

Seven Chimneys had changed in the time he'd been away. The yellow brick had lost its rawness and ivy had fanned out around the upper windows. The rose bushes had thickened and the flower bed outside the study been weeded and cut back so many times its earth had changed colour.

Even the huge brass lion of a door knocker had lost its brashness and been cleaned and polished into something that felt greasy beneath Kit's fingers as he lifted its heavy ring and brought it down with a bang.

He had to knock another three times before he got an answer.

'Who is it?'

'Me,' he said, before realising how ridiculous that sounded. 'It's Kit,' he said. 'I need you to look at something.' On the far side of the door bolts were drawn back, and when the door opened it was still held by a heavy chain.

'Who's she?' demanded Kate.

Neku sighed. 'Told you,' she said.

184

While Kit looked through the attics for a trunk or box that might take the little brass key, Neku and Kate made lunch, which mostly involved slicing tomatoes and sticking fat chunks of cheese between even fatter slabs of bread.

'Make a dressing,' Kate ordered. When Neku looked blank, Kate pulled wine vinegar, olive oil and black pepper from a cupboard and dumped them in front of the girl.

'Mix them,' she said. 'Then grate in some pepper.'

'What proportions?'

'How would I know?' Kate asked, dumping an empty mustard jar in front of Neku. 'My husband used to make it.' She nodded at the jar. 'He used that.'

Having poured oil and vinegar into the jar, Neku added black pepper and screwed the jar shut before shaking it hard. Then she drizzled the dressing over the top of the sliced tomatoes, because she couldn't see what else she was meant to do with it.

'It's pretty here,' she said.

Kate grunted.

Horses ran in a field beyond the kitchen windows and bees clustered around a vast spread of lavender that overflowed a stone trough next to a bench on the lawn immediately outside. The room itself was huge, with stone slabs for a floor and work surfaces cut from railway sleepers. The kitchen was too big for one person, almost too big for one family. It looked as if it belonged in a hotel.

'You and Kit,' Kate asked. 'What's that about?'

So Neku told Kate how she'd met Kit by accident while she'd been stealing a pen, notebook and ink from a shrine shop in Tokyo, because she had a story she needed to write.

'What's the story about?'

'A marriage.'

'Whose marriage?'

'Mine,' said Neku, 'to the son of a lizard prince.'

Kate raised her eyebrows. So Neku told Kate how she met Kit a second time on the streets of Roppongi, when he gave her a coffee one morning, because it was raining.

'Because it was raining?'

'That's what he said.'

'And when was this?'

'Last Christmas,' said Neku. 'He bought me coffee every day after that, and often daifuku cake. Stuffed with sweet bean curd,' she added, when Kate looked puzzled. 'I came to rely on it. The days Kit forgot I went hungry.'

'You couldn't just beg?'

'Maybe that would have been better,' Neku admitted. 'Less trouble for everybody, but it seemed wrong.' She told Kate how she'd actually had a coin locker stuffed with millions of dollars she was unable to use. And how taking coffee from Kit had somehow felt different. 'Anyway,' she said. 'I saved his life from an assassin. So that was repayment.'

'Seems to be catching.'

'What is?' asked Neku.

'Wanting Kit dead.'

Neku shrugged. 'He was fucking the wife of a gang boss and bikers used his bar to deal drugs, plus lots of *uyoku* felt Yoshi Tanaka should be married to someone Japanese. Then there's *chippu* he owed to the local police and unpaid bills from a Brazilian transvestite who mends his motorbike. It could have been anyone.'

Kate laughed. 'You tell a good story,' she said. 'Almost as good as Patrick. All the same, I'd like the truth next time.'

After lunch, Kate carried her own plate to the sink and ran it under cold water, leaving it to dry on a wire rack. It was the action of someone grown used to living alone, life reduced to simple habits. Neku did the same for her own plate, Kit's plate and the plate on which she'd put the tomatoes, washing each before placing it next to the plates already there.

Before enlightenment, chop wood, carry water. After enlightenment, chop wood, carry water ... Neku found it hard to remember which actions carried weight and which got lost as static and dust in the slipstream from other people's lives.

'I'm going for a stroll,' said Kate. 'You can keep looking,' she added, speaking to Kit. 'But there's no trunk here and no tuck box. Mary didn't go to that kind of school.' And, with this, Kate headed for the kitchen door.

Neku made to follow her.

'*Neku,*' Kit said.

'What,' said Neku. 'I'm not allowed to take a walk too?'

CHAPTER 39

Thursday 28 June

Cars locked up the M25, London's orbital. They crawled towards turn-offs, negotiated endless roadworks and slid gratefully away, like single fish leaving a shoal as they finally headed home to leafy and not-so-leafy suburbs. About ten minutes short of his own turn-off, Kit spotted a BMW up ahead and thought no more about it, filtering through the gap between the BMW and a white van.

As he did so, an arm reached through the driver's window and fixed a blue light to the roof. Sirens blipped and the BMW would have remained trapped in treacle-slow traffic if Kit hadn't obediently pulled over.

'Licence . . .'

Kit had already removed his helmet and dark glasses, so he smiled and nodded politely. 'I'm sorry. Is there . . .'

'Licence,' said the man.

'Of course,' said Kit. Without hesitation, he unzipped a side pocket and flipped open his wallet, offering the man a small square of plastic. The only instantly recognisable words were *Kit Nouveau*, everything else was in Japanese.

'What's this?'

'My licence.'

The policeman turned over the square of plastic. It was obvious from the irritation on his face that he found the vehicle categories outlined in kanji on the back equally incomprehensible. At least the front had a photograph of Kit, a reference number and something that looked like an end date.

'Where's your international permit?'

'I don't need one,' said Kit, careful to keep a smile on his face. 'This is good in the UK for a year.'

'Great,' said the man. 'I've got myself a lawyer.'

'Not at all,' Kit shook his head. 'But I checked with the British embassy in Tokyo before I left.' As a lie it was next to impossible to refute, and besides Japanese driving licences were legal in the UK, everyone knew that.

'What about her?'

Before Kit had time to answer, Neku produced a red and gold passport and handed it over. As an afterthought, she remembered to execute a small bow. A smile was fixed firmly on her face.

'How long's she been here?' demanded the policeman.

'Almost a week,' said Kit.

'And when she's due to leave?'

'Soon,' he said, pretending not to notice Neku's frown.

'Wait here,' the man ordered. A few minutes later he was back. Without a word, he returned Neku's passport and the Japanese licence taken from Kit, then nodded at the bike. 'You can go.'

Car after car had been crawling past even more slowly than traffic conditions demanded, as drivers braked slightly to stare in vague interest at whatever was happening. When the policeman raised his head to stare, a handful of faces of immediately looked away.

'Come on,' Kit told Neku, putting on his helmet and waiting for her to do the same. 'Let's go home.' He turned the Kawasaki in a slow circle and touched his rear brake as he reached the unmarked police car, slowing slightly to peer inside. Two men sat in the front. The one who'd just demanded sight of Kit's licence and Sergeant Samson, the police officer from a couple of days before.

'Evening,' said Kit. And left the Sergeant to his calls and the numbers he'd been reading to someone over a car radio.

Every city has its own night noises. The talking police cars in Tokyo. A foghorn from a freighter heard between New York's rumble of trucks. The braying of a tethered donkey in Tunis.

In London the late sounds were composed of lorries, banging doors and people fighting in the streets. At least, that was how it sounded to Kit as he lay awake and listened to the hours crawl by as slowly as that evening's traffic on the M25. It was noisy, if less noisy than Sophie had said.

As well as using the mews to piss, drunks stopped off to try their phones or slumped, half conscious against a wall, waiting for a call to remind them where they were meant to be. Couples dipped into its depths to kiss or fuck or squabble away from the main street. A typed note in a plastic folder – nailed to a door just under the arch, where it could be read by street light – assured punters that no prostitutes worked from any of the flats in Hogarth Mews.

(According to Sophie, a couple of Estonians had started conning tourists in Soho by giving them a key and an address in Hogarth Mews, with a promise that young and beautiful East European girls would be waiting. A Glaswegian trio tricked into visiting the non-existent brothel had been angry enough to kick down a door.)

For all this, Hogarth Mews was a good address. A quick look in the window of a local estate agent had told Kit just how good. Not central Tokyo prices, of course, because few cities in the world had anything approaching those, but Mary had still left him a flat worth more than he'd earned in the previous ten years.

And staring into the half darkness, Kit just wished he knew why. Apology, guilt, some weird attempt to make peace? Any of those would have worked, if only things had been the other way round. If he'd been the one offering Mary everything he owned.

Kit was still worrying at this question when he heard the door from the roof garden open and then the sound of Neku's key in the front door of the flat. This was not unusual because Neku often passed ghost-like through the hall on her way to get a glass of water or use the bathroom.

Only this time she stopped outside his room.

'You awake?'

'Yeah,' he said, watching his door open.

'Are you okay to talk?'

'It's three in the morning,' said Kit. 'Can't it wait?'

'No,' Neku said, shaking her head. 'Probably not.'

He caught the sweep of one hip, a shoulder and a curve of breast in silhouette as she turned back from shutting the door behind her. Absolute certainty of her nakedness came with a splinter of streetlight between her thighs as she walked towards him.

'I'm not going back to Japan,' said Neku. Sitting herself on the edge of Kit's bed she reached for the covers, her fingers tugging at the edge of his quilt.

'Neku.'

The tussle was brief and Kit won.

'Why?' she asked, when she'd done what Kit demanded and put on his yukata, tying its belt tight around her. She still sat on his bed, only now her legs were folded under her and only one foot could be seen.

Her arms were folded and she'd hunched inside herself, visibly furious with him.

'You're a kid,' said Kit.

Neku snorted. 'In some prefectures,' she said. 'The age of consent is thirteen. Anyway,' Neku added crossly. 'You wouldn't be my first.'

'Maybe not,' Kit said, 'but that's hardly the point.'

'So, it's definitely my age?'

He nodded.

'Would it help,' said Neku. 'If I told you how old I really was?'

'Probably not.' Kit had her pegged at fifteen or sixteen. Although, since Japanese girls could look young for their age she might be seventeen, though he doubted it. She behaved like a child, for all that she sometimes pretended to be something else.

'Well?' he said.

'I'm hundreds of years older than you.'

'Hundreds?'

'Thousands,' said Neku. 'Ten of thousands. I don't even know when this is, it's so long ago ...'

CHAPTER 40
nawa-no-ukiyo

'Where's Luc?' Lady Katchatka demanded.

'Being miserable somewhere,' said Nico. 'Knowing him.'

'And your sister?'

Lady Katchatka glanced at her three sons. Nico sat her feet, sharpening the blade of a katana said to be older than the family itself, while the two elder boys knelt by a wall, playing cards. Something simple, like clans.

'Well?'

'She was in the gardens,' said Antonio. 'Playing with her stupid cat.' Antonio dealt another card, only to swear when his brother scooped the pile.

'And when was this?' asked Lady Katchatka.

'After lunch.'

The old woman sighed. 'Nico?'

Her youngest son ran a sharpening glass down one edge of his blade, then wiped the metal with a finger, checking the silver dust he found there. 'She's asleep in the spire,' he said, without looking up.

Petro snorted.

'I thought it best to check.' Nico said coldly.

She was going to have to deal with this, Lady Katchatka decided. Only not now and certainly not before the wedding banquet was over.

'Sound asleep?'

Nico scowled.

'Well,' Lady Katchatka demanded. 'Was she sound asleep?'

'Dead to this world,' said Nico.

Also curled up in a corner. Although Nico didn't need to mention this, because everyone knew how Neku slept. She'd been curling up in stray corners from the day she was born.

How odd, Lady Neku thought. *Why would Nico lie about having gone to my room?* Shaking her head, the girl edged round a half pillar, looking for a better peep hole. Unlike the pillar's far side, which pretended to be marble, the side Lady Neku edged round was unpolished metal, with fat bolts that fixed it to the sheet steel beneath her feet. This was because Lady Neku was inside a hollow wall.

She'd been nine when she discovered the trick. A door into the Stroll Garden had been locked and Lady Neku wanted to be on the other side. So angry had Lady Neku been that she hit the door; not softly or in pretend anger, but hard enough to split the skin of her knuckles. Only the pain Lady Neku expected to feel on her second blow never came, because the door dissolved beneath her punch and she found herself with her arm stuck almost entirely through its surface.

When screaming produced no help, she tried reason. At nine, of course, Lady Neku could already out-think Antonio and Petro. Even Nico, who was used to being the most intelligent, had come to realise his sister was talented. Which was probably why he'd locked her out of the garden in the first place.

After reason failed, the nine-year-old began to push at the doors with her shoulder, finally falling through. Since this was obviously impossible, she decided not to mention it to her mother or brothers.

So began her travels. At first she simply walked through doors. Although this was a clumsy way to describe the intricate negotiation her body made with the physical boundaries around it. The following year Lady Neku realised that if she approached hollow walls face on and then stepped sideways, she could remain within the wall itself.

By then, she'd done some basic research and decided it was down to the molecules of her body negotiating *miu* space within the molecules making the wall. This was, she later discovered, almost entirely wrong. Whatever, Lady Neku increased her ability to wander, until even Nico became disquieted enough by the things his sister knew.

She became the family ghost, the halfwit others barely mentioned, wandering alone down abandoned corridors or climbing the sheer sides of cathedral-high hangars to hide on ledges for days.

Cold, hungry, lost and alone, they were some of the happiest days of her life. She discovered the drop zone, filled with pods designed to make one-way trips to the planet's surface. And having made her first drop, she introduced herself to her family's castle, which found it hard to accept she'd made no provision for her return.

'Really?' Schloss Omga asked.

'Really,' said Lady Neku, sounding remarkably unworried, given she'd forgotten to bring food and the heat inside the castle's shell was already gluing her shirt to her back. So the castle returned her anyway. Shifting the nine-year-old a hundred kilometres straight up, from ground level to High Strange, as simply as Lady Neku herself moved through doors.

Next time she did the drop, the castle said, *I suppose you expect me to do that again?* And Lady Neku simply nodded.

Mostly it was her silence and self-sufficiency that worried Nico, Antonio and Petro. She avoided physical contact, long talks, sympatico symbionts and all the other little tics that bound her brothers to her mother. She was herself, the original. Everyone else was just a copy.

'Okay, then,' Lady Neku heard her mother say. 'We're all agreed?'

The idea of her mother asking approval of her brothers was so surprising that Lady Neku hesitated on the edge of leaving and decided to stay where she was.

Looking up from his blade, Nico said. 'Are you sure about not telling Neku?'

'It seems best.'

'She's going to take it badly. You know she will.'

Lady Katchatka nodded, mostly to herself. 'Better this way,' she said. 'Neku's going to be upset whatever.'

'So we don't tell her about Luc?' That was Antonio.

'No,' said Lady Katchatka, 'we don't.'

Having carefully placed his cards face down on the floor, Petro glanced between his mother and Antonio. 'And we don't tell her about Lord d'Alambert either?'

'We don't tell her about anything,' said Nico. 'It's a secret.'

'That's right,' Lady Katchatka said. 'It's a secret.'

Antonio and Petro nodded.

After the two eldest boys returned to their cards Nico stood up and swished his katana through the air, listening to its note; then he wiped its blade one final time and sat himself at a window seat, staring out over the wastes of Katchatka segment below. A moment later, his mother joined him. Unfortunately, they were too far away for Lady Neku to hear what was said.

When their conversation was done, Lady Katchatka bent forward and kissed Nico carefully on the forehead. She left without bothering to say goodbye to the others.

Lady Neku half expected Nico to follow, but all he did was stroll over to where Antonio and Petro knelt and squatted beside them. At the end of that round, Antonio dealt the cards into fresh piles and all three brothers began to play.

'I don't get it,' said Luc, when Lady Neku eventually found him sulking in the Stroll Garden. 'Why do you dress like that?'

Protocol said he lived with her family for the time it took to complete the celebrations that ensured she would remain for the rest of her life within his. Luc made little pretence about hating every minute of his enforced stay.

'Why do I ...?' One of the things Lady Neku found most odd about Luc was the innocence with which he asked questions. Surely he'd been told that every question revealed more about the person asking than could be offset by knowing the answer?

Yet Luc simply asked. *Odd* was one word for it. *Stupid* was another. Because the other thing Lady Neku found strange about Luc was that he appeared to believe everything she told him. There was a third strangeness. Which was that Neku had begun to find herself giving truthful answers to the questions Luc asked, because tricking him and lying were just too easy. If nothing else, she found a novelty value in being honest.

'Dress like what?' Neku demanded.

'You know.' Luc flapped a hand. 'All this black. And that shirt.'

'What about it?'

'It's ...' He shrugged, then flapped his hand again. Lady Neku guessed he meant to indicate the rips. Luc went red every time he got embarrassed. *I mean,* she thought. *How stupid a modification is that?*

Lady Neku wore a skirt of crumpled silk ripped to show the layers beneath. The skirt was old and had been spun by tiny worms fed on starlight, so her mother said. It fluoresced in the daylight, but wear it at night and it became darker than the deepest shadow, a mere absence of light wrapped around the person inside.

It had been Lady Neku's favourite, until she mentioned this to her mother and Lady Katchatka had replied, dismissively, that she'd also loved it at her daughter's age. Now Lady Neku hated it, but continued to wear the garment to stop her mother from knowing the effect of those words.

Anyway, it was not the skirt that bothered Luc, nor the *neilo* bangles and memory beads around Lady Neku's wrists, it was her top. 'It's okay,' said Lady Neku. 'You can stare. Everybody else does.'

'Everybody?'

'Nico, Antonio and Petro.'

When Luc bit his bottom lip it made Lady Neku wonder what she'd said. And that was enough to push her into considering his question carefully. It was only after she'd dragged Luc to a tiny waterfall and sat him beside her on the grass, that Lady Neku wondered if his unworldly innocence were some weird double bluff, designed to manipulate her into telling him the truth. If so, then she was impressed, because it was working.

'What?' Luc said.

'Nothing,' said Lady Neku, 'I'm just not used to talking to people. So you'll have to listen carefully.'

'To what?'

'My reasons. Why I wear black.'

'I understand they're Katchatka colours,' said Luc. 'It's the way you all dress. You know, it's just the ...' A shake of his head, then one hand went up to rub his eyes.

If he'd only get his mouth fixed, thought Lady Neku, he'd be almost good looking. Pulling up her knees, she twisted her skirt decorously around her ankles and rested her chin on her hands.

Lady Neku was thinking.

'Okay,' she said. 'It goes like this. My mother likes torn clothes because they look good on her and my brothers dress the same because they follow my mother's example. I wear this shirt because it renders me invisible to them ...'

Lady Neku held up a hand, stilling Luc's question. 'Let me finish,' she said. 'The rips are house style. If I dressed as neatly as you I'd be making an exhibition of myself. Does that make sense?'

Sitting back, Lady Neku lowered her knees and unfolded her arms. 'What do you see when you look at me?' she demanded.

His blush was her answer.

'Exactly,' said Lady Neku.

'That's how you make yourself invisible?' Luc said softly. He nodded, then nodded again, considering her words. 'But I still don't understand. Who are you hiding from?'

It took Lady Neku ninety minutes to explain to Luc the background, history and internal politics of her family. And at the end, all he said was, 'You're hiding from the lot of them?'

And when she scowled, he nodded.

'Okay,' he said. 'I can see how that might work.'

Sweeping hair from his eyes, Nico slashed through the air and a dozen invisible enemies died beneath his flurry of blows, then a dozen more as he dropped, swept low with a particularly lethal cut and danced away across the duelling room. When he finally came to a standstill in front of Lady Neku, his brothers and Luc, he'd barely broken sweat.

'Sweet,' he said. Nico was talking about the blade.

'Let me try,' said Petro.

Nico shook his head.

'Come on,' Petro said. 'It's not even yours.'

'It is now,' said Nico. 'I found it. Go find your own.'

Only Petro wouldn't, because that meant the surface, tracking down an object of value and then wresting it from the original owner. And Petro grew sick simply thinking about surface dwellers and the plagues they carried. Not something that worried Nico, who time and again had returned with blood splattering his arms. 'Here ...' Nico tossed the katana to Luc, all three brothers grinning as Luc fumbled his catch. 'You can borrow it,' said Nico. 'I'm sure Petro would be delighted to fight you.'

Petro scowled, mainly because Luc got to try the blade and not him. Which, obviously enough, was why Nico gave Luc the katana in the first place. Lady Neku's family could be very predictable.

'I'm not that good,' said Luc, as he tried the katana for balance. He was rewarded with a laugh from Nico.

'Have a go, anyway.'

'Okay,' he said. Turning in a circle, with the katana held far too tightly to give him the fluidity he'd require, Luc practised a dozen of the simplest blocks and finished up facing Petro.

'What are the rules?' Luc asked.

Petro grinned. 'This is Katchatka,' he said. 'There are no rules. At least, not about things like this. You should know that if you're going to marry my sister.'

'So how do you score?'

Petro glanced at his brothers, who rolled their eyes rather more obviously than was necessary. 'Two people fight,' Petro said. 'One wins. How hard can that be to mark?'

It was time for Lady Neku to get involved. The question was how? Since coming up with a complex and emotionally satisfying answer would take longer than she had, Lady Neku chose the simplest option. Pushing herself away from the wall, she marched across to Luc and held out her hand.

'Let me see,' she said.

Luc did as he was told.

'Nice balance,' said Lady Neku, cutting air. 'Very nice indeed ....' Luc was still busy admiring Lady Neku's swordplay, when she spun away from him and slashed the blade hard towards her brother.

As Petro brought up his own blade to block her blow, Lady Neku twisted sideways, reversed her katana in one fluid move and struck fast and hard, the blade actually cutting her skirt as its tip lanced out behind her.

'Fuck,' said Petro, only just stepping back in time. He looked shocked.

'You've been practising,' Nico said, his voice amused.

Lady Neku nodded.

'Okay,' said Nico, 'my go.'

So Lady Neku tossed him the sword. The spin she put on the handle made the blade difficult to catch, but Nico caught it all the same. He grinned at his sister, nodded once to Luc and swept hair out of his own eyes.

'Why doesn't he just get it cut?' whispered Luc.

'Because then he wouldn't be able to flick it back ...' Lady Neku sighed, surely Luc could see how the floppiness of Nico's hair was reflected in the ruffles of his shirt and the wide hem to his trousers?

'Ready?' asked Nico.

Mouth sullen, Petro nodded. What had begun as fun at Luc's expense had turned into fun at his own. 'Of course I'm ready,' he said. Stepping forward, Petro swung his blade a couple of times and then stepped back. As Nico moved forward to begin his own warm up, Petro aimed a heavy-handed side slash that would have severed Nico's leg had it met flesh.

Nico blocked the cut with a smile.

Only, by then, Petro had launched the moves he really wanted to make. A quick reverse, a faint to the head and then the blow itself. Straight at Nico's throat.

'Idiot,' said Lady Neku.

Springing aside, Nico let the katana pass, before sinking his own point deep into Petro's chest. As his elder brother opened his mouth, in something halfway between pain and astonishment, Nico yanked his blade sideways, severing his brother's heart. Blood went everywhere.

'Nico ...!'

It was too late. By the time Lady Neku reached Petro's side his eyes were unfocused and his pulse had stopped. 'Mother's going to be furious.'

'He started it,' said Nico, suddenly sounding like the boy he was.

'Like that will make a difference.'

'Well, he did.' Wiping his blade, Nico returned it to the scabbard.

Lady Neku sighed. 'You know what Mother's like about hurting Petro's feelings.'

'Feelings?' said Luc.

Nico nodded. 'Petro is the oldest,' he said. 'So we're not meant to make fun of him. It makes my mother upset.' Nico paused. 'That's bad,' he added, as if this might be news to Luc. 'The problem is Petro's just rubbish at everything.'

'I suppose,' said Antonio, glancing at the blood. 'We'd better get this cleared up before anyone sees it.'

But Lady Neku was one step ahead of them both. Dropping to a crouch, she stroked the tiles next to Petro's body until they began to sag and opened into a body-sized hole. 'I'll let you two finish off.'

'Okay.' Nico nodded. 'Come on,' he told Antonio. 'Let's get it over with.' Walking across to where Petro lay, Nico and Antonio began to roll him into the hole.

'You'll get him back in two days,' said Lady Neku.

'What . . .'

'That's good,' she said. 'I had to negotiate to get it done that fast. The *kami* are working full out on tomorrow night.'

For once her brothers didn't mock her. 'Oh fuck,' said Antonio. 'Mother's party.'

She watched Nico and Antonio glance at each other.

'He'll miss the wedding banquet,' said Nico.

'I know,' said Lady Neku.

'Mother's going to be furious.'

Lady Neku nodded. 'You should have thought about that before you killed him.'

CHAPTER 41
Friday 29 June

Time was spherical, layered within itself, each layer actually a sphere when expanded into three dimensions, although it looked like two when seen from any perspective beyond four, most layers being climbed using a basic Einstein-Rosen bridge.

'Got it so far?' asked Neku.

Kit shook his head. The girl sat against the head board of Mary's bed, still wrapped in his yukata. Her shoulder was pressed into his arm and her eyes were shut. Neku smelt of soap, shampoo and marmite; the last being what Kit had put on the toast he made her.

He'd made toast because Neku began crying and he wanted to give her privacy; that either constituted cowardice or compassion. Kit could waste time later trying to work out which.

'Okay,' said Kit, 'But what's all this got to do with being upset?'

'Everything,' said Neku.

Settling herself, she brushed crumbs from her chin and started to sketch a jerky spiral in the air with one finger. 'This is time,' she said. 'Enormously simplified and seen from a different perspective. Think of it as steps circling a central well. Unfortunately the stairs only go in one direction.'

'Why?' asked Kit.

Neku sighed. 'Because they do,' she said. 'My brother said time is an infinite number of doors forever locking behind you.' Which showed what he knew.

'And what's at the top?'

'For me,' said Neku. '*Nawa-no-ukiyo*. The floating rope world. Everything else has gone.' She nodded towards Kit's window. 'All of those stars,' she said. 'They've shifted, the moon's been segmented and the gas giants drained for fuel. It was the Great White,' she added. 'Everything

199

that could be used was, to help humanity reach the other side.'

Neku spoke with such conviction that Kit found himself nodding. What she said was impossible. Worse than this, it was largely incomprehensible. But Neku believed it and that made it real for her. Kit had lived for long enough inside his own dreams to recognise someone else's.

No one should have to carry the ends of time or that quantity of dark dead space inside them. Without thinking, he hugged the child close and felt her hesitate, then snuggle closer to his shoulder.

'Finish your toast,' said Kit.

She chewed in silence.

'Thing is,' said Neku, when her mouth was empty. 'You only see this many stars because we're in your light cone. Even then, about a fifth of those are already dead. Nico says stars shift with time, until distance begins to look like absence.'

Kit nodded.

'And I'm not really sure why earth was chosen.'

'For what?'

'To house all the fugees. Because it was empty, I guess. A planet without a people for a people without a planet,' Neku sighed. 'It probably seemed like a good idea at the time.'

Together Kit and Neku watched the sky beyond his window get lighter and the stars, already faded by the city's sodium glare fade further, until they vanished into the perfect upturned bowl of an early summer morning.

Kit thought Neku was dozing until she suddenly spoke again. 'Okay,' she said. 'What are we doing today?'

'I'm seeing Patrick Robbe-Duras,' said Kit. 'To show him Mary's key. Pat says he doesn't remember Mary owning a trunk but I can take a look anyway.'

'Can Charlie come too?'

Kit was about to say, *but I'm going alone* ... And then decided to save himself the argument.

Quite why Pat expected Kit and Charlie to mow the lawn while Neku sorted buttons from a button box was never explained. Although by the end of the afternoon the grass was trimmed, raked and rolled and all of the buttons collected by Mary as a small child had been sorted by size and type.

As a reward, Pat gave them tea on the freshly-cut lawn. Charlie set up a wooden picnic table and Neku carried the china. She would have made

200

the sandwiches, but Pat insisted on making those himself, somewhat crossly.

'He's tired,' said Kit.

'No,' said Neku. 'He's dying.'

When Pat returned he found Neku and Charlie crouched by the river. Charlie was feeding digestive biscuits to the ducks, though every now and then he'd dip a finger into the water to take a bit of weed that Neku indicated. Just as Neku would discard a pebble from her mouth to taste another, when she found one she liked better.

Neither looked up when Pat got back.

'I've upset them,' said Pat, putting a plate of cucumber sandwiches on the rickety picnic table. 'I'm sorry.'

'It's okay,' said Kit. 'You're tired. Neku understands that.'

'Talk about me, did you?'

At Kit's nod, Pat sighed. 'People have been talking about me my entire life. Well, about Katie really. Speaking of which, she called yesterday to say you'd be in contact about some bloody key. So I told her you'd been in contact already.' He shrugged. 'Not sure if Katie was angry about my already knowing or glad you were pushing on with finding Mary.'

Pat held out his hand. 'I suppose you'd better show me.'

Taking the key Kit offered, Pat turned it over in his hands and pulled a pair of reading glasses from his jacket pocket to take a closer look.

'Recognise it?' asked Kit.

'No,' said Pat, handing the key back. 'Anyway, it's not like Mary went to that kind of school. You know why?'

Kit shook his head.

'Because the first private school we tried refused to take her. Oh, she passed their exam all right. Only someone told them about Katie and we had a very embarrassed letter from the headmaster saying he'd made a mistake with class sizes and he was really sorry, but there wasn't a place after all.'

'What happened?'

'Half the school burnt down.'

Kit looked at him.

'Before term began,' said Pat tiredly. 'No one got hurt.'

'Were you upset?'

'About Mary losing her place? Of course not. I was delighted. It was Katie who ...' He stopped as Charlie escorted Neku up the bank, her fingers closed tight around a dripping mass of leaves, petals and water weed.

'What's that?'

Neku smiled. 'You'll see,' she said.

When Neku and Charlie reappeared it was with a glass full of cloudy water and a tiny box made from neatly-folded paper. 'Drink this,' said Neku, putting the glass on the picnic table. And the fact Pat did showed either extreme faith or an unusual level of tact.

'God,' he said. 'That tastes vile.'

'Maybe,' said Neku. 'But it will help. My grandmother taught me about plants.'

'About plants?'

'Well, poisons ... They're close enough. It's what you do at the molecular level that matters.' Holding out her paper box, Neku showed how it opened to reveal one pebble. Kanji characters on each side of the box had bled into soft focus as ink seeped into paper.

'The box is meant to look like that,' Neku insisted.

'I'm sure it is,' said Pat. 'What does this charm do?'

'It summons the *kami*,' promised Neku.

Pat smiled.

CHAPTER 42
Friday 29 June

It was Pat's suggestion that Charlie and Neku travel back in Charlie's old Mini and Kit stay for coffee. 'It'll only take five minutes,' Pat told Neku. 'I just want a quick talk and Charlie needs to get home.'

'But I don't have front door keys,' said Neku, sounding put out.

'It's all right,' promised Pat. 'Kit will catch you up.' When Neku looked doubtful, Pat smiled. 'Charlie can drive slowly,' he said.

Charlie nodded.

'She's a good kid,' said Pat, once the gravel was empty and the Mini a memory of noisy horn bursts from the road beyond. 'And she's obviously worried about you.'

'Worried?'

'She told me you were in trouble. Something about Yakusa bosses and fire-bombing. Katie mentioned you had problems, but didn't tell me what. Katie always tried to keep that stuff from me.' Pat took a deep breath, then lost a whole minute to the coughing fit this induced.

'Shit,' said Kit, when he'd finished helping Pat inside.

Spitting into a tissue, Pat nodded. 'I'll live, for a while anyway. What I kept you back to say was I'm grateful for the help you're giving Katie, but if you're really in trouble then tell her. Katie has contacts. Call it payment.'

'Kate hates me,' said Kit. 'And the debt is mine.'

'You were kids,' Pat said crossly. 'It's time you forgave yourself.' He sat in silence for a while after that, watching Kit sip lukewarm coffee from a battered mug, while staring out of the window at the river beyond. 'I never liked how Katie lived,' said Pat. 'It was always a problem between us.'

He was talking about *the firm*, Kit realised, the web of criminal connections that Kate O'Mally inherited, built into something altogether grander and eventually passed to her nephew Michael, the man Kit half-blinded beside a hedge in Wintersprint.

'She told me once,' said Pat. 'That it was just a job.'

'What did you say?'

'That it was a job in which people died. She told me mortality was the human condition.' Pat sighed. 'I blame her priest. When I told Katie that wasn't good enough, she said at least it was the right people who died, and it was the only answer she had.'

'I should go,' said Kit, 'if I'm going to catch them up.'

'What I'm trying to say,' said Pat, sighing, 'is that Katie has connections. Global connections. The Yakusa, the Camorra, the 'Ndranghala, the Mafia ... Katie's mob might not have a fancy name but they still command respect. If you have problems talk to her.'

Kit shook his head.

'At least pretend to think about it,' Pat said.

Peeling off his gauntlets, Kit kicked the Kawasaki onto its stand and unbuckled his helmet. Charlie was already negotiating his battered Mini into the spot where the Porsche usually parked, so Kit guessed he was planning to see Neku inside.

The sun was low enough in the sky to be lost behind a tower block and Hogarth Mews stood in shadow, its front doors half hidden. Which might have been why Kit didn't spot the speltered-metal bust of Karl Marx, until he almost tripped over the thing. The door to Sophie's flat was also wedged open, only this time she'd used a small marble vase overflowing with five-pence pieces.

'You're back,' said Sophie, crushing a cigarette under heel.

'Yes,' said Kit. He caught her glance at the Mini. 'Is that a problem?'

'Someone was looking for you. Said they were from the police.'

'The sergeant again?'

'No.' Sophie shook her head. 'Plain clothes this time. A woman, claimed she knew you.'

Kit waited.

'Inspector Avenden ...'

'Never heard of her.'

'Whatever,' said Sophie, pulling a battered packet of Gauloise from her jeans. 'She wanted to wait. I said she couldn't. So now she's in Caffé Nero sulking, well probably ...'

'Probably?'

'As I said, she wanted to wait here. I suggested the inspector find a café in Charlotte Street and wait there instead.'

'Not fond of the Met, are you?'

Sophie's scowl was fierce. 'I'm old enough to remember them unarmed,' she said. 'Before the laws changed. So are you,' she added. 'I used to love this city. Now it's all fake threats and real guns.'

Beside them, Charlie and Neku had stopped to listen. Charlie was nodding, which Kit found interesting. The boy didn't look like revolutionary politics came high on his list of interests.

'You okay to take this up?' Kit asked Neku, holding out his helmet. 'There's someone I need to see. It won't take long.'

'Sure,' said Neku. 'I'll get supper on.'

'If he wants,' Kit said. 'Charlie can stay to eat.' The boy seemed pleased, although Neku looked entirely non-committal.

'I suppose you know what you're doing,' said Sophie, when Charlie and Neku had disappeared in a clatter of feet on the stairs. 'She's cute. And I know she beds down on the roof terrace ... I sleep with my window open,' she added, seeing Kit's face. 'I hear the kid stamping around in the night. All the same, she's in love with you.'

'No,' said Kit. 'She likes Charlie.'

Sophie shook her head. 'Charlie likes Neku. Neku likes you.'

'She's a child.'

'No,' said Sophie. 'She's not. Look at her. She's cooking, cleaning, wearing neat clothes. She's digging in for the long haul.'

Kit gave a sigh.

'Someone has to say it,' said Sophie. 'And whatever you're really doing in London, it doesn't feel like something that should involve a kid.'

A kid who's killed. One who gets an ex-gangster eating out of her hands in the time it takes to make cheese sandwiches, badly. Instead of saying it, Kit just nodded, because all of the above still didn't make Sophie's words untrue.

The ground floor to the café on Charlotte Street had three customers, all at a metal table outside. The counter itself was deserted, the only member of staff Kit could see leant against a stool, skim-reading that morning's *Metro*.

The floor above was almost as empty. A Chinese student made notes from a biology textbook at a round table at the top of the stairs. And, in the far corner, looking sullen in a black skirt, white shirt and plain jacket was a woman in her mid thirties, already climbing to her feet.

'Inspector Avenden?'

Nodding, the woman offered her hand, then let it drop. Maybe it was the way Kit's voice turned her name into a question. Or maybe it was the fact he refused to shake. Either way, her eyes went flat.

'You don't remember me, do you?'

'No,' said Kit, shaking his head.

Honesty, it seemed, was the best policy. At least where Inspector Avenden was concerned, because her wide face regained a fraction of its smile. 'Oh well,' she said, a Welsh lilt to her voice. 'You always were more interested in Mary O'Mally.'

He got it then.

A kiss that tasted of cheap cigarettes, a footpath fumble and a promise – still unfulfilled – to go clubbing when she got back from somewhere or other. Amy Avenden had hightailed it out of Middle Morton almost as fast as he had.

'Would you like …?'

'Let me get …'

Her laughter might be self mocking as their questions clashed, but her face was more relaxed than when Kit first appeared at the top of the stairs. He got the feeling this meeting was not entirely willing on her part. Which begged the question as to why it was happening at all.

'I'll go,' said Kit, and she let him.

When Kit returned Amy had put a small notebook on the table and placed a pen neatly beside it. There was something formal about that fact.

'Is this official?' Kit asked, putting down the lattes.

'If it was,' said Amy, 'that would be a voice recorder. Call it semi official …' She sat back and stared towards the ceiling, collecting her thoughts; collecting something anyway, because when she leant forward it was to tell Kit his name had been cross-linked on the computer.

'Which means what?'

'You sent an e-mail to Japan that put you on one list. A call you took from Kathryn O'Mally put you on another. When you came up a third time during a licence plate check with the DVLA the machine flagged you as someone to watch.'

'E-mail?'

'Sent from your flat to an e-address in Tokyo. The *bozozoku* have connections with motorcycle gangs in America, Scandinavia, Russia and Australia. When Scotland Yard checked with Tokyo's Organised Crime Section they discovered the e-address belonged to the girlfriend of a foreign resident. Enquiries to Australia showed Tommy Nadif had a criminal record, involving drugs.'

'Got it all sewn up, haven't you?' said Kit.

'You don't approve?'

'Not really ...' Kit shook his head. 'Although it's obviously good to see you again.'

Amy's mouth twisted into a wry smile. 'Always the charmer,' she said, her voice making it clear she meant exactly the opposite. She tapped a cigarette from a packet and fired up before Kit had time to offer.

'Can I ask you something?' said Kit.

'You can ask.'

'Is the fact you're here and we know each other a coincidence?'

Amy had the grace to look embarrassed. 'No,' she admitted, blowing smoke towards the ceiling. 'I got a call ...'

'So you were sent because you knew me?'

'Wrong again,' said Amy. 'I was sent because I knew Mary. My boss called the Canterville Gallery to see if anyone had been asking about Mary or Ben Flyte. Your name came up. That was the fourth time you got tagged and every tag shifts you up a level. We're used to looking for subtle connections and delicate webs of coincidence. Few people hit code red quite as fast as you did.'

Great, thought Kit, the words *frying pan* and *fire* coming to mind.

'I need to ask why you're in London,' said Amy. 'And what makes you think Mary O'Mally might still be alive?'

'I don't,' said Kit. 'But her mother does. Unless it's her father. I'm meant to help them find her.'

Amy sighed. 'What do you know about Benjamin Flyte?'

'The cokehead?'

'Her boyfriend,' said Amy. 'The one who mysteriously vanished around the same time. Had the two of you ever met?'

'Of course not,' said Kit. 'I was in Japan. You think Mary's disappearance has to do with Ben?'

'No,' said Amy. 'We think it's much more likely Ben Flyte's disappearance has to do with Kate O'Mally. He wasn't a nice man,' she added. 'And we've got a record of the police being called to more than one disturbance. Mary refused to press charges.'

The Chinese student near the stairs having made her final note and snapped shut her biology book, left in a tiny bubble of concentrated thought that prevented her from even noticing there were other people in the room. A girl in a black tunic arrived to clean up, carrying a broom and a washing-up bowl in which to collect the dirty plates and empty cups that still littered most tables. She seemed fairly surprised to see Kit and Amy. 'We're closing.'

Amy nodded. 'I'll just finish my coffee,' she said. 'Then we'll be gone.' She said this with such casual authority that the girl was nodding before Amy had even finished speaking. 'In fact,' said Amy. 'You might want to clean up downstairs first ...'

Kit watched the girl disappear, still carrying her bowl and broom.

'Unregistered, probably an illegal,' said Amy, with a sigh. 'Anyone who sounds as if they can cause trouble gets obeyed.' She shook her head, the first sign Kit had seen that Amy didn't think everything was great in the world of policing.

'Tell me about Ben,' he suggested.

'Okay,' said Amy. 'Some plod went to his flat in Chiswick to ask questions about Mary. The place was empty. I don't mean it was deserted, it was empty, five rooms gutted of everything except a bed and a built-in wardrobe, even then, the mattress was gone.'

'Which suggests what?'

'High level competence,' said Amy. 'The carpets were missing, the walls newly repainted. A local firm, paid in cash and instructed by phone. Worse than useless when questioned.'

'You think Mary organised it?'

Amy raised her eyebrows. 'We considered that,' she admitted. 'Only Ben Flyte was seen the day after Mary's suicide.'

'Where?' demanded Kit.

'Here,' said Amy. 'Well, at the flat you're now using.'

Another five minutes of conversation produced the following. The police had closed the case on Mary O'Mally's suicide. Amy had pulled the files. No, that wasn't entirely legal. Amy lived in North Barnet, near where her ex grew up. Yes, she was recently divorced, divorce being infinitely more common in police work than solved cases. No, this was definitely not an official interview. Yes, she'd be happy to grab something to eat for old time's sake.

On his way out, Kit remembered something from Sophie's argument with Sergeant Samson, the uniformed officer she left standing at the door in Hogarth Mews.

'What's Section 44?'

So abruptly did Amy stop that Kit almost ran into her. 'It's a clause from the old Terrorism Act that did away with the need for reasonable suspicion. Why?'

Kit shrugged. 'Someone mentioned it,' he said.

They ate in a Pizza Express, surrounded by young men in wire glasses and suits, a handful of neatly-dressed women who would have qualified as *office ladies* in Japan and a raucous table of students whom the first two groups would obviously rather weren't there. The only people to interest Kit were a couple who came in late, so obviously trying to be anonymous that it was impossible not to notice them.

'Famous?'

Amy shook her head. 'Just two people having an affair. Soho's full of them.'

'That what happened to you?'

She nodded.

'I'm sorry.'

'So am I,' said Amy. 'But I was the one who climbed into the wrong bed. Also goes with the job, apparently. So Steve told me.'

Steve must be the ex-husband, unless he was the ex-lover.

'You want anything else to drink?'

Amy glanced from the empty Soave bottle to her almost-empty glass. 'I think we've had enough,' she said. 'Well, I have.' A margarita pizza flopped virtually untouched on the table in front of her. 'Should have eaten some more if I was going to drink that much.'

Kit shrugged. 'It's not every day I meet an old friend.'

'Is that what I was?'

Something about Amy's voice demanded an answer, so Kit provided one. 'I think so,' he said. 'But things move on.'

'Which is what we should do,' said Amy. 'Or they're going to shut this place around us.'

Alcohol reduces inhibitions. Other drugs do it better, but alcohol works when these are unavailable. The man who walked up Charlotte Street, turned left opposite the print shop and cut through a narrow alley behind a pub knew all about drugs and inhibitions, having shared his life with both.

The woman who walked beside him also knew, though Kit was coming to realise her knowledge of both was mostly hypothetical. A dozen snatches of conversation came and went, signifying nothing but thinly-shared memories. It was hard to say exactly when lust crept in to Kit's mind, but creep in it did, arriving somewhere between a child's cry and the sight of two men scuffling outside the doorway of a 1980s concrete block.

'I should find you a taxi,' said Kit. It was late, Neku was at home, he'd already missed supper and Kate O'Mally was bound to phone before breakfast.

'Yeah,' said Amy nodding. And somehow her nod invited a kiss, the kiss turned into something more serious and Kit found himself with one hand on her breast and Amy's fingers holding him through his jeans.

'You know,' said Amy. 'We could always go back to Mary's flat.'

'No.' Kit shook his head.

Amy took a step back. 'I thought you'd want ...'

'The kid's there.'

She stared at him, eyes uncertain. 'I didn't know you had a kid.'

I don't. Well, thought Kit, *maybe I do. Only not in the way you think.* 'It's complicated,' he said.

Hotel3 was what you got if a London property company bought the gap between two Georgian town houses on the Eastern edge of Fitzrovia, then in-filled with a thin cage of ferro-concrete clad in smoked glass. The glass was mostly gone, replaced with panels of reconstituted limestone chosen to match the walls on either side, something the hotel's original façade had failed to do.

In fifteen years Hotel3 had gone from *uberchic* to *has been,* and was now halfway back, thus occupying a far more enviable place, as a comfort zone for those who'd originally made it fashionable.

'I'm not so sure that ...'

'This is a good idea?' Amy smiled. 'Of course it's not. You should be at home, I'm meant to be writing a report on you and we're both drunk. But since when did Kit Nouveau worry about things like that?'

Since always.

'Come on,' she said.

Their room was tiny. A chocolate-coloured box, with hessian walls that were either a retro joke or the cutting edge of new design. The bed was a hand-made cherrywood futon, while the kidney-shaped basin came from Syracuse in Italy and was cut from the same horsehair marble as the bath. A sign by the door told them so.

What the sign didn't mention was that their room looked out onto a fire escape, where kitchen staff gathered to smoke dope and swear loudly about the chef, the sous chef and the unbelievably shitty pay on which the rest of them were expected to live. When the litany of complaint began for a second time, Amy shut the window with a bang.

'You want a shower or something?'

Kit shook his head. 'You?'

'Not really,' said Amy, 'unless you think I should ...'

Her hair stank of cigarettes, anchovies and garlic from Pizza Express and grease from not having been washed in a while. Without even realising he'd made the comparison, Yoshi floated ghost-like and squeaky clean into Kit's mind.

'What?' Amy demanded.

'Nothing,' said Kit.

'Good,' she said. 'You might want to kill the lights.'

Amy stayed standing while he undid her blouse, finding each pearl button by touch, before moving to the next. After the blouse he unzipped her skirt and discovered through touch that she wore a thong. Her bra was pale in the half dark, underwired and undid at the front, because some things in life never changed.

Feeling one nipple harden, Kit cupped his fingers under a full breast, until she hooked her hand behind his head and pulled him close. Their kiss was deep and lasted for as long as it took him to slide his hand towards her knickers.

Amy groaned. A second later, she said. 'Don't smile.'

'Why not?' asked Kit.

They kissed again, his fingers trapped between her thighs and her hand still wrapped in his hair. And then, as Amy broke for air, Kit edged aside the silk of her thong and slid two fingers into her.

'Fuck,' said Amy.

He grinned. 'In a minute,' Kit said.

The kitchen staff came back sometime after midnight, to stand on the metal grid outside the closed window, insult each other and bitch about the chef. Although, after thirty seconds of listening to Amy, their bitching was reduced to the occasional whispered comment and stunned silence.

It was a command performance.

Having wrapped both arms around Kit's neck and hooked her ankles over his, Amy clung so tight that every time Kit tried to pull back, he simply lifted her off the mattress. Yelping turned to something more urgent, as Amy grabbed his hips, jammed her nails through Kit's skin and began to ram him into her.

Spitting on his fingers, Kit reached under to spread Amy's buttocks and eased one finger inside. So far as Kit could tell Amy's orgasm was real. Her scream certainly was.

'Shit,' she said, when she got her breath back. 'So that's what closure feels like, I always wondered.' And before Kit had time to think that one through, she rolled him onto his back and dropped her head to his lap.

CHAPTER 43

Saturday 30 June

The dirt tracks and dunes of his original dreams had gone. Where once trucks had been driven by skeletons, a ragged matrix of dimly visible silver threads patterned the bowl of a silver sky.

Kit didn't believe in souls or eternity, but was still blinded by both as they pulled tears from his sleeping eyes. His own soul had been lost in the sands, a voice told him. The last life taken in the cross hairs had been his own, each shot splintering a little of what made him alive, until finally there was nothing left to splinter at all.

He had blown through Middle Morton that summer like a ghost, hungry for forgiveness and angry at the weakness this signified. The voice told him nothing that was new. He'd heard it all before. The voice was his.

Trapped in a half world between waking and sleep where everything is possible only because common sense refuses to object, Kit opened his eyes to a tiny hotel room in Fitzrovia and tried to remember how he got there. And then he remembered.

The same way he usually did.

Amy lay across him, naked and snoring. A crumpled sheet was thrown back to reveal heavy breasts, a soft belly and a butterfly tattoo on her hip. She still stank of unwashed hair and cigarettes, only now sex and sweat had added themselves to the mix.

About the only thing they'd missed out was tying each other to the bedstead, and that was only because Amy shrugged it off when Kit hesitated, offering him something far filthier instead. If Amy had bruises on her thighs, then Kit had scratches across his back and a vicious bite below his neck. Kit was wondering whether to wake Amy, or just start again anyway when a shrill buzz from his phone rewrote his day.

Only three people knew the number – Kate, Pat and Neku. It was 8.00

on a Saturday morning, and even Kate would think twice about calling him that early.

'Me,' he announced, as he rolled out of bed.

All Kit got was silence.

'*Hello?*' he said.

'Hi, is that Kit?'

'Yes,' said Kit, realising he didn't recognise the voice. 'Who's …'

'It's Charlie. Are you still in London?'

'Of course I'm,' said Kit, then hesitated. Fire and ice, ripped sails where stars should be, the naked woman in the bed behind him, all irrelevant. He'd just remembered what the screen read when Charlie's call came up.

Neku.

'Where is she?' he demanded.

'I don't know,' said Charlie. 'But she's not here.'

'You slept over?'

'In your room,' he said, sounding instantly defensive.

'I'm not bothered about that,' said Kit. 'How did you …'

'*What is it?*' Amy demanded. When Kit turned, he found her sitting up in bed behind him, arms folded across her breasts.

'Trouble,' said Kit, returning to his phone. 'Look,' he said. 'Charlie … How did you discover Neku was gone?'

'You had a delivery,' said the boy. 'I went to get Neku because it needed a signature. The roof door was open but her hut was empty. This was about an hour ago.'

'An hour …'

'I thought she'd gone out. You know, to buy milk or something. So I waited to see if she'd come back. And then I noticed her bag on the floor of the little hut and thought I should call you.'

Charlie's voice had grown formal and it took Kit a couple of seconds to realise why. He'd heard Amy. So now he knew Kit had missed supper to spend the night with someone. Since he'd gone to meet a police inspector and not came back it didn't take genius to …

Kit sighed. 'I'm on my way,' he said. Grabbing his trousers, he found his shirt and struggled into both. Yesterday's socks were in a corner and his pants on the floor. He was just kicking his heels into his shoes when he caught sight of Amy's face in the mirror, all hurt and hollow eyes. Someone else bailing out of her life.

When did he get to know this stuff? wondered Kit, turning back. 'You coming with me?'

Amy shook her head, but some of the emptiness left her eyes.

'Look,' said Kit. 'The kid's gone missing. Think you can do something for me?'

'Maybe,' said Amy.

'I need the name of a police officer,' said Kit. 'Large, slightly fat with a moustache and greased back hair … What?' he demanded, seeing her smile.

'Describes half the guys I know.'

'He was in an unmarked car on the M25 with whoever made that call to the DVLA. Pulled me over a few days back. It wasn't the first time. A couple of days before that he came by Hogarth Mews asking about Mary O'Mally.'

'Section 44.'

'Yeah,' said Kit, 'that's the man.'

'I don't suppose you got his registration plate?'

Kit gave her what he could remember, which was the year, the make of car and a guess for the first two letters of what the plate might be.

'You want to know who he is?' Amy asked, jotting the details on a hotel pad by the bed.

'Also what he thinks I've done.'

'Maybe,' said Amy, 'it's what he thinks you're going to do. You know, a lot of people are surprised you came back.' She hesitated on the edge of saying something else. 'Take care,' Amy said finally.

'Say it,' said Kit.

'I just did.'

Peering from her flat, Sophie gave Kit one of the strangest looks he'd ever received and slammed her door without saying a word. A second later, she turned on her sound system and yanked up the volume, until whichever Rai mix she'd put on was loud enough to shake the stairs. Mixing with the enemy was obviously an unforgivable sin.

'Mrs O'Mally just called,' said Charlie, when Kit opened the door to the flat. 'I promised you'd call her back.'

Kit groaned, it was entirely instinctive. 'What did you tell her?'

'Nothing,' said Charlie.

'She want to know who you were?'

The boy looked sheepish. 'She already knew. Pat had called her last night. But I didn't tell her about Neku,' he promised. 'Well, not really. I said Neku was out shopping.'

'At eight-thirty on a Saturday morning? What did Kate O'Mally say?'

'You should call her back ... It's in here,' Charlie added, nodding to the kitchen. 'I signed for the package when I realised Neku had gone.' The teenager was torn between being cross with Kit and being worried, so far worry was winning.

Kit left the box where it was, on the breakfast bar in the tiny kitchen and went to look at Neku's hut and the roof garden. The ivy both sides of the door outside was undisturbed and none of the smaller pots had been knocked over. Neku's sleeping bag had been left open but the zip still worked. When Kit checked the bottom of the bag a passport, an A-Z of London and 1500 dollars fell out.

'Take these,' he said, giving the lot to Charlie.

A cheap laptop in the hut fired up the moment Kit turned it on and proceeded to download pages from *Asahi Shimbun*, news from BBC Asia and half a dozen e-mails, mostly from Micki.

Stand off continues in Roppongi ...Civil matter, says Tokyo's new mayor ...Opposition demand use of riot police... Dear Neku, No Neck and Tetsuo and Micki say hi ...

A lift-up latch had let Kit into the hut and the latch still worked. There was no sign of anyone trying to force the door.

'What are you trying to find?' demanded Charlie.

'It's what I'm hoping not to find.'

Charlie stared at him.

'Blood,' said Kit. 'Torn clothes, broken fingernails, ripped hair, all the signs of a struggle ...' He bent to pick up a bead from the boards. Blue, not threaded but held on a short length of silver wire by a complicated knot that allowed the bead to shift within a mesh cage without allowing it to fall free. It was the first sign that Neku had put up a struggle. At least that was what Kit thought, until Charlie told him otherwise.

'I don't remember Neku wearing a bracelet,' said Kit, considering.

'It broke. She said you gave her the beads back.'

'I thought those came from her wedding gown,' Kit said, and found himself explaining about *cos-play* and how Neku used to dress.

'She hangs them from her phone,' Charlie said. 'Only they fall off. She said so,' he added, when Kit looked doubtful. 'Shouldn't we open the parcel?'

'In a moment,' said Kit.

No one packed a box that big with something so light unless they were making a point. Taking a kitchen knife, Kit sliced away one side of the box, ignoring the tape holding the package shut.

'It might be a trigger,' he said, answering Charlie's unspoken question.

215

Inside the box was crumpled paper, pages from a South London freesheet, and in the middle of these was an envelope. The envelope contained a photograph and Neku's flat key. She was standing against a red brick wall in the picture, dressed in her jeans and black jersey and her eyes were open.

'Good,' said Kit.

'How can you say that?' asked Charlie, then stopped. 'Oh fuck,' he said. 'What were you expecting?'

Neku naked. Neku dead. Neku in chains.

'Nothing specific,' said Kit. 'But I can think of half a dozen shots that would be infinitely worse.'

The message on the back was simple, a telephone number and a time. A handful of words warned Kit what would happen if he went to the police. 'Are you planning to go home?' Kit asked Charlie, who stared at him.

'How can I leave now?'

'Good,' said Kit, 'because I need you here.' Someone had to be around to answer the phone and keep Kate at bay. 'But, are you meant to be somewhere else?'

Charlie shook his head. 'My mob are in Italy. Mum might call the house, but she'll be cool if I'm not around to answer. She'll just call my mobile to find out where I am.'

'And you'll lie?'

'Obviously.'

'Right,' Kit said, stripping off his shirt, choosing a new one and shrugging himself into one of Ben Flyte's old jackets. 'Keep the flat door locked. Don't answer the buzzer and if Kate O'Mally calls back tell her Neku and I have gone shopping.'

'That's what I told her last time.'

'Well, tell her again.'

CHAPTER 44
Saturday 30 June

It was hot, the air was sour and London stank of fried onions, too much aftershave, diesel and dog shit. Saturday morning shoppers filled Oxford Street, mostly tourists and teenage girls, every second one of whom reminded him of Neku.

Men in jeans and black T-shirts crowded a table on Dean Street, talking into their phones, checking their mail and skim-reading the headlines in that day's papers. The sun was out and people were smiling, as the city changed into something more relaxed and less English, which it always did at any pretence of good weather.

Tomorrow would bring thunder storms or smog to send everyone back to their shells, but most Londoners had grown blasé about the meteorological equivalent of mood swings, though that hadn't stopped a newsagent running his own news board for last Wednesday's *Standard* that simply read, *Weather Buggered*.

Kit was walking the streets in search of answers. He was looking for them inside his head, in the eyes of those coming the other way on crowded pavements, even in the mirrored world he could see in shop windows. So far he'd collected enough wrong answers to make him believe it was only a matter of time before he stumbled over one that was right.

According to Charlie, a mathematician at Cambridge once said that if people saw only the one-in-a-hundred answers that proved correct, then the answer obviously looked extraordinary, because the ninety-nine failures went unseen. It was like videoing yourself throwing four dice, and editing the result to retain only the times when every number came up six.

Kit had a feeling the boy meant to be supportive. In the three hours Kit had to waste before he could make the call, he stamped an unconscious pattern of anxiety into crowded streets from Euston Road in the north to Leicester Square and Piccadilly in the south, throwing dice in his head, making deals with God, wondering what he could offer in return for Neku's safety.

George Bernard Shaw and Virginia Woolf had both lived in the same house in Fitzroy Square, just at different times. An Englishman was once briefly king of Corsica. The dining club founded by artist Joshua Reynolds was now Blacks, a drinking den for journalists. Soho got its name from the Duke of Monmouth's habit of calling So-Ho when hunting. In between the dice and deal making Kit learnt back history from heritage plaques on the walls.

Every plan that came to his mind got dismissed, for one reason or another. Yoshi always insisted that ideas, like everything else, followed a path made from tiny steps, that looked obvious only in retrospect.

Every bowl she made was the result of a hundred bowls she chose not to make. It followed that every act, whether the finding of a new proof for a complex mathematical problem or a twist of vision that turned one school of art into another was a result of endless failure. It was the unconscious editing of the process that made the outcome look clever, not the process itself.

It also followed, at least it did to Yoshi, that every problem, no matter how intricate could be broken into smaller pieces. How these pieces fitted provided one with the answer.

Try as Kit might, he couldn't make it work. He had the problem, he had a willingness to shuffle endless permutations of what might be behind Neku's kidnapping, but he couldn't make his pieces fit. Who was he threatening by asking questions about Mary? Nobody, at least nobody Kit could see. So he tried to tie Neku's disappearance to what had happened to his bar in Tokyo, but that made even less sense than before.

Outside the French Protestant Church on Soho Square, while still worrying about what he should do, Kit realised it was after twelve and he was five minutes late making his call.

'It's me,' he said. 'I got your note.'

'Ahh … At last, my friend. You're a difficult man to find. Where are you now?'

'In Soho.' Silence followed. Maybe this was meant to make Kit nervous. If so, it worked. All the same, Kit made himself wait.

'I was sorry to hear about Mary,' said the man. 'She was a nice girl. Still, you seem to have found yourself someone else.'

'What do you want from me?' Kit demanded.

'Ben, come on. Let's not make this harder than it need be.'

'*I'm not* . . .' Common sense kicked in a split second ahead of Kit telling the man he wasn't Ben Flyte. Common sense, and sudden hollowness in his gut. Life had just got very messy indeed.

'You know,' said the voice. 'You and Sergeant Samson have to be stupid to keep jerking me around. Very stupid.'

The accent was foreign. East European, maybe.

'No one's jerking you around,' said Kit. 'Tell me what you want and I'll do it.' He heard muffled voices and an unexpected shriek of feedback, followed by a sharp command. The noise fell silent and inside the silence was music, a vacuum cleaner and the sound of glasses being stacked.

He was being called from a bar or club, somewhere with a sound system and an open mic. Not a huge surprise. In Kit's experience clubs were ideal for laundering money and fronting less legit enterprises. Drugs could be confiscated and recycled, girls hired as dancers and then required to diversify, protection rackets marketed as concern for the local good.

Always the first industry to embrace global opportunities, crime had taken the remains of the Soviet Union and created modern Russia, introduced the Balkans to free market values, plus bullets. Whole governments in Central America owed their existence to its patronage and it worked so seamlessly alongside religion and commerce that most barely noted the reality. Half of Japan still couldn't tell the difference between crime and politics.

'Mr Flyte, I want my consignment back. Otherwise . . .'

Yes, Kit knew about that bit. 'Let me talk to the kid.'

'She's sleeping,' said the man. It was the first thing he'd said Kit didn't believe.

'This consignment,' said Kit. 'What if it's not all there?'

'Then we kill her anyway,' said the voice. 'Call me when it's ready. You have twenty-four hours.'

'*Wait*,' Kit demanded. '*Please* . . .'

'Why?'

'It's going to take longer.' Kit needed time, more time than this man was going to give him. Much more. 'I need two days,' he said. 'What you want is hidden. It will take me two days to recover it.'

'Thirty-six hours,' the man said. 'Maximum.' A click told Kit the conversation was over. After a minute or so he remembered to close his phone.

The *South London Gazette* covered an area of fifty square miles in total, from Lambeth, through Southwark and across to Lewisham. It was a free sheet, delivered weekly to over 150,000 households. Kit knew, he'd talked to its advertising manager, a woman who sounded as if she habitually worked Saturdays and had been slightly displeased that Kit might think otherwise.

The paper used a basic flatplan, she told him, with the facility to swap stories at a local level. The version in which Kit was interested covered an area of 12,000 households on the Lambeth/Southwark borders. And yes, she'd be happy to e-mail him a distribution map.

Focus, Kit told himself. *Work out what you're going to do.*

He might actually have intended to return to the Queen's Head, an old pub in the shadow of the Telecom Tower, or it might have been an accident, his feet following a path so faded he only remembered the local landmarks when he saw them. Mary O'Mally had taken him here. It had been the O'Mally's local before Kate moved the family out of London.

At the till two members of staff were discussing a third. 'Plus,' said the man, 'he fucks anything that moves.'

'And you don't?'

'Well, nothing that goes *baa, moo* or *mummy.*'

The woman laughed. 'When I was a kid in Sydney,' she said. 'We fucked but that was just pretending to be grown up. It wasn't like we really liked them or anything.'

Speak for yourself, thought Kit,

Cutting between tourists, he chose a table that let him sit with his back to the wall, then took a long look around the pub. No one was smoking. Half of the clientele were drinking diet Coke or wine. The locals he remembered inhabiting the place had been reduced to a hard-core cluster of old men near the bar.

London wasn't a city Kit recognised any more.

Flipping open Neku's laptop, Kit logged into his mail. Anti-ageing drugs, Chinese porn, a note from the consigliere of a Brazilian crime family offering unspecified riches in return for borrowing Kit's bank account.

The note from Hiroshi Sato was brief.

A single link to an English-language news story on *Tokyo Today*. No Neck, Micki, Tetsuo and half a dozen others had been arrested and unexpectedly released. A teenager had been killed in a battle to retake the site, but since he was *bozozoku* no one was making much of a fuss.

A second note, from Micki, told the same tale in rather more breathless prose. What should Tommy and his friends do if things got really ugly? she wanted to know.

Well, No Neck wanted to know, really.

'Nothing.' His first reply seemed too abrupt, so Kit sipped his brandy and thought about it. What should No Neck do? More to the point, what could No Neck do? Other than marry Micki, find himself a proper job and walk away from his friendship with Kit ...

'There was an *uyoku* van,' Kit wrote finally. 'Gold sides, with the imperial mon picked out in black. See what Micki can find out about it.' Still too bald, so Kit added. 'And take care of yourself.'

The last e-mail Kit opened contained a map showing a tight jumble of streets in the shadow of a new flyover. Layers of history in a muddle of names, as old generals and battles – Napier and Mafeking – intersected with Nelson Mandela Drive. Somewhere in that jumble of streets was the bar where Neku was being held. All Kit had to do was find it.

He was aware just how absurd that sounded.

Clubs and pubs needed to be licensed. A place with live music probably needed a different type of licence again. Someone would have that list. It's all about small steps, Kit reminded himself.

Calling the police station where Amy worked, Kit hit his next problem, no one had heard of her. 'You say she claimed to work here?' The inspector on the other end was more interested in this than anything else Kit had to say.

'Yes,' said Kit.

'And you're definitely not a journalist?' The inspector was tapping away at a keyboard, so he had to be checking on Amy, unless he was simply getting on with his own work.

'I'm a friend.'

'Right,' said the man. 'Give me a number and I'll call you back.' Five minutes stretched into ten and then into twenty, when this became half an hour, Kit stopped bothering to watch the time and began watching people instead.

A Saturday crowd came and went, deals were done, four girls went to the loos together and came out looking much happier.

Money or drugs seemed the obvious answer to *what* Kit was expected to produce. A bar in South London was the *where*. In Japan, kidnapping was the preserve of hard-core criminals. Over here, Kit wasn't sure, maybe amateurs got in on the act as well. He needed someone who would know.

When his mobile buzzed he got her.

'You've been looking for me?' It was Amy, her voice guarded enough to give Kit pause.

'Look,' said Kit, 'I need some help.'

'Yes,' Amy said. 'I enjoyed supper too.'

I enjoyed?

In the background behind Amy a printer was clattering and half a dozen men discussed flak jackets, raising their voices to be heard above the noise. It sounded like any office, apart from the number of times *Guv*, *Ma'am* and *Boss* got dropped into the conversation. A conversation that stumbled when Amy said, 'No, there's nothing I need to tell you ...'

Someone sniggered. 'Hey,' he said. 'We've got ourselves a domestic.'

'Shut the fuck up,' snapped Amy, remembering to add, 'Sir.' Unless that was meant to be part of the insult.

Oh shit, indeed.

'I'm at work,' said Amy. 'Call me later.'

'This can't wait,' Kit told her. 'I need to know about Ben Flyte. Everything you've got.'

'Why?'

'Because whoever's taken Neku thinks that's who I am.'

'Unlikely,' said Amy. 'Ben Flyte's dead.'

'He's what?'

'Murdered,' she said. 'Six months ago. We just haven't released the news. If I call you back it will be in five minutes. Go somewhere private.'

A courtyard behind the Queen's Head was stacked with metal barrels and mixer crates full of empty bottles. Its walls were high enough to muffle traffic from the street beyond. No one stopped Kit when he walked through the kitchens and took up position against the wall.

'Kit,' he announced, answering his phone on the first ring.

CHAPTER 45
nawa-no-ukiyo

'I'm sorry,' said Luc.

'For what?' Lady Neku had never met anyone like the boy for apologising. He'd been sorry about tripping on the stairs, although she got in his way, rather than the other way round. He regretted taking up her time and not wanting to practise with Nico, Petro and Antonio in the duelling room. Now he was apologising again. Hadn't anyone ever told him never apologise and never explain?

'What am I sorry for?' said Luc. 'I'm sorry for everything.'

Lady Neku laughed. 'You can't be,' she said. 'No apology would be long enough.' She watched him think that through.

'You're not what I expected,' Luc said finally.

'Really ... What did you expect?'

Oh God, thought Lady Neku. Now she'd embarrassed him. They were loitering in a corridor that led from the duelling room to the archives, which was an old name for an area now mostly given over to rubbish.

'Antiques,' her mother called them. 'Heirlooms.'

Rubbish all the same.

'I don't know,' said Luc. 'Someone ...'

'Weirder?'

He grinned at that. 'How long do you think they'll be busy?' Luc asked, glancing at the entrance to another corridor. One that led to the throne room, where Lord d'Alambert and Lady Neku's mother were locked in discussion. It amused Lady Neku that Luc had such trouble orientating himself in her habitat. A lifetime of exploring corridors and levels had imprinted a mental map into her subconscious. Unless, of course, it had been imprinted earlier and she'd be born with the thing.

'Hours, I guess,' said Lady Neku. 'Maybe days if my mother is feeling difficult. It depends how much negotiating they have left to do.'

Luc looked shocked. 'What's to negotiate?' he asked. 'The major domos agreed everything in advance.'

Lady Neku was about to say this was the first she'd heard of it, only she'd been saying this a lot recently and it worried her to discover Luc knew things she didn't, so she swallowed her comment.

'Come on,' she said instead, 'I want to show you something.'

'What?' demanded Luc. He was still asking when Lady Neku reached the drop zone. A dozen opalescent pods sat gathering dust, the thirteenth was already releasing its door.

'Get in,' Lady Neku said.

'You're joking ...'

'Why would I do that?'

As Lady Neku watched, the door sprang open and its inner membrane began to nictate. The pods liked to do these things for themselves, so Lady Neku made herself wait. Once door and membrane were open, Lady Neku reached for a grab bar and hauled herself inside, sitting patiently while the pod grew straps.

'Yeuch,' said Luc, watching sticky tendrils tie themselves tight around Lady Neku's upper arms and shoulders.

'It brushes off,' she promised. 'Come on, climb in.'

Luc did, reluctantly, only realising too late that he should have entered from the other side; after all, that was where the pod had grown a door for him.

'It's okay,' said Lady Neku, as Luc began to climb down. 'Just clamber over me ... And hold tight,' she added.

Luc was about to say something when the door membranes finished regrouping, both doors sealed and the floor fell away, turning the pod through a hundred and eighty degrees, before releasing it towards the planet below; which had suddenly become the planet above.

'Warned you,' Lady Neku said.

Slow entry speeds were essential. Even so, the friction on the falling pod was sufficient to ionise its surface and create a luminous bubble that trailed colours behind them like a broken rainbow.

'Is this safe?' said Luc, looking at dials which had begun to spin wildly.

Such a child. Did he really think pods came with dials on the original spec? Lady Neku considered admitting the dials had been her idea and she'd demanded needles that spun, but decided not to bother.

'Well,' she said. 'This is my tenth drop and I'm still alive.'

Luc didn't seem to find this comforting.

After a while, Lady Neku flicked out the wings and had the pod roll through another hundred and eighty degrees, changing her descent to a wide spiral. The forces on her body felt more natural that way.

Cracks in the earth became ruined towns and those towns expanded to reveal districts and finally roads and even houses. Only the very largest buildings could be seen from this height, but half of one town was obviously buried by sand and an earthquake had ripped another across its edge like badly-torn paper.

'Welcome to Katchatka Segment,' said Lady Neku. 'Glory of Planet Earth.' Leaning forwards, she brushed one finger across the window and sat back as a living town spread itself across glass.

'Shit,' said Luc. 'What's that?'

'History,' Lady Neku said, removing the town with another brush of her finger. 'What used to be. How old are you really?' she asked.

'Sixteen,' said Luc, sounding offended. 'You know that.'

'And me?' She was going to have to do something about his habit of changing colour. Luc couldn't keep turning pink at every question, or her brothers would never leave him alone.

'Fifteen,' she told him. 'I'm fifteen.' Lady Neku paused. 'Do you believe that?'

Luc nodded. 'What's not to believe?'

'What if I'm a copy,' said Lady Neku. 'Then how old am I?'

Luc looked at her.

'Okay,' said Lady Neku. 'Think about it ... Fifteen, plus the age of my mother when the copy was made. Right?'

The boy shrugged.

'But what if my mother was a copy, then how does it work? My age, plus her age when I was copied, plus the age of her mother when she was copied? That would make me ...' Lady Neku began shuffling numbers in her head, only to abandon her sum when the pod caught the outer edge of a massive dust cloud.

'Turbulence,' she said. 'You might feel sick.'

'I already do.'

As she grinned, Lady Neku watched Luc make himself release his grip on the chair; he minded her noticing his knuckles had gone white.

'Don't worry,' said Lady Neku.

'I'm not ...' Luc caught himself. 'Of course I'm worried,' he said. 'We're falling out the sky in a pod the size of a large table and we don't seem to have an engine.' He looked at her. 'We do have a Casimir coil, don't we?'

'No,' said Lady Neku, shaking her head. She'd have shaken it whatever the answer, but for once the truth was on her side. The pods were strictly one use only and that was down.

'Oh fuck ...' Luc's voice was small.

Come on, Lady Neku wanted to say. *How can you miss it?* Surely Luc had spotted Schloss Omga by now. It was that enormous castle crawling up the side of a mountain.

'Luc,' she said, and when Luc stayed silent Lady Neku leant over to touch his shoulder. It was rigid.

'Leave me alone.'

'Come on,' said Lady Neku. 'You can tell me what's really wrong.'

Faded blue eyes turned towards her. A sky magnified by sadness and something else, something darker. 'I'm afraid.'

'Why?' asked Lady Neku, meaning, *why now, why here?* God, she knew what she meant.

'Because I was born afraid,' said Luc. 'And I didn't think it would happen like this.'

'What?'

'Death ...' Luc shrugged. 'She told me you'd try to kill me.' For someone talking about his own fate the boy seemed almost resigned. Afraid, but resigned, there was probably a term for it.

'Who did?' Lady Neku demanded.

'My mother, that's why she refused to come. She doesn't trust your family.' Luc shrugged. 'She told my father it was all a trick.' His broken smile was heartbreaking, and the really weird thing was that Luc obviously had no idea how heartbreaking. Nico would have been milking it his entire life.

'We're not going to die,' said Lady Neku. 'And I'm certainly not here to kill you.'

'But we're out of control.' He gestured at the altimeter's spinning needles. 'You said it yourself, we've got no power unit.'

'*Luc ...!*'

He wasn't listening.

'It must be odd,' he said, a moment later. 'You know, being able to back up and be more than one person. I find it tough enough just being myself.'

'I'm just me.'

'Yes,' said Luc. 'But there's another you back at High Strange. How did you agree which one should die?'

'*We're not going to die,*' shouted Lady Neku.

'Of course we are. You can't just fall out of the sky. Someone lied to you,' he said. 'About not crashing.'

'Luc,' said Lady Neku, grabbing the boy's hand. 'There's only one of me and we're not going to crash.' When Luc stayed silent, she gripped his fingers so hard he tried to pull them away. 'I've made this drop ten times,' she said fiercely 'It's going to be fine. The castle will catch us.'

'What castle?'

'That one,' she said, pointing down.

It took seventeen minutes to fall from High Strange to earth. The pods had enough strength to survive the howling winds that turned Katchatka Segment's lower atmosphere into a danger zone; after that it was simply a matter of sitting out the fall.

Each of the families had owned a land base and an overworld back in the early days. These talked to each other, even when the families themselves refused to communicate. Lady Neku had been so surprised by this she made Schloss Omga provide proof. A history lesson followed. The land bases talked to each other and to individual nodes on the filter, which was what Schloss Omga called the overworld mesh of *nawa-no-ukiyo*.

The glitch was not that the bases and nodes could talk to each other, it was that Lady Neku could talk direct to them, without needing to go through a major domo interface.

'Neku ...'

'What?' she said, dragging her thoughts back to the pod.

'We're slowing.'

'Of course we are.' Tapping the window Lady Neku woke it up again. 'Look,' she said. 'We've arrived.'

Spread out below was a massive spiral that twisted to a blunt point, while a leathery fringe around its base locked the castle to rock. A thousand people had lived in its upper levels. Eight members of the Katchatka family, a hundred military modifies and eight-hundred and ninety-two fugees who provided service in return for shelter.

'Wait,' Lady Neku instructed. 'And watch.'

So Luc stared intently at the shell below him. 'That's a *Viviparous malleatus*,' he said finally.

'A what?'

'A trapdoor snail. We've got them in our koi pond.' He glanced from Schloss Omga to the mountains on both sides and then at the altimeter dials in front of him, which had slowed to a lazy twirl. 'It's vast.'

Lady Neku smiled. 'Yes,' she said. 'It is.' Looking across at Luc, she wondered if the boy knew he was still clutching her hand.

CHAPTER 46
Saturday 30 June

Kit counted off the time by the bells from St Dominic's, a new church on the corner of Conde Street, in what had once been a carpet warehouse. After a single peal for quarter past two and a slightly longer peal for half past, the landlord of the Queen's Head finally arrived to see what the stranger was doing at the back of his pub.

Since the after-lunch staff had been stepping out for cigarette breaks on a regular basis and most had scowled at the sight of a stranger this was not unexpected.

'Police business,' said Kit, barely bothering to take his eyes from a narrow passage back to the road. He must have sounded convincing because the landlord turned back, and whatever was said when he got inside that was the end of the cigarette breaks.

Motorbikes, rickshaws, taxis and more white vans than Kit could count rolled down the road. The third time he saw the same shiny black Volvo, Kit left his hiding place and waited for its return at a pavement table on Conde Street.

'Where have you been?'

'Watching,' said Kit, although what he really wanted to say was, *Just who the fuck is this?*

'Afternoon.' Flipping up her arm, an old woman angled it backwards to shake, while simultaneously pulling away from the curb.

Amy shut her eyes.

The driver's grip was strong, though liver spots splattered her wrist like dung. Greying hair had been cut tight to her neck, and she wore heavy dark glasses to shade her eyes. 'Brigadier Miles,' said the woman, introducing herself. 'I gather someone thinks you're Ben Flyte?'

Kit nodded, catching her gaze in driving mirror.

'You're certain about that?'

'Yes,' said Kit, 'I'm certain.'

'Interesting,' said the Brigadier, turning her attention back to the road. Hanging a quick left, the woman filtered right at the lights and checked her mirror; whatever she saw satisfied her.

'Got a lighter?' she asked Kit.

He shook his head.

'Use this one,' she said, passing him something cheap and disposable, then followed it with a packet of Lucky Strike. 'I need a cigarette,' she added, when he just looked at her.

By the time the Volvo had put Piccadilly behind them and the city's open spaces had switched from Green Park on the left to Hyde Park on the right, the car was filled with smoke and Kit had worked out that the Suzuki up ahead and the Merc two vehicles behind were part of an escort.

As the Suzuki peeled off, to be replaced almost instantly by a different bike and the Merc fell back a place to allow another car in, before peeling off itself, he realised that at least four vehicles were shadowing this one and that a traffic helicopter overhead seemed to paying close interest in their route.

'Where are we going?' he asked.

'To have a quiet talk,' said Brigadier Miles, and left Kit wondering why Amy refused to meet his eye.

'Used to be bigger,' the old woman announced, a while later.

'What did?'

'Those.' She pointed at plastic cows on a distant roof. 'Used to be life size, only they kept causing crashes and had to be changed. Pity really.' Sliding down a side road, she took a roundabout rather too fast and roared back the way she'd come, leaving the cows a vanishing memory on the far side of a dual carriageway. 'It's about half an hour from here,' she said.

'What is?'

'Boxbridge ...'

A Lutyens copy of a small Elizabethan manor, Boxbridge House was built from red brick that had weathered to a shade of pink. Ivy softened its stark façade and its gravel had been racked to zen-garden smoothness in front of the main door. It was the house Seven Chimneys would love to be, and maybe would become if Kate O'Mally's home survived long enough to avoid developers and find its own soul.

But before Kit, the old woman or Amy could reach Boxbridge they had to clear the gate house. Also designed by Edwin Lutyens, this featured a pantiled roof and a central arch under which visitors must pass. The gun slit cut into the arch was definitely not in Lutyens' original plan and nor was the steel hut hidden beneath camouflage netting a hundred paces beyond.

Dipping his head a soldier with a sub-machine gun took a good look inside the Volvo, before nodding. 'Madam,' he said.

Brigadier Miles nodded back.

Two more soldiers waited at the front door and both carried H&K assault weapons and wore body armour. Kit was beginning to understand why flak jackets had been such a topic of conversation.

'Welcome to HQ Organised and Serious,' the Brigadier said.

The entrance hall was panelled in oak and its floor was marble, not large slabs but tiny black and white tiles set into patterns that looked Greek. A corridor led off the hall and it was down this that Brigadier Miles led Kit, with Amy following behind.

'My office,' the Brigadier said.

A small library from the look of it. Cloth-bound books ringed all four walls in faded shades of red and blue. A dark and over-varnished *Stag at Bay* above the marble fire place shed gilt like dandruff onto a mantelpiece below. A desk in the corner was buried under paperwork and old coffee cups. It looked too structured in its chaos to be entirely real.

'Please take a seat.'

Brigadier Miles indicated a wooden chair, so Kit chose a battered leather one instead, which was a mistake because it immediately put Kit lower than either of the others.

The old woman sighed.

'We have a problem,' she said. 'One that you can help us solve.' Glancing towards a collection of files, Brigadier Miles considered something and then pulled a packet of cigarettes from her jacket pocket, lighting one with her plastic lighter. 'The police photographs are ugly,' she said, exhaling smoke at a nicotine-yellow ceiling. 'So we'll spare you those ...'

Amy nodded.

'Let's start at the top,' said the Brigadier. 'Six months ago a corpse was found beside the M25. The body was male, aged somewhere between thirty and forty and had been badly mutilated. Its fingers were missing, someone had cut away the face and broken the lower jaw to make it easier to extract teeth. Scotland Yard tried for a DNA match but came up blank.'

'Ben Flyte,' said Kit.

'We think so. Actually,' said the Brigadier. 'We know, because seven weeks ago Scotland Yard finally asked a member of Flyte's family for DNA to help make a match. Our problem, at this end, is we thought he'd been killed by the man who telephoned you.'

Kit looked up. 'You know who that is?'

'Oh yes,' said the Brigadier. 'We know. And the fact he thinks Mr Flyte is still alive is extremely convenient. Now, Ms Avenden tells me this child is being held someone in South London, in a club … at least, so you believe. Do you want to tell me how you reached that conclusion?'

Kit scowled at Amy.

'What did you expect me to do?' she said.

Raising her eyebrows, the Brigadier asked, 'Is there anything about you two I should know?' It probably didn't help that Kit and Amy shook their heads at exactly the same time.

'Neku's photograph was packed in pages from last week's *South London Gazette*,' said Kit. 'The Lambeth edition. The box in which it came originally contained Walkers Crisps, 144 packets. When I took the call I could hear music and the sound of crates being shifted …'

'He's good,' said the Brigadier.

Amy's smile was sour. 'Yes, so I said.'

'We run a program,' said Brigadier Miles. 'It identifies someone who knows someone who knows someone we need to contact. It works by weighting age, location, schooling and background and then assigning a score. Amy came out on top. So we borrowed her …'

Kit blinked. 'From the police?'

Amy bit her lip. 'From Ceausescu Towers. I'm a recruiter on the university milk run. Come and work for Mi6, it's not dangerous and the perks are great. Olympic size swimming pool, own gym, discount shopping mall. Join us and you'll never need to leave the office again.'

She didn't sound too impressed by her job.

'Why not just call me yourself?' asked Kit, looking at the Brigadier, who ground out her cigarette and immediately lit another. Her smile made Amy's look positively sweet.

'You're a deserter,' she said. 'A known link to the Yakusa. You returned to Britain alongside last season's version of the Krays. A woman the *Sun* has managed to turn into the UK's most unlikely cultural icon. Just imagine your reaction if we'd called by Hogarth Mews suggesting a chat.'

'So you sent Sergeant Samson instead?'

'We'll get to him in a minute. But first, would you like some tea or coffee?'

'No,' said Kit, 'I'd like to know what you're doing about Neku.'

'Nothing,' said the Brigadier.

Kit stared at her.

'We know you friend is still alive,' said Brigadier Miles. 'And I've borrowed a pair of SBS to watch the club. If things look risky I'll have them extract her.'

'What are their chances of getting Neku out alive?'

In the background, Amy winced.

'They're the best,' the Brigadier said. 'Statistically, the SBS extract more hostages with fewer casualties than any other European force. You really want that child in danger I'll have them withdraw.'

He'd offended her.

Fuck it. Kit sat back in his chair. *Walk with a man a hundred paces and he'll tell you at least seven lies.* 'You know who Neku is, of course?' His voice was sharp enough to made both Brigadier Miles and Amy glance up.

'Who?' demanded Amy.

'Kate O'Mally's granddaughter.'

The Brigadier ground her cigarette against the bottom of a glass ashtray, until it was almost flat. 'For real?'

'Oh yes,' said Kit. 'I can just see it,' he said, 'if it all goes wrong. Kate O'Mally on the news, raging about her injured granddaughter and talking about how today's authorities aren't up to the job.'

Amy looked slightly sick. 'That's why Mrs O'Mally was in Tokyo?'

'Of course,' said Kit, meeting her gaze. 'She wanted to meet Neku.' It was all he could do not to cross his fingers behind his back.

'But she's ...' Amy was about to say *Japanese*. Only she put one hand to her mouth instead. 'Oh, fuck,' said Amy. 'We all got it wrong, didn't we? It wasn't you at all. Neku is Josh's kid.'

Kit smiled. He'd been dealt the weakest hand of cards possible, only to discover what actually counted was the pattern on the back.

CHAPTER 47
Saturday 30 June

Lighting a cigarette, Brigadier Miles threw her dead lighter and now-empty packet into a metal bin, ignoring the noise this made. A cup of Earl Grey tea sat on a desk in front of her, beside two biscuits so dry they might as well be made from cardboard. She seemed to be waiting for something.

After a while Kit realised it was his full attention.

The basic rule seemed to be that the Brigadier ran the operation and Kit did what he was told. Since this involved being fitted with a body mic and wheeling sixty kilos of recently-confiscated heroin into a lap dancing club owned by a murderous gangster he was less than happy with the Brigadier's take on this.

'It's not going to happen,' Kit said.

'Why not?' The old woman sounded genuinely surprised.

'Because I won't do it.'

Beyond the window a soldier mowed grass and beyond that a row of young oaks screened a high mesh fence, with rolls of razor wire along its top. A small Victorian folly behind the wire had been turned into a guard tower. Kit doubted very much if Boxbridge appeared on any of the official lists of government property or supported itself from a declared budget.

'You don't have much choice,' said Amy. 'Given that Brigadier Miles is all that stands between you and arrest for desertion. The MOD aren't wild about people who run away.'

'I didn't run,' said Kit. 'And they'll be even less happy when I've talked to the press.'

'No.' Brigadier Miles shook her head. 'Don't do that. The court will just double your sentence. I've seen it happen,' she added. 'Help me and we'll arrange an honourable discharge.'

'And if I refuse?'

'I talked to Whitehall this morning,' said the Brigadier. 'Desertion in war is a capital offence.'

Kit snorted. 'That wasn't a war,' he said. 'It was three weeks of televised bullshit, followed by as many years of avoidable chaos. More of us got killed by our own side or accident than by Iraqis. The real casualties came after the conflict supposedly ended.'

The Brigadier looked surprised. 'I didn't have you pegged as a pacifist.'

'I'm not,' said Kit. 'I just like my wars to have two sides and an adequate reason.' He was perched at the edge of his chair, fingers twisted so tight it felt like he might snap his own bones. *Sit back*, Kit told himself, but his body refused the command.

'Madam,' said Amy, 'do you think this is a good idea?'

'No,' she said. 'But he's the only chance we've got and, short of blowing down the door, Kit's our best way into the club. But if you want your doubts made formal, I'll have them noted.'

Amy shook her head.

'We need the owner to admit he's dealing drugs,' said Brigadier Miles, stubbing out her cigarette. 'Without that we're helpless. You have to get him on tape.'

'Why not just bug the place?' asked Kit.

'It's swept, the phone lines tested for central station taps. He's got fooler loops on every window and wall. Even if he didn't, the bloody music is so loud we'd have trouble isolating speech to a standard acceptable in courts.' Brigadier Miles sounded more irritated than angry. 'It's got to be taped *in situ*.'

'All I want,' said Kit, 'is Neku out of there.'

'You don't care about someone dealing heroin?'

Kit shook his head.

'We're still your best bet,' said Amy. 'The Brigadier knows this man. He's never left a witness alive in his life. That's why he's still jetting round Europe and she's here talking to you.'

Shutting his eyes, Kit tried to work things through. Four dice, a hundred throws, surely he had to hit four sixes soon?

What should he do?

'If you don't know,' said the Brigadier. 'I can't tell you.'

So Kit told her about his history of wrong calls. He really didn't mean to, it just happened. He started with the difference between an M24 weapons system and the earlier M21; both being bolt action, five shots in the magazine and one in the chamber.

The M24 came with a choice of sights, a night scope and the one he'd been issued, the basic 10x42 Leupold M3A, with adjustment dials for elevation, focus and wind. Kit's voice was so matter of fact he could have been discussing the man rolling the lawns outside.

'There are only a handful of things I'm good at,' said Kit. 'And running a bar and hitting targets top the list. I can take out a man's brainstem at five hundred paces, while he's still scratching his balls. Take out a child's too ...'

'A child?'

Kit nodded, then described his tenth kill. Exactly halfway down his second clip, ten hits in three days and not a shot wasted. A burning truck, with a boy at the wheel and the clown-faced corpse of a small girl beside him. Clown-faced because fire does that, it pulls back the face into a rictus grin.

He talked about the flames, the acrid smoke that hugged itself to a dip in the dunes and closed his throat. How a two-man patrol had found him blackened and voiceless, trying to pull corpses from the truck. It wasn't their fault they thought he was Iraqi.

'Were they British?' Amy asked.

Kit shook his head.

'American?' The Brigadier sounded worried.

'Not that either,' said Kit. 'I don't know what they were ...' He shrugged. 'Azeri, maybe; perhaps Georgian.' Kit felt ashamed, as if he should have known the nationality of the soldiers he killed.

Brigadier Miles gave a sigh. 'Could have been worse,' she said. 'Much worse. I wouldn't be surprised if they were Iraqi. In fact, I'm sure they were ... Almost captured by Iraqis,' said the old woman, trying the words aloud. 'Sent home, cracked up, went missing. Sounds convincing to me.'

Outside the window the rolling of the lawn had finally finished. Someone had brought fresh tea and biscuits and left them on the Brigadier's desk. All of the cups had been used and one sat empty next to Kit's hand, so he guessed he must have drunk it.

'We'll get Neku back for you,' promised Amy.

'All you have to do' said Brigadier Miles, 'is trust us.'

The first photograph showed a thin man in his early thirties. Curling black hair fell over the high collar of a leather coat that was cut like the jacket of a suit. He looked vaguely Arab, maybe southern European. 'This,' said Amy, 'is Armand de Valois.'

'French?'

'Originally Russian,' the Brigadier said. 'Well ... half Russian. His father was Sergei Akhyrov, a colonel in the Red Army. His mother came from Chechnya. She was the one who named him Armed.'

'I thought ...'

'He changed it,' the Brigadier said. 'And that wasn't all.' Fanning out three photographs, she pushed them across the desk. 'This is Armand in Bucharest, in Berlin and in Paris.'

It was easy to see the progression, because it involved more than just clothes or the cost of Armand's haircut, though these changed as well. His eyes got less wild, his smile more confident. Somewhere between Berlin and Paris he had rhinoplasty and his lips became fuller. The change was subtle, but it was definitely there.

'American surgeon,' said Brigadier Miles.

'De Valois flew to the US?'

'Too risky. The surgeon came to him. Armand switched nationalities around this time. He's currently using a passport issued in Rome and we've checked, it's genuine.'

'Really?' asked Amy.

'His notario had the right proofs. A Parisian birth certificate, marriage papers from Milan showing his mother was French and his father Sicilian. Also evidence of land holdings near Palermo, once owned by a great grandfather. It's easy enough, particularly in Italy.'

'I know drug smuggling was big business,' Kit said, 'but this is still ...' He swallowed the rest of that sentence because he'd just realised the obvious. 'This isn't about drugs, is it?'

The Lutyens mansion, with its rolls of discreetly-coloured razor wire, all those soldiers wandering around in flak jackets. He'd been right about the size of the budget and wrong about where it was aimed. What commanded this kind of money? What was the world's biggest growth industry on both sides of the fence ...

'He's a terrorist,' Kit said.

Amy looked up from a photograph.

'This isn't about heroin,' said Kit, 'At least, not directly.' Reaching for the folder, he fanned its contents across the untidy desk. At least fifty pap shots of Armand de Valois in a dozen different countries. Hair style and clothes changed, but the man and the woman at his side remained the same. In some de Valois smoked and in others he held a brandy glass. In one, the woman was absent and de Valois wore an astrakhan hat and smoked a small cigar through a very long ivory holder. The office block behind him was ugly, half-derelict and brutal enough to speak of decades of Soviet planning.

'Groznyy,' said Brigadier Miles, lighting up a cigarette of her own. 'Before Russia flattened it for the second time. He was buying plastic explosives.'

'Why don't you just arrest him?'

'We lack sufficient proof.'

'Then kill him.'

'It's been tried,' said the Brigadier. 'About eight months ago. On a section of the B1 between Tegel and Tempelhof. Airports in Berlin,' she added, seeing Kit's face. 'A motorcyclist and pillion, both Colombian. They killed his driver, his bodyguard and his son. Armand let it be known that he was also dead.'

'Which was when Ben Flyte's troubles began,' Amy said. 'Because he failed to pay for a consignment of heroin, thinking Armand wouldn't be around to collect the debt.'

'Only Armand was alive,' said Brigadier Miles. 'Busily arranging the death of an entire Colombian drug family, right down to the family pets. Those are photographs you definitely don't want to see.'

'Why not just do the job yourselves?'

'That's been suggested,' said the Brigadier. 'Unfortunately the Attorney General takes the view that as it's been suggested we can't do it. Apparently, had we just done it that would be entirely different.'

'Then subcontract the job to someone else.'

'Don't think we haven't considered it,' she said. 'Unfortunately life is not that simple. Moscow have decided Mr de Valois might make a good next president for Chechnya, and Russia is our friend.'

'And the Americans?'

'Reserving judgement,' said Brigadier Miles, sounding tired. 'As are the French. Which still leaves us with today's problem.'

'Why?' asked Kit, looking at women opposite. One reminded him, in some weird way, of an older, better-dressed version of Kate O'Mally. The other had trouble meeting his eyes.

Amy scowled. 'What do you mean, *why*?'

'Why would a man like de Valois waste time with this? I mean, what's one missing consignment of drugs to a future president?'

'Ah,' said the Brigadier. She glanced at Amy, as if about to say something and then changed her mind. What she wanted to say, Kit reckoned, was this friend of yours is less stupid than I thought.

'You noticed the woman?' asked Brigadier Miles.

Kit nodded.

'Ivana de Valois. Ambitious, ruthless and highly intelligent. Currently sulking in Bucharest. Armand and his wife share the first two of those qualities, but not the third.'

'I'm sorry?' Kit said.

'She's the brains,' said the Brigadier. 'Ivana is currently waiting for Armand to realise that.'

'Which is why she's in Bucharest?'

'Plus the kid's death caused a rift,' said Amy, shuffling papers until she found the sheet she wanted. 'Mr de Valois demanded the boy accompany him to Berlin. Ivana warned her husband it was dangerous.'

'It's been five months since they talked.' Sitting back, the Brigadier lit another cigarette and stared at the ceiling. When she glanced down again, Brigadier Miles was smiling. 'Every fuck-up he makes is worse than the previous one. Although few come close to flying into London to collect on a debt Ivana would subcontract to a local *vor v zakonye* without even bothering to think about it.'

'What are the drugs worth?' asked Kit.

'About a hundred thousand Kalashnikovs, three ex-Soviet tanks or more plastic explosive than you could load into a long-wheel-base Cherokee Jeep.'

'A million five street value,' said Amy.

'Forget street value,' the Brigadier said. 'You might as well multiply it by three and say that's the amount of crime you'd need to commit to get that level of profit ... It's an old argument,' she added, seeing Kit's expression. 'I use wholesale only and that's about fourteen thousand per kilo.'

'So little?'

The Brigadier's grin was sour. 'The weather's good and our friends in Kandahar grow little else.'

'And bodyguards,' said Kit. 'How many has de Valois got?'

Amy laughed. 'None,' she said. 'Immigration arrested two this morning on their way to work. The third was arrested when Mr de Valois sent him to find out what happened to the first two. He's reduced to using locals.'

CHAPTER 48
Sunday 1 July

Kit was given a suite to himself. It was beautiful, with high ceilings and long windows that looked out over immaculately-cut and rolled lawns. The kind of lawns where ghosts probably still played croquet.

The bed was high and rickety and creaked when he rolled over in his sleep. Or what would have passed for sleep, had Kit been able to sink deeper behind his eyes. For the first time he could remember, he spent a night beneath sheets, blankets and an old-fashioned eiderdown.

Peacocks woke him, which was when Kit realised he'd slept after all. Shrill and awkward and slightly insane, their cry cut through an open window and welcomed Kit to another Sunday, one unlike any other.

A bathroom to one side offered a tub deep enough to take a family and taps that looked original. A mirror above the basin was foxed and speckled so badly that shaving was reduced to a chase to find his own reflection.

He pissed, shaved, bathed and dressed.

Kit was tying his shoes when a soldier came to unlock his door.

The morning was spent going over the Brigadier's plans; until the church bells struck thirteen, and Kit deducted one from the total to reach the real time. Lunch was sandwiches in the garden. Kit was given an hour or so to read the Sunday papers, while Amy and Brigadier Miles talked intently, then it was back to the Volvo and Amy refusing to meet Kit's eye.

The call came when Kit was between Boxbridge and the outskirts of London. He was sat in the back, next to Amy, who cradled a silver suitcase stuffed with something unspecified. Amy and Kit had been doing their best not to bang hips every time the Volvo changed lanes or jinked from one road onto another.

'Does she always drive like this?'

Amy said nothing and neither did the Brigadier, although the old woman's smile got a little tighter.

'Phone,' said Amy, a mile or two later.

'Yeah ...' His Nokia had been buzzing for a while. That was how Kit had it set, go straight to vibrate, ring after thirty seconds and skip video function unless otherwise told.

'It's me,' he said.

'We've got someone who wants to talk to you.'

A burst of Japanese blasted from its tiny speaker, Neku's words slung into one long howl as if trying to cram in as many words as possible before the inevitable happened and someone ripped the phone from her hands.

'You see,' said de Valois. 'She's unharmed, for the moment.'

'Put me back on,' demanded Kit.

'Say please.'

Kit took a deep breath. 'Please let me talk to the kid.'

De Valois laughed. 'Keep it short.'

'There's only three of them,' said Neku. 'The others vanished yesterday. Bring me a gun ...'

'*Neku!*'

'I'm serious,' she said.

The Brigadier had turned off her radio and both she and Amy were listening intently to Kit's end of the conversation.

'Enough,' said the voice. 'Now tell me what the girl was saying.'

'That she's okay and I should do exactly what you say.'

'I'm delighted to hear that,' said Armand de Valois. 'Now, which do I get? My money or the return of my merchandise ...?'

'Your goods,' said Kit.

'Excellent.' Armand de Valois's praise came in a drawl that Kit hated, along with its owner. It went with the floppy haircut and expensive suits, the dark glasses and the chunky gold identity bracelet. 'Although,' said De Valois. 'I'm surprised I had to contact you. We've been expecting your call.'

'I've been busy ... reclaiming your consignment,' Kit added, in case de Valois decided this was an insult. Nothing he'd heard about the Chechen suggested he took insults lightly.

'But you've got it?'

'Oh yes.'

'And where are you now?'

In an unmarked car with a geriatric ex-Army chief and a spook so

241

memorable I can barely recall the first time we met, or forget the last. Where the fuck do you think I am?

'On a bus,' said Kit.

Armand chuckled. 'On a bus,' he said. 'With my missing consignment. How English.' The line went dead, leaving Kit to the rumbling echo of traffic on London's South Circular.

'Where are we headed now?' Kit demanded.

Eyes met his in the driving mirror. 'To the club,' said Brigadier Miles.

'What, directly?'

She shook her head. 'We need to stop on the way. Change cars and prep you for the meeting. Nothing difficult.'

Having swung the Volvo into a supermarket car park, next to a roundabout just off the South Circular, Brigadier Miles walked away without looking back or removing her keys from the ignition. And as Amy indicated that Kit should wheel the silver case towards a zebra crossing, a young woman pushed a trolley up to the Volvo and began bundling shopping bags onto the back seat.

'Here we go,' said the Brigadier, as an old SUV pulled up by a crossing. 'Meet Maxim, my deputy.'

A large Jewish man with full beard and cap welcomed them into his car. In the back, right in the middle of the seat, sat a small boy playing *Death Ice V* on the in-car console. He moved up grudgingly to allow Kit, Amy and her case into the car. The Brigadier sat up front, shuffling receipts she took from her purse.

'Expenses?' asked Maxim.

The old woman nodded.

'Do them every month,' he said. 'It's easier. Alternatively, save them up, but don't expect sympathy.' Changing down a gear, Maxim chugged the SUV out into the evening traffic and wound towards a roadblock. The nod he gave the soldiers got Maxim through the check point with no problems.

'Where do you want me to drop you?'

'The Cut.'

It was one of those soft Sunday evenings that felt as if it belonged only in memory, when a settling sun puts the world very slightly out of focus. The children who crowded the street corners wore hoodies despite the heat and hunched around their own toughness, but they greeted each other with nods and bobbed hidden heads to the music that flowed from open windows.

The kid in the car kept playing his game, Maxim smiling every time the boy twisted his hand-held console frantically, trying to make his sled corner faster.

'What are you thinking?' Amy asked Kit.

'About Neku.'

'Me too,' said Amy, then blushed ... Kit was still trying to work out why, when he realised that both Maxim and the Brigadier were watching from their mirrors.

The Cut turned out to be behind the main station at Waterloo, and their destination a nondescript flat above an Indian newsagents, with walk-up stairs and bars over all the windows.

'See you in a minute,' Maxim told Brigadier Miles.

The kid said nothing. Just got back into the car.

A table in the main room held local maps for South London and a manila folder full of forms that the Brigadier spent at least fifteen minutes signing, with a Caran d'Ache silver pen she pulled from a jacket pocket.

'What's all that?' asked Kit.

'Paperwork,' Amy told him.

'Yes,' he said. 'Obviously ... What kind?'

Amy's gaze slid to a shelf of cheap paperbacks and old magazines. A novel at the end seemed to hold particular fascination. She was wondering whether to tell him, or maybe she was just hoping he'd forget the question.

'Well?' he demanded.

'She's taking responsibility if it goes wrong. You know, if the Brigadier's plan fails and ...'

'I get killed,' said Kit, finishing Amy's sentence for her.

Amy nodded a little too fast.

Not just me, Kit decided. *Neku too.*

He spent the next few minutes looking at the paperbacks and magazines. Crime novels, thrillers and romance. A couple of back issues of *Cosmo* and an American edition of *Esquire*. A handful of locally-produced booklets about the area. Holding up a pamphlet, Kit showed Amy the title. *Necropolis Railway.*

'Great,' she said, and left Kit to his reading.

As the living crowded London to such an extent that speed limits were introduced for horse-drawn traffic, the dead began to take more space than the city could provide. In the winter of 1837 fever took victims so fast families had to stand in line in London churchyards to wait for the funerals ahead to finish.

So, when it was suggested that corpses be freighted out of the city and buried at a purpose-built necropolis big enough to take London's dead for a hundred years, funds were raised quickly, and work begun. Necropolis Station opened in 1854, allowing the dead to make their journey to the grave in three levels of comfort, first, second and third class.

'Interesting?' Amy asked.

'In a sick sort of way,' said Kit, putting down his pamphlet and looking round the room. 'Are we done here?'

'I reckon so.' She glanced to where Maxim and Brigadier Miles were folding up a huge map and talking into their phones, fingers in one ear and both obviously irritated by the noise they considered the other was making.

'Demarcation,' said Amy.

'Security forces and the local police?'

Amy looked at Kit. 'Fuck no,' she said. 'We don't involve them.'

'Five squabbling with Six?' guessed Kit, naming both security and counter intelligence.

'It's internal,' said Amy.

Kit scowled.

'What?' she demanded.

'You're enjoying this,' said Kit, 'aren't you?' He watched Amy begin to deny it and then stop. That was Amy, honest to a fault even with herself.

'Well ...' she said. 'It beats the milk run. Is that bad?'

'No. Of course not.'

'But what?' Amy said, voice flat.

'Nothing,' said Kit. He checked his watch, worked out how long he had until de Valois's deadline ran out and remembered Charlie all in the same breath. 'I need to make a call,' he said. 'I left a friend of Neku's at the flat.'

'Charles Olifard,' said Amy.

Kit looked at her.

'It's okay,' she said. 'He's fine. The Brigadier sent him home last night.' She caught Kit's expression. 'Charlie's on an Mi6 scholarship,' she said. 'He'll be working at GCHQ when he's done at Imperial.'

'Sweet fuck,' said Kit, more loudly than he intended.

Across the room Maxim and the Brigadier, who'd just been flipping shut their phones and smiling grimly, stopped looking pleased with themselves and glanced across.

'That's what Charlie was?' asked Kit, his words little more than a savage whisper. 'Someone to shadow Neku? Still, at least he didn't crawl into her bed.'

Amy slapped him.

'Feeling better?' Kit asked, watching her walk away.

'You want to tell me what that was about?' demanded Brigadier Miles, after Amy had slammed the bathroom door, leaving the entire flat ringing with silence.

'Charlie,' said Kit.

The old woman frowned. 'I doubt,' she said, 'Amy slapped you over Charlie Olifard. They've never even met.'

'You know Charlie?'

'No,' said Brigadier Miles.

'You didn't put Charlie up to meeting Neku?'

Dragging on her cigarette, the old woman shook her head. 'GCHQ and my lot don't really talk,' she said. 'Not these days. Still, he's obviously a good boy.' Brigadier Miles spoke with the Olympian detachment of someone at least four times Charles Oliford's age. 'And he left you a message.'

Kit scowled at her.

'Keep rolling the dice, whatever that means. Charlie called the police, you know, yesterday afternoon. When you didn't come back. Told them about the kidnap. Guess what they found?'

'Charlie?'

'$10,000 in used notes, wrapped in book covers, packed in the bottom of a kid's sleeping bag. You want to explain that to me sometime?'

'I can't,' said Kit.

'Of course not,' said the Brigadier, grinding out her cigarette. 'I imagine it belongs to your little friend. Word is, she takes after her grandmother.'

CHAPTER 49
nawa-no-ukiyo

The problem with boys was that they were easily impressed. The correct response on entering a cleft in the shell of Schloss Omga was interested boredom, where the interest was ice-thin and the boredom deep and obvious.

A casual comment from Luc that his family's castle was bigger or smaller, simpler or more ornate would also have been adequate: provided it was said in such a way as to turn any compliment inside out. Alternatively, he could just have mentioned the obvious, that Schloss Omga was dying and having crawled up the side of a high mountain, the vast mollusc had nowhere left to climb.

So sad, he could have said. *How awful. It must be terrible to watch.*

And since shells existed to create ideal internal conditions, as much as for protection, he could have mentioned that the hole at the tip of Schloss Omga, while undoubtedly making it easier for Lady Neku to land was not, in itself, a good thing.

Neku would have mentioned it. Casually, in passing.

'What are we doing here?' asked Luc.

'Arriving,' said Lady Neku, then smiled to show she was joking. 'You're about to meet my father.'

Luc's mouth dropped open as fast as if someone had cut a wire to his jaw. 'But he's ...'

'Dead,' said Lady Neku. 'Yes, I know.' Waiting for the pod to open, she reached for a grab bar and hauled herself from her seat, landing lightly on a mother-of-pearl deck below.

'Don't worry,' she added, when Luc slipped. 'It's always tricky at first.' She led him towards a leathery wall that opened as she approached, sealing itself behind the two of them, before opening again into a curving corridor beyond. In the handful of steps it took to enter Schloss Omga,

246

the air grew less sour and the ambient temperature dropped by several degrees.

'Fuck,' said Luc. 'How did you do that?'

'Not me,' said Lady Neku. 'That was my father. Most probably ... It might have been the castle. No one's quite sure what happens to nervous system state vector maps after they upload.'

Luc looked blank.

'Well,' Lady Neku said. 'What do you do with people in your family when they die for real?'

'Bury them,' said Luc.

The corridor they were in curved round and down, circling from the tip of Schloss Omga to a level where the shell of the walls became less rotten and the floor less treacherous. On the way they passed a dozen other flaws in the wall but none as large as the one through which Lady Neku landed her pod.

It seemed unfair to Lady Neku that something as beautiful as the mother-of-pearl patches closing the gaps should be the result of the castle's failure to heal itself properly. Although her mother would probably regard this as childishly naïve. All beauty, according to Lady Katchatka, had its origins in pain.

'Here we are,' said Lady Neku, opening a real door, the kind with hinges and a handle. 'This is where my father used to work.'

Huge windows looked down onto the wastes of Katchatka Segment. It was this view that drove their father mad, in Nico's opinion. This view that finally drove him to suicide.

The ground was yellow, with black rock spines. A mat of weed floated on top of the distant lake, a different kind of weed crawled from the depths towards the land, unless it was the other way round. The ruins of the old city looked very distant and battered enough to pass as natural. A giant sand devil was sinking into itself in the distance. This was the World she knew, the one she saw inside her head when people talked about Katchatka Segment.

Lady Neku had been given lessons on radiation, cell mutation, suicide genes, splicing and sickness. Splicing was what separated fugees from animals and her family from fugees. Those who stayed, her father said, were those who lacked the will, determination or strength to go elsewhere.

Nico, Antonio and Petro chose to assume he was talking about the fugees. Lady Neku was much less sure.

'Come on,' said Lady Neku. 'Let's get this over.'

It had been a gentle summons. A simple, *your father would be pleased if you were to drop by his study sometime*. Of course, the main advantage of being dead was never having to raise one's voice. Had he remembered she'd have to pod drop from High Strange, negotiate fifteen minutes of unsafe corridor and risk whatever her mother would do if she found out?

Hard to tell. And all Lord Katchatka said when she and Luc entered the study was, 'That was quick.'

'This is Luc d'Alambert,' said Lady Neku. She watched the boy look round the huge room, searching for the source of the voice. 'It's in your head,' she told Luc, when he started looking for a second time.

'How do you do,' Luc said.

'Well enough,' said the voice. 'All things considered.' It sounded amused about something. 'I've got a question for you.'

Luc waited.

'What did you see during the drop?'

What Luc can still see. It was all Lady Neku could do not to answer for him. She stopped shuffling her feet long enough to peer through a window in front of her. It was a very high window, arched, and with little marble pillars to support the curves where they dipped in the middle and then soared away.

'Sand,' said Luc, having considered the question carefully. Sand was all anyone saw when they looked at Katchatka Segment. Sand, mud, cracked earth and a rotting lake. There was life in the lake, so people told him. Mud skippers, maybe. Evolution was going backwards. At least life was being killed off in reverse order of appearing, or something. As he'd already told Lady Neku, that part of future history went straight over his head.

'What was there before the sand?'

'More sand?'

The room sighed. It seemed that before the sand had been mountains, formed when two continental plates collided. For a while, the lake had been a sea; not quite big enough to be an ocean, but perfectly able to support trade in a city that sprawled along its Western edge: until one of the overhead wires making *nawa-no-ukiyo* had snapped and the sky been torn, letting in what High Strange and every node like it had been created to hold at bay, the solar-induced disaster of a planet in decline.

End days, Lord Katchatka called it.

'You know why this happened?'

Luc blushed.

'It was before your time,' said the voice. 'Before even mine. The truth can be useful sometimes.'

'The sails,' said Luc. 'They broke.' He meant the sky sheets high above Schloss Omga, the ones controlled by Lady Neku's family. The 33.2 million square miles of mirrored gossamer that constituted Katchatka's responsibility.

'All sails break,' the voice said. 'Such is the nature of fragile things. Our failure was not to act until it was too late.'

'It's not,' said Luc. 'My father says the sails can still be mended ...'

'Using what?' asked the voice.

The boy shrugged. 'I don't know,' he admitted.

'You know what else puzzles me?'

It was obvious that Luc didn't, just as it was obvious that the voice had every intention of telling him. 'Why you are marrying my daughter.'

Opening his mouth, Luc shut it again.

'Yes, I know,' said the voice. 'You're marrying her because that's what you've been told to do. And that's also why she's marrying you.'

Lady Neku and Luc looked at each other. 'But that doesn't answer the question, does it? What would a family as cryozoic as the d'Alamberts want with one old woman, three boys and a halfwit girl. Because that is what's left of Katchatka's rulers.'

A voice woke her in the darkness. As unexpected as it was unfamiliar, until gut-level instincts caught up with the obvious and Lady Neku realised it was Luc, sounding close enough to be in the same room.

'You awake?'

Pulling herself out of sleep, she sat up and glared around her, even as she realised how absurd that was. Alarms would have gone off long before Luc reached this far inside her private quarters.

Only she was still in the castle. And a graphite silver night was visible through the high windows of her father's study. She seemed to be wrapped in a silver blanket and lying on leather cushions taken from three different chairs.

'You must be awake,' said Luc. 'You're sitting up.'

And then Lady Neku saw him, in the half darkness beside her, also wrapped in silver blanket. Although, she was glad to notice it was a separate blanket.

'Are you scared about tomorrow?' he asked.

No, thought Lady Neku, as she wondered what tomorrow was meant to bring and then remembered. Banquets, marriage and a public bedding.

Compared to most of her life, it would be simplicity itself.

'Of course not,' she said.

'I am.' Luc's voice was thin, unashamedly lonely. 'Tell me again,' he said. 'How your family was first chosen ...'

The idea to cut the moon into segments came from one of Lady Neku's ancestors peeling an orange, either that or it came from the province of Satsuma itself. One was a family holding in pre-Meiji Japan, later folded into the Kagoshima prefecture, the other a citrus fruit with a high tolerance to cold.

Japan, *Kagoshima* and *cold* Lady Neku knew only as concepts. She knew the whiteness of satsuma blossom and the smoothness of the leaves from personal experience. Almost all of the plantings in the Stroll Garden bore fruit, the few that didn't were saved by the medicinal qualities of their sap, leaves or bark. The original culling of plants had been carried out with a ruthlessness Lady Neku admired but wondered if she would be strong enough to imitate.

The Stroll Garden held *sukura*, plum and satsuma. The willow only survived because of its ability to lower fever, and even *kouyou*, the flaming red foliage of autumn, so loved by Lady Neku's grandfather, had not been enough to save the maple. She'd seen the pictures. Well, one of them. A woodblock print so ghostly that leaves fell across rice paper in a waterfall of fading ink.

It *was* possible that the idea to segment the moon came from Satsuma itself. A hard core of her family had taken to referring to the vanished province by its old name, which was their way of rejecting the original Meiji settlement and the abolition of the provinces.

The fact the destruction of the shogunate had happened in 1851, nearly seven hundred years before, they regarded as irrelevant. After all, the world was considering the first, and quite probably, the greatest exploration of time ever undertaken. What were a few centuries when millennia were about to be opened?

Lady Neku shook her head. So naïve. So ridiculously childish. Even a halfwit like her could see that opening up time was never going to work like that. All that shit about avoiding the Great White and sending humanity to explore its own future history. It was obvious what time shifting was really good for.

Where better to house every criminal and political refugee than here, the end of the world? As for exploring the future of human history, that might have been possible if whatever humanity became hadn't already left by the time their visitors arrived.

CHAPTER 50
Sunday 1 July

The area of South London through which Maxim drove was not quite suburb and not really inner city. A sea of small white-faced villas, red-brick shops and pubs filled the gaps between old Victorian houses, all of which had been converted to flats.

A handful of shops on a run-down estate were still in business and one of the pubs, but most of the ground floor flats stood empty, with studded steel plates sealing doors and windows against squatters. Signs warned that guard dogs patrolled the area and the estate was awaiting redevelopment. To judge from the faded state of the signs it had been waiting quite a while.

When Maxim turned up a narrow alley before exiting into a busy road, Kit felt obscurely relieved. As if the grey concrete of the estate behind him was one thing too many.

Time had not been kind to the local high street, or maybe it was town planners. The people who lived there, however, made do. East European *kabaks* had replaced most of the old kebab shops in the fifteen years since Kit had been anywhere near this part of the city, and newsagents had sprouted icons and window posters written in Cyrillic, although they still had the metal grilles. A Methodist church on the corner had been made over in Russian Orthodox style and a crowd of old women were spilling from its door.

Middle-aged men sat outside cafés, nursing tiny cups of coffee or shot glasses of vodka, which they seemed to be washing down with water, unless it was another clear spirit.

'Welcome to Little Russia,' said Maxim, opening the front door to another walk-up. 'Everyone's home from home.'

The club behind the flat was called Bar Poland. A naked girl clung to a pole on the sign above its door just in case the pun was over subtle.

Actually, she was three girls in silhouette and the neon was wired to twirl her endlessly round the pole as each silhouette lit in turn.

A young black man inside the walk-up seemed to be watching her with casual intensity. 'Classy, eh?' he said, stepping back to let Kit clamber over a tiny generator on his way to the window. It was beginning to look as if British intelligence provided one of the biggest markets for crappy accommodation in the city.

'This is Alan,' said the Brigadier, but Kit's attention was on the neon girl. She was retro kitsch, the kind of icon that had begun to spring up all over East Shinjuku and the bits of Roppongi not yet colonised by haute couture and impossibly-expensive estate agents.

'What's the latest?' ask Amy, sounding brightly professional. The one advantage of the SUV over the Volvo was that Kit and Amy had been able to sit with the suitcase flat between them. In the last hour Amy hadn't spoken one word to Kit; hadn't even looked at him, come to that.

'That CCTV camera above the door is live,' said Alan. 'We've jacked a feed. De Valois has a man at the top window watching the courtyard below. Since he's been there for the last six hours we figure he's shitting in a bag and peeing in a bottle.' Catching Amy's eye, Alan raised one hand in apology. 'That's the truth and it works in our favour.'

'Why?' she demanded.

'He'll be bored,' said Kit. 'Also pissed off. That's never good.' Turning to Alan, he asked. 'How about sound?'

'The phone bug went down again, when Mr de Valois ran a sweep. We've still got parabolics on his windows but the fooler loops are keeping us out. We can get it all back up by morning, if necessary.'

'Should we be worried?' said Brigadier Miles.

'I doubt if he even knows we're here,' Alan said. 'It's all pretty low level.'

The Brigadier smiled, as if the technician was about twelve and not a professional in his early twenties. 'And the Japanese kid ...?'

'Sat in one corner, drawing a weird-shit comic strip and talking to herself. At least she was last time we checked.'

'Which was how?'

'Man in suit.'

'We report noise to the local council,' Alan told Kit, 'then wait for a local official to come out to inspect the club or bar or whatever we're watching.'

'Isn't it dangerous?' Amy asked.

'Not really,' said Alan. 'We don't tell them anything in advance. Just grab them when they get back and debrief them out of sight. You'd be surprised how much a jobsworth with a clipboard notices. It's their blind ignorance keeps them safe,' he added. 'Even our best people can't fake it.'

Kit began by refusing to wear the flak jacket. This was more a vest than a jacket, made from woven kevlar and reinforced with callus-like pads over the heart and across the sides.

'Liver,' said Alan, producing the garment. 'And kidneys. More of a target than you think.'

'No.' Kit shook his head.

'Come on,' said Alan. 'It's regulations.'

'Not my regulations,' said Kit; so Alan went to fetch the Brigadier, and to give Brigadier Miles her due the first thing she asked was, *why not?*

'Because it will show.'

'Not if you wear a jacket over the top.'

'Think about it,' said Kit. 'It's hot, it's muggy, we're at the beginning of July. No way is anyone round here going to wear a jacket, unless it's a hoodie.'

'Which would look absurd on you,' said the Brigadier.

'Exactly.'

They compromised on clothing, Kit agreeing to wear black jeans and a white cotton T-shirt, one thin enough to make obvious he wasn't wearing a flak jacket, pocket recorder or receiver.

'Here's your gun,' said Maxim, producing a heavy-looking Colt automatic from his briefcase.

'What?'

'Ben Flyte always went armed. Stupid little prick. Besides ...' Maxim grinned and dropped out the clip, jacking out the first five bullets. 'We need you to take this inside for us.' Extracting what looked like the next five slugs, Maxim passed Kit a tiny tape recorder. 'Old skool,' he said happily, before reloading the clip and snapping it back into the gun.

'How does it work?'

'Noise activated,' said Maxim. 'It's already running.' When Brigadier Miles looked worried, the old man smiled. 'We need to check it's working. I'll reset the chip when he leaves.'

'I want another gun,' insisted Kit, before the Brigadier could say anything else. 'As backup, and a knife in an ankle sheath. If you want me to carry then we do this properly.'

Arguing this out took five minutes, with another fifteen wasted while a motorcycle courier collected the items and delivered them to the walk-up. By the time Maxim signed for the items, the sky had darkened through three different shades of blue and the neon girl outside cast enough light to turn net curtains purple.

Without even thinking about it, Kit dropped out the clip to check it was full. The Beretta was tiny, in better condition than the Colt, but so small it only took short-length .22. Clicking the clip back into place Kit spun the little automatic in his hand and then tucked it into a sock.

'You know how to use it?' Alan asked.

Kit nodded.

The blade was black, double edged, made from transformation-toughened zirconia, good for slicing, though not recommended for high-impact applications. It said so on a gold label that Alan peeled away, slipping the crumpled paper into his pocket.

'Sticky tape,' Kit demanded.

Even Amy was finally looking at him. And somehow Kit didn't think it was because he was stood on a dusty floor in a crappy little flat with one leg still rolled up like an initiate to the freemasons.

'The weapons are for show,' said Maxim. 'Okay? Nothing else ...'

As Maxim began to repack his briefcase and Brigadier Miles collected up her cigarette ends, decanting them into a small plastic bag, Amy took a call, glancing across at Kit before looking away.

'Yeah,' she said. 'He's ready.'

Kit shook his head, pulled the Colt from the back of his belt and put it on a table in front of Alan, who was adjusting a parabolic mic with a tiny screwdriver.

'I'll be back in a few seconds.'

That got everyone's attention.

'Nothing serious,' Kit said. 'Just ...' He nodded towards the bathroom. *I want to roll the dice.*

'Can't it wait?' said Brigadier Miles.

Kit should already have left. At least that was the Brigadier's plan. Out of this flat to a café on the corner, where he would wait for a passing uniform to ask the owner if she'd seen a missing teenager. His cue to move.

'No,' said Kit. 'I don't think it can.'

Armand de Valois answered Neku's phone on the third ring. It was probably too much to expect that Neku would be allowed to answer. It might also be too much to hope that Alan was telling the truth when he said the bugs were down, but it was all the hope Kit had.

'*Armand de Valois?*'

'Oui. Who is this …'

Who did he think it was?

'It's me,' said Kit. 'We're meant to be meeting.'

A moment of silence and then, 'Meant?' In the club a man stopped talking, probably shocked by the fury in that single word.

'It's a trap,' said Kit. 'I'm being used by the police and I'll be carrying a tape recorder …' Now was when Maxim, the Brigadier and, quite possibly, Alan and Amy should start breaking down the door. All Kit got was silence at both ends of the phone.

'You there?' he asked.

'Yes,' said de Valois, 'I'm still here, and I can tell you now, it's a bad idea to try to fuck with Armand de Valois. You bring my consignment tonight or the girl dies. No tricks, no more extra time.'

'But …'

'Now,' said de Valois. 'You bring it now. Because if you don't, then we kill you.'

'Neku …'

'Oh yes,' said de Valois. 'We kill her too. Only we rape her first.'

When Kit had finished vomiting, he splashed water on his face and rinsed out his mouth. He looked older than he remembered, hollow eyed and hollow cheeked, a long way from the Englishman abroad he once was.

But he'd discovered something.

The safety glass between himself and his past had cracked. In its place was a sharp-edged clarity that had Kit adjusting his mind for angle, distance and the wind drift of a life almost wasted.

Four sixes. Charlie would be proud of him.

'Are you all right?' Brigadier Miles looked worried.

'Oh yes,' said Kit. 'I'm fine.'

It felt odd to wheel a fortune in heroin between East European kids in jeans and leather jackets. Odd, but interesting. One of the older boys looked as if he might be reluctant to move, but something about Kit's certainty made him step aside. To save face the kid whistled, a staccato trill that announced he had drugs to offer.

Shaking his head, Kit kept walking.

'Someone should do something about them,' said a woman in the café.

'Someone will,' said Kit. Life expectancy among teenage drug dealers in South London was short. It had been that way for much longer than those kids had been alive.

Anywhere else the café's décor would be ironic. Pine tables and pottery mugs, leather place mats and a framed Bob Marley poster. A nod to the simplicities of the 1980s. A chrome espresso machine behind the counter was undoubtedly the most valuable thing in the place.

The West Indian woman who'd been complaining about drugs brought Kit a menu, having waited politely while he chose a table and parked his case. 'We're closing soon,' she said. 'But I can do you soup or toasties.'

Ackee, Red Bean, Pepper Pot ... Having dismissed the soups, Kit chose a jerked chicken sandwich and fries.

'Been somewhere nice?' the woman asked, after taking his order.

'Japan.'

She raised her eyebrows at this. 'Strange place for a holiday.'

'I live there,' said Kit, *well, maybe* ...

'Bet London's changed.'

He smiled.

'And not for the better,' she said, nodding beyond the window. When Kit said nothing, the woman sniffed. 'What do you want to drink?'

'Tea,' said Kit. 'I could really do with tea.'

'Coming up,' she said, unfreezing as quickly as she'd taken offence.

The tea was warm and weak and tasted as if it had been made from leaves swept off a factory floor, while the milk was so rich that fat skated like oily insects across its surface. All the same ...

Sentiment, he told himself. He didn't do sentiment.

And yet here he was sat in some crumbling café in an area known for its high levels of unemployment, prostitution and street crime, mourning the passing of a world he'd done his utmost to avoid. But which he might be about to leave, if that was what it took.

Kill me, so this thing I love keeps living ... The words Kate O'Mally had quoted beside the little waterfall in Shinjuku Park crowded his head. It made no sense. And yet it was true.

He would die if this was what it took. Worse than that, he would kill. *Why?* Because Mary O'Mally once told him every debt must be repaid. It had just taken Kit longer than it should to realise debts could be carried over and repaid to someone else.

What he owed Neku, what he owed Mary, what he owed himself.

'Here,' said the café owner, slapping down a poster. 'Take a look. He won't know,' she added, talking to someone behind her. 'He just got back from Japan.' The picture showed a young black girl. *Missing* was written across the top.

'Shit,' said Kit.

The West Indian woman frowned.

'You know her?' demanded the police officer.

Kit shook his head. He could feel their stares all the way from his table to the pavement.

CHAPTER 51
Sunday 1 July

Shut, announced a sign, *for renovation. Open soon!*

Three locks, a peephole and a camera above the door secured the entrance to Bar Poland. Kit wondered why, if the club was closed, the neon girl still swung in circles and decided it really didn't matter. There were bigger questions to answer, like how to retrieve Neku and talk his way out of there alive.

Three hours, he'd been given. After that it was out of the Brigadier's hands and Neku took her chances with an extraction team. Kit didn't believe the bit about it being out of the Brigadier's hands, though it had been repeated several times.

Having knocked, Kit counted to ten and began to walk away. The door to Bar Poland opened before he'd taken five paces.

'Oi,' said a voice. 'You Mr Flyte?' A teenage boy with cropped skull, checked shirt and tight jeans stood sneering in the doorway.

'What do you think?' said Kit.

'You got Mr de Valois's stuff?'

'All sixty kilos of it,' said Kit. 'Vacuum packed, grade A ...'

The boy scowled, then glanced round in case Kit's comment had been overheard, which it undoubtedly was, and taped as well, not to mentioned filmed from between the slats of blind covering a window high on a wall behind his visitor.

'Better let me in,' said Kit.

The young man stepped aside, slowly.

As Kit walked into Bar Poland, he heard the door shut behind him and the click of one lock after another. As a final touch, a steel bolt was slammed into place.

'Scared of burglars?'

The boy hit Kit hard, from behind.

Red carpet, with a worn strip down the middle where endless feet had headed towards velvet curtains beyond. On the far side of the curtains was a sound system, turned up loud. Kit knew this because its bass line was loud enough to shake the floor next to his ear.

'Up you come.' Hands dragged Kit to his feet. It was the boy, only now his sneer had become a smirk. He was rubbing his fist, although it was probably unnecessary, as the shot-weighted leather glove he wore looked designed to offer protection. 'We've got your girlfriend dancing,' said the boy. 'She's pretty good.'

'You've got ...'

'Hey,' he said. 'Be grateful. For Mr de Valois that's mild. It could have been so much worse.'

Could it? 'I'll bear that in mind,' Kit said.

Matters of great concern should be treated lightly. Matters of small concern should be treated seriously. So said the book Mr Oniji gave Kit in hospital. It said other things as well, but the most important of these he had worked out for himself. *Regard yourself as dead already.*

An old Killers track blared from hidden speakers. It was before Neku's time and quite possibly before de Valois's too, unless his youthfulness was just a trick of the light and a good surgeon.

'Ah, Ben ... So you came.' Mr de Valois smiled, his eyes visible behind lightly-tinted shades.

'I wouldn't miss it,' said Kit, reaching behind him.

'Kenka shinaide!'

'What?' demanded de Valois, then added, 'Keep dancing.'

Neku did as she was told.

So did Kit, who stopped reaching for his gun and wheeled his case across to Mr de Valois instead. 'It's all here,' Kit said.

'I certainly hope so.'

No way will I look at her, Kit told himself, then glanced anyway. Seeing a half-naked child draped in the glare of a cheap spotlight that lit every scowl on her face.

'Search him,' demanded de Valois.

The crop-haired man found the Colt first time, only finding the ankle gun when de Valois told him to search properly.

'Anything else?'

Kit shook his head.

'You sure?'

He nodded. 'I'm positive.'

'Good,' said de Valois. 'So you won't mind when Alfie breaks her

259

arms if we find something, will you?' He raised his eyebrows at Kit, who shrugged.

De Valois laughed.

'Check the cases,' he told Alfie.

Sixty individual bags of heroin. More oblivion than Kit could imagine. Each one heat-sealed along its edges and then wrapped again, in polythene so thick it looked like oiled paper.

'Well?'

'It's all there,' said Alfie, in a South London accent obvious enough to remind Kit of black and white films he hadn't even seen.

'Call Robbie down,' Armand ordered. 'Tell him to test it.'

A few minutes later a dreadlocked Rasta ambled from the shadows, holstering a gun as he came. His hair was thinning and had turned to grey. His red shirt had sweat marks under the arms. He looked almost as unhappy with life as Kit felt. So Kit guessed he was the man who'd been shitting in a bag.

'Ah,' said Armand. 'My friend …'

Producing a scalpel from his pocket, the Rasta chose a package from the middle and slit it open, carrying a little of the power to his tongue. 'Well,' he said. 'It's the real thing.'

Without needing to be told, Robbie slit open another five bags and carried them to a table near the stage. A small gas cooker, a glass beaker and a handful of bottles appeared, along with a small pair of scales. Although, in the event, the only pieces of equipment Robbie used were a laptop, a glass of water and a small white box with a glass lid.

'Residual alkaloids, some methaqualone, also traces of diazepam,' said Robbie, amending it to, 'Afghani, sixty-five percent pure,' when Mr de Valois looked irritated. 'Also, sugars for bulk.'

'It's been cut,' Kit said, 'ready for market.' This was what he'd been told to say. 'And I'm really sorry about the misunderstanding. I obviously had no idea …'

'That I was still alive?'

Kit nodded.

In the background Razorlight replaced Kaiser Chiefs and were replaced in turn by a dance track with a single looped vocal and an idiotically simple synth line. Golden oldies, what the punters would expect; and behind Robbie's table, apparently forgotten, Neku circling her pole in time to the music.

She'd lost weight again. Kit could see ribs beneath her skin and watch the muscles in her shoulders slide across each other as they propelled her round and round the same tight circle of misery.

'Pretty,' said de Valois. 'Isn't she?'

'She's Kathleen O'Mally's granddaughter. You know who that is?'

It was obvious he didn't, and equally obvious that Robbie did. So Kit suggested the Rasta tell Mr de Valois, who listened in silence to a bullet-point breakdown of Kate O'Mally's life, while Alfie looked increasing impressed in the background.

'This woman. She knows you're here?'

'Of course,' said Kit.

Mr de Valois shrugged. 'Not my problem.'

Kit caught the exact moment Alfie looked at Robbie; crop-haired thug and grizzled Rasta, whatever passed between them, it passed in silence.

'All the same,' said de Valois, gesturing towards Neku. 'The kid's good. Where did she dance before this?'

'Dance ...?'

'She has the moves, even has a couple that are new. I was just wondering where she's been.'

'Tokyo.'

'Ahh,' said de Valois. 'That would certainly help explain her lack of English.' He glanced at Neku, his gaze sliding over her naked breasts and tiny g-string. 'I think it would be good if you asked her to join me for a drink.'

Perhaps Kit was wrong to treat this as an invitation, because Mr de Valois's smile froze at his counter-suggestion that perhaps Neku and he should think about getting home; now Mr de Valois had his consignment and Kit had made his apologies.

'Not yet,' said de Valois. 'You see, we still need to agree a price.'

'There is no price,' Kit said. 'The consignment is yours. All I'm doing is returning it.'

Armand de Valois's laugh was loud was enough to make Neku flinch. 'Not a price for me,' he said, with a grin. 'For you, for causing me problems in the first place.' He nodded towards Neku. 'Also her, if you want her back I will require a transfer fee.'

'She's Kate O'Mally's granddaughter.'

De Valois looked irritated. 'Other people would kill you,' he said. 'I am being generous, very generous. In future you will work for me. As will she. But first, we have business.'

When the music stopped it left Neku frozen in mid swing. 'Tell her to come here,' de Valois said, looking at the girl.

Instead of climbing from the stage, Neku vanished through a door at the back and when she reappeared it was wearing a tatty silk dressing gown that reached her ankles and was tied tightly around her waist. Sweat dripped from her face and a pulse beat steadily in her neck. Kit could smell her from five paces away.

'I need a shower,' she told him.

'Later,' said Kit, keeping to Japanese.

'What did she say?'

'That she needs a shower ...'

Mr de Valois grunted. 'There'll be time for that later,' he said. 'Tell the girl I have a job for her. A very suitable job.'

So Kit did.

Neku's eyes were arctic, devoid of light and so cold they made Kit shiver. It would have been better if a sneer or scowl gave anger to her face, but instead she smiled, almost blandly. 'Tell him I'm always willing to help.'

Things moved swiftly after that.

From somewhere a chopping board was produced, along with a stained Sabatier knife and a chrome bucket full of ice. Armand demanded rubber bands and when these failed to appear announced that string would have to do.

'You ever seen this done before?'

She had, Kit realised, having translated Armand de Valois's question. Which was more than could be said for Kit, unless one counted films. Because he'd just worked out what was about to happen.

Kit only knew a gun had been pulled when he felt its muzzle touch the side of his ear, a cold kiss just behind the hair line. Alfie's hand was shaking. A poor start for someone holding an automatic so cheap it lacked a safety catch.

'Taking my drugs, trying to trick me and not showing sufficient respect. Three transgressions,' said de Valois, handing Neku the knife. 'That means you cut three times, one joint after another.'

He smiled while he waited for Kit to translate.

'My finger,' said Kit, meaning *my finger, not that man's throat.*

Neku weighed the blade in her hand.

'Just do it,' Kit said. 'And we'll get ourselves out of here.'

She knew exactly where to make the first cut. Placing Kit's left hand face down on the board and positioning her knife above the first joint of his little finger, Neku slammed her palm across the back of the blade.

Fuck.

The severed tip of a finger was rolling across the board before Kit even registered the pain, but by then Neku had his hand back on the board and her blade against the same finger, one joint lower.

A slam of her hand and two segments of finger rested beside each other.

'Take the last joint,' said Neku, 'and I'll have nothing to tie off …' Barely bothering to wait for Kit to translate, she held Kit's hand to the board and repositioned her knife.

'She's good,' said de Valois.

'The best.' Neku said, in fractured English.

Armand de Valois laughed. 'Okay,' he said. 'Tell her to have this one on me.'

Cutting a length of string, Neku bound the last section of finger and tied it off in a quick knot. 'One section you can re-attach,' she whispered, 'two is much more difficult.'

She was supporting him. Her single hand beneath Kit's elbow to brace his entire weight, should he needed time to compose himself.

'We're done here,' Kit said.

'Almost,' promised de Valois. 'But first, Ben … Your finger, it hurts?'

Of course it fucking hurts.

'A little.'

What was he meant to say? *A lot, hardly at all …* It was, Kit suspected, a question to which there only wrong answers.

'Luckily,' said de Valois. 'I have just the cure. Sixty-five percent pure and freshly delivered. Here we go …' Wiping the Sabatier on a beer mat, de Valois dipped the blade's tip into an open bag of heroin.

'Lighter,' he demanded.

Robbie held a flame beneath the blade, until the metal tinged orange and dreams began to spiral from the oily mess.

'Come on Ben,' said de Valois. 'Let's make friends.'

A million dreams twisted towards a nicotine-stained ceiling. A hundred thousand nightmares and every shade of longing in between. All Kit had to do was lean forward and inhale the smoke.

He made his decision without even realising there was a decision to make.

Twisting the hot blade from Robbie's fingers, Kit moved before anyone had time to react. A sizzling slash to the throat, a smoky drag across both eyes and Kit was almost done, his final strike hissing its way under de Valois's chin and through his soft palate, braising his tongue.

A thing done with moderation may be judged insufficient.

A cold click told Kit that the slide had been pulled back on Alfie's

263

gun. So this is the way the world ends, he thought. With a Chechen gangster blinded and a bullet through my head. *When one thinks one has gone too far ... One has probably gone far enough.*

'Let it go,' ordered Robbie.

Alfie hesitated, and in that moment of hesitation, Robbie leant forward and tapped the heel of his palm under the knife, driving the blade clean through the roof of de Valois' mouth and into his brain.

'Arsehole,' he said.

CHAPTER 52
Sunday 1 July

While Neku finished washing in the staff loo behind the stage, Kit ran through her parentage again, simplifying it, just to make things really clear. The more Kit iterated his points, the more convincing they sounded.

Walk with a man a hundred paces ...Kit's smile was sour. He was planning to walk far more than that in the company of Robbie and Alfie, assuming they all got lucky.

'Fuck,' said Robbie. He'd been a foot soldier when he originally met Kate O'Mally, standing silent while she ripped strips from some local Don. It was, admitted Robbie, unlikely Mrs O'Mally had even known his name, for which he remained extremely grateful. As for Alfie, the boy was too young to have those kind of memories. He'd heard of her nephew though. You didn't cross central London without getting Mike Smith's permission first. At least people like Alfie didn't.

'You mean,' said Alfie. 'The girl is Mr Smith's cousin?' It was an interesting update in the lexicon of fear.

In unspoken agreement, Alfie and Robbie moved to the bar and got themselves a whisky chaser, washing the spirit down with a bottle of Becks. Robbie lit the teenager's cigarette for him, because Alfie's hand was shaking too badly to work the lighter. Neither would look at Neku when she returned from rinsing out her mouth, splashing water on her face and whatever else she'd been doing in the staff bathroom.

'How many ways out of here?' asked Kit.

'Only one,' Robbie said. 'Why?'

'Because it's a trap,' said Kit. 'Gunmen are out there, waiting ...' He jerked a thumb over his shoulder towards the corridor. 'And we've got about half an hour before someone blows down that door.'

'Oh shit,' said Alfie. 'You were telling Mr de Valois the truth?'

'Yeah,' said Kit. 'It's a bad habit of mine.'

'But he had his own man in the drug squad.'

'I know,' said Kit. 'Only, Sergeant Samson has been suspended. I bet he didn't tell de Valois that.'

Alfie looked sicker still. 'How many ways?' Kit insisted.

'Front door, side windows ...'

'Both covered,' said Kit. 'Anything else?' The two men shook their heads. 'Over the roof? Across a back garden? Come on,' he said. 'There must be another way.'

'Attic,' Alfie said. 'Round here most houses have linked attics.'

'Probably walled up. Mortgage regulations,' Robbie added. 'My brother used to be a builder.'

'Then you know how crap they'll be,' said Alfie.

Having left on all the lights and restarted the music, Kit, Neku, Alfie and Robbie went up the stairs two steps at a time. And unlikely as it sounded, the rubbish stacked on the club stairs got worse the higher they climbed. The first floor had changing rooms, if such a label could be given to a room stripped of everything but a mirror, overhead bulb and a cracked lavatory in one corner.

'Mine,' said Neku, grabbing a handful of clothes in passing.

'Was mine,' Kit said, tossing segments of finger into the open bowl and pausing to check it flushed properly.

When Robbie and Alfie looked at each other, Kit wondered if it was the finger or discovering that Neku spoke proper English after all. So abandoned was the next level that its floors had been painted white with pigeon shit. A broken window showed where the birds got in. A short run of ladder led to the attic and a hole in the roof above revealed night sky.

'You go first,' Kit told the boy, who did as he was told. It didn't actually matter to Kit in what order Alfie and Robbie climbed. But simple commands, easily obeyed, kept the two men under his control.

Robbie was right, a wall had been built; and Alfie was right, because the brickwork was crap. Cheap breezeblocks had been stacked clumsily on top of each other and glued into place with cowpats of dripping mortar.

'Amateurs.' Robbie sounded personally offended.

'Makes it easier,' said Alfie, producing a lock knife and grinding it into a crack between two blocks. 'I'll need some help,' he said.

So Robbie stepped forward and together the two men sawed at the crude mortar, reducing it to dust. 'Buggered,' said Robbie, but he was talking about the blade.

'No matter,' Alfie said. 'We're done.' And he proceeded to kick down the wall with a quiet ferocity that spoke of current anger or a lifetime of unresolved issues.

The attic next door was also empty, in better condition than the one they'd just left and, best of all, not bricked up on its far side. A partition had been built, but this was made from flame-proof board and Alfie tore it down without even having to be asked.

'Okay,' he said, 'We're above the Golden Balti.' Catching Neku's glance, he added. 'That's the local take-out.'

Which left the Japanese girl little wiser.

A flight of steps led down to a small landing stacked with empty ghee tins and a large wooden crate, reading Rajah Spices. Someone had set up a canvas bed in a bathroom. A copy of a local Bengali paper lay open on the floor.

'Quietly now,' said Kit.

The floor below held a store room, customer lavatories and a bemused-looking waiter who was obviously wondering about the noise. When Kit put his hand to his lips, the man nodded.

No one challenged Kit, Neku and the other two as they filed through the crowded restaurant, squeezing between a large group waiting for takeaway near the door. And no one made a fuss when they reached the street outside, crossed the High Road and cut under a railway arch into a passage that led to a car park beyond.

'We're square, right?' asked Robbie.

Kit nodded.

'I mean, for real? It was a mistake, right? We didn't know she was ...' He glanced at Neku, who stared back. It was Robbie who looked away.

'I'm cool with you if she is,' said Kit.

After a moment, Neku nodded.

'That's settled then,' he said, turning to include Alfie in the conversation. 'None of us were here,' said Kit. 'You didn't see me and I didn't see you. If anyone asks you just stick to that.'

Somewhere away to his right a black helicopter came thudding low over the houses, a siren fired up three streets away and a thunderflash could be heard, rattling shop windows like fireworks. Brigadier Miles had obviously just told her boys to go in.

CHAPTER 53
Sunday 1 July

Trying to ride a motorbike with an amputated finger was a bad idea. The actual practice was worse. Every gear change made Kit chew his lip and fight to keep his hand on the bars. He'd probably have been crying with frustration if the night wind hadn't got to his eyes first.

The Suzuki belonged to Alfie and was the machine Kit would have expected. Cheap, flashy and done up with after-market accessories. On the plus side, the tank was full, the machine was licensed and Alfie had been pitifully willing to offer Kit its use.

It was the wrong side of midnight when Kit left the motorway. There was no need to kill the lights as he approached speed cameras but he did it anyway. Kit liked the way darkness turned the blacktop to an icy strip, lit by little more than the sodium glare of a village nearby.

At a service station south of the M25, he stopped to refill the bike and use the loos. As an afterthought, Kit asked Neku if she wanted a coffee. In return, she asked him a question of her own.

'Why did you kill him?'

So he told her.

Sat next to a glass window, in a café deserted enough to have been ripped from an Edward Hopper painting, Kit explained about the debts he owed. How he'd never really fallen out of love with Mary and why he let Kate O'Mally drag him back from Tokyo.

Kit realised halfway though his story that Neku knew none of this. And then he realised no one did, except No Neck, Micki and that other girl the day Mary's postcard arrived; and they didn't count, because he'd been drunk and they'd been careful not to mention it again. Almost everything that mattered to Kit in the last fifteen years had happened inside his head.

Conversations with ghosts.

He'd kissed a girl and it was the wrong girl or the wrong time. He'd lived badly and lived well and neither felt more real than the other, because everything after Josh was counting bells. Like Mary, Kit had just been adding and subtracting to keep the devil at bay.

All those lives snuffed out in the cross hairs of a M-24 sniper rifle needed shifting up one, to make space for the truth. Josh killed himself but Kit had provided the reason.

'You're sad.' Neku's voice was matter of fact.

'I'm cold,' said Kit, taking the coffee she offered. It was sweet and still hot, bitter from having stewed in a glass flask on a ring for the previous hour.

'Losing a finger does that,' Neku said. 'It's the shock. My brother ...' Whatever she was about to say got lost when Neku took herself to the restrooms. She was still wiping her mouth when she got back.

'How are you?' Neku asked Patrick Robbe-Duras, when Pat finally stopped fussing about the damp and cold and how Neku must feel after such a long ride in the middle of the night.

'I'm okay,' said Pat, sipping his whisky on the rocks.

Neku smiled. Their next discussion involved whether or not another coffee would keep Neku awake and her insistence that all Japanese girls hated hot milk, so that was out of the question

'No tradition of keeping cows,' she said.

Pat nodded, doubtful.

After this, as the conversation turned to biscuits versus cake, Kate caught Kit's eye and nodded towards the kitchen door.

'Good idea,' said Neku, hooking ice from Pat's glass. 'Chill your finger,' she told Kit. 'Then cut back the knuckle and sew the flesh shut.'

Kit took the ice Neku offered. Smiling, when he realised Kate's mouth had dropped open.

'I can do it later,' said Neku. 'If you'd rather.'

Leading Kit along a corridor Kate opened a heavy door to reveal a very traditional-looking study, lined with books Kit doubted she'd ever read and hung with a Gully Jimson nude probably chosen years before and barely looked at since. Cigarette smoke clung to a leather armchair, and a waste paper basket overflowed with newspapers. It looked like a room no one had bothered to clean in a very long time.

'You want me to do it?' Kate asked, nodding at Kit's injured hand.

Kit shook his head.

Kate O'Mally was surprisingly good with a knife. Well, surprising to

269

Kit, who'd always assumed her nickname of *butcher* indicated clumsiness, not skill. All the same, it hurt like fuck and there was no other way of putting it. Slicing back flesh, Kate cut free gristle and bone, flicking the remains onto her desk. It looked like one of those chewy bits of chicken.

She let Kit sew the ends together.

'Pat arrived this afternoon,' said Kate. 'Just turned up in a taxi, collected his cases and told me to pay the driver. Said he'd come back for good if I'd accept Mary was gone.'

'What about his own house?'

Shrugging, Kate said, 'I hardly dare ask. You need a drink?'

Kit shook his head.

'Don't suppose I should either.' Sitting herself at the desk, Kate rummaged through a drawer until she found a Partegas box. 'Want one of these instead?'

The cigars were dry and burned too quickly, but Kate and Kit still sat there and smoked them anyway, watching curls of smoke obscure the ceiling. Kit understood what Kate was doing. She was ensuring he understood this meeting was social. They were no longer enemies. In her own way, the rituals Kate O'Mally lived by were as rigid as those Yoshi followed.

'People have been calling,' Kate said, finally coming to the point. Sucking in a final mouthful of smoke, she let it escape between her lips and ground her cigar stub into a glass ashtray. 'A surprising number of people ...' She smiled. 'A man from the MOD, for a start.'

'What did you say?'

'Said I'd never heard of you. Anyway, you know Jimmy the Greek?'

Kit shook his head.

'That's good,' said Kate. 'You don't want to know him. Anyway, Jimmy was also on the line. He runs an outfit in High Barnet. One of his boys is called Robbie. Nasty temper, but a good chemist. Anyway, Jimmy's worried because he lent Robbie to a Russian and now the Russian is dead and Robbie's scared he and I have unfinished business.'

'I told Robbie it was cool,' said Kit. 'And the guy was Chechen.'

Kate reached for another cigar.

'Armand de Valois was Chechen,' said Kit. 'Not Russian. Although he was pretending to be French.'

'You were there when he died?'

'I killed him.'

'You? A Chechen mafia leader ... Feel like telling me why?'

270

He made the kid dance.

'Neku,' said Kit, and the old woman nodded. It was answer enough.

'The Greek wants a meeting.' Blowing fresh smoke towards the ceiling, Kate sat back in her chair. In anybody else this might be taken as a sign of relaxation, but Kit could tell Kate was worried about something.

'So send your nephew,' said Kit.

'That would make it business. I want you to go,' said Kate. 'Sort out the problem.'

Maybe laughing wasn't the right response. 'Look,' said Kit, when Kate had stopped scowling. 'I'll call Jimmy.'

'Call him?'

'That's my best offer.'

Kate pushed her mobile across the desk and waited while Kit punched in the number she gave him.

'Mr Giangos?'

A sleepy grunt from the other end and a woman in the background, followed by a snapped instruction to be quiet. One didn't need Greek to understand what was being said. 'Yes ...?'

'I'm calling on behalf of Kate O'Mally.'

'What?' Jimmy Giangos. 'She can't call me herself?'

'It's about Robbie,' said Kit, ignoring the question. 'Mrs O'Mally wants you to know there is no problem. In fact, everything is fine. She will tell her nephew this.' Kate raised her eyebrows.

'The problem was Mr de Valois. This has now been solved.'

On the other side of the desk, Kate O'Mally actually began to smile. Although, Kit's next words knocked the smile from her face and reduced Kate to frozen silence.

'What problem? He kidnapped Kate O'Mally's granddaughter.'

Jimmy Giangos actually gulped.

'Robbie didn't tell you that?'

'No,' said Jimmy the Greek. 'He forgot to mention that bit. We knew nothing about ...'

'Mrs O'Mally understands that,' Kit said. 'She sends her regards.' Shutting off the phone, Kit looked up to see Kate staring at him.

'Look,' said Kit. 'I had to say something.'

'So that's why Pat came back,' said Kate, barely listening. Pushing away her chair, she walked to the window and stared out into the darkness, only coming back to her desk to rummage for another cigar. 'He must have worked it out for himself,' she said. 'Why didn't you tell me in Tokyo?'

'Tell you what?'

'The truth.' Kate O'Mally shook her head crossly. 'Everything finally makes sense. Mary's postcards to you. Her leaving you the flat and her gallery. The reason she'd never talk about being pregnant and what happened while she was away.'

Any objections Kit might make vanished as Kate's phone began to buzz. Having listened, the woman nodded a couple of times and broke the connection without saying a single word. 'The police,' said Kate. 'It's time we got you out of here. Come on.'

But Kit was going over what Kate had just said about Mary writing to him. And wondered whether to tell Kate he knew where Mary was, assuming she was anywhere. *I always thought this is where we'd both end up*.

It was the *both* that gave her away. Vita Brevis – bass/vocals/lyrics. Not one to waste words, ever ...

CHAPTER 54
nawa-no-ukiyo

Her cloak stank of smoke and her knives were gone. High Strange was cold and empty and not at all as it should have been.

'Door,' said Lady Neku.

The door, however, said nothing. It just stood there, black lacquered and shining, in the middle of the wall, with great brass hinges and a handle cut from a single block of obsidian.

KATCHATKA STATION read a metal plate on the lintel. BUILT BY KITAGAWA INCORPORATED, SHINJUKU, IN ASSOCIATION WITH PEARL ISLAND ENTERPRISES.

Neku shook her head. That description was wrong. It wasn't the wall which had brass hinges. Well, yes, but not in the way her words sounded. And anyway, the door might be black but it wasn't *urushi* lacquer, being made from a single block of obsidian, which meant the handle had to be something else.

Details were hard to remember. *Continuity glitches*, that was the technical term and her life had been full of them. Crossing out three lines of *hiragana* script, Neku rewrote the door as obsidian and its handle as marble, changing this to diamond as being more likely. She made the hinges steel for the sake of it and because brass felt too predictable.

Sixty-four pages it said on the back of her notebook, which was also the front, depending on which script she used. So far Neku had written alternate pages, from front and back, using a mixture of *kanji*, *romanji*, *katagana* and *hirogana*, being *han script*, *roman script*, *man's script* and *woman's hand*. She regarded it as her duty not to make the truth too accessible, also safer ...

'Come on,' said Lady Neku, giving the door a kick. 'All you have to do is open.'

'You know,' said the door. 'I'm not sure that's a good idea.'

'Why?' she demanded.

'Because,' said the door, 'once opened, I'm open. Returning to a time when I was locked becomes impossible.'

'I can relock you myself.'

'That's not the same,' said the door. 'And you know it.'

'I'm going to hate what's inside,' Lady Neku said. 'That's what you're saying, right?'

The door stayed silent.

Every other door in High Strange had opened as Lady Neku approached. Only the council chamber stayed locked. Six sided, to reflect the high stations, the chamber had six doors, one for each family. Every sector had a council chamber and the layout was identical for each.

The door should have recognised Lady Neku instantly and opened itself. It was the grandest of the doors, because this was High Strange and that was how things worked. In the d'Alambert Sector, Luc's family would have the grandest door, such things stood to reason.

'You know who I am?'

'Of course.'

'So why won't you open?' Lady Neku demanded, resisting the urge to kick the door again.

'Because,' said the door, 'you're dead.' There were so many things wrong with that statement that Lady Neku barely knew where to begin, so she began with the most obvious.

'If I was dead,' she said, 'we wouldn't be having this conversation.'

The door considered that.

'Also,' said Lady Neku, 'I can see my reflection.'

'Do you look like you?'

'Yes,' said Lady Neku, rather too fast. 'At least, I look like the me I remember.' She stared hard at her reflection in the door's black surface. Her face was coarser, her hips slightly thicker than she'd like and her hair had been dyed silver, but she still looked like her, despite the tattered lace of her *cos-play* dress. Lady Neku could definitely see herself in the other girl's eyes.

'I am Neku Katchatka,' she said. 'You will open.' So the door did and it was right, she didn't like what was inside one little bit.

A spread of shingle was washed by waves. The water so cold that she could feel nothing, although that might have been memories draining from her head. A boy was on the beach behind her, half kneeling, he seemed to be looking for someone and Neku was afraid it might be her. He never saw the man who put a gun to the back of his head and ...

'Wrong,' said Lady Neku, covering her ears. 'All wrong.'

The audience chamber was colder than she expected and icy underfoot, but for all its frosty chill the air was tainted with corruption. None of the lights lit on command, and the windows remained shuttered against the sky beyond. Flakes of ice had drifted into patterns on the floor. Lady Neku could only see these because light from the corridor flooded a strip of tiles in front of her. The rest of the chamber was in darkness.

Lady Neku knew what answer there would be to her request for the shutters to open and the lights come on, but she asked anyway, refusing to be shocked, surprised or even disappointed when they stayed closed and the lights failed to work.

Instead she stopped at the nearest window, trying and failing to force its covering before moving to the next. High and lonely and arched into darkness above her, each shutter rejected her attempts. Their touch burnt Lady Neku's fingers and glued cold metal to her skin.

'Fuck,' said Lady Neku, ripping herself free.

Each window took her deeper into darkness, until the door by which she'd entered became a tiny smudge of light that vanished as she reached halfway around the chamber and some object finally obscured the smudge from sight.

She kept up her litany of swearing until she approached a window. Only to begin again when its shutter refused to budge. After a while, the words lost their meaning and Lady Neku's voice lost its fury and the hot sweat beneath frozen arms, and the pain in her fingers, told her to stop *doing* and begin *planning* instead.

Everything was linked. As surely as the solar system completed its orbit of the galaxy every 250 million years and fugees needed the floating rope world to protect them from being poisoned. *Everything was linked.* She could get somewhere with that thought, Lady Neku just knew she could.

Forcing torn fingers into the web of a fresh shutter, Lady Neku heard a click, echoed from eleven other windows. As she watched, each began to iris, preparing to reveal light through a wall of metal flowers. And though every single one glitched before it was even a quarter open, this was enough.

The obsidian door had been right; what was seen could not be unseen, and doors could be reshut but not unopened.

'*What?*' Lady Neku told herself. '*You're going to cry now?*'

She made herself cross the tiles to the table where her family still sat, their food as frozen as those who'd been about to eat it. She did this by the simple expedient of refusing to give herself an option.

Lady Neku's mother grinned at the world from a gash that opened her throat from ear to jewelled ear. She'd either been the first to die, or accepted her death without complaint, because the arms of her chair still touched the table and her glass of wine stood icy but undisturbed. Blood crusted the surface of her Maltese lace shawl like beads of jet, sewn into random patterns.

Her brother Nico had gone down fighting, his scabbard abandoned beside his half-seated body, his chair pushed back and twisted sideways. Antonio sat back and Petro slumped so far forward in his seat that his head rested on the table. Even his long black hair felt frozen.

Everyone wore their best clothes, black velvet and lace, jewelled cloaks. Only one member of the Katchatka family was missing. The one staring down at the table and its barely-touched wedding banquet.

So this was what death looked like, thought Lady Neku. A massive smear of shit across the surface of the world. She should have known. All this, just to remember why she'd first run away.

CHAPTER 55

Monday 2 July

So much of what Kit thought was right was wrong, starting with who killed Ben Flyte. The police had believed the killer was Armand de Valois, until Kit tripped up their conclusions while Kit himself had decided it was Kate O'Mally, a woman he'd always believed capable of anything.

It had been someone else entirely.

'*Ben?*' demanded Pat, pulling off a muddy track. His question was meant to be throwaway. A *sorry, what was that?* Only Kit had watched his shoulders tense.

'Mary's boyfriend.'

'Really?' Pat said. 'I'm not sure we ever met. They kept changing ...'

'Kate mentioned him in Tokyo.'

'He's probably with someone else now,' said Pat. 'Things are different these days.'

Kit sighed. 'You know,' he said, 'what your mistake was?'

Pat Robbe-Duras climbed out of the car. After a second Kit realised he was meant to follow. The sky was dark, the stars high and the moon half hidden by a flat scrap of cloud. A flare of a match and the restless tip of a cigarette were the only clues that Pat was walking towards an open-fronted hangar, watched by sleepy cattle from a nearby field.

'Tell me my mistake,' he said, when Kit caught up.

'Never once mentioning him,' said Kit, then asked a question that had been troubling him, really troubling him. 'No face, no fingers, no jaw, no teeth. How did you bring yourself to inflict that level of damage?'

'He used to hit her,' said Pat. 'Did Katie tell you that? Mary wouldn't let either of us interfere. We were just meant to live with it. And then she went missing.'

'The suicide?'

'Before that,' said Pat, disappearing into the hangar. When he returned it was to pick up his conversation where it left off. 'Mary was due to have lunch with me about a week before she took the ferry. She never turned up, but Ben did in that wretched little car of his.'

'Did he say where Mary was?'

'No,' said Pat. 'Hadn't seen her in days apparently, and didn't know where she'd gone, wanted my help getting her back.'

'So you killed him.'

'That was later,' Pat said. 'When I realised he'd brought his shit into my life.'

'*What?*'

'He arrived with a Chinese lacquer trunk he'd found Mary for Christmas. Asked me to store it until they made up again, lying little fuck. I gave him about ten minutes, to make sure he wasn't coming back and then hacked the lock. You know what I found?'

'Heroin.'

Pat nodded. 'So I called him up and said I knew where Mary was, but we needed to talk before I told him.' The old man's face was a cold mask in the moonlight. 'He came bouncing back, all smiles, promising to make everything right. And then he saw the open trunk ...'

Two men were leading a small plane out of the hangar, one of them walking ahead. The plane had both its engines going and was inching forward, running without lights. As Kit watched it angled itself along a darkened runway.

'You should go,' said Pat.

'Say goodbye to Neku for me. And tell her I'll see her soon. Tell her that's a promise.'

'Of course.'

Looking away, Kit said. 'You never told me how you made yourself mutilate Ben Flyte. What drove you, was it anger?'

'No one got tortured,' said Pat. 'We had a whisky while Ben waited for me to tell him where to find Mary. Only his glass was loaded with my painkillers. I put him in the freezer and hacked him up later, when he'd frozen. It was meant to make his body hard to identify.'

'It worked,' Kit said. 'And the drugs?'

'Into the river.' Pat looked sad. 'That was my big mistake,' he said. 'They killed the fish.'

The waters of the English Channel were dark beneath the plane. A sheet of oxidised lead hammered flat by moonlight and wind. A bank of tiny diodes on a console were the only lights in the cabin. Kit was pretty certain that flying dark was illegal but he kept his mouth shut and watched sullen lead turn into wild grass instead.

Dawn was an hour away. Which would give Kate's pilot time to land in France, turn around and be back over Kent before the sun clipped the horizon. A feat quite within the Beechcraft's capabilities, according to a tatty leaflet Kit had been reading before take-off.

The King E90 was a turboprop, once popular with air charter companies. It could stay airborne for six hours and was designed to seat eight, two pilots, four passengers in club chairs, and two bodyguards, chauffeurs or junior staff in seats at the back.

In the plane they used, someone had long-since ripped out the leather seats and replaced the carpet with sheet steel, unless that was the original floor. Over the steel had been taped polythene, now badly scuffed and somewhat torn. Whatever this plane usually carried it was unlikely to be business-class passengers, or their assorted hangers-on.

The pilot was a young Asian called Tony. At least that was how he'd introduced himself at the small airfield, where Kit had been dropped by Pat, who turned out to drive almost as fast as Brigadier Miles.

'Calais ... right?' It was the first thing Tony had said since take-off.

'Apparently.'

'Okay, I'm to give you this.'

The padded envelope contained euros, two credit cards, an EU driving licence, one of the new ID cards and a passport, all made out in a name Kit didn't recognise. Kate O'Mally had obviously spent the last half hour before Kit left pulling in favours. It said something for her reputation that the fakes were good.

'Computers,' said Tony, glancing across. 'Just drop in the photograph and hit print.'

The licence and ID looked perfect. The back pages of the passport, when Kit examined them in the light of a pencil torch seemed slightly ruffled.

'If anyone queries you,' Tony said. 'Say you got caught in the rain.' He shrugged. 'And remember, the credit cards are only for show. Your boss said use cash ...'

My boss? Kit laughed.

The wild grass gave way to French fields and finally to a small airstrip trapped between an empty railway line and the edge of a vast farm, one of those industrial outfits with tractors the size of small houses and pig pens the size of railway stations.

'You known Kate O'Mally long?' Kit asked.

'Never heard of her,' said Tony, adjusting the joystick to slide the Air King E90 between a narrow strip of lights. 'Never heard of you either. I'm not even here.'

There were slow trains to Paris from Calais, express trains and even a Eurostar, which stopped to take on passengers at a dedicated station nearby. A plane ticket was already waiting for Kit at Aeroport Charles de Gaulle. All the same, Paris, the ticket and Kit's flight to Tokyo would have to wait. There was somewhere else Kit needed to go first. He got there by lorry.

'Good for you I was passing.'

They'd been through this. It was good Philippe had been passing and even better that he stopped when Kit stuck out his thumb. So now Philippe wanted paying in English conversation and Kit was doing his best to oblige.

'It's a clear morning.'

The driver peered intently through his windscreen and then nodded agreement. 'Very clear,' he said.

'And the sea is blue.'

'Very blue. Also grey.'

Kit sighed. It was 370 kilometres from Calais to Amsterdam and so far they'd managed fifty of them. If Philippe was to be believed, his cargo was going the whole way. Although Kit had a feeling his original question might have been misunderstood, he'd find out in a while.

'Your hand it is hurt?'

This was a fair guess, given Kit was wearing a finger stall and had tape holding what remained of his smallest finger to the ring finger next door. 'An accident,' said Kit, folding his hand out of sight.

'Nasty,' Philippe said. 'You walking?'

'No,' said Kit. 'I'm in a lorry with you.'

Philippe laughed. 'I mean, are you *holiday walking*? Lots of the English visit Pas de Calais to walk. Also Amsterdam, where they hire bicycles.'

'Not walking, or planning to hire a bike in Amsterdam.'

'But you're visiting the city on holiday?'

'Yes,' said Kit. 'And I'm late.'

Philippe frowned. 'How late?' he asked.

At least fifteen years, thought Kit, but he kept the words to himself.

There were cities where Kit barely knew one place from another outside the area in which he'd lived. The squalor of a ghetto in Istanbul, an arid little suq in a town Sudanese rebels called their capital. Even Tokyo – where Kit could have told Roppongi from Shinjuku blindfold by street noise alone – largely remained a mystery to him.

And yet the city about which Kit knew most was the one he'd never visited. Empires had squabbled over it and Protestants besieged Catholics to claim its muddy flood-threatened streets. Home to Rembrandt van Rijn, the place where Descartes linked identity indelibly to thought, the city had fought against the British, French and Spanish, given England a king and been ruled by one of Napoleon's brothers.

Its canals were famous, it had two of the most famous churches in Europe, and yet all most tourists knew it for was brothels, endless bicycles and cafés where it was still legal to smoke dope.

Amsterdam had been Mary's idea. Although it was Kit who bought the map and found the first guide book. Mary was the one who bought the postcards, five in total from a charity shop in Newbury. All black and white, and showing views of a city that probably didn't exist even then. The Prinsengracht canal, Anne Frank's House and a solemn-looking Rijksmuseum, Rembrandt's *Night Watch*, and last of all a typical Dutch square overlooking a narrow canal.

Tulips grew in wooden tubs, an old man in clogs sat smoking a pipe … A girl in a dark coat and a young man with a beret pushed a pram beneath a row of poplars.

That was going to be them.

It took Mary and Kit a whole weekend to identify Statholder Square from a map. The bridge helped and the church opposite. They were going to become famous, sell millions of Switchblade Lies CDs and buy one of the narrow houses that stared from the square to the canal beyond. The dream lasted about seven weeks. Long enough to learn a handful of Dutch words, cut a demo, and decide they'd have a white cat and never see either of their families again.

All of this in the year before Kit stopped beside a hut above Middle Morton to crash a party to which he definitely hadn't been invited, and everything in his life suggested he'd have done better to avoid.

Seven narrow houses lined one edge of Statholder Square, a museum dedicated to the Goldsmith's Guild and a row of smaller houses stood opposite. The tulip tubs were gone and the poplars on the canal edge had sprouted wrought-iron cages to protect them from the world. And looking from the square's open edge, Kit saw five more houses and a wide-windowed art gallery where the original postcard had shown a print shop.

A steel grille protected the gallery window and a sign on the door read, *gesloten*.

Closed.

Taped to the window was a large poster of a semi-nude with wild blonde hair, a sour smile and dark nipples. The words beneath read *33/33 @ 3+30. A series of self portraits by Sophie Sullivan.* Whatever Kit expected, it wasn't this.

It took five knocks to earn a shout and another five before footsteps could be heard on the stairs behind the door. When the last of the bolts shot back, a cropped-haired woman blocked his way.

'Gesloten,' she announced, pointing to the sign and reading it aloud in case he was a complete idiot.

'I'm a friend,' said Kit, nodding to the poster.

'Of Sophie?'

'Yes,' said Kit.

The woman looked doubtful.

'Call Sophie,' he suggested. 'Say I'm here to see Mary.' When that failed to work, Kit added *please*, and somehow this was enough.

The conversation happened just out of earshot, with Kit on the doorstep. When the woman returned her eyes were hard. 'This Mary of yours is dead. Sophie says you know that already.'

'Except she isn't. Is she?'

It took another ten minutes and two more calls. The last call to Sophie sounded very much like an argument. 'She'll see you,' said the woman, not bothering to disguise her anger.

'Sophie?'

'The other one.'

I always thought this is where we'd both end up. So obvious, but only in retrospect. It made Kit want to punch himself.

'Which house?' he demanded.

The gallery owner looked puzzled.

'Where's Mary staying?'

'At the hotel, obviously ...'

Herberg Statholder was so hip it avoided signs and any clues it might actually be a hotel. A simple black-painted door, with a dolphin door knocker, opened onto stairs leading up to reception. The air smelt of scented candles and expensive leather. The Warhols on the wall looked as if they might be original.

A brass lift carried Kit down to an almost-empty sitting room, which looked over Statholder Square or the canal, depending on which sofa one chose. It was here he found Sophie, who clipped a bell on the table in front of her and ordered two espressos from the man who materialised, without bothering to check if Kit wanted coffee.

She looked older than he remembered, her hair unwashed and her nails bitten. Worry, anger or a migraine had closed down her face. 'So ...' Sophie said, when their cups arrived. 'You've come to see Mary.'

'Yeah,' said Kit.

'How did you find out?'

'Mary told me where she was,' he said. 'Only, I was just too fucking stupid to realise.'

'*She told you.*'

'I got a postcard before Christmas,' said Kit. 'An old card I thought she'd long since thrown away. It said ...' He hesitated. 'It said things that should have been said long ago. And it said here was where Mary thought we'd both end up.'

'I don't get it.'

'Nor did I,' said Kit. 'Not at first.'

'I think this is a bad idea,' Sophie said. 'Mary knows that. If Ben or the Russian follow you here ...'

'They're dead.'

Sophie put her cup down with a click.

'Ben Flyte died six months ago,' said Kit. 'The other one died yesterday.'

'What happened?' asked Sophie.

'I killed him.'

Sophie blinked. 'You killed Armand de Valois?' Her hands were shaking, Kit realised. Shaking so badly she halted on the edge of reaching for her cup. 'What about the sergeant?'

'What about him?'

'He was employed by de Valois. And Ben relied on the sergeant for protection. They'd been working together for years.'

Kit put down his own cup and looked round the elegant drawing room, rejecting a house phone that sat on a marble table near the door. 'You'll have to excuse me,' he said. 'I need to make a call.'

CHAPTER 56
Monday 2 July

The first phone booth was empty and working but took only credit cards, so Kit walked until he came to another, which was occupied. A quarter mile after that he found a third outside a café.

Everyone at a pavement table looked up, but this was probably because Kit had just entered a booth in a city where even tramps seemed to carry their own phones.

Feeding a twenty-euro note into a slot, Kit fed in another and then a third, making sure he had sufficient credit. He wanted to avoid the slightest chance of losing his concentration while making this call.

'Amy.'

Stunned silence gave way to a gasp. 'Shit,' she said. 'I can't believe you'd ...' And then Amy said nothing, although her silence was thick with worry, anger and unmade decisions.

'You could record this,' said Kit. 'Or you could give me the Brigadier's direct number.'

'I'm at Boxbridge,' Amy said. 'We were just talking about you.'

A briefer silence became the voice of Brigadier Miles. 'Mr Newton,' she said. 'I imagine you realise we're tracing this call.'

'I'm in Amsterdam,' said Kit. 'About ten minutes walk from Statholder Square, outside the Tolkien Café. Although I'll be gone the moment I hear sirens or see anything resembling a police car. I want to do you a favour. Do you know someone called Alfie ... Alfie Maran?'

'Not as well as I'd like. He's currently in South London, helping the Met with their enquiries. Apparently he was somewhere else when Mr de Valois got murdered. Alfie just can't quite decide where. You did hear about that unpleasantness, didn't you?'

Kit ignored the comment.

'And for some reason,' said Brigadier Miles. 'The Met are unhappy with us. They think we've been hiding things.'

'Which you have.'

It was Kit's turn to get ignored.

'Talk to Alfie,' he said.

'And say what?' The Brigadier sounded interested.

'Ask him about Mr de Valois' relationship with Sergeant Samson. You'll have to offer him immunity, but more to the point, tell Alfie it will make Kate O'Mally and Mike Smith very happy.'

'Will it?'

Kit shrugged, watching his money count down on a little digital window. 'It probably won't make them unhappy.'

'You know,' said the Brigadier. 'I'm beginning to believe the rumours that you're actually working for Mrs O'Mally.'

'I've heard those rumour too,' Kit said. 'All lies.'

'And if I did offer Alfie help, it would be immunity from what?'

'General wickedness, I imagine. Unless you know something I don't.'

'So he didn't knife de Valois?'

'No,' said Kit. 'He didn't.'

The Brigadier sighed. 'I was afraid of that. You do realise, don't you, that your prints are all over that blade?'

'Quite possibly,' said Kit.

'Anyway,' the old woman said. 'Let's get back to Alfie. What can he give me?'

'Something to upset the Met.'

'Really?'

Kit grinned. It was a tired grin, one that barely made it onto his face but it was still a grin. He felt it catch the side of his mouth like a hook setting. 'Thought that would interest you,' he said. 'Armand de Valois was paying Sergeant Samson in women as well as cash for information ...'

Brigadier Miles laughed.

'It gets better, ' Kit added. 'The sergeant and Ben Flyte were a team. In fact, I'd bet it was Sergeant Samson who told Flyte that de Valois was dead, right after that shooting in Germany. I can see the attraction. All that heroin with no owner. What's a crooked cop to do? Only, Armand wasn't dead. A bit like Ben Flyte.'

'Flyte?'

'Last seen in South London, I believe ... Sometime yesterday.'

He had the Brigadier's attention, the hook set as firmly into her mouth as it was set in his.

'What you've got,' said Kit, 'is a murdered terrorist, and a society drug dealer as your chief suspect – and providing Alfie talks – a currently-suspended officer from a South London drugs squad who's the only known connection between the two. If I were you, I'd offer Alfie anything he wants.'

'I'm going to make some calls,' said the Brigadier. 'Give me a number where I can call you back.'

'I need a favour in return.'

'A favour?'

'The name behind a construction company in Tokyo.'

Silence greeted this request. A handful of seconds of static and doubt. And then the Brigadier was back. 'And how do I get you that?'

'You must have friends,' said Kit.

'Not in Tokyo,' said Brigadier Miles.

'People like you,' Kit said, 'have friends everywhere.'

CHAPTER 57
Monday 2 July

All of the rooms at Herberg Statholder had double beds, their own glass-topped vanity tables, satellite television, discreet minibars, music systems and wireless internet. Laptops were provided for guests who forgot to bring their own.

Meals could be served at any time of day or night and in any place, although the Sky Café apparently offered unrivalled views across the slate roofs of Amsterdam, and all guests got preferential booking at a Michelin-starred brasserie less than three minutes walk from the hotel.

The Herberg Statholder had money. It had money because its guests had money and matching expectations. Herberg Statholder pulled off that difficult trick of offering the expensively shabby and casually exclusive. Although a wooden panel in the lift was cracked, the brass fittings were hand-polished and the lift's single picture was signed and numbered and came from one of Chagall's shorter runs.

Kit took the lift alone because Sophie refused to accompany him, her anger so obvious that he began to wonder if it was with Mary rather than him.

Room 12.

Herberg Statholder avoided numbering its rooms according to floor. With only twelve bedrooms such fussiness was irrelevant. The narrow corridor onto which Kit's lift opened led to the Sky Café in one direction, and to three bedrooms in the other: servants' quarters, made fashionable by their rooftop view and the tectonic shifts of history.

'Come in ...'

He would have known the voice anywhere. Kit was still wondering what to say when Mary pulled herself up and adjusted the pillows behind her head.

'Long time,' she said.

He nodded.

'I didn't mean you to find me,' said Mary, then added. 'Sophie called me, while you were on the way up. You read more into my card than was there.'

'No,' Kit said. 'I didn't.'

She looked at him.

'Why send it then?' demanded Kit. 'At least, why that card and those words?'

'To hurt you,' Mary said. 'So you knew what really happened. I was tying up my life's loose ends and you were one of them.' Her window was open on the other side of the bed, a vase of orchids stood on a vanity table and an open copy of *Vanity Fair* lay discarded on the floor. It made no difference. The room reeked of illness.

'Sit down,' said Mary, and that was when Kit realised he was still standing in her doorway.

'What is it?' he asked.

'A mistake, we shared needles. Ben was in remission and I didn't even know he was ill. I came apart in a matter of months.' She nodded towards a chair. 'Sit,' she said.

A child could be heard outside, chattering excitedly about nothing very much. A bicycle went past in need of oiling. A woman talked to herself, or on the phone. 'You hear all that?' said Mary, indicating her open window.

He nodded.

'It's called life. That's what I'm leaving behind.'

'I don't suppose,' said Kit, when he'd listened some more to the noises outside and seen Mary smile, 'there's much point my asking why you staged a fake suicide?'

'You don't know?'

'How would I?'

'Because you always boasted you knew me better than I knew myself.'

Kit shrugged. 'I must have been lying.'

Mary's laugh was thin. 'Take a guess,' she said.

'You were escaping Armand de Valois.'

'Why would I do that?'

'Because the man wanted his heroin back.'

'My choice had nothing to do with Ben,' she said, sitting back. 'Or that dealer of his. Anyway, I couldn't have told de Valois where his drugs were because I didn't bloody know.'

'If Ben wasn't the reason?'

'Oh God,' said Mary. 'Work it out.'

Sat on a chair, beside a bed in the attic of an absurdly over-priced hotel in Amsterdam, Kit did. It was a very Mary reason.

'You couldn't stand Pat and Kate watching you die.'

She nodded.

'You wanted to spare them the pain.'

Mary laughed, hard enough to set her coughing again. When Kit patted her back he felt mostly bone. 'Oh God,' she said, catching her breath. 'All that black leather and cynicism and fucked-up back history. And you've still got a heart of pure marshmallow. You've seen how my father is. You've seen how my mother fusses. I wanted to spare *me* the pain.'

They sat in silence, with a warm wind carrying sounds and a slight sourness from the canal through Mary's open window. The orchids were new, the paper open on her bed was that day's issue. Someone was obviously looking after her.

'Anyway,' said Mary, into the silence. 'Enough about me. Tell me about you. Are you married? What's Tokyo like as a place to live? Do you have kids?'

There was no easy answer to any of those. So Kit told her about Neku instead. About how *cos-play* dressed and how his bar had been a drinking club for *bozozoku*. And how he'd finally worked out the reason he liked Tokyo so much was that everyone spent most of their time pretending to be someone else.

'You met this child on the street?'

'In a Roppongi doorway. I gave her coffee. She cried.'

'And now you've got her at the flat in London?'

'It's not like that,' said Kit, explaining what it was like, as Mary listened intently and asked the occasional question, until she had what she needed to know.

'So you're using this girl to repay a debt you owe me?'

Kit nodded.

'I can live with that,' she said.

The metal tub in Mary's bathroom had clawed feet and stood in the middle of the room, on boards that had been sanded back to bare wood and then painted white, very crudely. A single curtain-less window looked up at sky.

'Not too hot,' said Mary, smiling when Kit tested the water with his elbow, as he'd once seen Yoshi do before bathing her nephew. Mary was far thinner than he remembered, her vertebrae sharp beneath his fingers as he soaped her back.

'Wash me thoroughly,' she said, kneeling up.

Kit did his best.

By the time he finished, the bath water was tepid and every inch of Mary's body had been soaped and flannelled clean. As a final gesture, he let the water drain away and used a hand shower to rinse her body. After that, he dried her carefully.

'Thank you,' she said. 'I can't persuade Sophie to do that.'

'Why not?'

'Too invasive,' said Mary. 'We're lovers,' she added, when Kit looked puzzled. 'Well, we're meant to be. It's been a while ...'

After he'd helped Mary back to bed, Kit spoke more about Neku and then about Tokyo, and he found himself telling her about the stand-off at the building site in Roppongi. Somehow that led to him telling her about Yoshi and the fire, not really being married and the night Neku killed a man.

'No one fights like that,' said Mary. 'Unless it's what they know.' Her voice was tired and her lips trembled, but she spoke with the certainty of someone facing death and refusing to look away. 'She comes from where I come from,' Mary said, before Kit could ask how she knew. It was the only time he could remember her mentioning Kate's profession.

'Ask yourself who really gains,' said Mary. 'Ask yourself how many of the things you believe to be true are lies. Find out what *really* happened that night ...'

'I'm sorry,' said Kit.

'Yes,' said Mary. 'Me too.'

Neither was talking about her family, Japan or the fact Mary was dying. 'About the bath,' she said. 'Don't tell Sophie.'

'I won't,' Kit promised, it was the last thing he said to her.

CHAPTER 58
nawa-no-ukiyo

She had betrayed herself, her family and Luc d'Alambert, everyone of
these by accident. So much for Lady Neku to remember, so much to
forget ...

'How does *that* work?' Luc had asked, finding himself standing in High
Strange, beside a recently regrown pod. He meant the fact that he was
standing there at all.

'Who knows?' said Lady Neku.

One second they were in Schloss Omga, the next Luc was asking his
question and Lady Neku was doing her best not to look smug. 'I mean,'
she said. 'How does High Strange stay up and what makes sky sails
change colour if the sun flares?'

'They're made that way,' said Luc. 'And we're high enough above the
ground to stay here.'

'No we're not,' she said. 'I've checked. We'd need to be at least three
times this height to stay in orbit, and then we'd have to circle the planet.'

Luc smiled. 'You really are strange,' he said.

Lady Neku sighed.

'I should go,' he said.

'Yes,' agreed Lady Neku. 'You should.' She watched him limp away, his
yellow cloak tangling with his heels as he walked. His foot, his lopsided
smile, that tic in his right eye; small problems, Lady Neku was pretty
sure he'd have them fixed if she suggested it.

'It's time you dressed,' said a voice in Lady Neku's head.

'What's the point?' she said. 'I'm only going to take it all off again. I
could always ...'

'No,' said the voice. 'You couldn't.'

The cloak was black, the dress was black, as was her belt and the shoes decorated with tiny beads. A black-bladed dagger hid inside a black velvet scabbard, the leather of its retaining thongs being the obvious colour.

'And the others?' Lady Neku asked.

'Already dressed,' said the *kami*. 'Going over the final arrangements. Do you want to see?'

Her brothers were in her mother's study, at the southern tip of the spire. Amber walls like frozen honey, a steel throne and a trio of wooden stools set neatly around it. Lady Katchatka wore a dress cut from spider's silk, the light-swallowing kind she professed to despise.

The boys wore doublets and cloaks sewn with black pearls. Petro was alive, looking pale and unsteady on his seat, Nico and Antonio supporting him at each elbow, neither prepared to meet their mother's eyes.

'You know what to do?' asked Lady Katchatka.

All three boys nodded.

'Nico moves first,' said Lady Katchatka. 'Until then, everyone behaves.'

Petro got ready to protest.

'*Nico does it,*' she told him. 'You're weak as a baby and Antonio is too slow. We strike fast, and hard. With d'Alambert dead the cripple will be useless. Antonio can have him. After that, kill anyone you want.'

'And the ships?'

'Old men and children,' said Lady Katchatka. 'We deny them air and food unless they surrender.' She smiled at Nico's raised eyebrows. 'All right,' she said. 'We'll deny it anyway.'

'What about Neku?' asked Petro, from a throat wet and barely formed.

'She'll get over it,' Lady Katchatka said.

The marriage ceremony was simple, the bedding embarrassingly crude. Mostly in the thinness of the mattress, the hardness of the actual bed and the wide-eyed enthusiasm of d'Alambert's retainers. As a sop to Lady Neku's modesty, Lord d'Alambert had allowed her a sheet. It came, almost inevitably, in a vile shade of yellow.

'We must talk,' said Lady Neku, as Luc slipped a robe from his shoulders and climbed self-consciously into bed beside her.

'Later,' he said. The boy was shaking, body taut as a karman wire.

'Now,' said Lady Neku, reaching up to wrap her arms around his neck and drag him close enough to bury her face in his hair. One of the retainers started clapping, and Lady Neku heard Nico groan.

'It's a trap,' she whispered.

Luc pulled back. 'What is?'

Grabbing his hair, Lady Neku yanked him down again, to general laughter from her brothers and a sigh from Luc's father. Only family were allowed close, retainers being kept at a decent distance by silken ropes.

'All of this,' whispered Lady Neku. 'Stay next to me at the banquet, I'll protect you.'

Startled eyes stared down at her. Luc wanted to demand answers, he wanted to scramble away. It was all Lady Neku could do to hold the boy in place.

'Whisper,' she said.

Luc leant close and someone started clapping again. 'What's a trap?' he asked, turning his head as Lady Neku's hands twisted into his hair and dragged his ear to her mouth.

'Everything,' she said. 'All of it.'

'Why?'

Lady Neku met his eyes. 'I don't know,' she said. 'I've only just found out. But you're in danger.'

'My father ...'

Shaking her head, Lady Neku felt her face against his. 'Too late,' she said. 'It'll be all I can do to save you.' A half dozen members of family stood watching, a hundred servitors waited behind a silken rope. The boy clung to her, his body protected only by the sheet. Anyone could have killed him with a single thrust, she should be grateful her brothers had spared her that.

'We have to go through with this,' said Lady Neku.

Luc's eyes widened. 'I can't.'

'Everyone's watching,' she said. 'You must.' *If you don't,* thought Lady Neku, *then Nico at least will know something is wrong and it will be much harder for me to protect you.*

His lovemaking was angry and brutal, as if it was her fault everything had already begun to go wrong. This was High Strange, once called Katchatka Segment. What did he expect?

Lady Neku whimpered and sighed, closed her eyes and clung to her new husband, burying her head in his hair. It was a command performance. So unexpected that she impressed even herself. When it was over, the face she presented to her family was streaked with tears. And the tears, at least, were real.

You did this, she told them, inside herself. *You took away my friendship with Luc. You made him hate me.*

Tradition allowed her to miss the banquet. In fact, tradition allowed her to hide her face from public sight for three days. Time for a new bride to live down the trauma of her public bedding. It was a d'Alambert family tradition. Lady Neku wasn't remotely impressed by what it said about them.

'You're sure you want to attend?' Lord d'Alambert stood with a cloak, ready to hide Lady Neku's nakedness. A moon-faced servitor, moist-eyed in sympathy for the tears drying on her new mistress's face stood ready to escort Lady Neku to a waiting ship. 'It would give you time to ...'

Lady Neku smiled her sweetest smile. 'I want to be with Luc,' she said, and all of the old man's resistance crumbled.

The cloak he offered her was a faded shade of red, with slivers of amber sewn in patterns around the hem. It was lined with yellow silk and weighed so heavily that Lady Neku's knees buckled as Lord d'Alambert draped it around her bare shoulders.

Having shown her mistress how to fasten the collar, the moon-faced servitor led Lady Neku to an alcove, so she could dress properly and compose herself. *Of course I'm shaking,* Lady Neku wanted to snarl. *You'd shake if you knew what was about to happen.*

'Leave me,' she demanded.

The servitor looked doubtful, which was interesting. Had the woman been from High Strange she'd barely have dared lift her eyes from the floor.

'I need time.'

Confusion, sympathy and apologies ... Lady Neku looked around the empty alcove and sighed. Struggling into her wedding dress, Lady Neku wrapped the ridiculous cloak around her shoulders and looked for the dagger she'd left under her folded clothes. It was gone.

'Oh great,' she said, just as Luc appeared in the doorway.

He blinked. A second later, Luc's father was standing behind him, concern on his face. 'Is everything all right?'

'I'm fine,' said Lady Neku, squaring her shoulders. It was only as she walked from the alcove to the candle-lit grandeur of the banquet that Lady Neku began to wonder how Luc's anxiety had produced his father in the door behind him, with no words being exchanged. She should have paid that thought more attention.

The major domo had excelled himself. A white tablecloth spread the length of a table. Silver candlesticks and oil lamps flickered and gutted smokily in the breeze from a recycling unit. Overhead lights could have been used, and food could have been pulled from the Drexie boxes, but this was a banquet, so fresh meat had been killed and old bottles had been opened.

Katchatka and d'Alambert. On the surface it was a triumph of diplomatic negotiation. Two families who had barely talked to each other in the time that anyone in the room had been alive now sat at the same table, preparing to celebrate their new alliance.

At one end sat Lady Katchatka, with Lord d'Alambert at the end opposite, in a chair of exactly-equal size. Luc and Lady Neku were on d'Alambert's right. Antonio, Petro and Nico on their mother's right, with Petro in the middle, so his brothers could support him discreetly, should Petro's new body proved too weak to cope with the meal.

It was the seating that protocol demanded.

'Lady Neku,' said Lord d'Alambert, raising his glass. 'Who will always have a place in our family.'

Raising her own glass, Lady Katchatka readied herself to make some equally facile reply and Lady Neku tensed, but all that happened was that her mother toasted Luc's strength and intelligence, and lowered her glass again. One course drifted into two and then three, bottles of old wine emptied and were replaced, until the room began to blur slightly and Lady Neku forced herself to drink only water.

Could she have misunderstood?

The image of her mother and brothers in the Amber Study felt so real that Lady Neku was still wondering when her mother nodded to Nico. 'If you would,' she said. 'We should give Lord d'Alambert his present.'

Lurching to his feet, Nico staggered to a side table and grabbed what looked like a cushion. Only, when he returned, Lady Neku could see that the cushion supported a tiny battered-looking bowl.

'I understand,' said Lady Katchatka, 'that you are interested in antiquity. This is the oldest artefact we possess. It is now yours.'

Nico put Yoshi's bowl on the table in front of Lord d'Alambert. And in that moment, as the old man's eyes fixed on fragile clay and Lady Neku began to rise from her seat, Nico struck, burying his dagger deep into Lord d'Alambert's heart.

At least, that was what was meant to happen. What Lady Neku thought had happened.

Only the old man took the blade through his wrist, wrenching the dagger from Nico's grasp with a single twist of his injured arm. From the expression on Lord d'Alambert's face he'd already moved beyond pain.

And as Antonio cried out and Petro tried to stand, Nico died, his chest opened in a single slash that sprayed d'Alambert with blood. It was a miracle the old man could see to reach for Nico's heart.

Lord d'Alambert killed Antonio with a single throw, catching him below the jaw and returning him to his seat. Petro died at the hands of Luc, who simply leant across the table to slit the throat of the man opposite, Petro being too weak, drunk or both to defend himself.

Sex and killing sounded the same, Lady Neku realised. All wet sucking and the slurp of broken vacuum. It even smelt the same, salt and sweet and shitty enough to leave her queasy.

'Wait,' she shouted, when Luc moved towards the final chair.

'She betrayed you,' he said. 'She traded you for a chance to kill my father. Why should she live?'

Because she's still my mother.

'How did you find out?' asked Lady Katchatka, with the calm of someone already dead.

'Your daughter told us,' said Luc.

Maybe he meant to be cruel, or perhaps he simply meant to tell the truth. Lady Neku watched her mother's composure falter. 'Wonderful,' Lady Katchatka said. 'Betrayed by the family idiot. How did she find out?'

'A *kami* told me,' said Lady Neku.

'AIs don't . . .' Cold eyes fixed on the girl. 'I should have drowned you at birth,' said Lady Katchatka. 'Make it quick,' she told Luc, her daughter already forgotten. 'Quick and clean.'

'Was that the death you intended to give us?' The voice behind Luc was thin with the pain of a skewered wrist.

'Yes,' said Lady Katchatka. 'It was.'

The corridor was empty, the statues silent, dust drifted in tiny eddies across the floor. It was cooler than Lady Neku remembered, which had to be the cause of her constant shivering.

'Go on,' she said, as she spun a handle. 'Open.' But the airlock door in front of her remained steadfastly closed. 'Just open,' said Lady Neku. 'How hard can that be?'

'It'll kill you,' High Strange said.

'That's fine with me.'

'And everyone else in the habitat.'

'Even better,' said Lady Neku, twisting the handle. When the great metal ring jammed in one direction, she reversed the spin, until it jammed in that direction as well. 'Open,' she demanded, dashing tears from her eyes. 'Stop fucking me around.'

The wound in her shoulder looked bad, but the truth was Luc had pulled his blow the moment Lady Neku threw herself in front of Lady Katchatka. Bleeding to death would take longer than Lady Neku was prepared to wait, assuming it was possible at all.

'Please ...' she said. 'Just open this door for me.'

'There are a hundred and thirty-five people on the habitat.'

'No there aren't,' said Lady Neku.

The voice gave her a list. It was right, of course, provided you counted servitors and retainers. She stood in the duct below the audience chamber, reached by the helix of stairs behind the unicorn. No one had seen her pull aside the tapestry and hide herself; they were all too busy watching Lady Katchatka die.

'Open,' demanded Lady Neku, more to banish this thought than any real belief High Strange might listen.

'And if I do?' it said.

'We die,' said Lady Neku.

'That's what you want?'

Lady Neku nodded her head.

'Say it,' the voice said. 'Name the people you think should die.'

'I don't know all their names,' said Lady Neku crossly, as she rubbed knuckles into her eyes and folded her cloak tight, to hide the sight of blood which was beginning to make her feel sick.

'So, you're saying you want people killed, but you don't actually know their names?'

Yes, that is exactly ... Well, Lady Neku thought about it. *Maybe not exactly*.

'You want Luc dead?'

Of course I want ... She hesitated. Killing Luc was her duty. Something to which she should dedicate the rest of her life. All the same. 'This isn't fair,' Lady Neku said.

'Nor is opening that door.'

For the rest of their conversation Lady Neku sat on the floor, her knees pulled up to her chin and her back against the door she'd been trying to open. She knew the discussion was mostly internal. High Strange just helping to pick through her thoughts.

'All right,' it said. 'I've opened the door. Only a fraction,' it added, as Lady Neku scrambled to her feet. 'The air is already thinner and your core temperature has begun to fall. That's why the bleeding is less. In a few seconds Luc and his father will begin to search for you. A short while later, they'll stop looking and make plans to abandon the habitat.'

'And me?' asked Lady Neku.

'Ah yes,' said High Strange. 'I need to talk to you about that.'

Her life was saved by a bowl. Along with the life of Luc, his father, their retainers, other families and people who clung to existence in parts of the world Lady Neku barely realised were inhabited.

The whole of humanity had been preserved because of a wafer-thin bowl barely larger than Lady Neku's cupped hands. It was old, it was cracked beneath the rim and it was the colour of burnt earth. It was also, according to High Strange, proof that humanity was capable of more than it seemed. That they were worth protecting.

'We are the ghosts,' said High Strange.

'Of what?'

'Your machines.' It smiled, she could hear it in the voice. 'We tied the knots for you and made the sails. We hold up your habitats. All you have to do is manage yourselves.'

'We've failed.'

'Katchatka failed. Lord d'Alambert will fold this station into his segment and grow new sails, with help from me. The weather will be stabilised. As your mother once said, everything comes at a price.'

'Her death,' said Lady Neku, eyes refilling. 'My brothers.'

'No,' said High Strange. 'You.'

Her cloak smelt of smoke and black ash formed moons beneath her fingernails, which were broken from having scrabbled through the rubble of a recently-burnt bar. The air in High Strange was thin and cold enough to make Lady Neku shiver, though that might have been the last of her memories falling into place.

Staring round the frozen chamber, Lady Neku saw the banquet table and her brothers where they sat. Lady Katchatka regal in a silver chair. Ice frosting the walls and the tiles and even the knives and forks on the plates laid out in front of the dead.

'Oh fuck,' she said. 'I came back ...'

She'd chosen exile. And offered her choice of time and place, had chosen where and when the bowl was made, because High Strange believed she would be happy there. Denied her own life, Lady Neku accepted a life that came frighteningly close.

Everything was possible in an infinite universe. That much was obvious. Less obvious, until one thought of it, was the fact that everything possible was possible twice, or three times, or as many times as anyone was prepared to throw the dice.

'I broke my memories,' said Lady Neku, wondering if this was excuse enough for her return.

'Neku,' said High Strange. 'We've been through this. The beads only worked while you were here with me. There's no *me* where you went, so no beads and no easy memories. Only you.'

'It's weird there,' said Lady Neku. 'No one is friendly and Kit's bar has just burnt down and the only normal person I've met so far is a cat.'

'Neku ...'

'I have to go back,' she said.

'Yes,' said the voice. 'You do.'

PART THREE

CHAPTER 59

Thursday 5 July

The limousine bus from Narita Airport was quarter full, as always. A Korean boy with spiky hair sat at the back, pointedly ignoring signs not to use his phone while the bus was in motion. Leant against him was a Japanese girl lost in admiration, but the boy was still embarrassed enough to be angry about something that happened earlier.

A customs officer had pulled him out of a queue in Arrivals and unpacked his luggage with excruciating slowness, carefully unfolding each item of clothing as the line looked on. It had been all the boy could do to bow when she let him go.

Rain hammered the bus, obscuring its windows. Behind the downpour hid trees and houses, a waterlogged crocus bed looking like a tiny paddy field. Half-seen factories stood back from the motorway, screened by sudden banks of earth. Just another summer's day in Tokyo, with its heat hanging on the edge of tropical.

Soon the bus would reach Odaiba and the artificial islands built to house Tokyo's overspill. Some of this area was still poor, but most had spawned wild architecture and ever-more-expensive shopping malls. It was the same city, Kit told himself. He'd been in love with its anonymity from the moment he first arrived; its anonymity and ability to change so fast it always remained the same.

It still was that city, but he was going to abandon it all the same, once he'd done what he came to do.

Having wrapped themselves around each other, the teenage couple behind him fell asleep, lulled by the warmth and that weird jet-lag dilation which means one's mind has trouble catching up with its owner after a long flight.

Kit's fake passport had carried him through customs. He suspected he had the Korean boy to thank for that. So disapproving had the smartly-dressed young officer been at the couple who'd preceded him that she gave Kit little more than a glance.

'Are you carrying drugs?'

Kit had shaken his head firmly.

'Why are you here?'

'Holiday,' said Kit. 'I'm only here for a week. At the Shinjuku Hilton.'

The officer nodded, as if this was where she'd expect someone like Kit to stay, stamped his passport and nodded Kit though. Both questions had been in English and Kit had been careful to answer the same way.

The hand in his pocket had been borderline rude, but he was *gaijin*, and besides being regarded as ill-bred was infinitely better than having a Tokyo customs officer wonder why his little finger was missing.

No Neck answered the phone first ring, his wide-cheeked face scowling from Kit's tiny screen. As Kit watched, the man dragged a smile from his memory. 'Media liaison,' he said.

'What?'

'English language liaison. 47 Ronin. How can I help?'

'It's me,' said Kit, flicking his Nokia to visual.

There was a sudden silence. 'Benny?' said No Neck. 'From *The Times*?'

In the split second before Kit decided to ask No Neck what the hell was going on, something about the old Rebel's eyes told him to shut the fuck up and listen instead.

'Liked your last story,' said No Neck, his voice matter of fact. 'You might also want to look at these. Oh, and Tetsuo says he's been offered cash for news of Kit Nouveau. And we've got a herd of rain-sodden lawyers down here trying to serve Mr Nouveau with cease and desist orders ...'

'Cease and desist what?' demanded Kit.

No Neck laughed. 'You name it,' he said and broke the connection. The URLs No Neck sent led to a dozen different sources of news, all carrying the same story. It wasn't the lead (because that was the stand-off between China and Japan), or even the second story (which alternated between storm warnings and unrest in Chechnya), but it was usually fifth or sixth and registered a respectable number of hits.

Stand-off in Roppongi. Hammerfest Hells Angels stand by Japanese 'brothers' ... That was from *Aftenposten*, the Norwegian daily. *The Washington Post* was more circumspect. *Tokyo mayor bides time. 'Civil matter,' he states. Opposition disagree.*

304

The occupation of a building site in Roppongi was now entering its tenth day. Questions had been asked in Japanese parliament. Several purchasers of the high-end apartments to be built on the site had already pulled out.

Pirate Mary's was described as a biker clubhouse, a bar owing more to Irish myth than any reality, and a *soi-disant* watering hole for Tokyo's self-proclaimed anarchic elite. (*Battered & Bruised*'s travel editor had been refused entry about six months before.) If anyone remembered a woman had died there they had forgotten to tell their readers.

Having checked the sites, Kit abandoned the protection of a Shinjuku bus shelter and braved the rain for a narrow doorway between electronic screens. Café Rikishi's windows had been sacrificed for profit, the advertising bringing in almost as much a week as selling beer made in a month. Besides, those who used the café were unlikely to miss daylight; they came for the *chanko nabe* stew, the beer and the memories it brought of a city only they remembered.

If the air outside was hot and wet, the café was worse. So humid was the tiny bar that condensation dripped like rain from its ceiling and ran in rivulets down black-painted walls. An old man in a sodden pork-pie hat sat at a table with five dead Kirin bottles in front of him. When not wiping sweat from his brow or gazing mournfully at his empty bottles, the old man shredded a damp napkin to make perfect paper moths.

'Ito-san,' said Kit, bowing deeply.

Since Mr Ito grew up in Shitamachi, a working-class area destroyed in the fire bombing of Tokyo, and since his generation kept a rigid demarcation between public and private behaviour, his shock at seeing Kit was quickly disguised.

Of course, maybe he was too drunk to recognise Kit at all. It could have been the shock of seeing a rain-soaked foreigner that Ito-san disguised, one brave or stupid enough to invade the sticky gloom of a café under the Shinjuku railway line.

Since Café Rikishi was barely larger than a broom cupboard, its crowd consisted of the owner and Mr Ito, Kit and a vast Korean mechanic who was stripping a Yamaha clutch at a table in the corner. When it became obvious he was not required to heave the *gaijin* back onto the street, the Korean went back to his gears.

'Mr Ito'

'Nouveau-san.'

So he *had* been recognised.

The old man stared at Kit, somewhat owlishly. 'You know,' he said, ripping a strip from his paper napkin and rolling it between his fingers. 'People said ...'

'I'd left Tokyo?'

Mr Ito twisted off another strip of napkin and folded both strips together, placing a tiny paper rifle on the table. 'You'd met with an accident.'

'Hardly,' said Kit, 'I've been on holiday.'

Mr Ito allowed himself to look doubtful.

'Let me buy you a beer,' Kit said, ordering two Kirin, and remembering to use enough polite form to make his request acceptable. The ex-sumo behind the counter glanced at Ito-san, who nodded.

All sumo learnt to cook, as did dervishes from half a world away, zen and sufi both considering it no stranger to look for truth in a bubbling pot than anywhere else. Kit had no idea if dervishes ran restaurants but half the sumo in Japan opened cafés as soon as the time came for them to hang up their ceremonial aprons.

The bottles of Kirin were so cold that steam from the *chanko nabe* condensed across their sides and began to trickle into damp circles. When Mr Ito returned his bottle to the table, he was careful to place it exactly inside the mark it made.

'Another?' Kit asked.

Mr Ito nodded. 'And maybe food?'

The stew was hot and filling and took the edge off the beer. It tasted of soy, garlic and rice wine, daikon and shimeji mushroom mixed with burdock root. The chicken and tofu were near perfect, the chrysanthemum leaves still slightly chewy. The udon came separately, in its own tiny bowl.

'Go chiso sama deshita ...'

Kit's simple thank-you earned him a slight nod from the ex-sumo, who then swept crude chunks of tofu into boiling broth. Obviously enough, the tofu wasn't really diced crudely, merely chopped in a fashion designed to look crude.

After a third bottle of Kirin, Mr Ito decided it was time to face whatever brought the Englishman to this café. So he sat back on his stool and signalled that Kit had his full attention. This involved little more than a slight change of expression and a relaxing of Mr Ito's shoulders.

'That night,' said Kit.

Mr Ito nodded, not needing Kit to specify which one.

'I have a question about the afternoon.' Kit had been thinking hard about this. *Look for the money*, Mary had told him. *Odds on, that's your motive.*

The insurance on Pirate Mary's was limited to what was required by law. So far as anyone knew he and Yoshi were married, he'd thought so himself, even *gaijin* in Japan got to inherit from their partners. The price of Yoshi's work might have doubled in the week following her death, but most of it was held in trust or owned outright by museums. It seemed a poor motive, assuming her death had been anything other than an accident.

Only the building value of the land made sense. And Kit needed Brigadier Miles to come through with a name on that. In the meantime . . . Kit had been landing at Narita when he remembered something Ito-san said.

'I was wondering,' said Kit. 'About that afternoon. You said you saw a car?'

'Yes,' said Mr Ito, 'And a policeman.'

'In uniform?'

Mr Ito shook his head. 'No, but he said he was police.'

'Can you remember how this man looked?'

Small, neatly dressed, somehow amused? The expression that always came to mind when Kit thought about Oniji-san. The face he'd seen the first time Mr Oniji walked through the door at the hospital and police officers stepped aside to let the oyabun see the foreigner who'd been fucking his wife.

Mr Ito leant back to think. Had he been in a chair this would have been fine. Unfortunately Ito-san sat on a stool, and for a moment Kit thought the old man might topple backwards. All that happened, however, was that Mr Ito lurched forward again as if on a spring, and finished up with his elbows on the table.

Mr Ito was drunk and slightly scared, which made Kit remember something else. So far as Ito-san was concerned Kit had knifed a homeless man and left his corpse against a cemetery railing. And that meant Mr Ito believed his beers were being bought by a killer.

Kit could understand how that might make him nervous.

'Was he small, this man? Smaller than you?'

Mr Ito shook his head.

'Are you sure?'

'He was big,' said Mr Ito. 'Like a Russian, and broad here.' He touched his shoulders, indicating width. 'That's the truth,' Mr Ito added, seeing the doubt on Kit's face.

'Japanese?'

Mr Ito appeared to think about that. Although it turned out he was considering, not whether the man was Japanese but what kind of foreigner he might be.

'Like me?' Kit asked.

A shake of Mr Ito's head.

'What then?'

'Maybe half Korean,' Mr Ito said finally. 'But dark.'

No one Kit knew came close to fitting both parts of that description. 'You're certain about this?'

'Yes,' said Mr Ito. 'Broad, bear-like, half Korean ...' His words were loud enough to disturb the ex-sumo behind the counter, who glanced across, considered things carefully and went back to dicing tofu.

Oh well ...

'Thank you,' said Kit, pushing back his stool. 'Let me buy you a beer before I leave ...' He waited for the huge ex-sumo to sweep diced scallions into his bubbling pot and reach for a notepad.

Seven beers, two bowls of *chanko nabe* – the seaweed crackers obviously came free. Sliding five thousand yen onto a small white tray, Kit took his change. It was as he turned to go that Mr Ito looked up from his final beer.

'The other man was Japanese,' Ito-san said.

Kit sat down again.

'What other man?'

'The one in the car ...' Mr Ito thought about it some more. 'Three men,' he said finally. 'Two in the car, one outside.'

'The big man, he got back in the car?'

Mr Ito shook his head. 'No,' he said. 'He arrived in the car and then the car drove away. This was in the afternoon, before ...'

'What were the two like?'

'One was young,' said Mr Ito. 'A *chimpira*.' He used the expression with disgust, as if things had been different in his day, which they probably were. Baby gangsters didn't dress like cut-price Hollywood stars for a start.

'And the other?' *Small, neatly dressed, somehow amused?*

'Swept back hair, expensive watch.' said Mr Ito. 'You know the type. Almost a *yanqi*, but older. Pale suit. Quite tall.'

Pale suit?

'This man,' said Kit. 'Did you get a good look at him?'

Mr Ito nodded. 'I see most things,' he said. 'Sometimes I see more things than exist, often many more things.' Sitting back, he shook his head, as if aware he probably shouldn't have said that.

'Cats talk,' said Kit. 'Girls disappear into thin air. For the last five days I've been throwing dice that don't exist, waiting for a winning number. I look into shop windows and see the reflection of someone else ...'

'Ahh,' said Mr Ito.

'I'm going to describe someone,' said Kit. 'He's tall, quite thin and has high cheekbones, a pointed chin and dyes his hair, which is swept back and slightly grey at the temples. He's Okinawan, so his skin is dark.'

'Is this man real?'

'Yes,' said Kit.

'Good,' Mr Ito said, 'because he sounds like the man in the car.'

CHAPTER 60
Thursday 12 July

It took Kit five days to decide he should call Amy, ten minutes to argue himself out of that idea and another four days to conclude his first decision had been right. In that time he changed hotels, followed the *bozozoku* stand-off in Roppongi and worked his way through Neku's translations of the original police papers, which she hid behind a site supposedly dedicated to a history of Emily Strange.

Neku wrote him e-mails, which Kit stopped collecting when he remembered Brigadier Miles and her comment about how Kit's name first came up on an international database. No one in England had his new number and he'd locked number display/ caller ID before phoning No Neck that first time, but Kit still changed his phone twice, dumping the second of three phones in the bin without having used it once. It didn't make much sense to him either.

The city looked the same and Kit looked different. The changes from London had rubbed off on him, his clothes were less formal, and he found himself looking at Tokyo through the eyes of someone who'd forgotten how to belong.

So much of how he defined himself had relied on Yoshi. With Yoshi gone, he'd begun to redefine himself, without even realising it. He checked into three different hotels and was taken for a tourist in each. At the Akasaka Prince he bought a hotel yukata, using it at the Shinjuku Hilton when he discovered the only thing on offer was a fluffy white robe. He might be assimilating, but things hadn't yet gone that far.

As he sat in the executive lounge on the thirty-seventh floor of the Hilton, looking out over one of the greatest night views in the world, while a Australian girl and her boyfriend huddled in front of a blaring laptop to watch children's films and polite middle-class Japanese families talked quietly, Kit decided he really needed to know why Amy had gone to bed with him. Maybe it just happened without reason.

Since a sign on his table banned the use of phones, Kit took himself out of the executive lounge and then, as an afterthought, out of the hotel altogether and into a taxi that was waiting at the door.

It was the day the BBC's news site announced that the Metropolitan police had issued an arrest warrant for Benjamin Flyte, a society drug dealer and ex-advertising executive. Mr Flyte was wanted for the murder of Armand de Valois, whose exact profession was left unspecified.

An ex-chief from intelligence was quoted saying she doubted Mr Flyte would ever be caught. Apparently, Brigadier Miles was allowed to say this, because she'd retired five years earlier. All her counterpart at the Met was prepared to say was he couldn't comment on individual cases, particularly when the question was speculative.

Evening in Tokyo translated as lunchtime in London and Amy was at her desk. Kit only knew this because he could hear the clatter of printers and the rattle of a train through an open window.

'Amy Avenden,' she announced, and Kit realised his phone still had its ID lock in place. When Kit kept silence, Amy repeated her name, slightly more forcefully.

'It's me,' he said.

She was about to ask who the fuck *me* was, because Kit could hear her draw breath and then she knew. It said something for her discretion that she didn't immediately say his name, although she did ask the obvious.

'Where are you?'

'In Tokyo,' said Kit, wondering if it was wise to answer. Although anyone who understood street noise would know he was in Japan from the sing-song jingle activated every time someone walked past a shop door. And anyone who understood jingles could tell he was outside a shop in Akihabara, Tokyo's eclectic town, where Kit intended to replace his phone the moment this conversation was done.

'Yes,' Amy said. 'That's where Kate said you'd be.'

'*Kate?*'

'She called, to see if we'd heard from you. Apparently the kid's worried.'

Kit took a deep breath.

'Things have changed at this end,' said Amy. 'The Brigadier ...'

'Did a deal,' Kit said, finishing the sentence for Amy, then wondering if he was right. 'I read about the warrant,' he added. 'It's why I called.'

Silence, then more silence. He'd offended her, again. 'It's not my only reason,' said Kit. 'But I do have a couple of questions. Are the police going to be waiting for me if I come back to the UK?'

'You deserted,' said Amy. 'What do you think?'

'Brigadier Miles offered me a deal.'

'If you helped us.'

'I did help,' Kit said. 'I got the kid back and de Valois won't be troubling you, I even left the drugs there for you to find.'

Amy laughed. 'Fuck,' she said. 'You're impossible. What was the other question?'

'Why did you go to bed with me?'

'Shit,' said Amy, and for a moment Kit thought she'd broken the connection. 'I'm at work,' she said. 'All work calls get recorded. That's just gone on my record.'

'What's the answer?'

'I was drunk. It was stupid. I'd broken up with Steve the week before. You were available.'

'That's all it was?'

'Oh for fuck's sake,' said Amy. 'I like you, all right? God knows why. People make mistakes. You were my biggest, both times.'

'But we didn't ...'

'No,' she said. 'We didn't. If we had then I doubt we'd be having this conversation. Anything else you want to know?'

She gave him the name Brigadier Miles had produced, offering to spell it out if Kit needed, but he already knew how to spell Tec Tamagusuku.

'You know him?' said Amy, it was only half a question.

Tall, quite thin, with high cheekbones, a pointed chin and dyes his hair ... 'Yes,' said Kit. 'I know him.'

Amy seemed surprised when Kit apologised. 'I mean it,' he said. 'I fucked up, both times.'

'What are the chances of you not fucking up a third time?'

Kit laughed, mostly at himself. 'Better than they were,' he said. 'Much better. Can I ask a favour?'

'What?'

'Would you thank Charlie for the dice and send my love to the kid? Say I hope she's okay. And she's to behave until I get back.'

'Why not tell her yourself?'

'If I call that number,' said Kit, 'someone at this end might link us. I want to keep her out of this.'

Out of what? Amy wanted to ask, but Kit was gone. Tossing his Nokia into a nearby bin, he fought his way into the crowded chaos of an Akihabara electronics boutique and bought himself another.

CHAPTER 61
Friday 13 July

Yuko's house was impressive, apparently. A copy in concrete and glass of a traditional Okinawan building, complete with red tiles on the roof and ceramic *shisa* lions guarding its rafters. Kit had never been, because Yoshi and her sister always chose times to meet when he was teaching or buying stores for his bar.

Everything he knew about the Tamagusuku family home he knew from Yoshi. It was big, the garden had its own waterfall and the gates were rather vulgar; although Yoshi had always been careful to blame this on Mr Tamagusuku and his southern heritage.

The house phone was gilt and alabaster, originally 1950s French, but refurbished by Mitsukoshi before being sold to Mr Tamagusuku. It sat on a marble table by the front door, or so Kit had been told.

As he sat in yet another café, nursing a cappuccino and watching morning commuters stream in their thousands out of a West Shinjuku metro entrance, he imagined Yuko Tamagusuku putting down her own coffee. Or maybe he'd got that wrong, perhaps she was handing her baby to the nanny and walking slowly to the phone as Kit counted the rings, wondering how many could go by before he had to accept she was ...

'Yuko,' said Kit, caught by surprise. 'It's me.'

He listened to Yoshi's sister struggle to put a name to his voice.

'I'm sorry,' she said. 'Who is this?'

'Me,' said Kit. She got it then. 'No,' he said. 'Don't put it down.'

Picking up again was Yuko's big mistake. If she really wanted to ignore him she should have left the phone ringing.

'We need to talk,' said Kit. He waited for a click, for the tone which would follow. It said something for Yuko's manners that she let the silence continue.

'Talk,' she said eventually.

'I know why Yoshi died.'

'That's no mystery,' said Yuko, voice cold. 'You abandoned her to the fire. I wouldn't be surprised if you did it on purpose.'

'*Yuko!*'

'Everyone knew you didn't love her anymore. All you really cared about was the bar and your mistress ...'

So Yoshi had known about Mrs Oniji. What's more, she'd told her sister. 'I'm sorry,' said Kit, bowing to his phone from instinct.

At the next table a Japanese boy glanced up, caught Kit's glare and hastily buried his head in an electronics catalogue. A second later he carefully extracted the exact change for his coffee and left the café.

'What are you sorry for?' said Yuko.

'Mostly for not being the person Yoshi thought I was. It was hard,' he added. 'And it got harder.'

'You knew who she was when it started. She showed you her studio and her ...' Yuko's voice faltered. 'Her equipment. You let my sister fall in love with you, then you abandoned her to a burning building and saved yourself.' Yuko was crying, her words no longer clipped with anger but swallowed along with her tears.

'It wasn't like that.'

'What was it like?'

'I was already outside when the bomb exploded.'

'*The what* ...?'

'There was a bomb,' said Kit. 'Something basic, like phosphorus and plastique packed in a cola bottle and detonated by walkie talkie.'

'No,' protested Yuko. 'It was an accident. I've seen the police report. You didn't even try to save her.'

Taking a deep breath, Kit said. 'I swear, I was already outside. No one could have saved Yoshi. The blast ripped my bar apart. She would have died instantly and so would I,' he added, admitting it to himself for the first time.

'Not true.'

'Yes,' said Kit. 'It's entirely true.'

He heard Yuko fight her tears, and when she finally broke her snuffling silence her words surprised Kit. 'You lasted longer than her first husband.'

'God,' said Kit. 'She'd been married before?'

'Yoshi never said?'

'No,' he said. 'I had no idea.'

Yuko sighed. 'Call me back later,' she said. 'I need time to think.'

CHAPTER 62
Saturday 14 July

The waves were high by the time Kit's taxi reached Kamakura. Families clung to their spots on the beach, but the atmosphere was sullen and no one seemed to be enjoying themselves. As Kit cleared a long stretch of sand, the rain arrived and people began to fold beach blankets and tidy away picnic ware.

'Storm soon,' the taxi driver said.

'*Hai*,' said Kit, nodding.

The driver smiled. Having decided Kit was new to Tokyo, he'd been busy pointing out shrines, famous buildings and women in kimonos ever since they left West Shinjuku. He'd even tried to teach Kit a traditional song about Lord Tokugawa, who turned the swampy village of Edo into his capital.

The directions Yuko had delivered to the Hilton were for a new marina on Enoshina, an island opposite the Oriental Miami, the most popular of the bathing beaches on the Shonan coast. She made no mention of the fact that Kit was staying at the hotel under another name.

'Here,' said Kit, indicating a roadside bar, where two Japanese boys were buying Pink Health, one of the newer amino-acid drinks. A double surfboard rested against a road sign beside them.

'See *Myo-on Benten*,' said the driver.

Kit looked blank.

'Goddess of karaoke and rock stars, many arms and very nude, also white and very detailed. You can see her . . .' The driver shrugged, leaving the rest to Kit's imagination. 'Very famous,' said the driver. 'Also lucky.'

Having thanked and paid his driver, Kit thanked him again, promised to keep the statue of Benten in mind and watched the car pull away. It left him standing in the rain, along with the surfers and a handful of tourists preparing to cross the bridge.

'Oxygen?' asked Kit, nodding to a small silver tank resting next to the upturned surfboard.

The younger of the two boys wore his hair like a Shinjuku Yakusa, but his accent belonged in Tokyo's western suburbs and he'd probably spent most of that morning just getting to the beach. 'Emergency floatation,' he said, patting the tank.

'Emergency ...?'

'Yank the cord and whoosh.' Unrolling a wafer-thin orange wet suit, the boy indicated a puffy white strip running along the spine and across the shoulders. 'Latest thing,' he said, 'very expensive.'

Nodding, Kit smiled his approval. And that was the way the three of them passed onto the bridge, talking and smiling, under the lazy eye of a local policeman, whose attention centred on an Australian girl in sodden T-shirt and high-sided briefs.

No picking wild flowers. No unguided cave trips. No dropping litter. No public indecency of costume ... In English the rules were blunter than their Japanese equivalents, though the message was the same. The Australian girl's outfit just about obeyed the law.

'There's going to be a bad storm,' said Kit, repeating what he'd been told by the taxi driver.

'Cyclone,' said one.

'Typhoon,' said the other.

Both grinned. 'It's going to be extreme,' they said together, then laughed at what was obviously a tag-line or shared joke. 'Everyone's here,' said the first, indicating other surfers lugging boards or heading towards the bridge. 'The call's been going out all morning. We want to get in the water before the police arrive.'

Fantastic Far View of Mount Fuji. By the time Kit and the two boys reached a teriyaki restaurant just beyond a Botanical Gardens, the rain had stopped and the café's canvas awning was dripping lazily onto the tiles of a small terrace. The far views of Fuji-san might well have been wonderful, but they were also obscured by cloud.

With its cafés and tourist shops Enoshina Island reminded Kit of Mont St Michel. Small islands off a mainland, their causeways hidden at high tide. Although in the case of Enoshina the bridge had dealt with that particular problem. And tourists, lots of tourists ...

'It's busy,' he said.

Both boys grinned. 'This is deserted,' they said, almost in unison. 'The storm warning has kept most families away.'

Kit left them at Fantastic Far View, paying the bill for three take-out teriyaki before he said goodbye. He'd arranged to meet Yuko at 2 p.m. and it was now fifteen minutes after that. It was time Kit worked out exactly what he was going to say.

Your husband did it.

Tamagusuku-san killed my wife. No, I have no real proof.

Even marinas in Japan had league tables to establish their status, and the new marina on Enoshina island was one of Tokyo's most exclusive, a sign at the entrance announced this fact. As did the uniform of the guard who stalked out to meet Kit, once it became obvious that here was where he was headed.

White gloves, a dark blue uniform and a officer's cap with high brim and a glistening gold and enamel badge, the guard's uniform was designed to impress and reassure in equal measures. The centre of the man's badge mirrored the emblem on the gate, a yacht silhouetted against a blood-red sun.

'Your business?'

Kit stared at the guard, and kept staring until the man finally blinked. Then Kit waited for him to ask again, using polite form. When Kit replied it was in near-fluent Japanese. His business, however, was his own.

'*Suijin-sama?*'

The guard gestured towards a far jetty in answer to Kit's question.

It would be. Named after a water god, the *Suijin-sama* had steel masts and gleaming brass work. The hull was black, with a white strip around the top, so it looked from the gateway like a floating tray of Guinness. A smartly-dressed woman with shoulder-length black hair stood on deck, staring towards Kit. Her nod ordered the guard to let him through.

Maybe it was looking identical that had forced the Tanaka twins to be so different in the choices they made. This woman wore Yoshi's face and body, but the expression of distrust was entirely her own. Yoshi would never have revealed herself to that extent.

Yuko Tamagusuku didn't offer to shake hands or even bother to walk down to meet Kit, she just stood at the top of the gangplank and scowled.

'Yuko,' said Kit, when he reached her.

After a second, Yuko nodded.

Their exchange was watched by a small man near the wheel. Unlike Yuko's husband, who habitually wore expensive suits and still looked like a *chimpira* pretending to be a Yakusa grandee, this man wore his like he meant it. A ruby ring glittered from one little finger and his watch was a Seiko, with a heavy gold bracelet, half a dozen dials and three winders. It was a point of principle for senior Yakusa to wear only Japanese clothes, jewellery and watches. Although what really gave the man's status away was a tiny and understated lapel pin.

What looked silver was platinum, and what looked like enamel was ruby, pearl and emerald, cut to fit and framed by the tiny circle of the pin.

Kit bowed.

The man bowed back.

'My uncle,' said Yuko. 'Nureki-san.'

A couple of teenagers appeared. The crew, Kit imagined. At least, they wore striped jerseys, blue chinos and deck shoes with rope soles; but they fumbled raising the sail and after a second the man waved them away and pushed a button on a console in front of him. Winches turned and the sail began to raise itself.

'My sons,' he said. 'You're Yoshi's English friend?'

'Husband,' said Kit.

Mr Nureki raised his eyebrows. 'More of that later,' he said. 'First we need to discuss her lamentable death.'

On the jetty below, the guard with the strange uniform had already unhooked a bow rope. Once the rope was discarded, Yuko's uncle tapped his console to winch it in.

'Wait,' said Kit. 'I just need a quick word with Yuko.'

'Too late,' said the man, glancing at the sky. 'Already the weather warning says stay in harbour. The rains will be back, worse next time. And besides,' he paused. 'You believe my niece was murdered. Is that true?'

'Yes,' said Kit.

'Then the conversation should not be quick.'

Turning away, Nureki-san tapped two more buttons, checked a readout on a tiny screen and spoke softly into a microphone. Engines fired into life below Kit's feet and the *Suijin-sama* began to turn itself.

'This yacht,' said Mr Nureki. 'Self steering, self navigating, gyroscopically balanced. You could send her round the world and she'd come back undamaged.'

'Impressive,' Kit said, wondering how much was true.

'Pointless,' corrected Mr Nureki. 'Such technology steals all purpose from our lives.'

The ocean hosted a battle between the rain, the wind and the waves; as torrential downpours tried to hammer flat seas that the wind kept scooping into white-capped peaks. Kit could see how belief in the nature gods might make sense. If he'd been a fisherman or farmer, he'd have been praying to the *kami* too.

Visibility was almost zero.

Actually, it was zero. So hard did the rain beat into Kit's face that the only way he could stand its sting was to close his eyes and hunch his shoulders. Of course, he could always have faced in the other direction.

'You,' shouted a voice. A hand tugged at Kit's arm, turning him. 'Yuko says come below.' It was Tsusama, the eldest of Mr Nureki's sons.

'I'm fine,' insisted Kit.

'You're sodden.'

'That's not a problem.'

'Suit yourself.' The boy shrugged, then hesitated. Glancing round, he checked they could not be overheard. Since his words were ripped by the wind from his mouth almost before he could say them his caution seemed almost comic.

'Did you love her?'

'What? Kit demanded.

'Yoshi … Did you love her?'

'Yes,' said Kit. 'I did. A lot, just not very well.'

Tsusama nodded. 'Yoshi was my cousin,' he said. Kit and the boy looked at each other and then the boy headed inside, scraping water from his hair. Whatever Tsusama said, Kit was left alone after that.

An hour later, with the wind less fierce, the torrential rain reduced to a drizzle and the clouds almost empty, the yacht reached a line of green hills rising steeply from the sea. A length of beach could be seen to the north, but most of the coastline seemed to be wilder, with inlets and coves guarded by dark rocks.

'Boso-santo,' said Tsusama. 'Beautiful, isn't it?' Nureki-san's eldest son was back. 'We've been coming here my entire life. Yoshi used to visit as a child. Well, she did according to father. That was before I was born.'

'What happens now?' Kit asked, standing in a puddle of water, his clothes glued wetly to his skin, trickles of rain running like tears down his face.

Tsusama shrugged. 'Not my decision,' he said. 'All the same you might want to get changed before you meet the high council.'

'Die smart?'

The boy grimaced, then patted Kit's sodden shoulder. 'Yeah,' he said. 'Something like that.'

A cupboard built into the bow of the *Suijin-sama* seemed to contain

319

nothing but suits. A roller drawer above held neatly-stacked shirts and a chrome rail inside the door hung with ties. Someone had even put silk socks into pairs next to the shirts.

Shaking his head, Kit said. 'I don't get it.'

'What's to get? Take a suit.'

Kit did as he was told, choosing black, because all the suits his size were in black. He matched the jacket to a black T-shirt, which was probably meant to be a vest but was all he could find. Wet or not, he kept the shoes he'd been wearing.

'No gun?' asked Tsusama.

In stripping to change Kit had revealed his lack of weapons.

'Why would I carry a gun?'

Tsusama shrugged. 'I just thought,' he said, 'you know ...' He nodded towards Kit's recently-severed finger. 'You were like us.' The idea of Mr Nureki's son considering any foreiger *like us* was so bizarre Kit wondered if the boy was mocking him. And then he realised something far more frightening, Tsusama was serious.

'It happened in London.'

'You owed a debt?'

'I paid a price.'

'There's a difference?'

'Oh yes,' said Kit. 'A big difference.'

'And this man you paid. Was he happy with the price?'

It was Kit's turn to shrug. 'I doubt it,' he said. 'He died before I could ask ...'

A single jetty jutted into the sea. Sun and rain had bleached its surface to a washed-out grey that designers around the world tried endlessly to imitate but never quite got right. It took years of weathering to achieve that effect. And though rain had darkened the wooden walkway its planks were already patchy where the puddles had begun to dry.

A narrow path wound between twisted pines beyond the jetty. About halfway up, a huge boulder broke through the dark and gritty earth and forced the path to change direction. At the top, four vermilion-painted cypress trunks formed a perfect torii gateway.

'We're at a shrine?'

'Among other things,' said Tsusama.

'What other things?'

'We have houses,' the boy said. 'A temple and family shrines. This is where we meet. There are rules ...' He hesitated.

'That sometimes get broken?'

'Only once,' said the boy. 'The cost was terrible.' Glancing at his watch, Tsusama nodded to himself. His father and brother had gone ahead, accompanied by Yuko. Tsusama was to deliver Kit to the ryokan exactly an hour later. This would allow sufficient time for the high council to meet. He was not to think, however, that the council met on his behalf. Their meeting and his presence on the island were coincidence.

The quietness is misleading, Mr Nureki had told Kit. *We are all in the eye of a terrible storm.* Kit was still wondering if the man meant it figuratively, literally or both.

'How long have your family owned the island?'

The boy smiled. 'Not my family,' he said. 'All of us, all the families, and this island is new.'

'Really?' Kit looked at the rocks, the dark volcanic sand of the little beach and the worn path leading to where black-eared kites soared above the battered torii. The broken earth was sticky with rotted pine needles, ruts in a track leading to the jetty suggested generations of carts unloading cargo. If its newness was true, the island was a masterpiece.

'Seven years,' said Tsusama. 'Mr Oniji bought a strip of cliff and had this island built half a mile offshore. It took three months to sink the foundations and another eighteen to landscape the island and erect the shrine, torii, ryokan and houses.'

'But that's old,' said Kit, nodding towards the distant torii.

A smile was his reply. 'Eleven hundred years,' he said. 'Probably the oldest now existing. Mr Oniji found it in Honshu.'

'And the temple?'

'From Sapporo. Also most of the houses, although Tamagusuku-san insisted on shipping his own from Okinawa.' Something clouded the boy's eyes and he turned away, their conversation over. At 6.35 p.m. exactly, silence having filled the remaining minutes, Mr Nureki's son checked his watch one final time and indicated the path.

'Go now,' he said.

Pine needles still crunched where heavy branches had kept the worst of the rain from reaching the ground. Mostly, however, the needles just slid wetly, like scabs of ground breaking free. Kit stopped at the torii to clap once and bow to any *kami* who might be watching. Behind him he heard Tsusama do the same.

CHAPTER 63
Saturday 14 July

In 1997, 'Beat' Takeshi directed a film about an ex-cop. He wrote the script, took the leading role, produced the film and included his own paintings as props to make visual points about life's strangeness.

A drop-out from university, whose nickname came from his days as a comedian in a Tokyo strip joint, Takeshi called his film *Hani-Bi*, which means *fireworks*, but uses a word that breaks into *fire* and *flower*.

And yet, what a thirteen-year-old Kit took from the film was not the lyricism of its camera work, nor an awareness that its script was so spare *Hana-Bi* could almost qualify as a silent movie. He took the image of Beat Takeshi as ex-cop Nishi, his face impassive and his eyes hidden by dark glasses.

Kit was reminded of this as he entered the ryokan, a lovingly-restored country inn. And he was reminded of how hard it could be to tell senior police officers, politicians and Yakusa grandees apart. So many dark suits, so many pairs of dark glasses, all those impassive faces.

He smiled.

Mr Oniji, Mr Nureki and Mr Tamagusuku sat at a side table. Tsusama and his brother stood behind them, both stony faced and obviously on their best behaviour. A couple of older men, who looked like senators or titans of industry, sat at another table. And on a chair between the two tables sat an old man with thinning hair. All of the men wore dark suits except the last, he had a simple yukata and rope sandals.

Kit bowed.

'You smile?' The old man lifted his head. Obviously wondering what this stranger found so amusing.

'What else is there to do?' asked Kit.

The man nodded. 'You may sit,' he said. When Kit remained where he was, the old man sighed.

'I am Osamu Nakamura ...'

The *kumicho*. The man Mr Oniji advised and Mr Tamagusuku obeyed. A man linked to the collapse of a major bank and the building of a bridge between Tohoku and Hokkaido, a project so grandiose no one had dared complain for fear of being regarded as unpatriotic.

An earthquake had seen to the bridge, along with the cranes, the bulldozers and most of those recruited for the project. The last thing anyone heard the *kumicho* had been too ill to appear at a court hearing. So his lawyers had demanded the trial relocate to Sapporo, where he lived. Somewhere in the middle of this muddle, the case collapsed.

'I'm glad to see you've recovered,' Kit said.

The old man laughed.

'You know why you're here?'

No, he could honestly say he didn't. Kit could take guesses, but few of them seemed likely and most were frankly improbable. Yuko had sold him out, this much seemed obvious. Apart from that ...

'Your friends have been causing us trouble.'

'My ...?'

'The 47 Ronin,' he said sourly. Someone snorted at the name, only to apologise before the old man could turn to see who it might be.

'You know about this, of course.'

Did he? Kit nodded. 'Someone destroyed their bar,' he said. 'My bar. Then Tamagusuku-san tried to steal my land. The *bozozoku* occupied the site to stop the developers moving in.'

'It's not ...'

Osamu Nakamura held up one hand to still Mr Tamagusuku's protest. 'So,' said the old man, 'you organised this protest.'

Kit shook his head. 'I didn't even know it was happening.'

Mr Tamagusuku snorted.

'That's what this is about?' said Kit. 'A bunch of bikers who want their bar back? That's why you've brought me here?'

'No one brought you here,' said Mr Nureki, glancing at Nakamura-san to check he was authorised to speak. 'As I understand it, you wanted to visit my niece Yuko. When she refused, you said the meeting could be anywhere she chose, that she could bring anyone she trusted. Well, she trusts me. And I trust this council.'

'You present a problem,' said the old man. 'This does not make us happy.'

No shit, Kit wanted to say.

'The choice is yours. You can be the solution or remain the problem. Either way, this matter will be solved.'

'Let me guess,' said Kit. 'You want me to stand down the 47 Ronin, tell them all to go home?'

The man nodded.

'And why would I do that?' asked Kit. 'Even if I could stand them down, which is doubtful. These people are a law to themselves.'

Like you, he thought.

'Because this situation is not good for any of us,' Mr Oniji said. His glance at the *kumicho* was part apology, part unspoken plea – let me handle this. 'You know how these things work,' said Mr Oniji. 'Tokyo is bidding for the Olympics. This kind of conflict is bad for everybody.'

'It's the camera crews,' said Kit, realising the obvious. 'So long as they remain you can't move the Ronin.'

'The press won't remain forever,' said Yuko's husband, his voice hard.

'But until they leave,' Kit said, 'you're fucked.' Looking round the low ryokan he saw impassive faces stare back. 'Where's Yuko?' he demanded.

'Why?'

'Because I came here to talk to her.'

'You can talk to me,' said Mr Tamagusuku. 'If you say anything of interest I'll be sure to tell my wife.'

There was one door into the inn and an internal door to the kitchens. That made two ways out at the most, in a room full of hard-core Yakusa, all of whom he could assume were armed.

'You're smiling again,' said the *kumicho*.

'Just thinking,' Kit said.

'About what?' Nakamura-san seemed genuinely interested.

'Among one's affairs should be no more than two or three matters of what one calls great concern . . .'

The old man smiled.

'*Hagakure*,' said Mr Oniji, he sounded surprised.

'This,' Kit said, 'is one of those matters. There are things my wife would want her sister to know.'

'She's not your wife,' said Mr Tamagusuku. 'Under Japanese law unregistered marriages are invalid.'

'You were married?' asked Mr Nakamura.

'In San Francisco.' Kit said. 'Fifty-five dollars, cash in advance. It worked for us.'

'But Yoshi Tanaka never registered it here?'

'So I gather.'

'And this is what you wanted to tell Yuko?' The *kumicho* sounded puzzled. 'That you were married to her sister?'

'No,' said Kit. 'Yuko knows that already. I mean to tell her who really murdered my wife.'

A dozen people started talking at once and fell silent the moment Osamu Nakamura slammed his hands together, the clap beginning in noise and ending in total silence. 'There was no murder,' he said. 'A gas canister exploded.'

'It was a bomb,' said Kit.

The old man shook his head, though when he spoke his voice was softer, almost regretful. 'No one doubts that you loved Yoshi.' Glancing at Mr Tamagusuku, he dared the younger man to disagree. 'But there was no bomb.'

'Mr Oniji knows it was a bomb.'

'No bomb,' said Mr Oniji.

'You told me it was.'

Mr Oniji shook his head. 'I made an error,' he said. 'An antiquated heating system exploded. It was an accident. I've seen the final report.'

'May I sit?' Kit asked.

Win first, fight later.

He took the stool indicated and buried his head in his hands, trying to arrange his thoughts. When he looked up, the whole room was watching him. Without knowing it, certainly without intending to, he'd got their total attention. He also had his final answer.

'Mr Tamagusuku tried to have me killed,' said Kit, his voice calm. 'When that failed, he planted a bomb.'

'Enough,' said Yuko's husband, pushing back his own chair.

'Sit down.' The old man's voice filled the room. Tamagusuku-san ignored him, and Kit caught the exact moment Mr Oniji and Mr Nureki exchanged glances. *Not clever,* thought Kit, watching Mr Tamagusuku stand alone, his hands bunched into fists.

'I couldn't work out how he could bring himself to murder Yoshi,' said Kit. 'Even if that meant getting rid of me. Only Yoshi's death was a mistake, wasn't it? You believed Yoshi was with Yuko. So when the first attempt failed ...'

'What attempt?' asked the *kumicho*.

'He sent a hit man.'

Mr Tamagusuku's first blow caught Kit in the shoulder, freezing his arm. The second just missed his throat and would have landed, if the *kumicho*'s bodyguards had not dragged Tamagusuku-san off in time.

'I ... know ... nothing ... about ... a ... hit man.'

'What about a bomb?' asked Mr Oniji, shrugging when everyone in the room turned to look at him. 'Just asking,' he said.

'Well?' demanded the old man.

Mr Tamagusuku hesitated.

It was enough.

Stepping forward, Kit kicked Tamagusuku-san hard between the legs, and would have kicked again, if not for the bodyguards. When they yanked Kit away from Mr Tamagusuku, they were less gentle than when it was the other way round.

'Take him outside,' said the *kumicho*.

And as fingers locked onto his elbow, Kit realised the old man had been talking about him. 'Wait,' he said. 'Please let me say something first.'

'No.' The *kumicho* voice was firm. 'This is not about you any more. You will wait outside while we make our decision.'

'One moment, if I may?' said Mr Oniji. He turned to Kit. 'How many people have you told about this?'

It was a question with only wrong answers.

'None,' Kit said, and watched Mr Oniji smile.

The last of the black-eared, high-circling kites had abandoning its kingdom to the stillness of the coming storm. Shingle shifted slightly as it was lapped by waves, and the Nureki boys looked at anything and everything except the man they were meant to be guarding.

It was hot, because Tokyo Bay in July was always hot, so the boys pulled at their shirt collars and played with their ties. After a while they held an intense and private discussion that resulted in them both removing their jackets. And through all of this the two boys clutched their guns clumsily, sometimes forgetting to keep the muzzles trained on Kit at all.

He was grateful for that.

Having sunk towards the Izo headlands the sun vanished behind Fuji-Hakone and Kit sighed and smiled. Staring at an unseen mountain, while thinking precisely nothing, Yoshi would have been proud of him.

'You're wanted,' said Tsusama.

Kit blinked.

'Take your time,' he suggested.

Nodding his thanks, Kit straightened himself and led the way back to the ryokan, hearing the boys whisper behind him. He entered the room first, with his head up and his expression firm. Kit had his own thoughts about what was coming. And any hope he might have was killed by the expression of regret on Mr Oniji's face.

'We have reached our decision.'

'Hai.'

'Don't you want to know what it is?'

Accept that you are dead already. Kit shook his head. 'Would my knowing change it …?'

He wrote the words Osamu Nakamura dictated, signing away all rights he might have in the building site in Roppongi, then wrote a shorter note to No Neck, putting the *bozozoku*'s real name on the front and adding, *by hand.* Someone would deliver it to the 47 Ronin in the morning.

'Now stand over there.'

The orange rope with which they tied his hands was nylon, meant for a use other than this and burnt as it dragged across his wrists. Tsusama tied the knots clumsily, refusing to look at Kit. His younger brother held the gun. This was their first real job, Kit could see that in their eyes.

'It's all right,' said Kit.

Opening his mouth, Tsusama promptly shut it again. Although he nodded to show that he'd heard and understood what Kit said.

'You know what must be done?' Mr Nakamura asked.

Tamagusuku-san nodded.

'Rip him open first.'

'Of course.' Mr Tamagusuku sounded irritated.

'We don't want …'

'I know, said Mr Tamagusuku. 'We don't want some idiot fisherman netting his bloated body.' This was not how one talked to a high oyabun, but the world was changing, this world as much as all others.

'See to it,' Nakamura-san said.

On Kit's way out of the ryokan he was stopped by Mr Oniji, who stepped in front of him and just stood there, scowling. Behind Kit, Mr Tamagusuku sighed.

'You've been an idiot,' Mr Oniji said.

Kit nodded. He didn't doubt it. There were a hundred things he would do differently given his life over again. A mere handful he'd keep the same. It was the handful which let him look Mr Oniji in the face.

'I imagine,' said Mr Oniji. 'You know what this is for.'

Sucker-punching Kit in the gut, Mr Oniji chopped him across the neck and dropped him to the floor. And then, kneeling on his victim's chest he slammed a final punch into Kit's kidneys. While Kit did his best not to vomit, and fought the fingers reaching for his testicles, Mr Oniji used his other hand to flip open Kit's jacket and tuck something into his trouser pocket.

It felt like a knife.

CHAPTER 64
Saturday 14 July

He was being drowned by slow degrees. Kit had a vague memory of pissing himself about an hour earlier, the urine warm as sea water and infinitely more welcome, proof that he remained alive.

Sometimes it was getting hard to tell.

He lived in the snatches between worlds, this one and others far stranger. Occasionally he'd refocus and the wind direction would have shifted or the waves risen higher. If Tamagusuku really wanted to drown him the man should have used longer rope, because the one tied to the rail of *Suijin-sama* was just about short enough to keep Kit's head clear of the waves.

Unless, of course, Tamagusuku didn't really want to drown Kit at all. Maybe the little shit just wanted to torture him.

Yes, that would be it. Obvious really. Having killed Yoshi, bombed Pirate Mary's and shopped No Neck to the police as the most likely suspect, Yuko's husband was now busy ...

Oh for fuck's sake, said a voice. *Are you just going to whine?*

Kit opened his eyes.

Well, are you?

Spray whipped his face as Kit glanced round, cursing the rope and the waves that stopped him from holding his head steady. Darkness was all he saw. Not even a light from the boat, which had run blind from Tokyo Bay. Certainly Kit saw no one close enough to speak. Assuming any voice could be heard above the howling wind and rain.

Tsusama and his brother, their father and most of the others had been left behind. Though the boys had protested for form's sake it was not very hard, and when Yuko's husband flatly refused to have them aboard, something very close to relief appeared in their eyes. They'd had trouble enough looking Tamagusuku in the face since bombs had been mentioned in the ryokan.

Let the grown-ups negotiate what came next.

The only surprise was the sudden appearance of Yuko, who arrived on the rickety jetty just as the boys were turning to go. Smiling at Tsusama, she patted him on his arm and indicated the path. 'Hurry up,' Yuko said. 'Baba's about to serve supper.'

She waited as two silhouettes turned on the path to see if she was still there. A quick wave from both and they were gone. Yuko smiled, though the smile barely reached her eyes.

'Why are you here?' Tamagusuku asked.

Yuko stared at him. 'Why do you think?' she said, stepping around both Kit and her husband.

'Wait,' he demanded.

'No,' said Yuko, turning to glare. 'My sister is dead,' she said. 'I'm going to see this through to its end.'

'Ask your husband how Yoshi died,' said Kit.

She slapped him.

Yuko and Tamagusuku left Kit bound on deck. Of course, since his hands were already tied with orange cord, all Tamagusuku had to do was secure Kit's ankles to the railings, while Yuko held a gun to his head.

'I'll be back later,' Tamagusuku promised.

Later turned out to be five minutes. Which was exactly how long it took Yuko's husband to put the propellers into reverse, back his yacht from the jetty and turn it to the open sea. This time round, the *Suijin-sama* made no pretence of running under sail.

'You've got an hour,' he told Kit, lashing one end of a tow rope to the railings and threading the other through Kit's bound wrists. Having knotted that end, Tamagusuku knelt to unlock Kit's ankle.

'An hour to do what?' asked Kit.

'Whatever.'

'Personally,' said Yuko. 'I'd recommend prayer.'

And so he trolled like fish bait behind the *Suijin-sama*. Dragged into rising waves for the time it took to turn himself, which lasted only as long as it took for the water to turn him back again. The sea was warm. Almost as warm as the springs in which he and Yoshi had bathed in the first year they were together. In the days when both of them cared about stuff like that.

It might have been better if the sea was cold. Cold water leached body heat until the brain shut down, a more attractive option than being dragged from the ocean like some thrashing tuna and gutted alive.

'I couldn't save her,' Kit told the waves. 'I couldn't ...'

Except he could.

All he ever needed to do was get home in time. The bar would still be burnt, Kit would be dead but Yoshi would undoubtedly be alive. So simple. She would have been at her sister's, admiring the new baby.

Oh, for fuck's sake, said the voice. *Enough ...*

Kit reopened his eyes.

Tears and snot and tiredness closed his throat. Every muscle in his body ached from fighting the rope and the waves. He found it hard to believe that he was still alive and part of him wondered if being alive was even true.

'Where are you?' Kit demanded.

The voice sighed.

'Okay,' he said, spitting water. 'Who are you?'

Who the fuck do you think I am?

'Don't know.'

I am a cat, said the voice. *As yet I have no name. Oh, for fuck's sake. Who do you think it is?*

'Neku?' said Kit.

CHAPTER 65

Saturday 14 July

One shoe was gone, water filled his pockets and his jacket had bunched at the shoulders to make a chute that yanked him back as the yacht dragged him forward. Climbing the tow rope was technically impossible, Kit was pretty sure of that. At least it was while his wrists remained lashed together with cord and friction spun his body in the water like bait for some monster beneath the waves.

Work on it, said the voice.

'I'm trying,' Kit said, but he was talking to himself.

By twisting his hands he could stress the orange cord binding them. Nylon stretched when wet and lost some strength. Sisal, on the other hand, just got tougher. He had Yoshi to thank for that piece of information.

The flesh on his wrists was blood raw, but Kit twisted his hands anyway, and having twisted them once did it again and again, until he could feel skin rip and the rope's sodden nylon fibres begin to loosen. It didn't matter if he cried, because there was no one to see and besides the waves washed away his tears. Anyway, it was just pain, nothing serious.

'And again,' Kit told himself.

And again.

If he pretended his wrists belonged to someone else, then twisting them until the sky red-shifted and blood drummed in his ears became almost bearable. He just pretended not to feel what he felt. And when that became impossible, he let himself taste the red shift and kept twisting anyway.

Yoshi had found purity in the middle of such behaviour. All Kit could find was pain, except not even that was true, because he found something else, something Kit should never have let himself lose.

He found himself.

Twisting his wrists until the bones locked and almost cracked, he forced the cord to stretch. 'Harder,' said a voice, and it was his. The skies shifted a final time and Kit wrenched a hand free, only just grabbing the tow line in time to stop a wave from tearing him loose. When Kit twisted this time it was to wrap the line safely around one wrist, so he could hold himself in place.

'Climb now,' Kit told himself.

And he did, not giving himself time to wonder how it should be done. He felt, rather than saw the sea change texture as he approached the propellers. Holding the tow line with one hand, Kit took a deep breath and reached as high as he could with his other hand, yanking himself up and over the wash.

'See,' he said.

It took Kit five minutes just to stop shaking. Five minutes in which he lay on the darkened deck gasping, as rain lashed his face and the sky rocked from side to side. And then Kit rolled onto his side and forced himself to his knees, digging into his trouser pocket.

The knife's sheath was sodden but its blade was razor sharp and slick with grease. So sharp in fact that Kit sliced skin while sliding it under the orange rope to free his bound wrist. Tossing the scrap of nylon cord after the tow line, he set his shoulders against the wind and raised a hand to keep the spray from his eyes.

All he needed to do was cross the ten or fifteen paces from the stern to the door of Tamagusuku's cabin without falling, slipping or dropping the knife. That had to be possible. Each step was made hard by exhaustion, and harder still by the shifting deck. As Kit got closer, the height of the cabin began to protect him from the spray, though the deck still shifted and a curling wind tried to drag him from his feet.

What now, he wondered.

Knock?

Well, why not . . .

Hammering on the door, Kit waited. When no one answered, he knocked again, much harder.

'Who?'

Kit laughed. Who the fuck did Tamagusuku think he was?

He stabbed his knife into the door frame for safe keeping, hammered one final time on the door and spun sideways, a split second ahead of Tamagusuku's first shot, slivers of cypress scything through the space where he'd had been standing.

One bullet down.

Instinct alone had saved Kit. Leaning forward, he smacked the door, dropped flat and rolled away, flailing for a grip to stop himself from sliding over the side.

Two, three.

Another couple of stars stood next to the first in the once-perfect door. Much more of this and Kit would be able to see what he was doing.

'Tamagusuku,' yelled Kit, dragging himself back to the cabin. 'Are you there?'

Four, five, six ...

With the sixth shot a cross brace in the door itself gave up the battle and a top panel dropped free, whipped away by winds and tossed over the side. So much light was released that Kit had to shut his eyes.

'Yuko,' he said. 'We need to talk.'

Another shot, making *seven.*

'There's nothing to discuss,' Tamagusuku shouted.

'It's not you I want to talk to. Don't you think it's time Yuko knew the truth?'

A shot splintered the frame near Kit's hip. *Eight* shots in total ... 'I'll take that as a no,' he said.

'What truth?' Yuko demanded.

A quick burst of Japanese, low and intense came from within the cabin, almost swallowed by the wind.

'Tell me,' Yuko yelled. 'What truth?'

'About Yoshi ...'

Tamagusuku's protests were harsh now. His voice was loud enough to compete with the exploding spray and the whistle of metal hawsers leading to high empty spars.

'I have the right to know,' yelled Yuko.

'Your husband,' Kit shouted, and felt the world twist sideways and the stars flare. Grabbing for the knife that still stuck from the door frame, Kit held himself up for as long as it took the blade to pull free.

The ninth shot had written itself across the inside of Kit's eyes.

Empty fingers told Kit he'd lost his knife, which was sliding like him across a slippery deck. This was shock, he realised. Black sky where the cabin should be, rain in his face and a jagged spike of wood jutting from his ribs.

The bullet had missed, the door frame it demolished had not.

Glancing beyond the spike, Kit found himself staring at rapidly approaching railings and felt his body change direction as one foot hit an upright and his whole body spun towards the waves beyond. His slide was broken by a wire he grabbed without even realising.

As the *Suijin-sama* crested a wave, the deck rolled and it was movement enough to tip Kit back under the wire. He slid wetly, breaking his slide just before he crashed into the side of the cabin.

Tamagusuku was five paces away, staring towards the stern. Yuko stood behind him, holding a whisky bottle. All either had to do to see Kit was turn round.

'You've killed him.'

'That was the plan.'

'But, I wanted to hear ...'

'I told you,' Tamagusuku said fiercely. 'Whatever he said would be lies.' His gaze swept across the door-lit gloom of the stern. 'We'll tell Nakamura-san I sliced the man open and threw him overboard.'

Kit took that as his cue to crawl backwards into shadow, only moving again after Yuko and her husband entered the cabin. The wind had lessened, the waves were less extreme, the rain however fell as hard as it ever had, washing blood down his shirt as Kit moved slowly towards the door.

'But what if the body ...'

'It won't,' said Tamagusuku. 'The waves will sweep it out to sea. Besides, Mr Nakamura won't remain a problem for much longer.' He paused, almost willing Yuko's question.

'Why?' she asked finally.

'Because I'm taking over.'

'This is agreed?'

'Not yet,' said Tamagusuku. 'But it will be. I'll give Kabuki-cho to Mr Oniji. Mr Nureki can have the fish market and the container port.'

From the safety of his new hiding place, Kit considered this; before gripping the jagged spike jutting from his ribs. He could remove it or not. One of those would be the right decision. Unable to decide which, he let it be.

He breathed deeply while Tamagusuku tacked a square of cloth across the broken door. He breathed deeply and considered his options. There was, Kit had to admit, a sense of relief in discovering that he didn't have any. All that remained was to go on.

Dragging himself right the way round the outside of the cabin, so he could approach its door from the other side, Kit took up his position. Only this time when he hammered it was with an outstretched arm, using the heel of his one remaining shoe.

Silence.

Kit gave it five seconds, then hammered again. Inside the cabin Tamagusuku swore.

'Yuko,' Kit said, voice raw. 'Your husband killed Yoshi.' He sounded like a ghost, even to himself, but then he felt like one too. 'An accident,' said Kit. 'But it still happened.'

'How, an accident?'

'He meant to kill me,' shouted Kit, clinging to the side of the cabin. 'But I was late home. So Yoshi stayed. You were right,' he added. 'It was my fault, but your husband planted the bomb.'

Inside the cabin, someone killed the lights and when the door banged open Tamagusuku's silhouette held a gun. A .38 calibre, to judge from the slightness of the damage to the door.

'I did not plant a bomb.'

'Oh no,' said Kit, 'that's right, you didn't. You had your bodyguard do it.' He watched Tamagusuku turn to find the source of Kit's voice. Watched as the man raised his pistol.

'Do it then,' Kit said, stepping away from the cabin. 'But you're too late. Yuko knows now.'

'*Enough.*'

'It's the truth,' said Kit, watching Yuko appear in the broken doorway behind her husband, still clutching the Suntory bottle.

'Yuko, if I could change it all I would.'

'It's a lie,' Tamagusuku shouted.

'Ask him where he was.'

'She knows where I was. In London. I bought her presents.'

'From Mitsukoshi,' said Kit. 'He's lying. If he was in London how come he was seen watching my bar?'

'When?' she demanded.

'About eight hours before Yoshi died.'

'Who saw ...'

'*Yuko, enough.*' Tamagusuku was furious, too furious. 'He's a liar. I'm not having this discussion.'

'You already are,' Kit said. 'So tell me one final thing. Why send a hit man if you'd already decided on a bomb?'

'I didn't ...'

'The homeless man,' Kit said. 'With the shabby suit and the expensive knife, a gun and a taser. All that hardware can't have come cheap.'

'I know nothing about this,' said Tamagusuku, and the weird thing was Kit believed him. He'd bombed the bar all right, but the thug who

336

came after Kit that night was the lid to a whole other can of worms.

'What man?' said Yuko.

Both Tamagusuku and Kit ignored her.

'Look at you,' said Tamagusuku, 'you're dying. All I have to do is wait, then tip you over the side.'

'We die everyday,' Kit said. 'It's called being human.' Taking a stumbling step towards Tamagusuku, he watched the other man steady his automatic.

'Yoshi,' said Kit, taking another step. *'I'm sorry.'*

Tamagusuku fired.

Kit must have imagined the click of an empty gun, because wind through the rigging would have drowned any noise that subtle. Yuko's husband slapped his gun, as if it had jammed, firing again. Tamagusuku was about to pull the trigger a third time when Kit reached for his throat.

'Wait,' Yuko said.

'Too late,' said Kit, tightening his grip.

The protest was slight, but Tamagusuku very definitely shook his head. Grabbing the jagged spike of wood still sticking from Kit's chest, the man twisted, and gulped air as Kit screamed.

Expecting the man to ram home the spike, Kit pushed at Tamagusuku's wrist and accidentally helped Yuko's husband do what he'd always intended, rip free the splintered piece of door.

Kit crumpled.

'Wait,' said Yuko. 'I want to talk to him.'

'No,' Tamagusuku said. 'Not this time.' Kneeling on Kit's chest, he reversed his gun and raised his arm, ready for a final blow.

'You killed her,' whispered Kit, and the darkness he awaited never fell. Because in that moment Yuko stepped forward and slammed her whisky bottle hard against the side of her husband's head. When the bottle didn't break, she hit him again.

'Yoshi was my twin,' Yuko said.

CHAPTER 66
September

The report in the *Asahi Shimbun* was suitably restrained. Under a heading *Yacht lost in storm, untimely death*, it ran a photograph of the *Suijin-sama*. A smaller picture, set to one side showed a serious-looking Tek Tamagusuku, wearing a dark suit, with his hair swept back and slightly grey at the temples. The caption announced, *Family in mourning. Irreplaceable loss to Japanese business, says Kisho Oniji.*

A small feature on page three mentioned that the *Suijin-sama* was one of thirteen Japanese-registered vessels lost in the typhoon, although it was the only one lost near Tokyo Bay. An editorial, opposite the letters page, put shipping losses in the context of wider damage, while the financial pages dealt with the implications of that damage for world risk/insurance ratios.

In passing, the feature mentioned an interview with a Texas-based academic denying Asia's worst cyclone had anything to do with global warming. (And the fact he'd got in trouble with his faculty for forgetting to refer to global warming as climate change.)

Local news shared space with stories from the wider world. A bomb blast in Baghdad, tension on the Chinese/Russian border, more riots in Mexico City, a possible, very tentative cure for breast cancer.

But the news that really interested Kit concerned the 47 Ronin. Men from the construction company had worked alongside *bozozoku* clearing rubble from Roppongi's streets, busily photographed by what remained of the camera crews. When the clearing was done, neither bikers nor builders returned to the site, and neither was prepared to say how such an agreement had been reached.

'What happened?' asked Kit.

No Neck laughed. 'Someone made a call to someone else, you know how it goes. Everything comes right if you wait long enough.' At his shoulder, Micki grinned, quickly covering her mouth with one hand.

Micki and No Neck had arrived with a huge pile of newspapers, going back weeks to the night of the actual storm. Being No Neck, he also carried a crash helmet and wore a ripped T-shirt reading, *Where are we going? And why am I in this hand basket?*

'You're lucky to be alive,' he said.

'Yeah,' said Kit. 'I know.'

'And you look like shit.'

'*Tommy* . . .' It was weird to hear No Neck called by his real name. Weirder still that he smiled sheepishly at the girl who used it. If No Neck didn't look out, his real name was going to prove catching.

'You look good,' Micki said.

'No,' Kit shook his head. 'Tommy's right, I look terrible.' He'd seen himself for the first time in a mirror that morning. His hair was greyer than he remembered and getting thin. Pretty soon he'd need to get it cropped. But then, pretty soon he'd need to do a lot of things, so he might as well start now.

'About the bar,' Kit said.

'Pirate Mary's . . .'

'No,' said Kit. 'That name's dead. You'll need a new one.'

'Me?' Tommy looked puzzled.

'The site's yours,' Kit said. 'Just as soon as I sign the paperwork.'

'Fucking hell,' said No Neck. 'You serious?'

'Yes,' said Kit. 'Very. I can even recommend a bank who might help you raise funds for rebuilding.'

'Except I'm Australian,' said Tommy. 'I mean, I'm grateful. But you know what they're like about that.'

'Put the land in Micki's name,' said Kit, glancing between them. 'And then make bloody sure you register the marriage.'

Micki grinned.

It was, Kit had to admit, a relief when the two finally left, all smiles and hands in each other's back pockets. Kit would have suggested they get a room, but his advice would have been completely redundant. From the way Micki and No Neck were glued to each other on the way out he imagined that was exactly where they were headed.

Kit was in the hospital ward he'd occupied before. The same Sikiyama cherry grew beyond its window, though the blossom was long gone. Behind the cherry, stood another just beginning to bloom.

'Autumn flowering,' his nurse had said. It seemed he was to get blossom after all. Two tubes fed into Kit's wrist and electrodes read off his heartbeat. He'd only recently got rid of the last catheter. This time round, the medical assistance had definitely been needed, Doctor Watanabe had been very clear about that.

The sliver of door frame had skewered his diaphragm. A little higher and Kit would have suffered cardiac tamonade, the membrane around his heart filling with enough blood to stop that organ from pumping. If not for Mrs Tamagusuku's quick action in staunching the wound Kit would be dead. It was, the doctor stressed, unwise to have been yachting in such weather.

A handful of cards sat on Kit's bedside table. Some were obvious, like the one from Micki and No Neck, others less so ... Mrs Oniji's card, delivered that morning, had been a surprise, its reference to Neku unexpected. There was even a card from Yuko. A simple snow scene in black ink on white paper, drawn with three quick flicks of the brush. Kit had been busy admiring it for most of an afternoon before he realised she'd drawn it herself.

The *Suijin-sama* had run aground and been broken by waves. Everyone knew the story. How Yuko Tamagusuku had left her dead husband to drag a badly-injured guest into the dinghy with her. Not everyone agreed with her decision but all were impressed by her bravery and the fact she fought to keep the foreigner alive.

A knock at Kit's door announced the arrival of Dr Watanabe, or so Kit believed until it opened to reveal Lucy, the nurse who'd removed stitches from his face three months before. 'You have another visitor.'

'Aren't visiting hours over?'

Lucy nodded.

A minute later an orderly came by to swap the high-backed chrome and leather chair in the corner for something simpler. At the same time, a second orderly removed Micki's flowers and replaced them with lilies. By the time the hospital administrator arrived to check the room was ready, Kit already knew who his visitor would be.

'How are you feeling?'

'Better than I deserve,' said Kit.

Mr Oniji smiled. 'An interesting choice of words.' Indicating the recently installed chair he said, 'May I?' And Kit found himself apologising for not having already asked the oyabun to sit.

'You got my letter?'

Kit had, it contained the paper he'd signed relinquishing all rights to the site in Roppongi. It had gone wherever shreds of paper go when flushed down a Tokyo loo.

'And they're treating you well?'

He nodded.

'Good,' said Mr Oniji. 'I told them to give you the best.' He glanced round the room, nodding at the flowers and smiling as he noticed the blossom in the courtyard outside. And then Mr Oniji's eyes alighted on a picture frame half-hidden behind cards on Kit's bedside table.

'If I may?' he said. Taking picture to the window, Mr Oniji looked at it very carefully. A minute or so later, he put it back.

'Very pretty,' he said slowly.

'Yes,' said Kit, 'I think so.'

'Anyone I know?'

'My daughter,' Kit said.

The photograph showed Neku in grey skirt, white blouse and navy blazer. The uniform of a school near Seven Chimneys. She looked very serious and ridiculously neat. Someone had styled her hair close to her head, *gamine* Pat would probably call it. A smaller picture, tucked into the frame showed her with her arms round Charlie, their smiles turned to the camera.

New term, announced Pat's scrawl on the back of the picture. *Me with Charlie*, read Neku's neater hand, in tiny letters across the rear of the snap. Her get-well card simply said, *Am fine, hope you feel okay. A friend will call.*

A letter had been tucked inside. The letter was short, the spelling random. In the ten weeks she'd been living with Kate and Pat her tastes had obviously changed. Gone was the Hello Kitty notepad and in its place a flimsy sheet of onion-skin paper, with a gold moon printed at the top.

I'm in a band, wrote Neku. *We're really good. Well, we will be. I've got Mary's old room and we're going to paint it purple next weekend. We is me, Charlie and Billie, his friend. I have a bass, Billie keeps forgetting to hold onto his drum sticks and Charlie can actually play – guitar, keyboard and violin!*

Kate says we have to practise in the garage and Pat says he doesn't mind where we practise as long as we get better, I'll burn you a CD. Kate sends her love. Pat says hello and I say goodbye, for now . . .

Only, maybe Neku's tastes hadn't changed that much. She signed her letter with a sketch of a cat.

'I didn't know you had a daughter,' said Mr Oniji.

'She's living at her grandparents' until I get home.'

Mr Oniji nodded. 'I see,' he said.

341

And then Mr Oniji didn't say very much for a long time. So Kit listened to the cars in the street and watched the sun turn a hospital wall from yellow to pink and finally to a pale and flintish blue.

'You know,' said Mr Oniji. 'She looks very like a child I used to know. Her name was Nijie Kitagawa.'

'The daughter of a friend?'

'An enemy,' said Mr Oniji, his face hardening. 'Who nearly cost me my life, also those of my colleague Mr Nureki and his eldest son.'

'Do I want to know what happened?'

'Many people died.' Mr Oniji's voice was flat. He glanced at Kit, considering. 'They were not good times.'

'You make it sound like history.'

Mr Oniji tapped the photograph. 'Maybe it is,' he said. 'At least, maybe it should be. But, you know ... One member of that family took something belonging to me.'

'A case,' said Kit.

Mr Oniji went very still indeed.

Looking from Mr Oniji to Mrs Oniji's card, Kit smiled. 'It might be worth trying the station lockers at Shinjuku Sanchome,' he said, reaching into his pyjama pocket for a key. 'I believe you have three days.'

ACKNOWLEDGEMENTS

Hayato Kato and Masato Inoue for translating lines from Yamamoto Tsunetomo's *Hagakure Kikigaki*. Without this help writing *EWB* would have been much harder. Also my thanks for their help in coming up with a suitable Japanese term for 'floating rope world ...' (All of the suggestions were excellent, but *nawa-no-ukiyo* caught exactly the right combination of history and artistic subversion.)

Monte Schumacher, owner of the Shogun Armory (*http://www. ShogunArmory.com*), for letting me use a photograph from his website on the front cover. The photograph shows an iron *jingasa* (samurai war helmet), dating from the mid Edo Period.

Timothy Gowers, Rouse Ball Professor of Mathematics at Cambridge. I took the four-dice idea from a brief interview he gave to *New Scientist*.

Everyone at the Akasaka Prince Hotel, the Akasaka Tokyu and the Hilton Hotel, Shinjuku. All of whom let me clog up their bars and lounges with my papers, laptops and general mess. Caffè Nero in Winchester and Blacks in Soho, for letting me use them as office space.

The lunchtime crew, even though the Islington SF lunches have gone the way of most things. *New Scientist*, for all-round greatness and articles on obscure subjects, which always seem to arrive in the nick of time (well, so far as I'm concerned).

Mic Cheetham (for agenting brilliance), Simon Spanton (understated editorial control), John Jarrold (copy editing), Jonathan Weir (publicity guru) and Gillian Redfearn (editorial admin).

And finally, Sam Baker, for reading the script, making pertinent suggestions and not minding when I zapped off to Toyko at zero notice.